Midwinter Turns to Spring

MARIA VELOSO

Copyright © 2005 by Maria Veloso
All rights, including performance rights, are reserved.

311 N. Robertson Boulevard, Suite 323
Beverly Hills, California 90211
http://www.thinkoutsidethebook.com

Grateful acknowledgment is made for the use of excerpts of Federico García Lorca's poems taken from *In Search of Duende* by Federico García Lorca.

All references in the novel referring to Pablo Picasso's work titled *Ruiz 1897* and the tambourine, as well as the events surrounding said items, are purely fictional. All similarities to actual people living or dead are purely coincidental.

Printed in the United States of America
Second Printing: December 2005

ISBN 0-9770751-0-9

Novel Editor: Diane Eble, author of *Abundant Gifts* - http://www.Abundant-Gifts.com
Cover Designer: Luciano Lorenzutti, TheNetMenCorp.com
Cover Illustration: Agustina Gramajo, TheNetMenCorp.com
Book Layout and Proofreading: Diane Mendez, Proof Plus

Dedication

With Profound Gratitude
to J.C.
who makes all things possible
and without whom
the words, the sentiments and the songs
in this book could not have been written.

Musical Soundtrack

Midwinter Turns to Spring is the first novel that comes with its own music soundtrack consisting of Flamenco-flavored pop ballads and instrumental theme songs. (See the companion CD attached to the inside back cover of this book.)

The songs are woven intricately into – and form a significant part of – the novel's plot. They serve to intensify the emotional involvement of the reader, much like a film score intensifies the emotional appeal of a movie. The author, Maria Veloso, also wrote the original song lyrics, and composed the music for five of the pop ballads.

The element of music was purposely included to highlight one of the central themes of the novel – that of the **power of music** to communicate love better than mere words can – as well as music's endless capacity for *healing, breaking through pain,* bringing us *together with those we love,* and *reconnecting us with our higher selves and our creator.*

The music CD soundtrack was produced, arranged, co-written and sung by Zendrik.

Some things that are hidden from view were meant to remain hidden, but others are preordained to reappear at destiny's prompting. An artist might conceal the fervent brushwork of his original sentiment under fresh layers of paint—but the underlying image often begs to resurface. Such is the sentiment of this story. Having been kept a secret for twenty-six years, it wants to live again.

PROLOGUE

Slumber through Oblivion

It was the third of August 2003. Gray sparrows crossed the somber sky toward Mendocino, and the late afternoon fog trembled as it flowed from the sea toward the bluffs. The fading twilight shed its last petals upon Larkspur Drive, while century-old cypress trees lamented the day's end. The road glistened, moistened by the mists of August, and the whitewashed walls of Mendocino Coast Hospital gleamed against the darkening sky at the tail end of Larkspur Drive.

Alfonso Madrigál walked through the sliding doors of the hospital, headed for the front desk, and inquired about Savannah's room number. He thus began his solitary walk down the long, relentless corridor toward Room 739, where he pictured her lying, still and silent, beneath sterile white sheets.

He knocked on the door, and a young blonde woman in her mid-twenties appeared.

"May I help you?" she asked.

"I'm Alfonso Madrigál. I've come to see Savannah Curtis." His voice turned soft and wobbly when he spoke her name.

The woman opened the door wide enough to let him in. "I'm Cassidy Hamilton, a family friend. Savannah's asleep right now, but please come in."

Alfonso walked slowly toward the bed, feeling the weight of his feet as he took the last steps of his journey toward Savannah Curtis, a journey that had taken twenty-six years of his life, over a distance far beyond miles.

He drew nearer to her as she lay sleeping, remembering a season when days were tender, muffled foghorns moaned, and the lament of a Spanish guitar touched the Mendocino wind. He drew nearer still,

1

hearing the cry of the wayward foam of the Pacific in the distance, listening to the waters grow deeper and deeper into a kind of delirium. He gazed at her, knowing that in the consuming frenzy of his life, hers was the face his heart always came home to each night.

He moved closer to her bedside, recalling the words he had written to her years ago.

> *Like the music of fresh fallen rain*
> *and of swallow's wings*
> *you are*
> *Like a young fern*
> *uncoiling leafy fronds into a thousand tomorrows*
> *am I*
> *Finding my way*
> *to the clearing in the forest*
> *and the serene, quiet shelter*
> *of you*

Of all the things he'd ever done, making his way back to Savannah made everything he had accomplished in his life grow dim by comparison. The face he saw in the mirror each day was that of a man changed infinitely by having known her, having been loved by her. Even on days when the agony of being without her was so great that death seemed seductive, his heart was made tranquil by the thought of her. The hope of seeing Savannah again was the only thing that carried him through the years, the only reason he had been able to endure great pain and sacrifice. Now, the fulfillment of his longing tasted sweet to his soul.

Alfonso reached out and held Savannah's hand as she slept, feeling grateful just to be near her, a soft smile creeping upon his lips. There were so many things he had yet to tell her, things he had failed to tell her, things he had not been ready to tell her – until now. How he had searched for her in the faces of a vast, undulant ocean of women in the concert stadiums, Flamenco bars, *tablaos* and *peñas* of his years. How there were times when he thought he recognized her elegance, her grace and her beauty in another, only to find poor facsimiles of her.

⁓

Cassidy Hamilton watched him from the corner of her eye, trying not to look directly at him. *Alfonso Madrigál.* The man of whom Savannah had spoken, of whom she had written volumes in her journal. There he was in the flesh, the man from the Andalusian province of Southern

Spain, wearing a sand-colored suit. He stood about six feet tall, his skin a deep bronze, his dark hair slicked back in front, peppered with streaks of grey, wavy locks spilling softly down the back, reaching halfway down his nape. Beneath the striking façade, there was a wildness that even his quiet demeanor could not conceal. The molten fire in his eyes spoke of a fierce temperament, but his unruffled exterior suggested just the opposite. He appeared to be in his early fifties, but his lean, muscular physique that peered out from under his black shirt, unbuttoned at the top, seemed to belong to a much younger man.

She observed him watching Savannah sleep. In his right hand, he held a large brown linen portfolio with expanding gussets and an elastic cord closure. Its contents bulged, as though containing odd-shaped articles that didn't quite belong in a slim case. She watched as he fiddled with the brown portfolio that he'd laid on his lap, feeling an intimate familiarity with this man, whom she had never met before today.

She knew of him only from what Savannah said and wrote about him, from listening to songs he wrote, and songs that were inspired by him. Yet she felt she knew Alfonso Madrigál better than her own flesh and blood.

Cassidy was startled when Alfonso suddenly turned his face towards her and said, "Please tell me, how is she?"

"Well, you probably already know she was in a car accident several days ago, and she's sustained a severe head injury. She was in a coma for a few days, but thank God she woke up yesterday. She's been sleeping mostly. Oh, and she's had a CT scan, and they've ruled out brain hemorrhage. Her doctor says she's in pretty stable condition."

Cassidy hesitated momentarily before breaking the news she dreaded telling him. "But I think I ought to warn you. She will not know you when she wakes up."

"*¿Perdóneme?* Excuse me, I'm not sure I heard what you said." She detected a trace of alarm in his voice.

"Savannah has amnesia."

A hush fell over the room as soon as the words escaped Cassidy's lips. She saw the light in Alfonso's eyes flicker and die, and in its place appeared a shadow of gloom.

Cassidy continued, "Her long-term memory has been damaged, and she can't remember most things that happened in her life prior to the accident. In fact, she doesn't even remember the accident at all. She remembers her own name, but very little else. The trauma has also caused her to have a–" she stammered momentarily, "–a different personality. Don't be surprised if she's not at all like the person you used to know."

After a silence that seemed to go on forever, Alfonso spoke again. "Is she expected to regain her memory?"

"The doctor says there's no telling. It may be a month. It may be years. There's also a good chance the amnesia may be permanent."

Outside, a thick blanket of fog rolled inland, allowing only the most fervent rays of the fading sun to shine through. Alfonso turned his face toward the window. His shoulders hunched as he rested his elbows on his thighs, his head bowed as he pinched the inner corners of his eyelids with his thumb and forefinger, not saying a word.

Cassidy's heart grieved with him as she tried to imagine what thoughts must be going through his mind. She could not begin to fathom the deep emotions he must be experiencing, the kind that only an Andalusian soul, such as that of Alfonso Madrigál, was capable of feeling. Looking at him from across Savannah's bed, she thought she heard a desolate cry coming from him, although his lips did not appear to move. It was as if some profound pain emanated from his body—pain that made her recall a fragment of a poem by Federico García Lorca—words that Savannah had often quoted:

We only know that he burns the blood
like a poultice of broken glass ...

She thought of the many things about Savannah that Alfonso had yet to know. The real reason why Savannah ended their relationship, why she had gone to live where he could not find her, the circumstances that led to the car accident, and how everything she ever did was somehow predicated upon him, without his knowledge. She wondered what Alfonso would do if he knew the painful secrets Savannah had kept to herself all these years. And now that Savannah was bereft of memory, who would tell him? Who had the right to tell him?

⌒

Alfonso continued to gaze at Savannah, searching for a glimmer of light from her closed eyes, but found none. A sharp blade of grief plunged between his ribs as his mind pondered thoughts too deep for tears. He felt like a lone bird condemned to the emptiness of the sky. He feigned composure over the news of Savannah's amnesia, all the while secretly rebelling against the injustice of it all. How unfair that he should be robbed of his one remaining joy—to be reunited with the woman who had given his life its meaning.

How could he have possibly come this far, only to find Savannah beyond his reach? How could she slumber through oblivion, untroubled, while he stayed awake, tormented by the impenetrable distance that separated her from him?

He began to roll words over in his mind, words he longed to tell her. *When you open your eyes, Savannah, you'll still have the same face, the same name — but you'll be someone else. You'll look at me through a stranger's eyes, and I'm not sure I can bear it.* Believing that Savannah loved him, even while they were apart, was the only thing that had kept him alive all those years. What would become of his life now that she won't even know who he is?

Alfonso looked down at the brown linen portfolio on his lap, which contained things he had wanted to show Savannah, lamenting the futility of bringing them with him. He began to pluck at the portfolio's elastic cord as he would a guitar string, making an eerie sound that echoed in the silence of Room 739 at the Mendocino Coast Hospital.

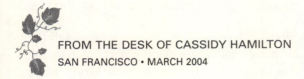

FROM THE DESK OF CASSIDY HAMILTON
SAN FRANCISCO • MARCH 2004

At first, the events that began in the fall of 2002 had seemed nothing more than a string of coincidences. But what ensued proved beyond doubt that they were anything but that.

On October 16, 2002, I moved from a modest flat in the university district of Berkeley into a Victorian apartment in the Pacific Heights area of San Francisco. I leased a splendid high-ceilinged "painted lady" with a turret-like corner tower, gingerbread millwork and bay windows that had breathtaking views of the bay.

Two days later, while unpacking boxes full of crystal and silverware, and putting them away into a built-in china cabinet, I came upon a hidden drawer tucked behind the baseboard of the cabinet. Inside the drawer was the journal of a woman who once lived there.

I examined the handsome journal covered in handmade mulberry paper, unsnapped its gleaming brass closure, and glanced through its pages with only lukewarm interest. The journal belonged to a woman named Savannah Curtis. On the front flyleaf, she had written the words:

*I'm certain there are occasions
when silence speaks better than words
— but I have yet to know them.*

Skimming through a few more pages, I surmised that the events described in the journal happened in 1977.

At the time, the only thing that caught my attention was a verse scribbled somewhere in the middle of the journal:

Sparrows fly on their way to you
   and if I knew the way
   I'd hurry, too
Midwinter turns to spring
   and I remember things I never said to you.

I laid the faded journal on the mantel above the fireplace, reminding myself to revisit it later, after I finished putting everything away.

The next day was Saturday, the 19th of October. The sky turned exceptionally luminous after the early morning fog had burned away.

It's too lovely a day to spend indoors, I thought. I couldn't face the drudgery of unpacking more boxes after having done the same for the better part of two days. The picturesque park across the street beckoned, and I responded to its call.

As I walked across Pacific Avenue on my way to Summerhill Park, a silver blue convertible came barreling down the street with its radio blaring. When it came to a full stop at the nearby intersection, I heard a song playing on the radio. "Sparrows fly on their way to you …" a voice sang. As the car drove away, I heard the tail end of the lyrics. "… and I remember things I never said to you."

What a strange coincidence, I thought, remembering the verse in the journal I had found the day before.

Yet I didn't give it any more thought until I came home later and saw the journal lying on the floor next to the fireplace. It had apparently fallen from where it was perched on the mantel.

Now, I'm not one to read into the significance of coincidences, but the synchronicity of events intrigued me enough to open the journal once again.

It was half past eleven on Saturday morning when I reclined on the living room sofa to read what Savannah Curtis had found the need to write about. After what seemed like several minutes later, I looked up at the clock on the kitchen wall. *Four forty-five.* I had been reading the journal for more than five hours!

I hadn't had anything to eat since six that morning, but even hunger couldn't pull me away from Savannah's story, which I had now read three quarters of the way through. There was something riveting about the story, not the least of which was a mysterious painting upon which the story unraveled—a painting that may or may not have been the work of Pablo Picasso.

My first impression was that the story was a clichéd portrayal of love and romance—not unlike the kind depicted in romance novels and films. An attractive female art professional from San Francisco meets a handsome Flamenco guitarist from Spain named Alfonso

Madrigál one sultry Indian summer in 1977. The story could almost write itself.

But as I was drawn further into the story, something began to happen. This story was somehow much more than just another love story. It began to stir a calloused space in my heart and overcome my cynical side, the side that detested the infatuation-driven, formulaic paradigms of love that were always long on romance and short on substance. I didn't know where it would end, but already I sensed an unraveling of my self-imposed belief that true love no longer exists in the modern world—a belief shaped by deep wounds inflicted upon me by what I used to believe was love.

I continued reading the journal straight through to the end, but was dismayed to find that the story ended abruptly. It climaxed in nothing but unanswered questions. The story tugged at me long after I had put it down. It was particularly spellbinding because a significant part of it happened right there in the Victorian apartment where I now lived. Over the next few days and nights, without any conscious plan, I found myself doing things to uncover the mysteries left unsolved by Savannah's journal.

On Monday morning, while having lunch at my desk at Morgan, Wellington & Linden, where I worked as a paralegal, I found myself launching my Internet browser, going into a search engine and typing in the words:

midwinter turns to spring + song lyrics

The search results appeared a few seconds later. They displayed the lyrics of a song produced in 1978. The lyrics contained the verse that Savannah had scribbled in her journal. The title of the song was *Midwinter Turns to Spring*. The recording artist was a man named Zendrik. No last name.

I clicked on a link on the webpage to hear a sample clip of the song…

> *I remember autumn years ago*
> *The amber days and nights of indigo*
> *Oh my love*
> *All the time left in the world*
> *Will never bring you back to me*

… the voice sang. When it played the refrain, I knew it was the same song I had heard on that car radio on Saturday.

The contact information for Zendrik was displayed on the webpage. He owned a company called Zendrik Music, which was based in Sausalito, California. My heart leaped, although I was still unsure why I should care about this one way or the other. I wasn't even sure at this juncture whether or not this artist named Zendrik had anything to do with Savannah and Alfonso. Or whether or not he had the answers I was looking for.

I dialed the telephone number that was on the *Contact Us* page. Got the answering service. I left a message for Zendrik, asking if he knew Alfonso Madrigál or Savannah Curtis. Zendrik called back later that day. He told me he was a friend of Alfonso's, but that he had lost touch with him years ago.

I asked if I could meet with him in person. He was happy to oblige, and at the end of the work day on Tuesday night, I drove across the Golden Gate Bridge and into Marin County to meet Zendrik for cocktails at the Sausalito Bar & Grill.

Zendrik was unlike anything I expected, although I wasn't exactly sure what I was expecting. A rock star, perhaps? Being half Portuguese and half Filipino, his face had exotic Eurasian features. He looked like a man in his late thirties, although he told me he was forty-nine.

Zendrik first met Alfonso in 1976 when Alfonso had just started performing at *Club La Cibeles* as a Flamenco guitarist. They became friends because of their common love of music. Zendrik spoke of Alfonso's childhood days, growing up in the coastal town of Málaga in the south of Spain. He spoke of the esoteric aspects of Flamenco culture to which Alfonso introduced him—a culture steeped in splendor and mystery that not too many people truly understood. But most of all, he spoke of Alfonso and Savannah. He seemed visibly moved every time he talked about them. He spoke of them with a kind of reverence reserved for heroes and saints. Zendrik had never met Savannah, and yet he seemed to know everything about her through his conversations with Alfonso.

Much of what I had read in Savannah's journal began to come full circle now that Zendrik revealed the other half of the story. I sensed a growing familiarity with Savannah and Alfonso, as seen through the eyes of one who not only knew Alfonso but was deeply affected by Alfonso's brief affair with Savannah. As Zendrik spoke, sentiments and emotions I could not comprehend arose in me. I couldn't quite understand why I had come to care about the fate of two people I didn't even know—two people I never even knew existed until three days ago.

Before Zendrik and I parted that evening, he reached into his jacket pocket, pulled out a CD in a plastic jewel case and handed it to me. It was the CD version of the *Midwinter Turns to Spring* record album, on which Zendrik sang the lead vocals together with a female vocalist. He said, "I wrote these songs. When you listen to them, you'll understand everything."

I glanced at the picture on the face of the CD label. It was an aerial view of Mendocino and the cove that cradled the bay. I recognized the foreground as the exact location Savannah described in her journal as Heaven's Bluff.

While driving home from Sausalito on that October night in 2002, I played Zendrik's CD on my car stereo. The music conjured up vivid imaginings of amber days and nights of indigo during one Indian summer in 1977.

I knew then why the story of Savannah and Alfonso tugged at my heart, refusing to be silent. It was prompting me to bring their story back to life.

It was in late October 2002 that I, Cassidy Hamilton, unwittingly embarked on a journey that would fling me headlong into the lives of Alfonso Madrigál and Savannah Curtis. During the weeks and months that followed, I would find myself becoming an integral part of their story in a way that could only be described as destiny. It was then that I began to understand why Savannah's journal remained unfinished. The story was yet to play itself out to a conclusion that no one could have predicted.

I'm convinced that it's impossible to read the story of Alfonso and Savannah and remain unchanged. If you've never been moved by a song so deep that it touched places in your heart you didn't know existed … if you've never heard a guitar weep, or lost yourself in its tears … if you've never been swept up in the delirium of a love that defies all odds … their story will open your eyes to what's possible when one dares to love.

If you're willing to set aside all your preconceived notions about love, and read this story as if it were told to you by a wise and trusted friend, it may heal whatever part of you is broken, and enrich your life … as it did mine.

CHAPTER 1
Luminous Winds and Opaline Doves
FRIDAY • SEPTEMBER 23 • 1977

Alfonso Madrigál stepped out from behind the wheel of his brown Buick sedan onto the campus grounds of the University of San Francisco on a warm, cloudless Saturday in late September. He was thankful for days like these that San Franciscans call Indian summer, that unseasonably warm spell that arrives in mid-autumn and lasts for several weeks. The thermometer was rising, the air crisp and fog-free, and sun-starved locals were flocking outdoors to snatch the last warming rays of the year before the season remembered what the calendar already knew.

Days like these reminded him of home. "Home," he muttered under his breath, wondering if it was still what he could call the city of his birth, Málaga. He pulled a lilac-colored flyer out of his shirt pocket, reading it again for the second time that morning.

THE HIDDEN MASTERPIECES OF PABLO PICASSO
Sutton Hall – University of San Francisco
September 23, 1977 – 9:00 a.m. to 12:00 p.m.

He glanced at his watch. He still had thirty-five minutes before he had to be at Sutton Hall. He slowed his pace down to a leisurely stroll, enjoying the summer-like weather, wondering how the sun affected the thoughts, the disposition and the aspirations of the people who were walking past him. He looked back on the events of this very day, a year ago. *September 23*. The date brought back a flood of memories. It was a year ago to the day that he first set foot on American soil. Just another immigrant from Spain, full of hopes and dreams, eager to erase the past and start anew.

The very thought of the word, *Spain*, brought ambivalent feelings of nostalgia, anger, joy, shame and scandal to him. He thought of Málaga, where he was born and spent all of his growing years, a proud Andalusian province in Southern Spain. All he had to do was close his eyes and he could still feel on his skin the humid breezes from the Mediterranean that rolled into his sleepy coastal hometown on the Costa del Sol.

In the summer, the parched coastal plains of Málaga quivered in the billowing heat and a delicate breeze from the Sierra Nevada ushered the fragrance of the citrus groves, while Malagueños looked out from shaded *terrazas* upon the glittering Mediterranean.

Alfonso was certain that if he were blindfolded and taken from one city to the next around the world, he would know instantly the moment he stepped foot in Málaga just from the aroma and the sounds of the city—that curious mix of fish frying in oil in the *marisquerías* of Pedregalejo and El Palo, the scent of sugarcane, bananas, citrus fruits and olives growing on the *vegas*, the smell of fresh baked bread wafting out of the ovens of the *panaderías*. Then there was the chirping of swallows overhead, the prevalent strains of flamenco sometimes accompanied by rapid rhythmic clapping, the constant sound of people shouting from the street, the eerie pan-pipe of the wandering knife grinder, the muffled splash of the Mediterranean on the coastal shores, and the clang of the church bells every hour.

Even as he yearned for his hometown, painful memories haunted him still. It had been six years since he left Málaga for Madrid, and then later, San Francisco. Oceans separated him from his past, yet random thoughts he didn't care to remember found their way to him now and again, making his stomach clench itself into tight knots.

He turned his thoughts instead upon Doña Carmen Madrigál, his grandmother, who raised him until he was ten years old. The years he spent with her were the happiest times of his life.

Doña Carmen Madrigál was the widow of the late Eugenio Madrigál. Don Eugenio and Doña Carmen had started a small fruit-growing enterprise, *Compañía Andalucía*, when they were newly married in 1912. Over the years, *Compañía Andalucía* made Eugenio and Carmen Madrigál a small fortune by becoming one of the leading citrus fruit orchards on the fertile irrigated coastal plains of Málaga called *vegas*.

When his grandfather, Don Eugenio, died in 1937, Doña Carmen took the helm of *Compañía Andalucía* and single-handedly expanded the enterprise into a conglomerate that became known not only in Andalucia but throughout Spain. That was something that no other woman of her time had been able to accomplish, particularly in the sleepy, sun-drenched landscape of Málaga.

When Doña Carmen's two older sons, Ricardo and Anselmo, were in their late teens, they started working at *Compañía Andalucía*. Neither of them demonstrated the keen business acuity for which their mother was renowned. Therefore, Doña Carmen did not promote them to responsible positions in the company. Even after Ricardo got married and started raising a small family, and Anselmo did the same, their positions and earnings at *Compañía Andalucía* still remained below what people would expect for the heirs of the Madrigál fortune. Doña Carmen's youngest son, Francisco, was born more than ten years after Ricardo and Anselmo.

Born at the height of the Madrigál enterprise's boom, Francisco was spoiled by both Doña Carmen and Don Eugenio, while he was still alive. Francisco grew up wild, capricious and hot-tempered. When he turned into a young adult, he was known throughout Málaga as a playboy who liked women, cigars, bullfights and the nightlife. Ricardo and Anselmo often regaled their friends in Málaga society with stories of Francisco's youthful escapades. Unlike his brothers, Francisco was never required to work at *Compañía Andalucía*, and neither did he learn to do an honest day's work.

In stark contrast to Doña Carmen's close-fisted treatment of her two older sons, she was uncharacteristically liberal in indulging Francisco with whatever he wanted. At the age of twenty-three, Francisco met Esperanza Manzano, a beauty queen from the neighboring province of Sevilla. She came from a family of modest means, and was swept off her feet when Francisco wooed her with extravagant gifts and ostentatious tokens of affection. Three months later, Francisco announced to his mother that he wished to marry Esperanza, and Doña Carmen threw the young couple the most lavish wedding the province of Andalucia had ever seen.

Alfonso was not certain how he came to be Doña Carmen's favorite grandson. He was neither the eldest, nor the youngest, nor the smartest, nor most talented of her eight grandchildren. Alfonso never considered himself anything more than ordinary, so he thought that perhaps it was because he was the only child of Francisco, on whom Doña Carmen doted. Later, when Alfonso was old enough to understand, Doña Carmen told him that she had sensed a spiritual kinship with him that she could never quite explain.

It was a rare day indeed when Doña Carmen, the grand matriarch of *Compañia Andalucia*, and lady of the palatial estate known throughout Málaga as Villa Madrigál, walked through the doors of Hospital de los Remedios on the morning Alfonso was born. It was the middle of a work day, and she had never been known to pull herself away from her business affairs for anything but the most pressing emergencies, least of all to attend to something as unmonumental as the birth of her eighth grandchild.

Alfonso's eldest cousin, María, daughter of Anselmo, never tired of telling the story of how startled she was to see the usually stern face of Doña Carmen beaming brightly as she took baby Alfonso in her arms, and said, *"Bienvenido, angelito mío." Welcome, my little angel.* Such displays of affection were not in Doña Carmen's nature. At the sound of her voice, baby Alfonso put forth the first glimmer of a smile.

Francisco Madrigál and his wife, Esperanza, were young and carefree. They weren't ready to settle down and raise their son, but preferred to travel, frolic in the jet set playgrounds of the world, and pursue the extravagant lifestyles of the vainglorious elite. Alfonso was left in the care of his grandmother, Doña Carmen, and his nanny, Margarita. While the request might have caused Doña Carmen consternation, had it been made by Ricardo or Anselmo, she joyfully welcomed the prospect of taking custody of Alfonso.

Alfonso felt a deep warmth creep over his chest whenever he thought of his grandmother, whom he endearingly called *Abuelita*. She was already seventy-one when he was born, but she had the energy of a woman in her forties. One couldn't find a single wrinkle on her flawless, honey-colored complexion that was marred only by a small brown mole above the left corner of her upper lip. Her dark, luxuriant hair, which showed only a few strands of gray, was always wound into a tight bun at the nape of her neck, further dramatizing the widow's peak on her front hairline. She was a handsome, magnificent-looking woman. At the height of her youth, she was one of the most beautiful women of Málaga. The sepia-toned pictures in silver frames that graced the mantel in her living room showed her astonishing beauty.

Even though Francisco and Esperanza's trips often lasted for several weeks or months, Alfonso never begrudged them for their absence during his growing years. Abuelita more than made up for his lack of parental attention and love. Abuelita was more of a mother to him than Esperanza ever was. He hardly missed his mother's presence, nor his father's, for that matter.

Back in the late fifties and early sixties, when more than a quarter of the people of Málaga were unemployed and poverty was prevalent, Alfonso lived a privileged existence, insulated from the harsh realities of the coastal city in the south of Spain.

He remembered Abuelita's house, the only place he ever called home. The huge black wrought-iron gate topped with a huge arch bearing the words, *Villa Madrigál*, in ornate script letters. The long driveway ending in a *rotonda* encircling a majestic fountain. Her splendid house was filled with hand-carved woodwork and floors of colored marble mosaics, the work of local artisans, and the windows were adorned with *rejas*, curvaceous black wrought-iron window bars. Everything in Abuelita's two-story mansion had seemed enormous to Alfonso as a young boy—with seven huge bedrooms, a large dining room, a magnificent living room, a spacious kitchen and a *terraza* that wrapped around the entire second floor of the house. There was a lot of room for young Alfonso to roam, but he spent most of his time in the east-facing *terraza* overlooking the Mediterranean. It was on the *terraza* that he learned to play the guitar at the age of seven. He often pleaded with Abuelita to accompany his guitar-playing with the tambourine that she always kept in a glass case.

She would always say, "That tambourine is not to be played like an instrument. It is a work of art, can't you see?" And she would point to the surface of the tambourine on which an exquisite bouquet of flowers was hand-painted. "That's why I keep it in this glass case."

On more than one occasion, however, he caught sight of Abuelita taking the tambourine out of its case, gazing at it intently, then holding it up against her cheek, a faraway look in her eyes.

Alfonso also loved spending time in Abuelita's mahogany-paneled living room filled with plush furnishings and beautiful paintings hanging on the walls. Alfonso liked one painting in particular. It was a portrait of Abuelita sitting on a grassy knoll, with a beautiful seascape in the background. The painting was signed *Ruiz 1897*. Alfonso liked the painting because it had a view that he had often seen with his own eyes. The artist's angle of vision was high, from the top of a hill–the same hill where Abuelita often took him to watch the sunrise. It was apparent to Alfonso that it was painted at dawn's early light because of the muted play of lights and the penumbra of the sunrise on the horizon.

When Alfonso asked Abuelita who painted the picture, she nonchalantly replied, "A friend of mine whom I haven't seen in a long time." Alfonso got the feeling her answer was purposely vague, although he didn't know why at the time.

Málaga seemed unremarkable compared to the high-profile neighboring resort cities of Marbella and Torremolinos on the Costa del Sol. Therefore, the townsfolk never missed an opportunity to elevate the status of Málaga by telling visitors that Pablo Picasso was born there. Indeed, Picasso was born less than two miles from Abuelita's villa, and spent ten years there before his family moved to Corunna, and then Barcelona.

Abuelita also liked telling visitors that Federico García Lorca, the renowned Spanish writer, poet and distinguished folklorist of popular Spanish songs, had described Málaga as his favorite town. Alfonso came to know and love Lorca's works because Abuelita used to read them to him as a young boy growing up in a culturally starved city. There was a verse in one of Federico García Lorca's poems that Alfonso particularly remembered, written in 1935:

> "*It will be a long time, if ever, before there is born*
> *an Andalusian so true, so rich in adventure.*
> *I sing of his elegance with words that groan,*
> *and I remember a sad breeze through the olive trees.*"

Suddenly, unpleasant events started to move across Alfonso's memory. It was inevitable. He could never think of Málaga without remembering them.

He was ten when Abuelita died. It was the summer of 1963, and he remembered the last time he saw her. It was Tuesday morning, and it was one of those rare occasions that Alfonso awoke early enough to see her leave for work. He rarely saw her on weekday mornings because she was always gone by daybreak to oversee operations at *Compañia Andalucia*. That day, Alfonso awoke early and while still in bed, heard her voice barking orders to the household staff. He remembered thinking that for all her fiery temperament that instilled fear in those who hardly knew her, she was as loved and respected as anyone could be—not only by her employees and servants, but almost anyone who spent any time with her. Beneath the arrogant façade was a heart that was as warm as the summers in Málaga.

Alfonso thought about going downstairs and seeing her off, but he remembered how Abuelita did not like unnecessary interruptions to her routine, especially when she was getting ready to leave for work. So, instead, he scrambled to the window just in time to see her get into the car and pull the door behind her; and Genaro, the chauffeur, pulled away around the *rotonda*, down the long driveway, past the wrought iron gate, and beyond. *I'll see you this afternoon, Abuelita,* he had murmured under his breath.

Just before noon, the school principal interrupted Alfonso's class, and asked the teacher to excuse Alfonso for the rest of the day. While the principal and Alfonso walked down a long hallway, she told him that Margarita had come to take him home. Margarita was waiting outside the principal's office and when Alfonso saw her face, he knew that something terrible had happened. He was soon told that Abuelita had died in a car accident when Genaro lost control of the wheel and drove the car off a cliff on the south side of town. Her body was so severely burned and disfigured by the accident that they had to keep her casket closed at the funeral wake.

Alfonso had never experienced a death in the family before and he was not prepared for the grief he felt after the death of Abuelita. He felt utterly alone without her. He remembered feeling orphaned, even though his parents were alive and well, vacationing in Switzerland when the tragic accident happened. Abuelita was the only parent he had ever known. He never dreamed how empty life would be without her. But even as he mourned Abuelita's death, he had no idea of the nightmare that was yet to come.

Doña Carmen Madrigál had bequeathed the bulk of her estate to her three sons, Anselmo, Ricardo and Francisco. To Alfonso, she left the painted portrait that he loved so much–and the tambourine on which a beautiful bouquet of flowers was painted.

Doña Carmen had left a handwritten will that was drawn up without legal advice, and it was full of loopholes that anyone could easily exploit. What ensued after the reading of her will was a mad scramble for a bigger portion of the Madrigál estate and a jostling for control over the Madrigál business enterprise by Ricardo, Anselmo, Francisco and their greedy wives. Ricardo and Anselmo took over the management of *Compañia Andalucia*, but because of their ineffective management, the estate that Don Eugenio and Doña Carmen Madrigál had worked all their lives to build collapsed in less than five years. The Madrigál brothers were forced to sell *Compañia Andalucia* to a competitor, and liquidate all other assets, including Villa Madrigál, at a tremendous loss.

Alfonso was old enough to remember the disgrace of losing a family fortune, the public scorn that followed the shame, the never-ending quarrels and conflicts that arose amongst his uncles, aunts, and his parents, and the horror of being forced to live a meager lifestyle to which he and his parents were not accustomed.

Francisco's consumption of liquor accelerated as fast as the family fortunes dwindled, and he soon took to the habit of beating his wife, Esperanza, and Alfonso for any provocation. Esperanza, in turn, having grown increasingly disgruntled over her miserable life, started taking her misery out on Alfonso.

Alfonso remembered the first time his mother slapped him across the face with a force so strong it resounded in his ears. Her heavy backhand flung him clear across the living room and he crashed onto the coffee table, shattering the glass tabletop into countless pieces. His left shoulder was dislocated during the fall, and splinters of broken glass lodged themselves into the gaping wounds that covered his arms and legs. He remembered lying in the ambulance on the way to the hospital, the smell of his mother's excruciatingly sweet French perfume with spicy undertones still in his nostrils. Agonizing as the pain in his body was, all he could remember as he lay in the ambulance was the sting of a thousand invisible needles on his cheek where his mother had slapped him. Tears welled up in his eyes. To keep them from falling, he bit hard on his lower lip until drops of blood trickled out.

In the blink of an eye, Alfonso's privileged life had turned into the kind of nightmare the likes of which he had only seen in tragedies portrayed in the cinema. His adolescence ushered in the dark days of his life when he rebelled against his parents, his family and all figures of authority. He began to run around with the wild *gitano* boys in the underbelly of Málaga.

Alfonso's only redemption came in the form of frequent visitations from Abuelita. The first time she visited, he thought he was dreaming. It was the week after her funeral, and he was sitting alone in his bedroom, looking out the window at oncoming storm clouds. Suddenly, from the far end of the sky came a dense cloud that appeared to be illuminated from within. It slowly made its way toward him, getting brighter as it got closer. Just when its brightness became too blinding, Abuelita emerged from the cloud. In an instant, she was standing right in front of him. He felt the warmth of her breath on his face, smelled the sweet fragrance of her talcum powder and the citrus scent of her hands. Her lips moved, mouthing words he couldn't hear, and then she was gone, along with the cloud of light that brought her. It was the kind of apparition that would send anyone running and screaming "Ghost!" But Abuelita's presence did not scare him. It gave him a semblance of peace in the turmoil that had begun to overrun his life.

Abuelita appeared to him once every fortnight in the months that followed her death. Her visits became less frequent as Alfonso turned into a wild adolescent. In his seventeenth year, he remembered her visiting him only once.

In the summer of 1971, the day after Alfonso turned eighteen, his mother, Esperanza Madrigál, died suddenly. Her death became a citywide scandal because she was rumored to have been having an affair with a wealthy older gentleman from Granada. The rumors started when Esperanza Madrigál started frequently visiting her hometown of Sevilla without her husband, Francisco. The townspeople kept track of the number of trips she made to Sevilla and the fancy jewelry she always brought back with her to Málaga, which she claimed were given to her by her parents who, according to the gossip-mongers, couldn't possibly afford such luxuries. Stories abounded that her visits to Sevilla were thinly disguised trysts with a man from Granada, who spoiled her with lavish gifts the way Francisco did when the Madrigál family had means.

One Saturday, earlier that summer, Alfonso caught sight of his mother with a tall, mustachioed, well-dressed gentleman in a fancy sports car driving off the beaten track in the outskirts of town, and he didn't tell a soul.

Three weeks later, Esperanza Madrigál was dead of a cerebral hemorrhage, and the townspeople whispered their suspicions that the abusive Francisco may have had something to do with her death. They said something about Francisco inducing her brain hemorrhage by lacing her wine with a drug called methylthionate.

Even worse was the malicious gossip that the two older Madrigál brothers, Anselmo and Ricardo, may have had something to do with the accident that took the life of Doña Carmen Madrigál. Rumor had it that Anselmo and Ricardo got tired of the paltry salaries and meager financial dole-outs their wealthy mother gave them, and they devised a plan to get a jump on their inheritance. Some of the rumors went on to say that the brothers paid a local mechanic, Arturo Marquez, to tamper with the car that sent both Doña Carmen and her chauffeur, Genaro, to their deaths. Since then, Arturo Marquez was nowhere to be found, and the gossip-mongers used his disappearance to prove the validity of their suspicions.

Alfonso didn't care to know, didn't want to know.

Grief, shame and disillusionment over the family scandals and misfortunes brought an end to Alfonso's good-natured personality. He became combative, hostile and calloused. He cared for nothing, trusted no one, loved no one, and found nothing worthy of his devotion. Finding no reason to stay in Málaga, Alfonso left home a week after his mother's funeral without saying a word to his father, armed only with his guitar, a few thousand pesetas that he had earned from playing his guitar for tourists on the piers of Málaga, Abuelita's painting, the tambourine and a few garments he owned. Without looking back, he boarded a bus and headed for Madrid.

On the bus, Abuelita appeared to him again. This time, he heard the words she said. *"Buen viaje, angelito mío."* Bon voyage, my little angel. It was the last time he ever saw her.

～

Alfonso's thoughts were interrupted by the siren of a police car in the distance. He glanced at his watch. *Ten minutes until nine.* It was his cue to start heading towards Sutton Hall.

Sutton Hall was almost filled to capacity when he arrived. Nearly a hundred people were already seated, a few stood in the back, and a few stragglers came through the door. Alfonso found an aisle seat in the last row of chairs. He had never been to these lectures, and hadn't expected this one to be so well attended. He was glad he didn't arrive a minute later because it seemed there were more people than there were seats to accommodate them.

Promptly at nine, a tall, bespectacled man, who introduced himself as Rupert Blackwell, gave an overview of the lectures that were to be given that morning. The subject was the collection of authenticated paintings of Pablo Picasso that surfaced after his death on April 8, 1973.

The moderator introduced the first speaker by name: Savannah Curtis. He referred to her as being a sought-after expert on the art of Pablo Picasso, a fine art consultant and appraiser, former director of the famed Somerset Gallery, and now an artist in her own right.

Upon being called to the podium, Alfonso observed a woman in the front row gathering a stack of papers and transparencies. Her head was bowed down as she riffled through her materials. Then, she slowly walked towards the podium.

From where he sat, Alfonso noticed that she was a lovely woman with hazel eyes, high cheekbones, with mahogany-colored hair that was upswept into a French chignon at the crown of her head. She reminded him of a European debutante. She appeared to be in her mid-twenties, which did not fit his idea of an art expert. She stood about 5-foot-6-inches tall, with a statuesque figure, and wore a conservative brown suit that had a contoured silhouette and a hemline that was just an inch below the knee. To Alfonso, her beauty was beyond shape or form. It appeared to be glowing from within. As she walked to the podium, she seemed to glide across the floor with a regal demeanor.

For all her serenity, Alfonso found something disquieting about her. He didn't understand the strange effect she had on him, and why he was having trouble taking his eyes away from her. He looked around the room to observe whether other people had a similar reaction to her, but everyone else seemed unaware of the quiet beauty of Savannah Curtis.

When she took her place behind the podium, she reached into her pocket and pulled out a pair of copper-colored, wire-rimmed glasses which she quickly put on. The glasses made her look quite scholarly, which came as a strange relief to him.

When she started speaking, it was evident to Alfonso that Savannah Curtis possessed extensive knowledge about the art of Pablo Picasso.

"Unlike many artists that develop a mature style and stick with it for the duration of their careers, Picasso possessed not one signature style, but worked in more than one style at any given time," she said, projecting transparencies of Picasso's work during various periods of his career.

"However, the challenge in authenticating works that surfaced after his death did not lie in the abundance of styles to which one must compare the works, but in Picasso's practice of selling his signature for a fee." An audible gasp arose from the audience.

"Now that I've got your attention...," she said with a smile, "...don't be alarmed. The practice is not as deceitful as it sounds. It's all a matter of market value–and that of determining what defines an original Picasso–not whether the work was created by him or not. Let me explain. It's a well known fact that unsigned works of Picasso, although original, command considerably lower prices than signed works of the same caliber. Oftentimes, an art dealer buys a group of unsigned prints at low unsigned prices. Picasso was known to oblige dealers—who knew how to catch him on a good day—by signing such prints. That then sends the total value of the prints to astronomical heights. Here are examples of pieces that were originally marketed unsigned, which Picasso signed afterwards. Note the differences in the market value." She placed another set of transparencies on the overhead projector, and the audience buzzed.

She had the audience in the palm of her hand. Seeing their fascination with the vagaries and whimsy of market prices, she proceeded. "Let me tell you a story. In 1969, Pablo Picasso received a large shipment of painting supplies at his studio, and the supplies were packaged in corrugated cardboard boxes. Instead of throwing out the cardboard panels—twenty-nine in all—Picasso made canvases out of the blank side of each of the panels and painted portraits on all of them. A few of France's leading lithographers made a series of lithographs from those originals. Picasso did not generate the lithographs directly. Certainly, the images were created by him, but transforming them into colored lithographs was not. Proofs of the lithographs were subsequently submitted to Picasso, who approved them—but he did not sign the prints, which the printers numbered. An image of his signature, however, appears as part of the lithograph. The question, therefore, is—are the lithographs considered originals?"

The rest of her hour-long lecture was lively, intriguing and eye-opening. Not at all what Alfonso expected from an art lecture.

Towards the end of her segment, she removed her glasses and replaced them in her pocket. Almost as soon as she did, the uneasiness arose again in Alfonso. He figured it was because he had an innate reverence for beauty, and Savannah Curtis's kind of beauty intrigued him. He had known many attractive women in his life, but there was something about her that was different. His eyes followed her as she walked from the podium back to her seat, while the audience applauded.

The rest of the morning was a blur. The two speakers that followed, a museum curator named Nigel Kendall and an art authenticator named Lindsay Morgan, were also quite knowledgeable, but their lectures came across as being academic and bland to Alfonso. *Not quite as engaging as the lecture of Savannah Curtis.*

The lecture series ended promptly at twelve. People poured out of the lecture hall and started milling around in the foyer. The hall was half empty now.

Alfonso sat in his chair watching Savannah Curtis, who was still seated in the front row talking to the other lecturers. He began to sense strange words arising from somewhere inside of him. Elegant, lyrical words and phrases of unknown origins flooded his consciousness like an overflowing stream. Words that spoke of luminous winds, opaline doves and cerulean skies woven into some kind of heaven.

He searched his pockets for a scrap of paper, and found the lilac-colored parchment flyer in his shirt pocket. On the blank side of the flyer, he started writing the words that were coming at him. For in the twinkling that the muse waved her wand, a barren landscape of paper pulp and fiber became a blank canvas on which something half-forgotten and half-remembered was coming alive.

He looked up from his writing just as Savannah Curtis and the other two speakers got up and headed for the back door. He thought he heard a faint sound of an eerie chime as she drew nearer to him. He sprang to his feet.

"Excuse me, Miss Curtis."

Savannah turned around and looked at him. "Yes?"

Up close, he noticed her creamy complexion that set off her exotically slanted hazel eyes.

"I'm Alfonso Madrigál. I enjoyed your lecture very much."

Savannah was riveted by his voice and his accent, which she immediately recognized as being Spanish. His words were friendly enough, but she sensed a fierce temperament in him–a brooding disposition with an almost palpable rage simmering underneath the surface.

"Thank you," she replied, lowering her eyes, not knowing why she felt embarrassed by the compliment.

"Miss Curtis, I hope it's not too much trouble, but I have a favor to ask you."

She motioned to her companions, who had walked several steps ahead, and said to them, "How about if I meet you there? I'll only be a couple of minutes."

Nigel Kendall answered, "Okay, see you there then."

She turned back to face Alfonso. He was standing two feet away from her, a little too close for her comfort. She took one step backward to where she felt more at ease talking to him.

"What sort of favor, Mr. Madrigál?"

"I own a painting that I'd like you to look at. I think it's the work of Picasso."

"What makes you think so?"

"It's signed *Ruiz 1897*. I'm not an expert like you, but I think the painting has a similar style to Picasso's works during that period."

Savannah was deep in thought. At the turn of the century, Pablo Picasso used the name *Ruiz Picasso* to sign his paintings–Ruiz, being his father's name, and Picasso, his mother's maiden name. Later, he just dropped Ruiz and signed all his paintings as Picasso.

"And how do you happen to own this painting?" she asked.

"We've had it in the family since the beginning. In fact, the painting is a portrait of my grandmother–with a view of Málaga in the background. You probably know that Málaga is Picasso's birthplace?"

"Yes. The paradise city–isn't that what Picasso called it?"

"Not many people know that, but you've obviously studied Picasso a lot, Señorita Curtis. Have you been to Málaga?"

"No, I haven't. The closest I got to Málaga was Barcelona–when I went to the *Museo Picasso*."

"How did you like Barcelona?"

"It's one of the most beautiful cities I've ever been to. So much history. The *Catalán* culture is fascinating."

"My great grandparents were from the *Cataluña* region. In fact, I remember my grandmother being able to speaking the *Catalán* dialect fluently."

Savannah thought she saw a momentary spark of delight in his eyes. But the spark was gone almost the same moment it appeared. He became withdrawn once again.

She glanced at her watch. *Twelve twenty-five.* "Listen, the other lecturers are expecting me to join them for lunch. I hate to be abrupt but…"

"May I invite you to have coffee tomorrow afternoon, then? I'd really like to continue our conversation…and show you the painting, if you like."

It wasn't her habit to accept social invitations from strangers, but she found a legitimate enough reason for her to agree to meet with him. She was more than a little intrigued by the painting he mentioned. "Okay, then. Let's meet at 2 p.m. at Café Marcel tomorrow. Do you know the place?"

"Yes, I'll be there. Thank you, Señorita Curtis."

She held out her hand to shake his. Both his hands closed around hers, and he gently brought her hand to his lips and kissed it, never taking his eyes away from her face. She was taken aback by the intimacy of his gesture. No man had ever kissed her hand before, at least not the way he did.

"Until tomorrow then."

"I'm looking forward to it."

She turned to go, feeling his eyes upon her as she walked out of Sutton Hall, through the foyer, and out into the September sunshine of the Indian summer. And though neither of them knew it, events from that day forward would conspire to irretrievably change both their lives.

CHAPTER 2
When Innocence Bloomed

SATURDAY MORNING • SEPTEMBER 24 • 1977

*S*avannah Curtis awakened in her room, which was still dim in spite of the blossoming day outside. It was just the way she liked it. The thick drapery that hung over her large window worked perfectly because she enjoyed gradually waking up from the pitch darkness of sleep, to a half-tone light instead of the blinding assault of a day in full bloom.

She stretched her arms and legs until she was sufficiently awake, then drew the curtains, and looked onto a dazzling San Francisco morning. Today, as always, she looked out of her north-facing window, and gazed at the leafy imprint that the rising sun was casting through the trees upon the house across the street. On mornings when the fog didn't roll in, the exterior wall of the house next door provided a wonderful and ever-changing canvas on which the sun unfolded its artistry. The overhanging trees told their story in a slightly different way every day.

Over the years, she had learned to use the wall as her very own sundial. She could tell the time and the season just by looking at the shadowy imprint on the wall. Right now, the wall said the time was seven o'clock in the early fall.

It was Saturday, and she didn't have to be anywhere until two. She relished the stretch of time she had to savor her morning coffee and even take a leisurely walk outside. She smiled as she imagined thousands of sun-starved San Franciscans contemplating the same idea. Having seen enough of the damp, foggy days and cold, windy nights that defined summer in the Bay Area, she had no doubt everyone would be flocking outdoors to enjoy the glorious warmth of fall known as the Indian summer.

Walking to her bedside table, she pressed the Play button of her answering machine, as she gazed at a framed picture of herself as a child, standing behind a white birthday cake that had black tap shoes with red bows decorating the top. The green lettering on the cake read: *Happy 7th Birthday, Princess!*

She listened to Russell's message. She had already heard it the previous night as the call came in, but she had not felt like picking up the phone and talking to him. "Hello sweetie, it's me." Russell's voice on the answering machine was spirited. "It's almost ten…

where are you? How did your lecture go? I hope it went well. Listen, I'll be back in San Francisco on Sunday of next week. I'm looking forward to seeing you. Miss you." Click.

The message was so typical of Russell. Brief, to-the-point, no unnecessary verbiage, almost business-like. Not one word more, or less, than necessary. It was hard to believe she had known him for almost four years, and yet she didn't feel any closer to him than she did when she first met him. She felt a distance from Russell that she couldn't quite understand. She thought that she ought to be feeling close to him, especially after they became engaged. But there always seemed to be a wedge that kept her from feeling connected to him.

She thought about him now. Russell Parker. A dyed-in-the-wool American, the only son of a former Lieutenant Colonel in the U.S. Army, who later made a fortune in commercial real estate. Sensible, straightforward Russell with the boyish good looks, sandy blond hair and hazel eyes.

They had met at the Somerset Gallery in 1973. Savannah had just become the Gallery Director at the time, and he had attended the cocktail reception to celebrate the opening of Dakota Lansbury's one-man show. He had bought a few of Dakota's paintings and sculptures, which came to a hefty price tag, for his new offices. She wondered whether Russell had bought the pieces to impress her–for that was Russell's nature. He was given to the arrogance of privilege and of conspicuous consumption, and was only too willing to flaunt his advantage. He was a successful investment banker with an Ivy League education, earning a high six-digit income, and he came from the well-to-do Parkers of Connecticut. He had a lot to flaunt–and he was a perfect catch, by most women's standards.

"Russell Parker is a *mensch*," her friend Kimberley would often say, which in Hebrew meant someone to admire, someone who had everything going for him.

If asked to name the quality that attracted her most to Russell, beyond his obvious attributes, Savannah would say it was his dependability. Russell was sensible, even-keeled and predictable– and was not one given to erratic behavior. His past relationships with women had always been long-term and exclusive, and she found that strangely comforting. She had a need for constancy and safety, which he fulfilled.

Yet there were also undesirable things she couldn't ignore, not the least of which were Russell's ego, which was as big as all outdoors, and his adamant need for control. He had to have things his way, or not at all. In many ways, Russell had inherited his father's regimented lifestyle. Everything he did was calculated and well thought out. No spur-of-the-moment, impulsive decisions–ever. All the way down to his choice of socks or restaurants. He even mandated the clothes Savannah wore—down to the fabrics, the brand and the style. He preferred tailored—never frilly—neutral-colored outfits on her, subdued make-up, leather pumps, understated jewelry, natural fabrics with soft patterns. He absolutely forbade her to wear anything with neon colors, or with checkered, houndstooth or dotted prints.

At first, Savannah had enjoyed dressing the way Russell wanted her to. It gave her the sense that she couldn't possibly go wrong—that she couldn't displease him if she looked exactly the way he required her to. The last thing she wanted to do was to displease Russell. She often wondered about her chronic need for approval—especially from the men in her life. But as the years went by, she silently rebelled against the Stepford wife/Geisha girl routine she had allowed herself to fall into, and felt that it stifled who she really was. But she continued to obey Russell's wishes anyway.

"Do you know how proud I am of you?" he had asked her after a party, wherein he had introduced her to his family and friends.

And deep inside, Savannah said wryly to herself, *Sure, why shouldn't you be? After all, I'm a creature of your own design.*

When they got engaged a month earlier, that too was a much deliberated decision. Russell had felt it was the right thing to do at the right time: he was at the right age and had the right financial circumstances to settle down—and he had the woman that would fill the wifely position quite nicely.

There was no marriage proposal per se. While riding in Russell's car one day, he had unceremoniously said to her, "We should marry." It was neither a question nor a proposal. It was an announcement. The following day, he slipped a velvet-covered box to her after dinner at his parents' home in Connecticut. Inside the box was a 3-carat diamond engagement ring with a note that read: *Savannah, I'm looking forward to spending my life with you. Love, Russell.*

Later that evening, he announced to his family that Savannah and he had just gotten engaged. Savannah was flattered, at first, but realized later what Russell was really saying. *There's no need for me to pop the question. You'd be crazy not to want to marry me.*

She rebelled over his conceited presumption. In reality, had he popped the question, she might have said she'd give the matter some thought.

Now, she wondered whether she had once again allowed herself to be bulldozed into a corner that wasn't her choosing. Although she did not love Russell the way she thought a woman should love a man, she did care about him and felt safe with him. Settling for a loveless relationship in exchange for safety was a trade she was willing to make.

She thought about the other men with whom she'd been involved, and they all had one thing in common. None of them had the power to hurt her. She had to be certain that if she lost them, for any reason—if they died, if they disappeared, or if they just decided to get up and leave—that she wouldn't fall apart when they were gone. So far, she was satisfied with the safe choices she had made over the years, and that included Russell.

Now that she was facing the prospect of being married to him, Savannah was no longer sure that it was the kind of life she wanted. She felt as though she was about to be trapped in a prison of protocol and circumscribed behavior—smiling endlessly at his business associates and their wives until her jaws hurt, cooking gourmet meals to suit his fancy, vacationing wherever he wanted to go, and doing things he wanted to do—which always seemed to be different from what she wanted to do.

Their wedding date had not yet been set, but Russell had said they'd talk about it when he got back from Chicago on Sunday. She secretly delighted in the eight more days that she had all to herself.

Her delight worried her.

Savannah walked over to her desk, which was tucked against the windowless corner of her bedroom. *It's about time I wrote to Sabine,* she thought. She usually exchanged letters and phone calls with Sabine, her adoptive mother, a few times a month, but it had been three weeks since she had written. She took a couple of pieces of monogrammed linen note paper from her stationery drawer and began to write.

Dear Sabine,

I received your package the other day. Imagine my surprise when I opened the box and found your latest collection of poetry printed on antique parchment, bound in pine bark and raffia. I'll treasure it always.

The packaging is exquisite, but your poetry is breathtaking. It is by far the most provocative work you've ever done. Your publisher must be thrilled.

There's something about a change of season that brings back memories. The first rain, the first falling leaf, the first frost—they always seem to remind us of other firsts in years gone by, when innocence bloomed and life was untouched by turmoil. Yesterday was the first warm day of the Indian summer and it reminded me of another day like it long ago—one that brought with it a hint of the coming cold. On a day like yesterday, I thought the world was perfect, and nothing could possibly go wrong. It was a day that Daddy and I happened to be walking by a colorful bazaar in Chinatown. I was mesmerized by a trinket sitting in a small glass case outside the store. It was a globe-shaped silver charm dangling on a silver chain. The charm gave out an eerie muffled chime from inside whenever you shook it. I didn't ask Daddy to buy it for me, but he did. Yesterday, I recalled what he said when he put it around my neck. "Savannah, whenever you hear that little chime, remember that I'm always with you—even when I'm away from you." I didn't know then that it was his way of saying goodbye. That day, he also bought me the green Chinese silk dress that he said matched the color of my eyes—the one he said I should wear on my birthday. You know the one, Sabine—and you also know the rest of the story.

Sabine, it occurred to me recently that agreeing to marry Russell may have been my way of bringing Daddy back, filling the void that he left. Now, I'm not too sure. Russell has been in Chicago for the last few days and he just called to say he'll be there for another week. Instead of being disappointed, I felt relieved to have another week all to myself. I'm happy to have this time to think. We haven't set a wedding date yet, but we'll discuss it when he returns. Russell thought a June wedding might be nice. Why am I not surprised?

Yesterday, I gave a lecture at the university on the hidden masterpieces of Picasso. The lecture was no different from the way most of my lectures go, except that something unusual happened. When the lecture series was over and I was leaving the lecture hall, a man from Málaga came up to me. He had dark piercing eyes, burnished bronze skin, a sovereign nose, and dark, shoulder-length hair with a lock spilling onto his forehead. I had noticed him sitting in the back row when I was standing at the podium. He had a morose expression and a permanent scowl on his face—and he seemed determined not to smile. He said his name is Alfonso Madrigál. We had a brief conversation, and he asked me if I'd take a look at a painting that he inherited from his grandmother. He seems to think it's a Picasso.

I agreed to meet him for coffee this afternoon. He makes me a little nervous. Maybe because he seems so serious. I'm not even sure why I'm telling you about him, Sabine. I guess I'm more than a little intrigued by this painting he speaks of—but I also have a strange feeling he'll somehow figure in my life in some important way. I'll let you know what happens the next time I write.

Love always,
Savannah

Savannah's fingers closed in around the globe-shaped silver charm that dangled on a silver chain around her neck. As always, it gave out that old familiar muffled chime. As she had done countless times since her childhood, she once again closed her eyes and tried to feel that her father was with her. Once again, she failed. Yet, she wore it every day, tucking it behind the neckline of whatever she wore so that no one would see it.

Slowly, she folded her letter to Sabine, and opened her desk drawer to get a matching envelope out of her stationery box. As she did, her eyes caught sight of a hard-bound journal in the far corner of the drawer. It was a blank journal covered in handmade mulberry paper that she had purchased a few months ago, intending to make it a diary of her thoughts. Thinking this was as good a time as any, she pulled the journal out of the drawer and wrote these words on the front flyleaf:

I'm certain there are occasions
when silence speaks better than words
— but I have yet to know them.

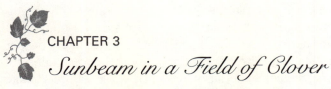

CHAPTER 3
Sunbeam in a Field of Clover

SATURDAY AFTERNOON • SEPTEMBER 24 • 1977

Savannah arrived at Café Marcel at a minute before two. She looked around the café, which was half empty. There was no sign of him yet. The strong aroma of roasted coffee beans permeated the air inside the cozy coffee house. She found a small table by the window and sat herself down. *What now*, she thought.

All day she had felt like a silly young girl. She had spent an hour trying to figure out what to wear and how to fix her hair. She decided on her chartreuse-colored silk dress that was simple but flattered her figure without being provocative. She wanted to look effortlessly pulled together, so she thought of wearing her hair down, fastened with a pearl-studded gold barrette, and putting on just a little make-up.

She had taken her time choosing from among her perfume bottles before deciding on *Ambrosia*. All the while, she wondered why she fussed at all—and reminded herself this was nothing more than a casual business meeting.

"*Hola*, Señorita Curtis." His deep, masculine voice came from behind her.

She turned around in her chair. It was Alfonso. "*Hola*," she said holding her hand out to shake his. "Savannah. Please call me Savannah."

He took her hand and kissed it. Blood rushed to her face. He had kissed her hand the day before, but today, the level of intimacy seemed more magnified within the confines of the coffee house than it did in the lecture hall.

"You're a sunbeam in a field of clover, Savannah."

"*Muchas gracias,*" she answered. It was not the kind of compliment she was used to hearing, nor one she expected from someone whose first language was Spanish. But he seemed to say the words with the same ease with which another man would say, "You look pretty." She allowed herself to savor the compliment, and felt warm towards this stranger who spoke to her in metaphors. His hand was warm, almost hot, to the touch. His face was only a few inches away from hers as he leaned forward from a standing position, his left hand resting on the back of her chair, and she could smell the citrus scent of his aftershave. If she had thought him attractive yesterday, today in his prairie cheesecloth shirt that he wore over khaki slacks and leather sandals, he looked stunningly handsome. The cream-colored collarless shirt, with its long sleeves folded carefully to just below his elbows, made his skin seem to take on an even deeper Mediterranean shade of bronze. He was about six feet tall, and through the translucent material of his shirt, she could just make out his well defined shoulder and chest muscles, his taut belly.

"May I get you a cup of coffee?"

"Yes. *Café au lait*, please."

"Would you like a scone or a pastry with your *café au lait*?"

"No, thank you. The coffee will do just fine." There she was, feeling nervous again.

"*Muy bien.* Please excuse me. I'll be right back."

Alfonso walked to the counter and ordered two cups of *café au lait*. A few moments later, he walked back to the table. Her fingertips felt the warmth of his skin when he handed her the cup. A faint current ran through her body as she murmured her thanks.

They both sipped coffee quietly for a few moments. She noticed that every now and then, he would push his hair away from his face with his hand and she would see the contours of his face, which reminded her of a savage version of a Michelangelo sculpture. He had a well-defined forehead, night-black hair, a noble nose, and a strong, cleft chin. His lips were exquisitely crested and had a provocative shape, with the color of faded crimson. There was something in the fierceness of his eyes that was disconcerting to Savannah, but at the same time, she sensed a profound sadness that lurked behind them and in the lips that seemed reluctant to smile.

"So tell me about Málaga, Alfonso."

Alfonso's eyes darted sideways. For a split second, she thought she saw his face grimace with pain. Looking at his face, she could almost discern the footprints of some dark, enormous woe pacing across his mind.

Then, in a voice that seemed emotionally vacant, he said, "Málaga is a city on the Mediterranean coast in a region of Southern Spain called Andalucia. When I was growing up, it was just a quiet agricultural and fishing village. Málaga is the capital of Costa del Sol. You have heard of Costa del Sol, no?"

"Oh, yes. Isn't that the area where all the resorts are? Marbella, Torremolinos......" She trailed off trying to remember other resorts in the south of Spain she had read about in travel books.

"*Exactamente.* Also Fuengirola and Estepona."

"Those were the resorts I was trying to remember. Yes, I'm familiar with Costa del Sol and its reputation among the jetsetters. When I visited Barcelona a few years ago, I planned to go there but I ran out of time."

"Maybe you'll find the time to visit one day. Málaga is about ten miles from Torremolinos and thirty-five miles from Marbella. Costa del Sol has the warmest temperatures in the Iberian Peninsula, especially in the wintertime. That's why our sleepy fishing village didn't stay sleepy for long. Tourists started coming into our city in cruise ships that docked in the port of Málaga. Or they flew into the Málaga airport. That's what Málaga is famous for now—the resort beaches, the sweet wine and the best fried fish in Spain."

It surprised Savannah that Alfonso described his hometown with such emotional detachment, as though he was reading a description of it from a travel brochure. As though he never lived there.

"The Gudalmina River divides the city in two," he continued. "On one side is the wealthy Málaga and on the other, the western side, the poverty-stricken city areas of La Trinidad and El Perchel."

"On which side did you live?" Savannah's question just came out on impulse. The moment the words left her lips, she regretted how thoughtless her question was.

Alfonso didn't seem offended by the question. "I lived the first ten years of my life in the rich half. Afterwards, I lived in the poor side of town. I was raised in my grandmother's house until I was ten—in her estate called *Villa Madrigál*, less than a mile from where Picasso lived. When she died, my parents and my uncles squandered her wealth and we ended up poor. I left Málaga for Madrid when I was eighteen."

She sat quietly, sipping on her coffee between conversation breaks. There was no joy in Alfonso's eyes as he spoke of his childhood. He seemed fiercely private and purposely avoided further details. Savannah didn't push it.

Then, as though reading her thoughts, he said, "I think I've talked enough about me. If you don't mind, I'd like to know a little about you."

She was thankful for the opportunity to dispel the nervousness she felt from being around him. So she talked. Told him about her father, Lyndon Curtis, a second-generation Welsh immigrant whose parents were born in a small fishing village in Swansea, Wales. Lyndon was raised in Coal Creek, Tennessee, an area with a well-established Welsh community, and met Elaine Jones, her mother, in nearby Knoxville. Lyndon married Elaine, moved to San Francisco, and two years later, she was born. They gave her the name of Savannah, which was her Welsh grandmother's name, derived from a boat her great-grandfather once sailed, called "The Savannah." Her middle name, Karenina, came from one of Lyndon's favorite novels, Leo Tolstoy's *Anna Karenina*. Told him that her mother died of a brain aneurysm when she was only nine. Told him about Sabine, her mother's best friend, the free-spirited poet with whom she spent the latter part of her growing years after her mother died–until Sabine moved to Switzerland when Savannah turned eighteen. About her art education, how she became the youngest director of the Somerset Gallery, and how she later decided to become a full-time artist. She talked about Russell, and how she just recently became engaged.

As she had done many times before, she remained silent about her father walking out on her mother and her. She had practiced it often over the years. Mastered the art of glossing over the painful subject by shining the light on something else–anything else.

To her relief, no one ever asked her the question she dreaded. Yet Savannah knew it was inevitable. She just didn't know Alfonso would be the one to ask, "So where's your father now?"

She stammered for a few seconds. It was the moment of truth. "Oh ... he remarried and moved away." With her eyes lowered, she struggled for something to say, wished she could at least name the city where her father had gone to live, but nothing came.

After what seemed an unbearable silence that stretched forever, she changed the subject and said, "So, I see you brought the painting with you?" She gestured with her eyes at the large black portfolio he had brought with him, and had propped against one of the table legs.

Savannah was aware that Alfonso had been searching her face, and she knew her evasion of the subject of her father's whereabouts did not escape his notice. Nonetheless, he didn't press her for a more definite answer.

"Oh, yes. I almost forgot," he said.

He leaned down and unzipped the nylon, soft-sided portfolio, reached into it, and pulled out the painting that he had carefully wrapped in brown paper. As he did, Savannah noticed that something fell to the floor.

She stooped to pick it up. It was a large postcard that had a collage of pictures of Flamenco dancers, Spanish *tapas* and wine, and Alfonso playing a guitar. On the bottom right-hand corner, the words: *Experience an Evening in Spain at Club La Cibeles.*

"You didn't tell me you were a singer, Alfonso."

"No, no, I'm not a singer. I'm a Flamenco guitarist. Flamenco comes in three forms. *Canto*, which is Flamenco singing, *Baile*, which is Flamenco dance, and *Guitarra*, which is guitar playing. Flamenco guitar playing–that's what I do."

"You mean like Paco de Lucía?" she ventured.

"You've heard of Paco de Lucía?" Alfonso appeared surprised.

Although Paco de Lucía was already famous in the Flamenco world, he had not yet become well known to the mainstream world.

"I just saw a film clip about him on TV. He's an incredible guitar player."

"Yes, he's definitely *the* virtuoso of Flamenco guitar. I don't pretend to be even half as good as he is."

"How long have you been playing at *La Cibeles*?"

"For almost as long as I've lived here in San Francisco. I arrived here a year ago yesterday." After a short pause, he said, "If you like Flamenco music, I wouldn't mind at all if you came to the club one night."

"I just might do that. Thanks."

There was something in his brooding countenance that intrigued her. It was as though some unfathomable, restless tragedy paced ceaselessly across his mind. During their conversation, he would often fix her with a sidelong glance, with his head cocked to the side, and his eyes burrowing through to her soul. There was something unsettling about the way he gazed at her from that oblique angle that made her insides jump every time he did it.

She couldn't help observing his articulate way of communicating in English, considering he had lived in the United States for only a year. She felt as though she did not have to alter her conversation to limp along in sympathy with his limited knowledge of the English language the way she had to with other foreigners.

"Where did you learn to speak English?" she queried.

He told her that Málaga had an academic atmosphere that attracted a significant number of international students who came there, wishing to learn Spanish. The students were always looking for a means of livelihood, and his grandmother hired an eighteen-year-old American girl named Joanne Hennessey from Boston, Massachusetts, who was fluent in both English and Spanish, to become his private tutor.

"Joanne taught me English, literature and art appreciation for two summers, and on weekends during the school year–until she went back to the States in 1962. I was nine when she left, but her teaching paid off. I became the only member of the Madrigál family who knew how to converse and write in English.

"I remember her telling me stories about America that ignited my imagination as a little boy. I think that's when I got the desire to come to America one day. When I moved to Madrid, I continued studying English for a few more years. The owner of the club where I used to play encouraged it so that we could communicate with the English-speaking tourists. By the time I left Madrid for San Francisco last year, I spoke English fluently."

"That's interesting," she said, pondering his privileged childhood. After a few moments, she asked, "Do you also sing, by the way?"

"No, I don't sing. Not in public anyway. I only sing to my daughter, Cristina."

Savannah was startled when he said the word *daughter*. It hadn't occurred to her that he might be married, much less have a child. Something inside her secretly wished he wasn't married. Finding out he was married made her feel a little more than disappointed–and that worried her.

When he spoke his daughter's name, there was a momentary glint in his eye, and for a split second, Savannah saw his eyes turn tender. His face, nonetheless, remained guarded.

"How old is she?"

"Cristina's four years old," he replied as he pushed the coffee cups aside, set the painting on the table, and proceeded to peel off the brown wrapping paper.

"Tell me about Cristina."

Again, Savannah saw his eyes turn gentle as his face formed an expression which, on some other man, might have ripened into a smile. He pulled himself back in his chair and combed his hair with both hands. He turned pensive.

"Ella es muy preciosa. She's a precious child," he said, with a touch of pride in his voice. "She's only four years old, but sometimes the things she says humble me. God gave her a unique pair of eyes."

"What do you mean?"

"She prefers to look at things that are made by God and not by man. Other kids are impressed by skyscrapers. She's impressed by the sky. She could sit and watch a rainbow or a blade of grass longer than she could sit and watch cartoons. I took her to Disneyland a few months ago, and she was more fascinated by the variety of flowers and trees that were there than she was of the rides and attractions." Alfonso shook his head, as if in awe. "She's a special little girl."

"Probably because you're doing a good job as a father."

"Oh, I doubt that very much. There are days when I think she teaches me more than I teach her. She has a deep intimacy with the world, and she hasn't lost her connection to divinity."

He turned reflective again, as though lost in his thoughts. "Cristina has taught me the ability to be enchanted by the present moment, something I'd given up a long time ago. I see a more expanded view of the world when I see it through her eyes."

Savannah marveled at the way he spoke of his daughter. Seldom had she heard a parent celebrating the divine nature of his child.

Parents don't often pay attention when their children talk about imaginary worlds, and they frequently dismiss children's imaginings as make-believe, even nonsense. What they're often preoccupied with is how many gold stars their children are getting, or how many A's on report cards—or some other petty rewards that give them the unworthy satisfaction of knowing that their child is better than other children. But rarely do they extol their divine aspect.

"It seems that Cristina is a highly evolved human being," she ventured.

"In the spiritual sense, yes. She's still… *cómo se dice*… unadulterated."

The intelligence and sensitivity she sensed in Alfonso struck a chord in her. Unadulterated was how he referred to Cristina. Unfettered by the trappings of worldly living. Innocence in the midst of chaos. Savannah longed for the simplicity of childhood, while grieving how far removed she was from that innocence.

"She also has a special gift. She has what you would call extrasensory perception."

"Really?"

"*Sí*. Sometimes, she can sense people's thoughts and feelings when she touches things that belong to them. She can't do it all the time. Usually only when the emotions attached to the things are particularly strong. Sometimes she doesn't even have to touch the things… just be near them."

"Like what, for instance?"

"Last week, I took her with me to a bookstore downtown. There was a poetry reading in the back of the store. I noticed that she stopped to listen as the poetry was being read. After the reading, she walked over to the woman who wrote the poem and asked her, 'Have you ever been in a small room with shuttered windows, a ceiling fan, blue-and-white checkered wallpaper, and an old man lying on a bed?' The woman broke into tears right there in front of everyone. Later, she told me that the poem was inspired by her dying grandfather whose room was exactly the way Cristina described it. That was the actual image that was in her mind when she wrote the poem."

"That's amazing!" Savannah had heard of others who possessed such exquisite intuition, but had never known any personally.

"Another time, Cristina was in day care. She and the other children were drawing with crayons. When they finished, their drawings were hung on the back wall of the room for everyone to see. Next to Cristina's drawing was a drawing done by a girl named Soo-Jen, a five-year-old Korean girl. When Cristina looked at Soo-Jen's drawing, she started crying loudly. The preschool teacher, Miss

Luisa, came over to see what was the matter. She told the teacher that someone has to stop Soo-Jen's mother from beating Soo-Jen with a broomstick. What Miss Luisa couldn't understand was how Cristina could have known that from looking at a drawing of trees on mountains with bright colors. Later, it was discovered that Soo-Jen was an abused child, and her mother always beat her with a broomstick."

"Incredible," was all Savannah could say. She couldn't help but wonder about this man who seemed fiercely private about his life but could speak so spiritedly about his daughter.

Just then, Alfonso peeled the last layer of brown paper off the painting. "Are you ready?" he asked. The painting was lying face down on the table.

"Oh, yes. Let's have a look."

Alfonso carefully grasped the sides of the painting and turned it over. Then, he gently pushed it toward her so that she could have a better view. Savannah's fingers brushed against his as she lifted the painting off the table and set it in an upright position on her lap. It was just a brief contact, but again, she felt the blood rush to her face.

As she gazed at the painting, she noticed that Alfonso never took his eyes off of her, studying her every move, analyzing every facial feature. She quickly concealed her uneasiness by pulling a magnifying loupe out of her purse. She began to examine the painting the way she normally would as an art professional.

It was an oil on canvas, framed in gilt-edged, hand-carved wood. About 25 inches high and 30 inches wide. The painting was that of a young, raven-haired woman with a mole above the left corner of her upper lip. Her long dark locks cascaded down her shoulders like tendrils of a vine, and her heart-shaped face was further emphasized by the widow's peak on her hairline. The woman was wearing a red dress, sitting on a blanket spread out on the grass, and behind her was a seascape. The sky was painted with luminous gradations of light that suggested daybreak.

Savannah sat quietly for a couple of minutes, first viewing the artistic virtues of the painting, then analyzing the mechanics.

She carefully lifted the painting with her left hand, and with her right, she brought the magnifying loupe up to her eye to take a closer look at the signature in the bottom right corner. *Ruiz 1897.* Then, she set the loupe down on the table, grasped the painting by both hands and tilted it backwards until it was almost in the horizontal position in mid-air, simultaneously lifted it to eye level, and examined it from that perspective. From the corner of her eye, Savannah noticed that Alfonso had nestled his chin on the crook of his left thumb and forefinger, while biting the left side of his lower lip, as if pondering a great mystery. There was something adorable about the way he did that. Everything Alfonso said or did seemed to give rise to something in her that she was not prepared to entertain.

After a few minutes, she said, "I'm just inspecting the canvas and the paint that was used. Also the style and intensity of the brushwork. Obviously, I will have to analyze the age, the craquelure and the patina of this oil painting further... but do you want to know my opinion at first glance?"

Alfonso nodded, with a look of anticipation in his eyes.

"The woman is painted in the style of the earlier works of Picasso. Those done in the late 19th century like *The Communion* and *Science & Charity*, both painted in 1897. There was a time when Picasso painted landscapes and seascapes, wherein he introduced his own innovations to the formal techniques of French landscape painters. Those innovations are apparent in the seascape of this painting. The penmanship of the artist is strikingly similar to that of Picasso's."

⚬

Alfonso looked at her, watched her lips move as she spoke. There was nothing more appealing to him than a beautiful woman with great intellect and knowledge. He had known many pretty women before, but had never remained attracted when there was nothing beneath the lovely facade. He hadn't met very many with the intelligence, grace and elegance of Savannah Curtis.

From across the table, he looked upon the profile of her face—the curve of her eyelid, the upturned, aristocratic nose, the full, sensual lips shaped like a guitar, the delicate chin. The afternoon sun streaming through the window made her hair of rich mahogany dazzle in the muted lighting of the café. In her golden-green dress, she looked softer, more feminine, and less severe than she did in yesterday's suit. To him, she had an air of confidence, yet he sensed a fragility about her. And her voice had a cadence and a sound that somehow calmed the ever-present turbulence in his soul.

He listened intently, without saying a word, nodding his head to acknowledge what she was saying.

"It's too soon to render a professional opinion, but I'm convinced there is a possible authenticity here. I need to put it through a more in-depth stylistic and technical analysis, but if this painting is authentic, it would probably be worth quite a bit. I suppose you want to know what this painting is worth, don't you?"

"It's worth the world to me, Savannah. Of course, it would be nice to know its market value, but I would never consider selling it.

I'm more interested in finding out an important part of my grandmother's life. Aside from the tambourine, the painting is the only thing of hers I own."

Savannah glanced at him with a look of surprise on her face. Then she said, "To authenticate a work of art like this that has no documentation whatsoever is an involved process. I'm an appraiser myself, and I can do a stylistic and technical analysis of the work using the wood lamp test, an infra red test–and comparing it with other works of Picasso. I can also analyze the penmanship further, study the pigments used, but even that may not be enough. I may have to call on other experts to confirm authenticity."

"It doesn't matter how long it takes or how much it costs, Savannah. This is very important to me."

She looked at him again with the same look of surprise. "Alright then," she said, opening her purse. She pulled out her business card, scribbled her home address and phone number on the back, and handed it to him.

"My card only has my mailing address and a telephone number that rings through to my answering service. But I've written my home address and phone number on the back. Why don't you bring the painting to my home on Monday? That's where I have my studio, along with the form I need for you to fill out to consign the painting to me while I work on it. I don't live too far from *La Cibeles*, so maybe you can stop by before you go to work. Would five o'clock be okay?"

He took her business card, and looked at the address she had written. 201 Pacific Avenue. He really didn't need any paperwork to consign the painting to her. He would have been willing to just entrust her with the painting with no reservations. But the lure of seeing her again was impossible to resist. Especially seeing her again at her place.

"Five o'clock on Monday is perfect," he declared, as he pulled out his wallet from the back pocket of his pants and tucked her card into it. "Thank you for doing this, Savannah," he said. "And by the way, Monday night is the only night I don't play at *La Cibeles*."

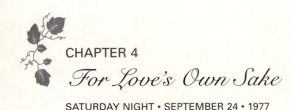

CHAPTER 4
For Love's Own Sake
SATURDAY NIGHT • SEPTEMBER 24 • 1977

Club La Cibeles was always bustling on Saturday nights. Alfonso arrived just before seven, looking forward to having his favorite dinner of Spanish paella, jabugo ham, Pacheco cheese and a glass of red wine, before playing at nine.

He liked working at *La Cibeles*. He enjoyed walking into the curvy entryway, with its Spanish murals and metal sculptures on the wall. He liked the stunning, multilevel dining room with muted lighting that cast a romantic hue on everything. He liked the smell of *tapas calientes* wafting in from the kitchen and the heady aroma of *marzuelas*, the seafood soup *La Cibeles* was famous for, next to its creative versions of Spanish *paella*.

"*Hola*, Gonzalo!" Alfonso exclaimed as he strolled in.

Gonzalo Arguelles, the owner of the club, was rattling off instructions to the kitchen staff. He turned his head and nodded at Alfonso, then quickly looked away, continuing to give orders. A moment later, his eyes darted once again at Alfonso, who seemed to him to be in unusually good spirits.

"*¿Qué pasa?*" he asked. "What's going on?" Gonzalo was a second-generation Spanish immigrant whose parents came from Avila, just north of Madrid. Gonzalo was born and raised in California, and spoke just enough Spanish to make him dangerous. The staff made a sport out of correcting his pidgin Spanish.

Alfonso shrugged his shoulders.

"Don't give me that, *paisano*. I can tell," Gonzalo said, peering closely at him. "You look...happy."

"I'm just having a good day."

"Oh, yeah? What's her name?" He winked at Alfonso.

"You already know my daughter's name. Cristina."

"Okay, if you say so. But I've never seen you in this kind of mood before. I'm sure something's going on."

"*Por Dios.* Is there a law against being in a good mood?"

"*Si, Señor*. When it comes to you, there is a law. I'm afraid if you smile, your face might crack," he said, contorting his face and crossing his eyes. "You've never smiled before. You never know what could happen. Your head could explode—*kaboom!*"

Miguel, the chef, Paco, the *sous chef*, and Ricardo, the head-waiter, who were standing within earshot, chortled with gusto.

Gonzalo was a natural comic, and he had never known anyone like Alfonso, who seldom laughed or smiled. But he was bent on trying. It had become a running joke among the club's staff.

Alfonso's face remained sober, although there was a bounce in his step and a gleam in his eyes that couldn't be missed.

"Hey, maybe our Flamenco boy's in love," Paco said, making exaggerated gestures with his hands, pretending his heart was bursting out of his chest like a Hanna-Barbera cartoon character in love.

"Exactamundo," Gonzalo said.

"*Exactamente*–not exactamundo," Ricardo said. "There you go again speaking Spanish like the Fonz." Miguel and Paco burst out laughing again.

"No problemo. I'm gonna make our boy from Málaga laugh yet. I feel it coming," he said.

"*No problema*," Ricardo corrected his Spanish again.

"Well, if you want to be a stickler about it," snorted Gonzalo.

༄

At the tail end of Alfonso's second set, Zendrik walked into the Club and seated himself at one of the bar tables. Alfonso joined him at his table when he finished playing.

"*Hombre!*" Zendrik said, giving Alfonso a handshake.

"*¿Cómo estás, amigo?*"

"Just great, man. My band just started playing at the *Grease Monkey* last week."

"*Espera*, I thought you were playing at the *Vicious Circle?*"

"Just finished that gig a couple of weeks ago," Zendrik said, taking a gulp of his Spanish *cerveza*. "The *Grease Monkey's* a helluva better gig. Much better pay, too."

"What days are you playing?"

"Tuesdays, Thursdays, and Fridays."

"Too bad. I work on those days. Can you believe, I've known you for almost a year now, and you've heard me play so many times but I haven't been to even one of your gigs?"

"That's because you're working all the time, *hombre*. Hey, you came to one of my band rehearsals last year, didn't you? We have an entirely new line-up from the one you heard, though. Some originals, some covers."

"Let me know when you start playing on Monday nights. You know that's my only night off."

"Sure, man," Zendrik said, taking another gulp of beer. "There's a chance we'll open for Len Gastineau at the *Trocadero* next month. I think that's on a Monday. I'll let you know."

"Fantástico!"

Just then, a cocktail waitress carrying a tray topped with cocktails came by their table. "A *Cosmic Shaman* for Zendrik, and a shot of *Moscatel* for Alfonso. Compliments of Diego," she said, placing the drinks on the table.

"Thanks, Carla," Zendrik said, pulling a five dollar bill out of his wallet and handing it to her.

Then, he turned towards the bar and waved at the bartender. *"Muchas gracias, amigo!"*

"De nada," Diego replied, grinning back at him.

Zendrik was well liked by the staff at the Club. They enjoyed having him around because he had an innate ability for making everyone feel good about themselves, and knew how to regale those around him with stories ranging from his escapades as a young musician, to out-of-body experiences, to everything profound, spiritual, weird or wacky. He also knew how to rustle up a good time at any given moment without being drunk, obnoxious or stoned like other party guys tended to be. Gonzalo called him *Hermano*, referring to him as the brother he never had. The bartenders, Diego and Enrique, called him *Cosmic Shaman* because he always engaged them in deep conversations about metaphysics and the occult. They even named a cocktail in his honor–*Cosmic Shaman*, which was a traditional margarita on the rocks with a splash of dark rum.

Zendrik had been a patron of *Club La Cibeles* long before Alfonso was hired as the main performer. He was at the Club when Alfonso auditioned for the job in the fall of 1976, and he had urged Gonzalo to hire him on the spot after he heard him play.

To the casual onlooker, the friendship that developed between Zendrik and Alfonso was not in the stars. They were as mismatched as friends could be. Zendrik was outgoing, flamboyant and fun-loving, while Alfonso was reserved, private, brooding and joyless. Yet they bonded like brothers because they shared a love of music that transcended their differences.

Alfonso felt comfortable with Zendrik from the first time he met him at the Club. He felt that they somehow had a psychic connection of some kind–one that enabled Zendrik oftentimes to know what he was thinking even before he said a word. It was not unlike the psychic connection that exists between identical twins. Alfonso also felt that Zendrik was the kind of person in whom he could confide, and to whom he could tell anything without fear of recrimination or judgment. But not until that day had there been anything private enough or important enough in his life to confide.

Alfonso downed his shot of *Moscatel* in one gulp, after which he pulled a piece of lilac-colored parchment paper out of his pocket, placed it on the table, and pushed it towards Zendrik.

Zendrik picked up the piece of paper and read what Alfonso had written on it. "Did you write this?" he asked.

"*Sí.* I just want you to look it over to make sure that it reads right in English...that it doesn't sound awkward."

"Awkward?" Zendrik gasped, looking astonished. "This is freakin' splendid, man. This could have only been inspired by a woman. In fact, I bet my life it was a woman who caused you to write this."

Alfonso was silent. He wasn't surprised that Zendrik had zeroed in on his thoughts, but he decided to play dumb. "Why would you think this has anything to do with a woman? My words don't say anything about a woman."

"I just know. I also know this woman has a name. What is it?"

"Her name is Savannah Curtis," he said, noticing the fracture in his own voice when he said her name.

Zendrik peered at Alfonso curiously and said, "Plato was right."

"About what?"

"He said, *'At the touch of love, everyone becomes a poet.'*"

"Who said anything about love?"

"You certainly didn't. But it's there in between the lines."

Alfonso had never thought of himself a poet of any caliber. He liked poetry. Not just those of Federico García Lorca and Pablo Neruda, but those written by English poets–Wordsworth, Byron, Keats. He had dabbled in poetry writing when he was a child, during his summers with his private tutor, Joanne Hennessey, and when he took advanced English during his years in Madrid. He wrote poetry whenever he felt a certain spiritual electricity--the kind he felt every time he saw the sun rise or set, every time he gazed at the ocean, the mountains, a cloudless sky, or a thing of grandeur or beauty. The same spiritual electricity he felt when he first laid eyes on Savannah.

"Well, whoever this Savannah Curtis is, she must be pretty amazing," Zendrik said, shaking his head in mock solemnity, all the while grinning at Alfonso mischievously.

"You could say that."

⁂

*L*ater that night, after playing his last set, Alfonso said goodbye to Zendrik, packed his guitar into its well-worn case, and drove his 1975 Buick slowly down Portofino Boulevard under pale moonlight. He turned left onto Pacific Avenue. He read the odd numbers on the right side of the street, one by one, as they came into view–

191, 193, 195, 197. Spotting a vacant curbside parking space right in front of 199 Pacific, he steered his car into it and turned off the engine. Just up ahead he saw Savannah's Victorian apartment. *201 Pacific*. The address marker was up lit and bordered in an ornate wrought iron scrollwork. It was perfectly visible from where he sat.

His heart pounded hard now, though he could not understand why. To his left was a small park with a playground. He gazed at it for a few moments before he turned his attention once again to the Victorian apartment where Savannah Curtis lived. It had a typical enclosed garage at street level, next to a long flight of stairs that led to her front door. The front door was partly obscured by an overhanging beam. On the second floor, a bay window revealed a part of the living room, and next to that was a large window that ran from the ceiling down to about two feet from the floor, with its curtains drawn. *That would be her bedroom*, he mused, noticing that the light was still on inside. He felt something stir inside him as he realized how close he was to her sleeping quarters, then quickly perished the thought. He sat in his car with his eyes transfixed on her bedroom window, watching for some movement that would allow him to know she was there, maybe catch a glimpse of her shadow—yet wondering why he was doing this when his wife and daughter slept no more than two miles away. He stared without moving for fifteen minutes until he saw her light turn off. He looked at the clock just beneath the dashboard—12:20.

His thoughts turned to his days as a teenager growing up in Málaga. His friends had used the word "love" so loosely. They would tell their girlfriends they loved them, and have no qualms about saying the same to the next few girls that came along. He often wondered whether it was the hormones speaking. He remembered asking his friend, Luis, "Why do you tell Corazon you love her? Do you even know the meaning of the word?" And Luis told him it's what the girls want to hear. He said if you want to have your way with them, you have to say you love them.

That always bothered him. That was so disrespectful of women, who to him were special beings that needed to be adored, cherished and celebrated. As a result, he never said, "I love you" to a woman, not even to his wife, Isabel. Because although he had "known" many women in the biblical sense, he never did love a woman, at least not in the way he thought a man ought to love a woman.

At first, he had equated beauty with love. If a man found a woman who was beautiful, he would proceed to fall in love with her. And it worked the same way for women, too. At least, that's the way he saw it in the movies. But then, he started thinking, if that's what love is, with the great number of beautiful women out there, he would be in love with a new woman every day. He would even be in love with his wife, Isabel, who most people considered quite beautiful.

No, love couldn't be equated to beauty, he had concluded. All he had to do was remember his parents. His father, Francisco Madrigál, fell in love with his mother, Esperanza Manzano, because of her beauty. To him, she was a trophy, not the love of his life for whom he'd forsake everything or give everything. Francisco himself was handsome, and was an heir to the Madrigál fortune. It must have been easy for Esperanza to fool herself into believing that she loved Francisco. They had a mutual infatuation for each other, and they were deluded into believing that they looked good together and made the perfect couple. In truth, it was nothing but the vanity of two young people giddy on having everything. As a boy, Alfonso had sensed no real love between his parents–not when the family fortunes were good, and definitely not when they went bad.

He had often spent time on the dockyards of Málaga, looking towards the glistening Mediterranean, wondering what love really meant. Now, as he thought of Savannah, he remembered that far out in the untraveled back roads of his mind lay a far-flung ideal from his boyhood that he had almost given up for lost. He had once imprinted it into his brain, and now he recalled every word of it.

> *If I must love a woman, let it be for love's own sake. Let it not be for the mere loveliness of her face, the way she speaks, the silhouette of her body, or for a quality that falls in well with mine, that makes a day or a season magical. For these things might not linger, and love thus made may be unmade just as swiftly. Let me not love for superlative things that she is or isn't, that she has or hasn't–for how easy would it be to find another who embodies such things and more, and lose my love thereby. But rather, let love carve in me an unchanging heart that chooses every moment to be amazed by her on any day, in any light, in any season, and any night. Let me love with spellbound fascination over her soul touching mine–that forever I may stand in the radiance that is her.*

As Alfonso looked at the darkened window of Savannah, a woman he met just a day ago, a small voice within him told him there was hope yet for the kind of love he dared to imagine in his younger days.

He drove home in silence. It was half past midnight. He wondered how he could wait two days before seeing her again.

CHAPTER 5
The Music of Fresh Fallen Rain
MONDAY AFTERNOON • SEPTEMBER 26 • 1977

It was already 4:30 and Savannah had not found anything suitable to wear. Alfonso would be at her apartment in thirty minutes.

Dressing for Russell was easy, because Russell always had clear-cut likes and dislikes. She always knew how to please him. *What is it with me?* she wondered. *Why do I spend my life trying to please other people instead of just being myself?* She admonished herself for the fussiness over perfection that had characterized her life. Sabine had told her on many occasions that her obsessive quest for flawlessness–not only in the way she looked, but the way she behaved, the way she furnished her home, and the choices she made in life– stemmed from her deep-seated need for approval. A need that was dangerously bordering on neurosis. A need that started with her misconception that her father wouldn't have left if she had only been a perfect little girl.

Sabine had always been perceptive and wise, but she constantly pointed to things Savannah wasn't ready to face. Today, Savannah decided she was going to put things in their proper perspective. Alfonso was virtually a stranger to her–someone she has known for only three days. He was coming to drop off a painting that she's having expertly authenticated. He's a married man with a daughter, and she herself was engaged to be married. *This is not a date,* she reminded herself. *Therefore, I don't need to dress as though I'm going on a date.*

She went through her closet one more time. Tucked behind rows of suits, dresses, blouses and slacks neatly hanging from scented, satin-covered padded hangers, she found a summer dress she had forgotten she bought at the end of last year's summer season. She had never had a chance to wear it this year because the San Francisco summer was damp, cold and foggy. It was a cornflower blue silk chiffon dress with a shapely silhouette and a flouncy hemline that rode up two inches above the knee. It had white spaghetti-thin straps with tiny white satin rosebuds running from the straps down to the scooped neckline and back.

She remembered falling in love with the dress, but thinking she could never wear it around Russell for there was nothing about the color, style or length that he would like. She had bought the dress anyway–just to please herself. The dress was a little more coquettish than she wanted to appear to Alfonso. *Forget about what anyone thinks,* she reminded herself. She tried it on and concluded that she liked the way it flattered her figure, showed just enough of her shapely legs under the hemline, and just a subtle whisper of cleavage beneath the scooped neckline. The dress made her feel girlish and carefree.

The doorbell rang at exactly five o'clock. She walked to the door and opened it. Alfonso stood for a moment looking awe-struck, but all he said was, "*Buenas tardes*, Savannah."

"*Buenas tardes,*" she replied, opening the door wide to let him in. She had told herself she didn't care what he thought of how she looked in that dress, and that she had worn it only because it made her feel good. But she couldn't help but revel in his unspoken admiration. His eyes couldn't hide their appreciation, and it gave her a warm feeling in her belly.

⁓

Alfonso stepped into Savannah's apartment, bending over to lean the black nylon portfolio against the wall after she shut the door. He tried not to look at her for she looked too captivating for words, so he let his eyes roam the interior of her apartment instead.

He remembered thinking what a pleasant surprise it was to step into a Victorian apartment and find he'd been transported to Asia the moment he got inside. It was like stepping into a visual feast of exotic persuasions that was at once warm, inviting and sensual. A large moon-shaped black lacquer screen with inlaid mother-of-pearl pagodas formed the backdrop of the living room, creating a dramatic contrast with the kidney-shaped sofa upholstered in a golden bronze silk fabric with a faint Oriental pattern. Off to the side stood an 8-foot bamboo tree in a reed basket. The round, glass-topped coffee table encircled with braided hemp that could have only been handmade in Indonesia, had a few art books on top of it neatly arranged in the shape of a fan. Next to the books sat a white orchid plant in a Chinese porcelain planter.

A long canister-shaped Japanese lantern made of translucent silver-speckled rice paper hung from a curved bamboo lamppost, dimly lit. The warmth of the day had released a tantalizing fragrance into the air. "What is that wonderful scent?" he asked. *"Maravilloso!"*

"You must be talking about the Kahili ginger flowers," she said, pointing to a flower arrangement on a narrow rattan table by the door. It was a stunning bouquet of long-stemmed yellow flowers with red stamens covering 18-inch stalks. "I try to have them around the house when they're in bloom. They're at the end of their season now. We won't be seeing them much until next July."

Once again, Alfonso thought he heard the sound of an eerie chime—the same one he heard as she walked toward him at Sutton Hall. He dismissed it as his imagination.

Savannah motioned for him to sit, and he sat himself down on the sofa, leaning back easily, putting one arm on the sofa back. He stretched his legs, crossing them at the ankles. He readily acclimatized to his surroundings, but there was an uneasiness inside him. Savannah was unlike any other woman he had ever met. To him, she was almost like deity–to be revered and glorified. One who would most likely steal his heart, perhaps already did. He had never been speechless around women. For some reason, women always seemed to find his brooding ways and dark conversation quite charming. But with Savannah, he didn't quite know how to act or what to say.

"Your apartment reminds me of an oasis in the middle of a desert."

"Thank you. I'll take that as a compliment," she said, smiling at him.

"That was how it was intended."

He looked at the framed pictures sitting on the side table. His eyes fell upon a photograph of a tall, good-looking blond man wearing hiking attire. "Is this Russell?" he asked.

"Yes, that's Russell," she replied, her eyes glazing over as she stared at the floor. "I took that picture of him when we went to Yosemite last summer." Shortly thereafter, she asked, "May I offer you something to drink? I have tea, soda, wine…."

"I'll have a glass of wine, *por favor*."

"I'll be right back," she said.

As she walked into the kitchen, he watched her. It was his first opportunity to really look at her. He had not wanted to look at her directly before—not wanting her to see the masculine longing in his eyes. *Qué exquisita! My God, she's exquisite,* he thought, forcing himself to view her as the delicate work of art she was, rather than the object of his masculine inclinations. How could he tell her how remarkable she was to him, how pleasantly engaged he was in her presence, how delighted he was by her conversation and exuberance, and how intoxicated he was by her elegance, grace and beauty? And how could he tell her that beneath her regal bearing, he sensed a palpable sensuality, which she could never quite hide from his view?

Savannah returned in a few minutes carrying a tray with a flagon-shaped bottle of Mateus Rosé and two wine glasses. She set the tray on the coffee table.

"Please let me do it," he said when he saw her reaching for the wine bottle. He poured the pale pink rosé into the glasses, handed her a glass, and lifted his glass to her.

"*Salud, amor, pesetas, y el tiempo para gozarlos,*" she said. *Health, love, wealth and the time to enjoy them.* It was a toast she had learned when she visited Spain.

"*Bravo,*" he said, taking a sip of the Portuguese wine, savoring its light and fruity spritz on his tongue.

Alfonso looked at her sitting across from him in the cane side chair–looked at her with exploring eyes. Her feminine modesty gave her an air of detachment, but that subtle sensuality of hers made his blood race and intensified his desire. He found himself fantasizing about stroking her hair, kissing her lips, caressing her body and taking her into his arms. He tried to think of something else– anything else to occupy his mind.

"Do you like classical music?" she asked presently.

"*Naturalmente.* Of course."

She walked to the bookshelf, which was next to her stereo rack. She pulled out a long wooden box neatly filled with cassette tapes, searching for Tomaso Giovanni Albinoni. Behind her glowed the long canister-shaped Japanese paper lantern, and from where he sat in the dimly lit side of the room, the light seemed to dissolve her silk dress into sheer gossamer. He watched, entranced, as Savannah's shapely figure emerged through the fabric made diaphanous by lamplight.

He thought of the time he lived in Madrid, particularly after General Franco fell from power. The air was charged with unencumbered freedom and the Spaniards gladly threw the old society's moral embargoes to the wind, exposing a new sexual liberation. There were countless pretty *señoritas* in the city looking for a little love, who found romance in his handsome face, his sensitive disposition, and the strains of his acoustic guitar. For some time, he enjoyed the attention of all those *Madrileñas* who were sophisticated and worldly–some of them beautiful as well. He dated many women and plunged into more short-term sexual encounters than he could count. Promiscuity and carnal indulgence was a way of life for most single *Madrileños.* Yet through it all, his soul had hungered for something more. He had never lost his heart to a woman the way he secretly wished he would. His soul never played a romantic rumba when he looked at a woman the way he thought it would when one falls in love.

Now, looking at Savannah silhouetted in the glimmer of the Japanese lantern fashioned out of translucent rice paper, something clutched at his heart and wouldn't let go. It was a feeling that was too far removed from anything he had ever felt with a woman before.

Savannah had found the cassette tape she was looking for, and played it for him. Tomaso Giovanni Albinoni's *Adagio in G Minor* slowed his heartbeat down, something for which he was thankful. There was something about early 18th-century Venetian classical music, the glow of a Japanese lantern and the scent of Kahili ginger flowers that framed Savannah in a way no masterpiece of art ever could.

Words were coming at him again. A river of words. Pouring themselves into neat little stanzas.

> *How is it that you have come to prevail*
>   *upon my soul?*
> *And what compass, what map, and which star*
>   *guided you to where my heart has hidden itself?*
> *And how is it that we've come to a place so swiftly*
>   *where time is as it never was*
>   *and yet is as it has always been?*
> *How is it that volumes have been spoken between us*
>   *without words*
>   *and without the complexities of pride and artifice?*
> *All day I seek the gentle sweetness of your voice*
>   *and the perfect clarity of your heart*
>   *without knowing why, or how,*
>   *or from where the fever came*
> *I fly, as sparrows do,*
>   *knowing I'm coming home to you*
>   *and I long to see your eyes when dawn pours its brandy*
>   *into the earth's bosom.*

The thoughts were so strange that he hardly recognized them as his own. It felt as though he were reciting words from a poem written by someone like Federico García Lorca.

༄

Savannah didn't know whether it was the effect of the music and the glass of wine, but she felt a tenderness for Alfonso Madrigál that she couldn't explain or understand. *What am I doing?* she thought. Deep inside she was secretly happy he chose the wine, instead of the soda or tea that she also offered him. It would give him a reason to linger. She didn't want him to leave too soon. She was afraid of risky possibilities, but didn't want the night to be over. She worried about how she should handle the rest of the evening. But he was a perfect gentleman making no advances. *Why should I worry?* she thought.

"By the way, there's something about your painting I want to tell you about. Can we take a look at it so I can point it out to you?"

"Of course," he said, putting his wine glass on the coffee table and walking towards where he had left the nylon portfolio.

"I'll go get the easel," she said, disappearing into her bedroom, and reappearing shortly thereafter carrying the wooden easel and setting it next to the bay window. Alfonso set the painting on the narrow easel shelf.

She drew the curtains, letting the fading afternoon sun stream through. Then she stood next to him, examining the painting. "Have you noticed that mysterious stain against the seascape?" She pointed to the area to the right of the woman's head, two inches up. It was a nebulous shadow that had an indefinite shape, the size of a silver dollar. It had a greenish tint.

"Yes. Even when I was a boy, I noticed that on the painting. It was much smaller then. The size of a thumbnail. I thought it was just a discoloration."

"Well, you may be partly right. My guess is that it's a *pentimento*."

"Hmmm ..." Alfonso was familiar with the literal translation of the word. In Italian, it meant *repentance*. But he was unsure what it meant in the context of art.

As though sensing his unspoken question, she explained, "In the early days, artists sometimes created an oil painting and then changed their mind and decided they didn't want to keep it, or they preferred to create another painting instead. When that happened, they frequently painted over the old painting beneath it."

"Why would they paint over it instead of just throwing the old one and starting with a fresh canvas?"

"Canvas was not as readily available as it is today. It was probably expensive back then, too. The problem is that if the artist doesn't use a scraper to remove lines or colors that are darker than the new paint and smooth out any thick impasto in the underlying image, it tends to reappear later. That's what a *pentimento* is. An artist's repentance coming back to haunt him."

"So you're saying that this work of art may have a *pentimento* beneath it?"

"It's quite possible. Look," she said, pointing to a dark pattern emerging through the pale colors of the seascape. "A *pentimento* becomes apparent as a painting ages. That's why the shadow is larger now than it was years ago when you saw it during your childhood."

"Does that mean that in a few years, the painting the way we see it may be completely replaced by the painting underneath?"

"More like a few decades. And it seldom happens that perfectly. Parts of the new painting may remain while parts of the underlying image–particularly those with strong brushwork and *impasto*–start to appear. Like a photo that's double exposed. Two pictures with unrelated subjects. Sometimes, though, the artist's original intention, as far as the composition of the painting goes, shows through. It's amazing when that happens. For instance, I saw one wherein the new painting was that of a woman sitting all alone on a rocking chair. The *pentimento* that emerged was that of the same woman holding a baby on her lap, sitting on a stationary chair. So the only thing that changed was the composition. It's pretty awesome to see because it's as though you're a secret witness to the artist's change of heart."

"Now-you-see-me-now-you-don't." It was Alfonso's attempt at being humorous. Savannah laughed. Not because it was particularly funny, but because it told her that there was a glimmer of light beneath his melancholy exterior.

"Is there any way to know–without waiting a few decades–what image lies underneath?"

"Yes, actually there are a few things that can be done."

"What would you do, exactly–I mean with the painting?"

"Well, there's infra-red reflectography, X-rays, ultraviolet photography…" She trailed off, as though losing herself in the painting. "I have an infra-red lamp here in my studio, but I'll have to send it out to be X-rayed. I don't want to bore you with the technical details, but yes, we can get an idea as to what the underlying image is."

"It's not boring at all. In fact, it's fascinating."

"I've studied some examples of Picasso's *pentimentos*. In the *Arlequín de Picasso* there is a change of position of the legs–a change that was obvious to the naked eye and later confirmed by the X-rays."

∽

*S*avannah continued talking for several minutes about other interesting *pentimentos* she had come across over the years. Alfonso listened intently, amazed at the amount of knowledge she had.

During a break in the conversation, he asked, "Would you mind if I took a look at your paintings, Savannah?"

"Not at all. They're in my studio…upstairs. Follow me."

Savannah turned and walked toward the wooden staircase and began climbing the stairs, with Alfonso walking right behind her. When she reached the fourth step, she said, "Watch out, now. The fifth step creaks loudly." She giggled softly as she reached the fifth step, which indeed let out a long, spooky creak that sounded as though the house was groaning.

When they reached the landing at the top of the stairs, she led him into a large guest room that she had converted into a studio.

"*Voila*. Here's my humble studio," she said. "It has a northern exposure, which is the kind of light I like to have when I paint."

From the doorway, he peered into her studio. A laminated work surface was mounted onto metal wall tracks with brackets. Perpendicular to the work surface against the wall hung a fabric-covered tack board pinned with notes, sketches and paraphernalia. Two mini speakers were mounted on tracks in two opposite corners of the room. A magnifying lens with an articulating arm was fastened to the metal wall track. A swivel task chair and a wooden bench were situated next to the work surface. Six of Savannah's paintings hung on the walls. The studio was tidy and uncluttered, except for a sketch notebook, pencils, a tool caddy and a red suede drawstring pouch sitting on top of the work surface.

"It doesn't look like a painter's studio. It's too ..."

"Clean? Yeah, I guess it looks very clean right now because I'm not presently working on a painting. I have a one-woman show in Los Angeles in a couple of weeks, and I've shipped off most of the paintings except for those six," she said, pointing to the ones hanging on the walls. "When I'm working, this place is covered with drop cloths, splattered with paint–dozens of brushes and a thousand tubes and cans of paint all over the place. It's a mess."

"May I take a closer look at your paintings?"

"Sure, step right in."

Alfonso spent a great deal of time looking at each of her paintings. She explained to him that these were the last of the pieces she would be exhibiting at her show in Los Angeles. She'd started working on them when she returned from New Zealand last March. Every collection she created was always inspired by a place that she had visited. Sometimes she painted an entire collection while still on location, like the one she did in Bali. Oftentimes, she painted from memory, the way she did these paintings of New Zealand forests.

After looking at all the pieces hanging on the studio wall, Alfonso said, *"Magnífico."* He said it under his breath; he wasn't sure if Savannah heard it.

Alfonso wasn't given to excessive displays of delight, yet he marveled how spiritually connected he felt to Savannah's art. He sensed a profound tranquility in each piece, yet with an undercurrent of desperate sadness bubbling beneath the surface.

"New Zealand has an ethereal kind of beauty that makes you feel like it's not of this world. The landscape there is so diverse. They have spectacular fiords, ancient rain forests, snowcapped mountain peaks, glaciers, pristine lakes, mountain ranges, and beaches. They have eighty-five species of ferns and volcanic landscapes—I could go on and on. It's an artist's paradise."

"When did you first realize you could paint?"

"I wasn't one of those who could draw or paint at a young age. Picasso, for instance, did his first masterpiece at the age of fifteen. I didn't create my first painting until I was twenty. But I remember what got me started."

"What was that?"

"When I was studying Picasso, I came across a story he once told when he first entered the School of Fine Arts in Barcelona. That was in 1895. He was seventeen years old. One of the first things he was taught at the school was to write in a notebook— *'One must learn to paint'*—and to repeat it several times. Picasso did it, but in reverse. Instead, he wrote in his notebook, *'One must not learn to paint. One must not learn to paint. One must not learn to paint.'*"

"And how did that get you started?"

"Well, what I gathered from Picasso's story is that it's so easy to lose one's spontaneous creativity when one is overly taught. When we have to abide by too many rules, we sometimes lose the joy of creating and we start being afraid of making mistakes. This stifles creativity. I think art needs to be approached from the spirit. Instead of learning the mechanics of painting, you have to let the Spirit move in you to tell you what you need to express through your art. Anyone can be trained to learn the mechanics of creating art—even a monkey or a robot. But the result would also be mechanical, lacking soul, lacking heart."

Her words stirred Alfonso. He sat quietly in deep thought, trolling her words over in his mind as his eyes once again fixed his gaze on one painting in particular. The painting was of a forest filled with primeval trees, swathed in a ghostly mist—and in the foreground the single frond of a fern tree extending into a luminous clearing. It seemed so real to Alfonso that he could almost smell the heady scent of the forest, and feel the cool mist on his skin.

"This one has no title," he said presently.

"What title would you give it?" she asked.

"I would call it *A Fern in the Clearing*."

"*A Fern in the Clearing* it is, then," she said. "I can see you like this one the most, don't you?"

"I like all of them, Savannah. They all have a quality that is... *cómo se dice*...unearthly. But this one speaks to my soul. That's because it has a picture of something I've been thinking of lately."

"I painted this on impulse just two nights ago–from my memory of the Manuka Forest in New Zealand. This is not part of the collection I'm sending to Los Angeles." She smiled at him. "I want you to have it." She proceeded to take it down from the wall.

Bewildered, he protested, "No, that's very kind of you, but I cannot possibly accept this."

"I've always believed that a work of art exists for the sole purpose of doing something to us deep within–changing us in some way. This painting speaks to your soul. There's no better reason for you to have it. That's what I've always told my clients when I worked at the Somerset Gallery. Please accept it as a gift from me."

"In that case, *muchas gracias*. You don't know what this means to me." He gave her a sideways glance, and noticed her face turning a deep crimson. She turned her face away and walked towards the filing cabinet in the far corner of the studio. Again, he heard the sound of an eerie chime as she walked.

༄

Savannah slid open a drawer and took out a large padded manila envelope. The painting was only twelve inches high and ten inches wide–small enough to slide into the pouch. She pulled the adhesive backing off the flap, sealed the envelope and handed it to him. Then, she opened another drawer and pulled out the form Alfonso needed to fill out to consign the painting to her.

"*No es necesario*, Savannah. There's no need for that. I don't need a receipt. I'm giving you unconditional custody of the painting."

Savannah was taken aback. She wondered once again about this dark stranger from the south of Spain who, despite his joyless façade, was capable of loving his late grandmother so much that he would never consider selling one of the two things she left behind– not for all the money in the world. It had occurred to her that this kind of sentimentality seemed incongruous to his aloof personality. Now, here he was, entrusting her with this article that means the world to him–one that could potentially be worth a small fortune, if it turned out to be a Picasso.

The practice of granting verbal custody of a work of art was not customary in the art world, but more than that, the implications of Alfonso's consigning his painting to her with no kind of paperwork in place spoke of an intimacy that was a little too close for her comfort.

She started to protest, "I really need to give you a receipt, just for your own protection...."

"Savannah, if you think I need to protect myself from things you might potentially do with my painting, then go ahead and give me a receipt. Otherwise, your word is good enough for me. I would not entrust this painting to just anyone. I'm entrusting it to you."

"Okay, Alfonso. We'll do it your way."

They walked back to the living room, and Alfonso poured more wine into their glasses. Savannah once again sat on the cane side chair, a comfortable distance from where he sat on the sofa. She felt a need to keep a modest distance from him.

Just then, the cocktail napkin she was holding underneath her wine glass dropped to the floor. As she stooped to pick it up, she became aware that the neckline of her dress heaved forward from the thrust of her breasts, and the hemline rode up her thighs a bit. She felt his eyes upon her and immediately rose to her feet. Secretly, she reveled in having him look upon her as a woman. All the while, Albinoni's Venetian music played on.

She began to have warm feelings toward Alfonso Madrigál. She wanted him to stay and never leave. While somewhere else inside of her, everything screamed the impropriety of it all. She still had the strength to put an end to all this. She wished she didn't have to be the one to decide.

Just as she was contemplating inviting him to stay for dinner, the phone rang. It was her friend, Kimberley, calling about a book Savannah had borrowed. She said she needed it back by Monday. Savannah was relieved that the decision she had been grappling with had been made for her, and all she needed to do was play along.

"Oh yes, Kimberley, that's pretty serious. How can I help?"

"Savannah, are you alright? You're not making any sense."

"Yes, of course, it's okay. Listen, I have a client here with me right now, but you can come over at seven, if you want. We can have dinner together, and we'll talk then. Or better still, I'll call you when I'm done here, and you can come over then, okay?"

"Alright, obviously something's up and you'll tell me later, right? I'll wait for your call."

"Yes, it won't be longer than fifteen minutes or so. Bye."

Alfonso had overheard her side of the conversation. He drank the rest of his wine, and got on his feet.

"You're expecting company, so I'd better go. I've done what I came to do. The painting is in your hands, so I'll say *adios* for now."

If he had fallen expectations or was disappointed about having been given the cue to leave, she didn't notice.

Maybe I'm more disappointed than he is, she thought.

Feeling the need to end their meeting on a neutral note, she said, "I'll go ahead and do my preliminary analysis of the painting, and if you call me on Friday, I can probably give you some feedback by then."

"Thanks again, Savannah," he said, picking up the padded manila envelope containing the painting she had given him. "I'll call you on Friday, then."

She followed him out the door to his car and waited until he got the engine started. Then she waved goodbye, walked back into her apartment and closed the door behind her. She leaned against the door, listening as the low rumble of his engine grew faint as he drove down Pacific Avenue and turned right on Larson.

Outside the clover swayed in the breeze, birds perched themselves on lampposts, and crickets complained of the coming fog.

Savannah walked to the coffee table, put the empty wine glasses on the serving tray to take everything back to the kitchen—when something caught her eye. A lilac-colored piece of parchment paper was tucked under the vase containing the Kahili ginger flowers. She pulled it out and read the handwritten words.

> *Like the music of fresh fallen rain*
> * and of swallow's wings*
> *   you are*
> *Like a young fern*
> * uncoiling my fronds into a thousand tomorrows*
> *   am I*
> *Finding my way*
> * to the clearing in the forest*
> *   and the serene, quiet shelter*
> *   of you*

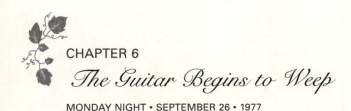

CHAPTER 6

The Guitar Begins to Weep

MONDAY NIGHT • SEPTEMBER 26 • 1977

The air was still warm when Alfonso came home to his Potrero Hill apartment at 10:47 after having spent a few hours at Zendrik's house in Sausalito, listening to his band rehearse a new line-up of songs. He alighted from his Buick, closed the garage door, and pushed the wrought iron pedestrian gate whose hinges had lost their will to turn. Dust and humidity coalesced on the cement steps as Alfonso walked up to the front door, making a mental note to grease those squeaky hinges. With Indian summer heat having the propensity to linger in enclosed spaces, it was warmer and twice as humid inside the apartment.

He unbuttoned his shirt as he walked into the living room carrying the padded manila envelope that contained Savannah's painting. Sweat dripped down his back and his forehead glistened with moisture.

He assumed Isabel was asleep. She had always been an early-to-bed-early-to-rise kind of person, whereas he was a creature of the night. The door to their bedroom was shut and he could hear no stirrings from within. He popped his head into Cristina's bedroom door and she, too, was asleep.

After getting a bottle of cold beer out of the refrigerator, he opened all the windows in the living room, sat himself on the sofa, and took off his shirt, slinging it on the arm of a side chair. A damp, warm breeze blew in as he sat quietly, taking occasional gulps of beer. He never thought San Francisco could be this hot and humid. He recalled the weather man talking about the day's record heat that hadn't been seen since 1906.

The mantel above the fireplace held an assortment of framed pictures. There was one of Isabel and Cristina that he had taken last summer at the *Great America* theme park. A photo of Cristina, with a white rabbit on her lap–taken in a studio when she was three. There was no picture of their wedding, but instead, there was a sepia-toned photo of Isabel's parents' wedding in 1950. Next to their wedding picture was a large collage containing pictures of Isabel's entire family–three brothers, four sisters and parents–taken in Barcelona, where Isabel was born and raised. There were pictures of aunts, uncles, cousins, nieces and nephews from her father's side of her family, as well as her mother's. Photos that weren't on display on the mantel were neatly organized into a dozen photo albums that Isabel kept in the drawers of the side tables.

Isabel considered pictures to be some of the most important things she owned. Given the opportunity to save one possession in the event of a fire, after saving loved ones, she would save her photos. Like most people, she felt that pictures represented priceless, precious and nostalgic memories, which are irreplaceable. In contrast, Alfonso was only eager to replace his memories with new ones. There was not one picture of himself when he was growing up, not a single picture of Málaga. He had deliberately left all the pictures behind, along with the nightmares they represented. The only picture he would have liked to have was one of his grandmother, Doña Carmen Madrigál

His thoughts turned to Isabel. Isabel Montez was twenty-four when they met; he twenty-five. It was 1975 in Madrid, just after the fall of the dictatorship of General Francisco Franco. Before 1975, when the power of Franco was still in full swing, only nationalistic platforms were politically accepted as "Spanish" cultural forms. Expressions of folkloric culture, such as flamenco, were suppressed. When Franco's regime fell, a slumbering country awakened to full bloom. The popularity of movies like *Blood Wedding* and *Carmen*, the most famous tales of Andalusian pride and passion, caused a huge boom in flamenco and elevated it to high society.

It had become chic in Madrid and most other cities to see flamenco performances. Since Alfonso made his living as a flamenco guitarist, accompanying flamenco dancers and singers, he too was shoved into the limelight. The society's emerging fascination with the gypsy culture ignited the curiosity of the pretty *señoritas*. Upper crust *Madrileñas*, who would never before have dreamed of dating a *gitano* or anyone remotely associated with flamenco, found themselves fascinated and curious about these dark strangers from the south. Isabel was one of those who took a fancy to the brooding, mysterious Alfonso Madrigál.

Alfonso met Isabel in a club where he performed with a flamenco troupe. She was a statuesque, buxom woman with ebony hair and large, doe-shaped eyes. While most people considered Isabel quite beautiful, in the context of the small universe of beautiful women in Madrid, she seemed unremarkable to him. He dated her occasionally, while maintaining liaisons with a few other ladies at the same time.

Women were in abundance in the flamenco circles of Madrid, and to be committed to one woman was not one of his priorities. But Isabel pursued him tenaciously and he fell into the routine of spending more time with her than any of the other women he knew.

He realized he wasn't in love with her, but she seemed deeply devoted to him, and that appealed to him.

Before long, Isabel told him that she was pregnant with his child. Alfonso thought that marrying her would be the right thing to do. The prospect of having a child seemed agreeable to him at the time.

They were married in a civil ceremony in Madrid, followed by a small reception. She had wanted a fancy church wedding in Barcelona but he had insisted on a modest, no-frills wedding that he could afford–even though her parents had offered to pay for all the wedding expenses. In all, twenty-five people attended their wedding. Nineteen of them were Isabel's friends and family, and six were Alfonso's friends from the flamenco troupe. When Isabel's relatives inquired why none of his family members were in attendance, he told them he was orphaned at an early age, and that the only living relatives remaining lived in the Ballearic Islands, and they couldn't afford to travel to Madrid. He could tell that Isabel's parents only half-believed his fabricated story, but felt he had spared them the sordid truth about the family in Málaga he had disowned.

Almost as soon as he married Isabel, he knew he had made a big mistake. Isabel became demanding, increasingly intolerant of the modest income that Alfonso made, and resentful of the limitations to her freedom that her pregnancy was causing her. In a burst of anger, she told him she regretted not marrying a wealthy suitor of hers from Aragon instead of him. Alfonso found himself married to a woman he didn't love, who was carrying a child that he wasn't absolutely certain was his. He had thought of leaving her, but decided to support her until the baby was born. In the middle of a particularly harsh winter in Madrid, Cristina was born, and from the moment Alfonso saw her, he knew he couldn't leave her.

Alfonso's relationship with Isabel continued to deteriorate as time went on. Every day, their marriage became more tumultuous, even while his fondness for Cristina grew. He had his mind set on moving to America–had felt for a long time that he would find his fortune there. Against Isabel's protests, he left for San Francisco on September 23, 1976, and told her he would send for them after he got settled. Three months later, after he got a job at *Club La Cibeles* and found an apartment on Potrero Hill, Isabel and Cristina came to join him.

Unlike Alfonso, Isabel spoke very little English, and therefore, had limited job opportunities. She did know enough Italian to get a job as a chef's assistant at a North Beach Italian *trattoria*. Isabel suffered from culture shock, was disgruntled about life in the United States, and felt degraded by her menial occupation. She made no bones about comparing her miserable life in America with the lavish lifestyle she enjoyed with her parents in Barcelona. On several occasions, she told him it was a mistake to marry him, and that she deserved much better than he could give her. Alfonso suspected that Isabel purposely told him hurtful things because she felt unloved by him and was jealous of his love for Cristina.

Alfonso sat on the living room sofa thinking how his life would have turned out if he hadn't married Isabel. Then, he might have a chance with Savannah. But even as he indulged in the luxury of the thought, he knew that if it weren't for Isabel, he wouldn't have Cristina. He decided to perish the thought.

He carefully slid Savannah's painting out of the envelope, and propped it on the tweed-upholstered side chair to take a better look at it. His thoughts turned to Savannah. Her face was a window that opened to a bright outdoors. Her voice a wand that turned every sound into music. The pitter-patter of footsteps, the clanging of the clock tower, the pulsating rhythm of a train, the waves lapping against the shore, the sound of children playing—everything turned into a symphony of beautiful themes that came alive because of her.

Without any conscious plan, he reached for his guitar and allowed his thoughts to bring him a song. *Empieza el llanto de la guitarra*, he said to himself, recalling the words of Federico García Lorca's poem. *The guitar begins to weep.*

He started to play a melody that came to him spontaneously—a beautiful melody that bore no resemblance to anything he had ever played before. It was a Spanish ballad, not a flamenco piece. His fingers plucked on the guitar strings as if they had a mind of their own. He surrendered all conscious direction and allowed the creative force and inspiration to work through him. He was mystified by the phenomenon that was occurring, and yet dared not question why and how it was happening. Moments later, he started to sing along with the melody that he played on his guitar. Profound, poetic lyrics, with the cadence and vibrancy of life itself, escaped his lips—and he hurriedly wrote the words down lest he forget them. Even as he wrote, he realized what a liberating experience it was to write them down. Writing the words was more than living—it was being conscious of living.

He began to wonder if all music was written this way, with little conscious control on the part of the songwriter. He recalled the words of John Keats:

> *Sweet are the pleasures that to verse belong*
> *And doubly sweet a brotherhood in song.*

As though in a hypnotic trance, Alfonso played, sang and wrote for close to three hours before realizing that he had written a complete song. For the first time in his life, he felt a profound joy, as though some seemingly random deity happened to pass by and redefined who he was. He didn't want to give the surreal experience a name, but he knew the song could have only come to life because of Savannah Curtis.

In the bedroom, Isabel was awakened by the sound of Alfonso playing his guitar and singing a song out in the living room. She looked at the clock on the nightstand. 3:41. It was a strange thing for Alfonso to be doing at this hour. She got off the bed and walked out into the living room. His eyes were closed as he sang his song, and his face had a blissful expression she had never seen on him before.

"What are you doing, Alfonso?" she asked, rubbing her eyes with her knuckles. "Do you know what time it is?"

Alfonso opened his eyes and looked at her vacantly. "I've just written an entire song–both words and music. First time I've ever done this," he said. Then, he closed his eyes and continued playing his guitar without singing.

"It's almost morning. Won't you come to bed?"

"In a moment."

Isabel walked back to their bedroom and shut the door behind her. She lay in bed awake, turning her face to the wall while listening to Alfonso play. Then, she buried her face in her pillow and began to weep.

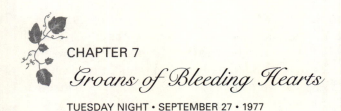

CHAPTER 7
Groans of Bleeding Hearts
TUESDAY NIGHT • SEPTEMBER 27 • 1977

It was 8:30 when Kimberley handed her keys to the parking valet at *Club La Cibeles*. Savannah walked with her into the club to find that the restaurant was unusually busy for a weekday night. All but two tables in the large multi-level dining room were occupied by patrons who were having dinner and drinking Spanish wines.

They grabbed the last table at the bar, located to the left of the elevated stage and the small dance floor. A magnificent wood carving of *Cibeles*, the goddess of fertility, sitting in her lion-borne chariot, was perched above the bar.

After ordering a round of drinks, Savannah looked at her watch. 8:50. Alfonso was scheduled to start playing at 9, but she still hadn't caught a glimpse of him anywhere.

"So you say this flamenco guitarist is a client of yours?" Kimberley asked, as she sipped a sangría.

"Yes. I'm helping him authenticate a painting that he owns. You know the one that was on the easel in my studio?" Savannah felt satisfied that she could put a professional designation on what Alfonso was to her. A client, that's just what he was. It gave her a good excuse for asking Kimberley to come with her to *La Cibeles* this evening.

A spotlight was switched on, focusing on the high stool at the center of the stage. Lights dimmed at the bar and throughout the dining area. Kimberley was talking about something that happened to her at work, and Savannah only half paid attention. Her eyes were roving for any sign of him.

Finally, at two minutes before nine, Alfonso emerged from a back room on the opposite side of the stage from where they sat, walked slowly with guitar in hand, and sat himself down on the stool at center stage. His eyes quickly swept over the entire dining area, and then the bar area. The spotlight was in his eyes, and the room was quite dark. He didn't see Savannah.

But Savannah saw him. In the darkness, she had the luxury of viewing all of him for the first time–without being conscious of his eyes upon her. He moved with the gait of a proud stallion, and wore a black drawstring shirt, with suede strings crisscrossing down the V-shaped neckline, that made him look every bit like a Spanish *caballero*. It was as though he had just stepped out of a different time and place–a time and place where Spanish cavaliers wooed lovely *señoritas* in the Spanish heartland. He greeted the audience briefly with a voice that sounded like midnight in a foreign cave.

"Is *this* the client you were talking about?" Kimberley winked at Savannah. "No wonder you dragged me here tonight."

Savannah barely managed a weak smile. Her attention was riveted to the sound of his guitar as he began to play. His fingers danced over the strings, moving with effortless speed. His guitar-playing had the vivacious, rhythmic power which made flamenco so riveting. He radiated energy as he played a piece with a festive cadence. All the pieces he played in the set had jubilant, bouncy melodies and rhythms that put the audience in a jolly mood. It made her ponder the stark incongruity between the joyful music and his melancholy personality.

Alfonso continued to play for forty-five minutes, and Savannah used the break from Kimberley's chatter to think about him. Alfonso was not the first handsome man she had ever met. She wondered what it was about him that made her feel enchanted, even enamored. Even as she wondered, she scolded herself for contemplating what was quite obvious. Here was a dashing Latin stranger with smoldering passion hiding behind brooding eyes, who wrote poetry and played exotic melodies on his guitar. *What woman's heart wouldn't be racing?* she said to herself. She smiled as she thought of the stereotypical Latin lovers portrayed in the movies who always had pretty young women swooning around them. Rudolph Valentino only needed to gaze at a woman and utter some tired, old amorous cliché and she would immediately be in the throes of ecstasy. It would be comical, if it weren't so true.

Savannah thought of all the handsome men she had met before. She often found them self-centered and uninteresting. They usually had very little substance because they never had to work hard at anything, always getting by on their looks or their special way around women. Intelligence, spirituality, sensitivity and the ability to discern real value amidst artifice were qualities in a man that she was more interested in. These were things she sensed in Alfonso.

It was ironic to her that, except for intelligence, Russell had none of the qualities she sought in a man–but she did feel safe with him. Alfonso had everything she wanted–and yet with him she felt dangerously at risk. He was married, after all, and had a child. He was a performer by profession, so he belonged to his public, and was exposed to the temptations that came along with his work. He was handsome, and probably the object of many women's affections. Then, there was the reputed chronic infidelity of Spanish men. Looking the way he did, Alfonso was probably a habitual heart breaker. The very thought of having her heart broken always put her in a state of panic, as if faced with an impending doom.

Alfonso approached the end of his first set. He alternated plucking and strumming with dexterity, let his fingers tickle the strings, and ended his last piece with a few dramatic thumps on the soundboard with his right hand. The audience applauded enthusiastically.

Kimberley excused herself to go to the powder room, as the lights went back on and Alfonso announced that he'd be back to play his second set in fifteen minutes. As he began to walk off the stage, he spotted Savannah and turned around to approach her. When he reached her side, he ceremoniously put his right hand out towards her, his left hand behind his back, waiting for her to give him her hand.

"*Señorita* Savannah, what a surprise to see you," he said, as she gave him her hand and he kissed it.

"It's good to see you, Alfonso. You played wonderfully."

"*Muchas gracias, Señorita.*"

"I want to thank you for the poem. Did you write it?"

"If you liked it, I did. If you didn't …"

"Oh, I liked it very much." She didn't tell him it took her breath away. "I didn't know you wrote poetry."

"Now and then," he said, "…when I'm inspired. I haven't written any in a long time."

"I found it interesting that your poem was about a fern in the clearing, which happens to be …"

"… the subject of your painting? *Si.* That's why your painting spoke to my soul."

Just then, Kimberley returned from the powder room. Clearly, she had dolled herself up in anticipation of meeting Alfonso. She had put on a fresh layer of lipstick and a little blush, fluffed up her long blonde hair a bit, and spritzed herself with perfume. Looking at Kimberley in the flattering pinkish light of the club, Savannah's heart sank. Kimberley looked ravishing. Heads turned to look at her as she sashayed back to her seat, pretending not to notice Alfonso standing by Savannah.

Maybe she's more Alfonso's type, Savannah thought ruefully, looking at her blonde, blue-eyed, buxom friend in her figure-hugging black knit dress with side slits that showed off her pretty legs.

Alfonso glanced at Kimberley briefly, then quickly turned his eyes back towards Savannah. "Kimberley, this is Alfonso Madrigál. Alfonso, this is my friend, Kimberley."

Kimberley held out her hand, and to Savannah's relief, he shook her hand and didn't bring it to his lips.

"*Mucho gusto.* It's a pleasure to meet you," he said.

"The pleasure's mine," Kimberley said in a voice an octave higher than her usual speaking voice. "You're a great guitar player, Alfonso. I really enjoyed your music."

"*Muchas gracias, Señorita.* I guess I did okay."

"Oh, don't be so modest. You're fantastic."

Savannah always knew when Kimberley was on the make. She flattered men's egos and coquettishly batted her long eyelashes at them. And she flirted shamelessly. Had it not been Alfonso she was flirting with, Savannah would have just laughed and called Kimberley a hoot–playing her usual game. But tonight, she was a bit annoyed by her flirtation.

Kimberley was not one who would horn in on a man Savannah was interested in, but to her, Savannah was off the market since she was already engaged to be married. So she felt at liberty to go after Alfonso.

Savannah smiled sweetly, not wanting to let on that she was irritated by Kimberley's aggressiveness, and not wanting to make it seem as though she were competing for Alfonso's attention. She also didn't want Kimberley to know that Alfonso was anything more than a client.

Kimberley completely monopolized Alfonso's attention, which was her nature with just about anybody she happened to be with. Savannah watched as Alfonso politely conversed with her, but noticed that while talking to Kimberley, he would cast sidelong glances at her, which made her pulse quicken.

When Alfonso excused himself to play his second set, Savannah saw Kimberley slip him her business card. She tried not to be bothered by it, reminding herself that women probably hand Alfonso their telephone numbers and business cards all the time.

Just as Alfonso began to play his guitar again, a cocktail waitress came and brought them a round of drinks and a platter of Spanish *tapas*, saying that they were compliments of Alfonso.

"Oh, he's a dreamboat," Kimberley cooed.

"He's a married man, Kim."

"Oh, darn it! The best ones are always married …"

"… or gay," Savannah said, finishing her sentence. They both giggled.

Halfway through Alfonso's second set, Kimberley looked at her watch. *10:30.* "Savannah, I think we better get going. It'll take me at least half an hour to get back to the East Bay. It'll be almost midnight by the time I get to bed, and I have to be up by 4:30." Kim worked as a Trading Assistant at a downtown stockbrokerage firm, and had to be at work at 6 in the morning.

"I still don't know how you keep these hours, Kim."

"I'm used to it. Shall we go?"

"You go on ahead. It's such a warm evening, I think I'll just walk home later. It's only a few blocks."

"They're steep blocks, Savannah. Are you sure?"

"I need to talk to Alfonso anyway–about his painting."

"Okay, I'll go ahead then. Tell Alfonso I said *adios*, and thank him for the food and drinks for me."

"Drive home carefully, Kim. You haven't had too much to drink, have you?"

"No, I'm good. See ya."

As soon as he finished playing, Alfonso joined Savannah again at her table. He sat on the seat Kimberley had vacated. Savannah expected him to ask where Kimberley had gone, but he didn't.

"When did you start playing guitar?"

"I was seven when my grandmother bought me my first guitar. But I didn't learn *guitarra flamenca* until after she died in 1963. I think learning it was my form of escape from my parents' frequent fights. I was a wild teenager and I started running around with the *gitanos*, the gypsy boys who lived in the outskirts of Málaga. Ruben Marquez, one of my *gitano* friends, taught me how to play flamenco guitar."

His eyes had a wistful, faraway look. "I remember the lessons so well. Ruben and I would sit chair-to-chair, face-to-face, guitar-to-guitar. Ruben would begin to play and I learned to read his hands backwards, like looking in a mirror. I imitated everything he did. Sometimes, he used to take me to one of the bars or *peñas* where flamenco guitar was performed so that I would learn a variety of styles and melodies. It was in the Peña Salgado that I learned about *duende*."

"*Duende?* What is *duende?*"

"If I could describe it, it wouldn't be *duende*. *Duende* is the essence of the flamenco culture. It is that indescribable spell or trance that a flamenco singer or guitar player casts on the listener. Goethe defined it as a mysterious power that everyone senses but no philosopher can explain. It's the quality that transforms both the artist and the listener from the inside out. It's a gift that some flamenco musicians have. It can't be taught, even with endless hours of training, nor can it be inherited. It's a gift from God. *Duende* is the heart of true flamenco music."

"Well, you seemed to cast a spell on your audience when you played. Does that mean you have *duende?*"

"Oh, no, no, no," he answered, shaking his head woefully. "Unfortunately, this music you've heard me play tonight is not even close to what true flamenco music is about. What I play is just a watered-down, sanitized version of the real thing. I play the kind of Flamenco that fits the American idea of what Flamenco is. Did you notice that the music I played tonight had a fast and cheerful tempo?"

"Yes, much like the kind of flamenco music I heard when I visited Madrid."

"Exactly. The flamenco clubs in Madrid are designed to please tourists so probably the show you saw was very commercial and upbeat–complete with clacking castanets. To a certain extent, I've sold out to that commercially adulterated brand of Flamenco–the kind you heard me play here tonight. But it does not have the genuine Andalusian spirit."

"What exactly do you mean by *Andalusian* spirit?"

"Flamenco music originated from the gypsies–we call them *gitanos*. Most of them lived in the province of Andalucia in the south of Spain where I am from. The most valued of all flamenco music is the *cante jondo*, the deep song of the *gitanos* which speaks mostly of loneliness, grief and the tragedy of the gypsies in naked and extreme emotion. This is music that tells of the loss of many mothers and the ruin of so many sons on the long Gypsy journey from their original home in northern India. Authentic flamenco music is not commercial at all like the lively tunes you've heard sung by gypsies in polka-dot costumes living in picturesque whitewashed villages. Not at all like the kind you see in the cinema either."

"So I haven't really heard authentic flamenco music then?" She laughed at his amusing comment, but noticed that he was not smiling. His voice conveyed a serious desire to educate her on the essence of flamenco music.

"No, you haven't. *Cante jondo* is the soulful music of voice and guitar. I remember when I was about thirteen or fourteen years old, my friend, Ruben, took me to the *Peña Salgado*. It was a dank and dreary club not far from my home. It was there that I first experienced *duende*. First, the flamenco guitarist strummed the melancholy rhythms and melodies. When the music reached a comfortable tempo, an unknown singer emerged from the darkness, stood with closed eyes, and began to moan from the back of his throat. The audience turned quiet, knowing that the improvised cry to follow would never be heard again. Suddenly the singer took a gulp of air, threw back his head and sang an extremely high, haunting note, a gut-twisting wail that made the people in the audience close their eyes, clap their hands and throw back their heads as though possessed or in a trance. There were cries of *"Olé! Olé!"* and *"Viva Dios!"* alternating softly, and then loudly, from the audience. After delivering such a display of emotion, he started singing the first verse of the song."

Alfonso continued, "I also experienced *duende* when I went to the Sports Palace in Madrid to see Jose Monge Cruz, who was known as *Camarón de la Isla*, one of the greatest flamenco artists of all time. He poured waves of emotion over everyone who was watching or listening. Ever since then, I have always had this burning desire to be able to affect people that way–to stir people into a kind of transcendence that is profoundly spiritual."

"Do you think you have *duende*?"

"I am a flamenco at heart. I am Andalusian after all. But *duende* encompasses a domain much larger than that. It imposes extreme emotional demands on the singer who wants to master it. Very few ever do. But *quizás, Señorita* Savannah, maybe one day."

She was intrigued by the passion with which he described the Flamenco culture, as well as the deep emotion that was the undercurrent of it all. Visions of *peñas* and *tablaos* tucked behind dark alleys in the outskirts of Málaga swirled in her head, and out of them drifted the melancholy groans of bleeding hearts. Indeed, Alfonso seemed to have the wild, defiant, wanton streak of legendary gypsies.

"There are not many places where you can listen to authentic *cante jondo*, not even in Madrid. You'd have to go deep into the heart of the Andalusian province to hear it. But if you're really interested, I know a place where you can experience true flamenco music."

"Really? Where?"

"It's not a flamenco bar, a *peña*, a *tablao* or a public place. It's at the home of a friend of mine–Manolo Aragon. He's invited me to his home in Mendocino on Saturday. They're celebrating his wife's birthday, and both he and his wife are authentic Flamencos. There will also be other flamenco aficionados performing. Would you like to come as my guest?"

"I would love to," Savannah replied. The words slipped out of her lips before she had a chance to think. She knew propriety should have caused her to ask why he chose to bring her, instead of his wife and daughter, to Mendocino. Somewhere in the back of Savannah's heart dwelled guilt pangs she was reluctant to confront just now. *What am I doing?* she thought. *I'm entertaining this flirtation, and it could lead where I don't want it to go. He's a married man and I'm engaged to be married.* But she chose not to entertain the thought. She knew that a four-hour road trip with him to Mendocino had an unspoken intimacy associated with it, but she ignored it.

"*Fantástico,*" he said. His delight was apparent, and for the first time since she met him, she thought she saw the beginnings of a smile.

～

*W*hen Savannah stood up to go, Alfonso escorted her across the club, through the curvy entryway, and out the front entrance.

"I wish I could walk you home, Savannah, but my last set starts in five minutes. I don't think I'll get back here on time. Are you sure you don't want to stay for my last set, and afterwards I can drive you home?"

"I'd like to stay, but it's really getting late. And it's not necessary for you to walk me home, Alfonso. It's only a few blocks, and it's such a warm evening. It'll be a nice walk. But thanks, anyway."

As he stood by the doorway of *Club La Cibeles*, he watched as she walked away. Her hair cascaded in soft waves around her shoulders and back. She swayed her hips ever so delicately in a gentle rhythm, and her blue dress embraced her body just enough to reveal graceful curves and a flash of her slender legs as she began her descent down Portofino Boulevard. As she proceeded walking down the hill, all he could see was the top of her body, and he felt his heart sinking right along with her. It was the kind of feeling he got whenever he watched the sun set–never wanting to let it go. In an impulse, he made a mad dash for the stairs that led up to Gonzalo's office. He bolted up as fast as he could, two steps at a time, until he reached the second floor landing.

He looked out the small window on the west side of the landing and watched her, not wanting to let her out of his sight one moment sooner than he had to. The lamplight cast a glow on her long mahogany hair, and for a brief moment, she turned around to look back at the club. He may have imagined the look of disappointment on her face when she didn't see him at the door, not knowing he watched her from upstairs. He smiled as he relished the thought. Being with her brought him so much gladness, but it grieved his soul to watch her move away from him. Further down Portofino Boulevard she walked until she disappeared completely from view. He could find no words to explain the ache and the inexplicable loneliness he felt at that very moment. For as long as he lived, no single vision of a woman could ever affect him the way watching her walk away that night could. Half-understood feelings swirled around him. He was being held prisoner by a force from which he could not break free since the day he first met her. Of one thing he was certain--whatever was happening to him, whatever Savannah was doing to him, he was totally powerless to stop it.

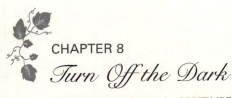

CHAPTER 8
Turn Off the Dark

WEDNESDAY MORNING • SEPTEMBER 28 • 1977

Daybreak was still an hour away when Alfonso stepped in behind the wheel of his Buick sedan. He got the engine started and waited half a minute for the car to warm up before he pulled it out of the garage and pulled up next to the street curb. Leaving the engine running, he climbed the stairs of his Potrero Hill apartment.

Cristina was sitting on the living room sofa, wearing blue jeans, a hooded fleece jacket over a blue T-shirt, white sneakers, and a small white plastic shoulder purse slung across her chest. She rubbed her eyes when she heard Alfonso come in. "I'm still sleepy, Papa," she said, with a yawn, her corkscrew curls tumbling over her cheeks.

"You told me to wake you up while the invisible rain is still on the leaves, remember? You can sleep a little more in the car and I'll wake you up when we get there."

"Isn't Mama coming with us?"

"She has to go to work, so it's just you and me."

Cristina rolled herself off the sofa and walked out the front door while Alfonso switched off the lights. Just before he shut the door, he caught a glimpse of Savannah's painting on the back wall of the living room, where he had hung it the day before. Even in the dark, *A Clearing in the Forest* had a luminescent glow.

He smiled as he locked the door behind him, held Cristina's hand, and walked down the stairs to the car.

Cristina climbed into the passenger side of the Buick. Alfonso watched as she sat herself down and she started stretching her right arm to shut the door.

"Remember what I told you, Cristina...."

"... to keep your feet, hands and clothes away from the door so that you don't slam on them," she finished his sentence, going through all the motions for his benefit. "Okay," she finally said and shut the door. Then, she reached for the seat belt and strapped herself in.

Alfonso walked around the back of the Buick to the driver side. He got into the car, turned to Cristina and said, "*Muy bueno*, Cristina. Well done."

She dozed off almost as soon as Alfonso pulled away from the

73

curb. The city lights were still ablaze, looking like gleaming rhinestones against the black velvet tapestry of the city as he descended Potrero Hill and drove towards Market Street. He enjoyed this time of day and remembered the countless occasions Abuelita had taken him on a similar excursion to watch the sun rise from atop the highest hill in Málaga.

He drove along Market Street, past the Castro district, and into the hills. Then, he headed east on Portola Drive and made a left turn onto Twin Peaks Boulevard. From that point on, it was a twisting, curving climb to the top. He pulled into the parking lot, still empty save for a few birds. He was thankful that the tourists that paraded through this lot every day, and the vendors who sold souvenirs and T-shirts to them, were still asleep at this hour.

The sky was beginning to turn peach on the eastern horizon, and there was hardly a cloud or a whisper of fog anywhere. It was going to be yet another warm Indian summer day, but the remnants of chilly night winds were still blowing. Alfonso reached for a knitted blanket in the back seat before unfastening Cristina's seat belt.

"*Estamos aquí.* We're here, Cristina," he said, shaking her hand gently to wake her.

Cristina's eyes flew open, looked out the window, and squealed in delight. She then reached over to open the car door and found it locked.

Alfonso lifted the latch to unlock the door, and said, "*Esperame.* Wait right here. I'll come get you." He alighted from the car, blanket in hand, walked around the back and opened her door. After folding the blanket lengthwise, he put it around her shoulders and she grasped the ends with both hands in front of her chest.

"Is the invisible rain still on the leaves?" she asked.

Invisible rain was how Cristina referred to the moisture that turned into the morning dew upon the leaves.

"Of course, *cariño*. Look, the sun hasn't come up yet to dry it all up."

She squealed again as she ran to a grassy area about fifty feet from where Alfonso had parked the car. When she got there, she carefully uprooted the longest blade of grass she could find, blew on the drop of dew that lay upon it. She then raised her other hand, letting the blanket slip off her shoulders, and watched the drop of dew falling into her palm.

Holding out her palm towards Alfonso, she said, "Look, Papa. Doesn't it look like a jewel?"

"It certainly does, Cristina."

"I'm going to collect a lot of jewels today." She proceeded to pluck a leaf from a nearby bush, blowing its dew into her palm.

Alfonso picked up the blanket that had fallen on the grass, remembering the days when he beheld the world with a wonder much like Cristina's. He looked at the underside of the blanket that had touched the grass and sure enough, there they were. Droplets of dew perched upon the woolen fibers of the blanket, and in the light of dawn, they did look like jewels sewn into the fabric.

He watched Cristina running around merrily, collecting her jewels before the sun came up and dried them all away. Meanwhile, the sweeping view of the city unfolded before him. From this, the highest point in San Francisco, with an elevation of nine hundred feet, he could see the downtown skyscrapers, the rooftops of all the houses that comprised half of the city, the Golden Gate Bridge, Alcatraz, Yerba Buena Island, Angel Island and parts of Berkeley and Oakland. It was enough to take anyone's breath away. But not Cristina's. She was not enamored by the bells, whistles and activities of the world. It was as though her eyes glossed over anything made of steel and concrete, and saw only the wonders of nature—the wonders to which most people rarely paid attention.

She had such a connection to all living things, the splendor of the earth, the promise of each new dawn, and the joy in beholding the simplest natural things. Although he was often tempted to silence her childlike musings, he knew there were enough thieves of innocence that could shatter the enchantment of her childhood—and he was determined not to be one of them. By learning to tune in to Cristina's musings, he had begun to appreciate the wisdom of her words. Among other things, Cristina believed that all living things are sacred, and have a beauty and value in their own right that goes far beyond their usefulness to human beings.

He let Cristina freely explore the enchanted world she perceived, and allowed himself to observe and be engaged in her experience. They spent many a time walking in the rain, watching a rainbow until it disappeared from view, blowing bubbles and standing astonished by the bubbles' changing colors, and watching the moon and the stars come up in the sky.

"The sun is about to rise, Cristina."

"Yippeeee!" she said gleefully. Alfonso wasn't sure what excited her more—collecting the morning dew or watching the sunrise.

Making sure to keep her left hand cupped so as not to spill the dew, Cristina reached into her T-shirt, tugged at a yellow cord attached to a yellow plastic oversized heart-shaped locket. She carefully pried the locket's lid open and poured the dew that she had collected into the box. Then, she blew kisses into it, snapped the lid shut and put it back in her pocket.

"I'm ready," she said, and Alfonso took her hand and led her to the panoramic viewing deck. A few early-rising tourists, carrying cameras and binoculars, were already there ahead of them, and he noticed that a few other cars were driving into the parking lot.

The sun rose at five minutes past seven, and they stood quietly, watching the landscape turn golden as it began to bask in the early morning rays. It always amazed Alfonso to see the sunrise arrest Cristina into silent contemplation–as though she was rendered speechless every time she looked upon it. He remembered Abuelita being similarly entranced by the rising sun, and whispering under her breath, *"Mira la majestad de Dios."* Behold the majesty of God.

Whenever Cristina turned contemplative, Alfonso allowed her to be alone with her thoughts and her communion with the world– and with God–for as long as she wanted. It didn't matter that the tourists were chattering noisily in the background. Nothing disturbed her solitude, and it was just the way he liked it. He wanted her to continue being connected with the higher endowments that made her the divine being that she was. He had known too many parents who were only too eager to snap their children out of their innate spiritual wanderings and rush them into the earthly, mundane realm they called the real world.

Just then, Cristina closed her eyes, raised her right hand in front of her with her palm perpendicular to her chest, fingers outstretched, and bowed her head ever so slowly, as if in deep reverence to some invisible deity. After a few moments, she opened her eyes, lowered her hand, looked at Alfonso and smiled.

A family of four pulled up in the parking lot, and two young boys alighted carrying colorful kites. When they managed to get the kites in the air, Alfonso said, *"Mira,* Cristina. Look at the kites," as he pointed upwards.

Cristina looked up, and suddenly her jaw dropped as she appeared mesmerized. Alfonso noticed that she wasn't paying attention to the kites at all, but to a flock of geese flying in the distance, far beyond the reach of the kites.

"I want to be a bird," she said. "Birds can fly anywhere and they're not tied to strings."

She had a way of uninhibitedly making connections between everything she saw or experienced, and distilling them into words more profound than any philosopher could articulate. Cristina's insight about the birds, compared to the kites, made him think of how often people marvel at things of their own creation when they only need to look beyond their frivolous handiwork to see things that are truly miraculous. He shook his head when he realized that he, too, had allowed his awareness of the magic of God's hands to diminish–and it often took Cristina's words to bring it back.

"How do they do that?" Cristina asked.

"Do what, *cariño*?"

"Fly that way," she said, pointing to the geese flying in "V" formation.

"Geese have to fly very far. Sometimes they fly from Alaska all the way down to California, or even Mexico–and then all the way back to where they came from. That's a long way to go. If they fly alone, they can't get very far. But if they fly with a group of other geese in that V formation..." he said, touching the fingers of both hands together to form a V, "...they are all able to fly farther. As each goose flaps its wings, it moves the air in such a way that it lifts the geese behind it in the V formation. Then, all of them get to fly almost twice as far than if each goose flew alone."

"Uh, huh .... so the geese help each other to fly."

"*Cierto.* That's correct, *mi hija.*"

"Why do they have to fly from Alaska to California or Mexico?"

"Alaska gets very cold in winter. So every autumn, they leave Alaska to go to places where the winter is warmer and where water is open–not frozen–and where they can find plenty of food. Then, in the spring, they start flying back home to Alaska in time for summer."

Just then, the geese began to honk as they flew further into the distance.

"Do they honk like that all the way?"

"The geese in the back of the flock honk sometimes–not all the time. That's their way of encouraging the geese flying in front, cheering them on to keep up the speed. That's because the geese in front have the hardest job–they flap their wings harder to help the ones behind them."

"What happens if they get tired?"

"When the goose in front gets tired, it goes to the back of the flock where it doesn't have to work so hard–and another goose goes to the front."

"Uh, huh...so they take turns being the leader?"

"*Cierto.* And do you know what happens when a goose gets sick or wounded and can't fly any more?"

"What, Papa?"

"Two of the other geese fly down to the ground with the sick or wounded goose to help or protect it. They stay with the goose until it is able to fly again. Then the three of them start another V formation or join another flock of geese."

"Wow, geese know how to take care of each other!" She was awed by the realization. "God made geese so smart."

"Yes, he did," Alfonso replied.

A few moments later, he asked, "Are you ready for breakfast, Cristina? Do you want to go to the Lotus Garden?"

"If it's not too expensive, Papa."

~

The queue of people outside Lotus Garden Café extended halfway around the block. That was a common sight to see every morning when the small Chinese café opened at seven. The café was not much to look at from the outside, and the interior consisted of just one long, narrow space with three tables, lots of Chinese lanterns hanging from the ceiling, and bamboo decor on the walls. People rarely came to sit at the tables, but instead they'd pop in to buy some of the city's best Chinese pastries and assorted *dim sum* items displayed in the glass counters and bamboo steamers situated at the front end of the café—and walk out minutes later with their purchases encased in pink cardboard boxes tied up in red string.

Cristina loved the egg custard tarts, the *har gow* shrimp dumplings, and the *charsiubao*, white, fluffy steamed buns stuffed with savory pork. Alfonso found a parking spot right in front of the Lotus Garden Café. They stood in line for ten minutes, and Alfonso ordered what she wanted, along with half a dozen *siu mai*, steamed duck-filled wonton wrappers, and a few Chinese pancakes. Walking back to the car, he let Cristina carry the pink cardboard box while he carried a tall Styrofoam cup of jasmine tea with a plastic lid, and a small paper bag containing paper napkins and a small carton of milk.

"Let's have our breakfast at the park," he said, as they got in the car.

"If you don't mind, Papa, can we eat this food right now? It smells so good, and I'm starving." She flashed a wide grin at Alfonso.

"Okay, you can eat in the car. *Después*, we can go the park."

He sipped on his tea, watching Cristina biting into the flaky pastry surrounding the warm egg custard, and then happily munching on the *charsiubao*. He noticed that a car had pulled up behind them, waiting to take their parking spot. Alfonso put his Styrofoam cup on the retractable cup rack and started the engine.

Cristina noticed that he was about to give up his parking space for the other car. She said, "*No preocupe*, Papa. I'll feed you while you drive."

She took a paper napkin out of the brown paper bag and laid it on his lap as he pulled the car away from the curb. Then, she took one of the *siu mai* and raised it toward his mouth, as far as her seatbelt would let her. He playfully snapped his jaws at her, pretending to bite off her hand, and she recoiled, giggling hysterically.

Alfonso drove out of Chinatown, passing Union Square along the way. Any other child would have pressed their nose against the car's window to look at the window displays at *Macy's* and the *City of Paris* department store. Not Cristina. She paid no mind to the window displays, or the St. Francis Hotel looming up ahead, or the other colorful attractions at Union Square. She was staring at a homeless man in tattered clothing, crouched on the northeast corner of the Square, coughing, and begging for alms.

"Who's that man, Papa?"

"He's a homeless man, Cristina." Alfonso realized that Cristina had never seen a homeless person before.

"You mean he has no house to live in like we do?"

"No, he doesn't."

"But who takes care of him?"

"He's a grown man, not a child. He takes care of himself."

"But he's sick, Papa. Look…," she said, pointing, "…he's coughing and he needs to take a bath and get new clothes. I'm sure he's hungry, too. Won't someone take care of him?" She had a tone of desperation in her voice, and her eyes were saddened.

Alfonso said nothing. Sometimes Cristina asked questions for which he didn't have answers.

"No, it can't be. We can't just leave him like that," she said. *"Espera un momento,"* she cried, quickly closing the pink cardboard box that still contained three pieces of *siu mai*, two *charsiubao*, a few egg custard tarts and a Chinese pancake. Then, she quickly unfastened her seat belt and opened the car door.

"Cristina, what are you doing?" Alfonso demanded as he brought the car to an abrupt halt.

In a flash, Cristina picked up the pink cardboard box with her left hand, grabbed the unopened carton of milk with her right, and dashed to the homeless man, who was now only a few steps away from the car. She handed the box and the milk carton to him, then unzipped the purse that was slung across her chest, pulled out all the dollar bills that were in it–seven in all–and gave them to him. "This is all I can do right now," she told him, after which she turned around, ran back into the car and shut the door, keeping her eyes fixed on the homeless man.

Horns were honking on busy Geary Boulevard as the drivers of the cars behind them impatiently urged Alfonso to get going.

"Fasten your seatbelt," he said, taking a quick glance at the homeless man, who had stood to his feet with his mouth open, watching them drive away.

"I hope you don't mind that I gave our food away, Papa."

"Why should I mind, *mi amor*? You've done a good thing. I'm proud of you. But never open the car door again while the car is moving, okay?" Then, as an afterthought, "Since you gave away all the money you were saving to buy a new goldfish, I'll buy you a new goldfish–to keep Bubbles company."

"Bubbles will be okay without a playmate. We have to feed the homeless people first."

Sometimes the things Cristina said humbled him. She was a far more spiritually mature human being than he ever was. And she instinctively knew how to prioritize things, never putting trivialities ahead of important things.

He remembered what Savannah had said about Cristina. That she's a highly evolved human being.

As he drove away from Union Square, he could see her still looking out the window at the homeless man. Then he heard her say just under her breath, "Geese are smarter than people."

༄

*L*ong-hibernating dreams rose from the pavement like the billowing heat of the parched coastal plains. Unspoken sentiments mandated the direction of a Buick's steering wheel… Alfonso found himself driving in the direction of Pacific Heights.

"Where are we going, Papa?" Cristina's voice was puzzled as she looked curiously around the unfamiliar neighborhood. "Aren't we going to the park?"

"We're going to a different park today, not the Golden Gate Park. This one is just a small park–but it has a playground."

"Okay!" She never seemed to tire of going to parks, whether the park had a playground or not.

Alfonso parked the car on Bayview Road, on the opposite side of the park from where Savannah lived. He couldn't decide whether he wanted her to see him or not. He hadn't planned on seeing her today. All he knew was that he had an inexplicable desire to be near her.

Summerhill Park was a shady park, sheltered by a lacework of foliage and overhanging trees. Cristina dashed toward the playground. Alfonso sat on a park bench and watched Cristina as she played in the sandy area equipped with two swings, a slide, a seesaw, a plastic tunnel and a merry-go-round. She always liked slides best and she amused herself on them as he watched.

Alfonso's eyes turned to 201 Pacific, searching for any sign of Savannah. He gazed at the bay window where he stood next to her three days ago, examining the *pentimento*. Then, his eyes traveled to her studio window. The curtains of her studio were completely open.

His eyes turned away momentarily to check on Cristina, who had now made her way to the plastic tunnel and was chatting with two other kids who were playing there. He then looked again upon Savannah's Victorian apartment.

He didn't know how long he had been sitting on the bench, transfixed. Suddenly, he was startled to see Cristina standing near him, her eyes darting back and forth between him and the house at 201 Pacific, drawing unspoken conclusions that troubled him.

"Cristina, do you remember where you put your camera?"

"I put it in the little cabinet in the car."

"The glove compartment?"

"Yes, Papa."

"Okay, you stay right here while I run and get it."

Alfonso headed towards the car, keeping an eye on her as he walked. He found the miniature instamatic camera. He remembered the day he took her to Fisherman's Wharf, and she was infinitely mesmerized by the sea gulls' cry, muted by fog, and how he imagined her thoughts being as vast as the Pacific. He had bought her the camera so that she could take pictures of the sea gulls and the sail boats. He took the camera out of the glove compartment and walked back to the playground, where Cristina sat on a swing, clutching the chains.

"There are only two shots left, Cristina. Let me take your picture so that we can have the film developed, okay? Why don't you stand over there," he said, pointing to the grassy area next to the sand pit.

"You don't want to take my picture here on the swing?"

"No, I want you to stand right there, Cristina," he said, and she walked over to the grassy area. As she did, she stared once again at the Victorian house at 201 Pacific.

"Turn around so I can take your picture," he said, and Cristina obeyed.

"Okay, now smile!" He brought the camera lens up to his eye, making sure that Savannah's Victorian apartment was in full view in the background. Cristina had a bewildered smile on her face when he took the picture.

"Let's take another one, *amorcito*. This time, I want you to give me a big smile like you always do. This is the last shot."

"Okay," she said, giving him the widest grin she could manage.

Just as Alfonso clicked on the shutter button, he saw Savannah through the camera's lens looking out through the parted curtains of her upstairs studio. After snapping the picture, he quickly looked up at the window of her studio. She was gone.

Even if it was just a fleeting glimpse of her, a wave of jubilance swept over him. Looking down at the camera, he checked the film counter, which indicated that he was at the end of the film. His hands instinctively reached for the camera's rewind dial and began rewinding the film until it reached the end.

Cristina was peering at him closely now. Alfonso's quick glance at the Victorian house did not escape her notice. She was familiar with every feature and every expression on her father's face, but at that moment, there was something unfamiliar about him. Something unfamiliar, but nice.

"Papa, you're smiling."

It was half past four when Alfonso and Cristina returned home. Alfonso pulled the mail out of the mailbox before he put the key to the front door.

The sun was still high above the horizon, but the apartment was dark when they walked in. A leafy oak tree shielded their windows from the sun at this time of day, and the blinds were drawn.

"Turn off the dark, Papa," Cristina said, as she stood on tiptoe with an outstretched arm trying to reach for the light switch. "Turn off the dark."

Alfonso switched on the light in the living room, drew the blinds, opened the windows, and tossed the mail onto the coffee table. An early Christmas card catalog was on top of the mail pile, and it caught Cristina's eye. She plopped down on the carpet, crossed her legs, and began to thumb through the glossy pages of the catalog. Before long, she came upon the picture of a Christmas card that had a Nativity scene in front.

"Look, Papa, "she pointed with her chubby finger. "Here's Mary, here's Joseph, and here's baby Jesus."

Alfonso nodded as he looked at the picture she was pointing to. Cristina continued. "And these are the three wise guys."

"Three wise men," he said, laughing a deep hearty chuckle that seemed foreign to him. It sounded like a boy's laughter echoing in the halls of a mahogany-paneled house in the hills of Málaga.

"Isn't that the same thing?" Cristina asked.

"Not exactly. The three wise men were the three kings that brought Jesus gifts when he was born. Wise guys are gangsters–bad men who do bad things."

He was still laughing when he walked into the kitchen, took out a pitcher of apple juice and poured it into two glasses. He gave a glass to Cristina, and took fast gulps out of his glass. Seeing that Cristina was preoccupied looking at the pictures of Christmas cards in the catalog, he picked up his guitar and started playing.

"*Estaba la paloma blanca,*" he began to sing. "*Sentada en el verde limon.*"

Cristina squealed for she loved it when Alfonso sang this *cancion infantile*, a Spanish song for children. She clapped her hands in time with the song's rhythm, and tried to follow along wherever she knew the lyrics, laughing as she did.

"*Dame un besito,*" he sang, whereupon Cristina kissed his lips, gleefully obeying the words of the song. "*Sobre tu boca.*"

He sang through to the last line, "*Porque te quiero a ti,*" and strummed his guitar to signify the finale, unaware that he was looking fixedly at Savannah's painting as he played. Cristina's eyes followed his gaze.

Before long, she was standing in front of Savannah's painting, scrutinizing it closely, her back towards him. Alfonso sat on the sofa, strumming softly as he watched Cristina.

Cristina's body began to tremble and Alfonso heard muffled sobs coming from her. Alfonso put down his guitar, walked towards her and picked her up in his arms. Tears were rolling down her cheeks.

"*¿Qué pasa, mi amor?*" he asked, carrying her back to the sofa and putting her on his lap.

"There's a missing piece. There's a big hole and it's empty right around here," she said, pointing to her chest.

"*¿Qué dices?* What are you saying, Cristina?"

"The lady who made the painting," she said in between sobs, "...her daddy's gone away and her mama died of a broken heart." Her little fists were clenched tightly and her body was quivering.

Tearfully, she continued talking. "Her daddy left her when she was seven years old–and she doesn't know where he is. He didn't say goodbye. She doesn't know if he's alive or if he's dead but she still waits for him. She thinks no one can love her–even her daddy didn't love her."

Alfonso's face turned pensive. He remembered the look of panic and helplessness Savannah had on her face at Café Marcel when he had asked her where her father was. This must be the secret woe she had been keeping–the fragility he had sensed in her. She had been abandoned by her father.

He could hardly comprehend the crippling grief Savannah must have suffered, must still be suffering. He recalled his own grief when his grandmother died. Even though Abuelita was separated from him as a result of her death, losing her hurt him deeply. He could only imagine the hurt Savannah must have had to endure, having been abandoned on purpose by the one she loved most.

All the half-understood, undeclared feelings that he had felt since the day he met her, the searching for the reason for his existence, the need to care about someone far beyond himself, coalesced at that moment. The rage, the void, the grief, and the aimlessness of his life trembled in Savannah's presence like corrupt magistrates unworthy of their posts. A lifetime of songs he never sang, dreams he never dared to dream, possibilities he had failed to realize, all the meaningless liaisons with women he cared little about, and all the things from which he was escaping–all culminated in her.

There was no denying now that he had fallen in love with Savannah Curtis. She was the one his heart chose to love–more than she could ever think it was possible for a man to love a woman, more than her daddy convinced her she deserved. He felt the need to protect her and overcome the fears that dominated her life. At that moment, Alfonso knew that if it was the last thing he did, he was going to love Savannah Curtis all his life.

CHAPTER 9
Pain Made Flesh

SATURDAY MORNING • OCTOBER 1 • 1977

Saturday dawned bright and splendid, without a trace of fog. Alfonso parked his Buick in front of Savannah's apartment at seven. From the foot of the steps leading up to her front door, he saw her look out of the bay window in her living room and wave at him. In a few moments, she came out of her front door and locked the door behind her.

From where he stood, Alfonso watched her descending the steps towards him. She was wearing a champagne-colored cotton sundress with soft floral prints, a tapered waist, a full skirt that reached just below the knee, and a halter neckline that tied in the back of her neck, revealing her graceful shoulders, arms, and much of her upper back. Flesh-colored sandals, a beige sweater slung on her right arm, and a small purse with bamboo handles in her left hand. Her skirt billowed in the wind as she walked down the long flight of stairs.

"*Hola*, Alfonso."

"*Buenos dias, señorita*," were the words he said. But there were words from the eloquent realm that spoke of the way she looked that morning. *You are the effervescence that escapes the goblet of angels and mortals—and your eyes are the sanctuary where my savage spirit longs to dwell.*

As she approached, Alfonso opened the car door for her, wondering if there would ever come a time when she would be anything but dazzling in his eyes. Savannah got into the car. Before closing the door, he took her hand and kissed it gently.

He walked around to the driver's side, stepped in behind the wheel and started the engine. Savannah laid her purse on the floor of the car, and her sweater on her lap, and pulled on the seatbelt. It was jammed.

"Is it stuck?" Alfonso asked, noticing her struggling with it. "Let me help you." He had already pulled away from the curb, so he stopped the car and shifted to neutral. He reached over to her side to loosen the seat belt from its spool.

After a few tries, he finally freed the seat belt from its jammed retractor spool and pulled it across her chest.

"Thanks," she murmured. Alfonso noticed that Savannah's cheeks deepened to the shade of dark claret.

Alfonso maneuvered through the streets of Pacific Heights, skillfully scaling impossible gradients and turning corners that revealed yet another stunning view of the city, the bay and beyond.

San Francisco never looked more like a picture-postcard. The city sparkled and the wind whistled between the neat little rows of colorful Victorian houses. Faces peered from behind bay windows as they drove down Larson Boulevard, through Fort Mason where the brisk breezes rippled the wayward banners. When they crossed California Street, a cable car lurched around the corner filled with tourists in T-shirts and Bermuda shorts with cameras dangling from their shoulders.

On the Marina Green, dozens of tank-topped, shirt-sleeved, summer dressed, sneakered and shirtless people were already out in the early morning sun strolling, flying kites and enjoying the unseasonable weather.

Savannah opened the car window all the way, then unfastened the barrette in the back of her head, letting her hair cascade down her delicate shoulders and halfway down her back. Alfonso watched from the corner of his eye as her hair defied gravity in the playful wind, and the sun turned its color into a vivid chestnut. He smelled the alluring fragrance of her perfume, and delighted in watching her gaze, dreamy-eyed, upon the city's scenery.

⁂

*A*lfonso turned on the radio. He adjusted the tuning dial and came to a station that was playing the Bee Gees's song, "How Deep is Your Love."

"I like this song," Savannah said, as the opening riff played, and she hummed along with it. The song always put her in a good mood.

Just ahead, the Palace of Fine Arts loomed grand and majestic against the blue sky, with its pageantry of wispy clouds in the distance. They headed north on the 101 Freeway through the great sweep of the Golden Gate Bridge, while underneath the San Francisco Bay lay calm and unruffled.

When they reached the other side of the bridge and descended into Marin County, just before it sank into the bosom of Mill Valley, a nostalgic shiver ran through Savannah's body, the way it did every time she passed that slice of highway. She remembered a few weekends in her childhood when her father took the family to Sonoma on day trips.

"You're not in Kansas anymore, Princess," her father used to say, quoting from her favorite tale, *The Wizard of Oz*, whenever they passed that bend in the road. She had always felt transported magically to a distant place and time whenever he said those words.

San Francisco was only a few miles back, but it seemed lost forever behind that bend in the road. A part of Savannah wondered if there would ever come a time when she would stop waiting for her father to come for her. Another part of her wondered if there would ever be a day when her face wouldn't get flushed every time Alfonso kissed her hand.

"We can get to Mendocino in three hours," Alfonso said. "But if you don't mind, I'll take Highway 1. It will take us an hour longer to get there, but it's a more scenic drive."

"I don't mind. We're not in a hurry, are we? We don't have to be there until lunch time."

"That's right."

Savannah relished the long stretch of road that she would be traveling with Alfonso. Gone was the nervousness she had felt around him during their first few encounters. In its place was a keen, pulsating sense of being truly alive.

All her senses awakened whenever he was near her. When he had unjammed her seat belt and pulled it across her chest, his fingertips had only brushed against the top of her bare shoulders ever so lightly, and yet she felt a warmth spread through her body, as if feeding some secret fever. Even the faint whiff of his raw, savage scent mingled with a fresh citrus fragrance made her body respond in ways that were more suited to a hormone-dominant adolescent girl.

"So tell me...what was it like growing up in Málaga?"

Savannah was surprised when Alfonso actually began to let her into the world of which he seldom spoke. He told her about his childhood years in Málaga, about Abuelita, Villa Madrigál, his parents, his love of poetry, soccer, Flamenco music, and swimming in the warm waters of the Mediterranean. The good days.

Savannah realized that the side of him she saw today was a far cry from the fiercely private individual she had met at Sutton Hall just a few days ago. She noticed how he was far more willing to open up. She listened with fascination to his stories that seemed to leap out of some foreign epic movie. Even as she listened, she wondered how someone who had lived a charmed existence had so much rage and sadness hiding beneath his brooding façade.

Alfonso had much more to say. He began to tell her about the Madrigál family scandal, its fall from grace, the suspicious deaths of his grandmother and his mother, the physical abuse he endured, why he left Málaga for Madrid, and his stormy marriage to Isabel.

Savannah felt tears sting her eyes as she listened to his story. She knew instinctively that it was a story he seldom, if ever, told anyone. She suddenly felt a kinship with him, and what she had previously perceived as aloofness, she now understood as the barriers he had put up between himself and the hostile world. She began to understand what made Alfonso the kind of person he was.

While driving through Sonoma County, they spotted a train in the distance.

"What kind of cargo do you think the train is carrying?" he asked her.

"Oh, I don't know. I imagine grapes from nearby vineyards on their way to market."

"I think they're taking flocks of wild eagles with injured wings …to a place where they can find their fragment of the sky—and learn to fly again."

There was something about the way he elevated something as commonplace as a train's cargo into something transcendent. His metaphors bordered on magic, like a fresh pair of eyes with which to view the world.

"Have you ever been to Mendocino?" he asked, as he took the exit marked 128 West, Fort Bragg, Mendocino.

"No, I haven't."

"This is where the road begins to twist and turn as we get closer to Mendocino."

"How much longer from here?"

"About an hour and a half to Highway 1. And then we'll head north another ten miles to Manolo's house."

Highway 128 meandered for sixty-five miles through the Anderson Valley wine country. The two-lane road then cruised through fifteen miles of redwood forest. As they approached Highway 1, Savannah caught glimpses of the ocean and the dramatic coastline. Then, it was a leisurely drive through the seacoast towns and villages of Gualala, Anchor Bay, Point Arena, Manchester, Irish Beach, Elk, Albion, and Little River.

"You haven't spoken of your childhood," Alfonso said.

"There's not much to tell. I lived most of my growing years in Tiburon with Sabine, my mother's best friend, who adopted me after my mother died. It's a small, peaceful town and there were barely seven thousand residents when I lived there. When I went off to college, Sabine moved to Switzerland, and she's lived there ever since. I went to USF and got a degree in Fine Arts, and well…you know the rest."

After delivering the *Cliff Notes* version of her childhood, Savannah admonished herself. *Badly done, Savannah.* She realized how just a few days ago at Café Marcel, she had quickly judged Alfonso when he spoke of his hometown in a detached manner, as though he was reading a travel brochure. Now, pondering her extremely abbreviated summary of her youth, she wondered what Alfonso must be thinking.

"You prefer not to talk about it, then?"

"I guess not," she replied, relieved that he was sensitive enough to discern her reluctance to divulge more about her childhood than she was willing to.

"Manolo's house is still a couple of miles north of here. But since you've never been to Mendocino, let me drive you into the village so you can see a few of the sights, *esta bien*?"

"*Esta bien.*"

To Savannah, Mendocino was the most enchanted place she had ever seen–the land at the rainbow's end, the horizon where heaven and earth crystallized. The road to the unspoiled New England style village was sprinkled with spectacular coastal gardens and wildflowers in abundance. The sea-swept headlands, dotted with quaint little inns and century-old cypress trees that danced to the cadence of the ocean's tide, was a feast for poets. The ambrosial air seemed perfumed by God himself. The majestic swells of the Pacific, and its roar upon the bluffs, were a rhapsody unto themselves. Thirty proud wooden water towers from bygone lumber mill days still graced the landscape of the village, and downtown Mendocino was sprinkled with dozens of shops, art galleries, restaurants and the veneer of civilization. Nearby parks had scenic hiking and biking trails.

"I've been told that Mendocino is famous for its artist community," Alfonso said as they drove by a few art galleries in the heart of town. "It's a haven for professional artists and art students."

"I can see why. Anyone's imagination can take wing in a place like this. I just might live here someday."

⁓

*M*anolo Aragon's craftsman bungalow looked quaint, silhouetted against the azure sky. Its low-pitched roof with wide eaves, and a front porch with square columns, reminded Savannah of the house in Cape Cod where she vacationed with her parents when she was six. Inside was a stone chimney, boxed-beam ceilings and half-a-century-old hardwood floors–oak on the main floor and old-growth fir in the upper floor. The main floor had an open living room with built-in bookcases, and an adjoining dining room. The living room was already filled with people when Alfonso and Savannah arrived.

Manolo and Matilde Aragon were as unmatched a pair as a couple could be. Manolo's face, lined with creases, looked like a topographical map, his hair almost completely gray. He sported a rotund body, a jolly disposition, and a hearty chuckle. Matilde was a tall woman–at least six inches taller than Manolo–with a smooth, porcelain-like complexion, wavy, jet-black hair that reached down to her waist, a gaunt face and figure, an imperious nose, bulging eyes, and an air of arrogance about her.

"Matilde reminds me of my grandmother," Alfonso whispered to Savannah. "Not in the way she looks but in how she comes across to others. Outside, she has a stern appearance that strikes fear in people, but inside that icy exterior is a heart of gold."

Alfonso was right. Matilde was a warm and gracious hostess who had a way of making her guests feel right at home.

It was Matilde's fiftieth birthday, and the buffet table overflowed with Spanish fare. There was a prawn-and-paprika fish stew with tomato rice, *paella*, an eggplant dish with caraway, button mushrooms with chorizo and vinegar, salt cod puffs, *Tabahajah*, an Andalusian lamb dish, fried, salted almonds and Spanish olives.

Sangría flowed freely, and they served more varieties of Spanish wine than Savannah had ever seen. A friend of Manolo's named Alejandro Medina brought two bottles of *Molino Real Moscatel*.

"*Especialmente para ti,*" Manolo told Alfonso.

"*Molino Real Moscatel*—how did you get your hands on this?" Alfonso asked, surveying the wine bottle Manolo handed to him.

"I have my sources," Manolo replied, chuckling. "Alejandro here can find practically any Spanish wine you can think of."

"You didn't have to go to all the trouble. *Pero muchas gracias, amigo.*"

Alfonso explained to Savannah that *Molino Real Moscatel* was a special wine made from grapes grown only in a small vineyard above the Málaga coastline, and that Manolo had ordered it especially for him.

A friendly energy filled the house—partly because Manolo's thunderous laughter reverberated throughout, partly because Matilde fussed incessantly, making sure everyone was taken care of— and also because the other guests were all spirited and determined to have a great time.

After the sumptuous lunch, everyone gathered together in the spacious terrace in the rear of the house. The noonday sun streamed in through the rafters. Manolo hauled out a wooden stool from the kitchen, sat himself down, and put his guitar on his lap, resting his hands on the curves of the guitar. The terrace became quiet.

"You're about to hear music you've never heard before, Savannah. And you will never hear this song quite the same way again. *Duende* doesn't repeat itself any more than do the waves of the sea during a storm. *Escucha.*"

Robert Frost, thought Savannah, remembering the words of the famous poet. *Never again would birds' song be the same.*

Manolo's fingers began to dance over the guitar strings. They moved with great speed, piercing the air with a tragic, spine-chilling melody. Savannah sat transfixed. Suddenly, she heard a sound akin to the trill of a wild bird—it seemed to be coming from the back of the room, or even the adjoining room, she couldn't tell. Then, the sound began to waft into the room like a slow, prairie wind blowing across the sierra. The trill gradually turned into what sounded like the long, uninterrupted crowing of a rooster, that later turned into a gut-wrenching human scream that could make the mercury ooze out of every looking glass. The hairs on Savannah's arms began to stand on end. She realized that the peculiar sound was coming from Manolo. He continued to play in a rapid tempo while his voice prolonged the ghostly cry that sounded like a heart plunged in pain.

It wasn't melodic in the strict sense of the word, but rather a primordial kind of music that resonated with the listener, drawing him into the pain of the singer. It was something that climbed up inside her, from the soles of her feet. Savannah shuddered when she realized that there was no longer any separation between herself and the agony in Manolo's voice. She had never felt anything like it before.

Manolo ended his song explosively, with a final wail of anguish and a spirited jaunt on the guitar strings.

Shouts of "*Olé*" reverberated through the rafters. Many stood to their feet in thunderous applause. Savannah was still in a trance, feeling as though all her blood had drained right out of her body, unable to understand what just happened.

Alfonso could tell by the expression on her face that she caught it. "There it is. What I told you about, Savannah. *Duende*. Pain made flesh."

He summed it all up in those three words, Savannah thought. *Pain made flesh.*

---

*N*one of the other guests were professional Flamencos like Manolo and Matilde, but they were all aficionados, eager to give their individual renditions of flamenco singing, dancing or guitar-playing. Whoever had the desire to perform—and the nerve—took a turn.

"Aren't you going to play for them?" Savannah asked Alfonso.

Alfonso shook his head. "I'm just a watered-down version of Flamenco compared to Manolo. He's a hard act to follow."

After a few of the other guests took their turn performing, Manolo once again picked up his guitar. This time he did not intend to sing, but to accompany Matilde's dance. Manolo began to play a melody on his guitar that began tenderly, and then started escalating into a mysterious, incomprehensible series of chords played to a rapid tempo, while people clapped their hands in synch with the complicated rhythm. Matilde appeared, wearing a long, red dress with a fringed, black silk shawl dramatically draped over her shoulders, cascading in waves almost to her feet. She tensed her fingers open as her arms floated away from her sides until they were arched at shoulder level. It seemed as though an invisible sorcerer controlled her from invisible strings above. As she held the pose, motionless, she was not unlike a leviathan rising from the abyss.

Manolo's guitar virtually burst into fire as Matilde danced with grace and elegance across the floor, arching her upper torso, moving her arms and hands with skillfully executed tension, twisting her waist, and letting her dress whip against her body. Then she broke open like flames dancing on the floor with circling wrists, intricate hand movements, feet moving faster than the eyes could follow, and virtual fireworks exploding at the clatter of her heels. She moved with smoldering sensuality, controlled passion, while keeping time with the staccato rhythms of her footwork. Her dance aroused raw, human emotions.

Savannah was delighted she had agreed to accept Alfonso's invitation to come to Mendocino. Alfonso was right. This was a far cry from the Flamenco most people would ever experience in their lives. It was impossible to walk away from it with one's wits still intact.

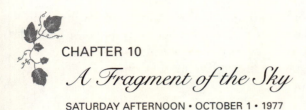

CHAPTER 10

A Fragment of the Sky

SATURDAY AFTERNOON • OCTOBER 1 • 1977

It was a quarter past three when Alfonso and Savannah said goodbye to Manolo and Matilde. Savannah felt inebriated. Her spirits were buoyed not by the alcohol, for she only had one glass of sangría, but from the spine-tingling emotions that she had experienced.

"Are you okay to drive? I wouldn't mind driving," she offered, since she had noticed he'd had a few glasses of *Molino Real Moscatel*.

"I'm perfectly fine," Alfonso replied. Savannah wondered whether she offended him by implying that he may be too drunk to drive. "*No preocupe*, Savannah. Don't worry. I would never drive if it meant putting our safety at risk."

Savannah smiled, remembering someone telling her that Spanish men could hold their liquor better than almost any other people. This owed itself in no small part to the fact that Spain ranked among the world's top consumers of wine per capita.

The sun was still high up in the sky as Alfonso drove further north on Highway 1.

"Don't we have to head south to get back home?" she asked.

"If you don't mind, I want to show you a beautiful place I discovered not far from here."

"I don't mind at all as long as you're sure we'll get back to San Francisco in time. You do have to work tonight, don't you?"

"I forgot to tell you. There's a private party at the Club tonight. The celebrant has hired a band that plays dance music, so I have the night off."

"Oh, I see," was all she could say as she felt a quiver running through her pelvis. It was a quiver that sprang from possibilities that the night presented. Possibilities that were at once frightening and provocative to her.

After driving a few miles up the coast, Alfonso pulled up next to what appeared to be nothing more than a grove of trees on the periphery of a dirt road. "It's just a short stroll up ahead and I promise that there's a view like you've never seen," he reassured her.

It was a stroll of about a hundred yards through the grove of redwoods and pine trees with filtered rays of the sun streaming through a cathedral-like overhang of branches. The smell of pine and redwoods was exhilarating. Alfonso walked beside her and slipped his hand around hers. It seemed a harmless thing for him to do. Yet Savannah was fully aware of how warm his hand felt to her, and how his touch ignited a fire within her that spread through her limbs and her lower belly.

"It's just up ahead," he said.

Suddenly, the grove thinned out and dramatically opened up into an oceanfront promontory jutting out into the steel blue Pacific. Savannah gasped. The panorama offered an unfettered vista of the ocean with its surging waves crashing upon an endless string of dramatic bluffs stretching to the north and south. *This must be the pinnacle of the world,* she thought to herself. The horizon that blurs the lines between heaven and earth in surreal splendor.

"It's absolutely breathtaking!" she gushed, watching sparrows begin their glorious journey toward the sun. "Does this place have a name?" she asked.

"If it does, I've never heard of it."

"In that case, I'll call it Heaven's Bluff."

∽

Alfonso gazed intently towards Mendocino Village to the south, and then north towards Noyo Fishing Village. "This scenery reminds me of the seaside villages on the Mediterranean coast. Look," he said, pointing to the north. "Noyo Fishing Village even looks like the *Pedregalejo* area of Málaga—with its fishing boats and seafood restaurants lining the shore."

"Have you ever gone back to visit Málaga since you left?"

"No," he replied.

He drew a long breath, reflecting on the changes that had happened to him over the last several days. Had he looked upon this scenery two weeks ago, before he met Savannah, he would have been haunted by the same unspeakable rage and sorrow that accompanied his memories of Málaga. Today, it was somehow different. He was able to look squarely upon the memories and not cringe from the turmoil in his heart.

He turned his gaze upon Savannah's face and saw the tranquility that had tamed the caged beast in his soul since the day he met her. *So help me God, I love this woman*, he said to himself. Had he not been bound by matrimonial ties, and had she not been engaged to be married, he would not have hesitated to tell her—tell the world—that he loved her.

But he knew he needed to tread with restraint. He sensed a greater measure of propriety in her than he did in himself, and he didn't want to scare her away. He would tell her in time.

Savannah had moved a few steps away from him. Alfonso, looking upon her and seeing her silhouetted against the vast blue sky, with the wind frolicking with her hair and her dress, knew she was the embodiment of everything that was beautiful to him. Nature's landscape imitated her. From the resplendence of the sun, to the curvaceous majesty of the hills, the undulating outlines of the coast, the splendor of the redwoods and the pine trees, and the fragrance of the ocean, nature imitated her. And yet she stood there, oblivious to how beautiful she was to him. Not knowing how worthy she was of being loved, and how his life was being changed by her.

"Savannah," he said suddenly. "Please wait for me right here. I'll be back in a few minutes."

"Alright."

He returned shortly with his scuffed leather guitar case in one hand, and a woolen blanket in the other. He laid out the blanket on the ground and bade her to sit down. Then, he opened his guitar case and carefully lifted his guitar out of it.

"Savannah, I'd like you to meet *Guernica*." He held his guitar with his left arm outstretched, while pointing his right hand to the guitar, bowing his head in mock formality.

"A guitar with a name. How delightful," she said. "And I suppose you named it after Picasso's *Guernica*?"

"*Si*. Picasso's *Guernica* was full of anguish. My guitar is full of anguish, therefore, the name."

Savannah pondered *Guernica*, perhaps Picasso's greatest work–a disturbing piece created in 1937 depicting the tragedy and drama of the Spanish civil war and, in particular, the pillage of the little town called *Guernica*. It was a stark masterpiece in which the artist refrained from the use of color, but resorted instead to the use of black or bluish gray to capture the anguish. Picasso made dramatic use of women and animals screaming in terror, including the figure of a weeping woman holding her dead child in her arms. There was something appropriate about Alfonso naming his guitar *Guernica*. It seemed a good match to his melancholy character and the sense of tragedy she sensed in him.

He sat down on the blanket facing her, and began to pluck and strum the guitar to tune it.

"Now, Savannah, I want you to close your eyes, listen with the ears of your heart and just float. When I start playing, just go where the music takes you, and just receive what the music gives you."

Savannah closed her eyes as Alfonso began to play. The sentimentality of the opening riff immediately engulfed her in a cloud of tenderness as he tugged at her emotions with fingers that traversed the octaves in undulating sequences. The tantalizing Spanish melody seemed to abolish time and space, and she felt the sensation of flying into the wide blue sky, gliding through meandering wind streams in a surreal dimension. Then, he began to sing with a voice so liquid that it reminded her of a country stream—sparkling, gentle and cool to the senses. The silky resonance of his voice rocked her gently to and fro like a raft on the emerald harbor of shimmering guitar strings. She hardly understood the Spanish lyrics, but so superb was the tapestry of his song and his voice that they swept over her with a language that her heart could understand. She rode the melodies as though they were invisible waves that were rising, falling, twisting and turning.

The song took her through narrow streets, wide thoroughfares, plazas, fountains, across oceans and across market squares and crossroads to discover deep emotions she had been waiting to feel. The music spoke of a heartfelt love—a desperate, fervent kind of love, longing and sadness. It was as though the music revealed her innermost secrets. At that moment, she was so overwhelmed that she could neither control nor explain the tears that rolled down her cheeks.

When Alfonso finished singing, he opened his eyes to find Savannah trembling and crying. He laid down his guitar and sat next to her, put his arms around her and held her for several minutes. She looked up at him, slowly coming back to her senses, and noticed that he was watching her with a devotion that startled her. But as soon as he became aware that she was looking at him, he reverted back to his usual sober expression. He looked away and fixed his gaze on the horizon.

Savannah was well aware of Alfonso's arms around her, and she savored the moment. Something in the back of her head protested that she was playing with fire. But at that moment, she didn't care and would not listen. Instead, she listened as her heart loosened the tight grip with which she held on to ancient fears. If she had refused to admit it was happening before, now there was no denying that she had fallen deeply in love with Alfonso Madrigál.

For the first time since she met him, she saw a smile ripen fully upon his lips. It was a bashful smile, but she sensed with delight that he was beaming like a peacock displaying its plumage, and the furrows on his brow softened.

"The song was written by a Malagueño singer," he said.

"Tell me what the words mean, Alfonso."

"The words are a little difficult to translate," he replied. "I promise to write down the translation for you sometime soon."

"Maybe it served me well that I didn't understand the words. It made me tune in to the sentiments of the song instead. I sensed an innocent joy in it–like that of a first love. But I also sensed a feeling of sadness and despair. The sentiments of this Malagueño singer were so deep that they brought me to tears."

This time, a broad smile crossed Alfonso's lips, like a bright flare slicing through darkness. "I guess you understood the words of the song after all."

"And you, *Señor* Alfonso, have an amazing singing voice. I'm surprised you haven't sung professionally."

He didn't respond to her compliment. He stared out into the distance, silent.

"Alfonso," she said softly. "Could it be that you have *duende*?"

"Why do you say that?"

"Just now, when you sang for me, something strange happened. I felt transported and mesmerized. I could hear you singing, but I scarcely knew whether I was listening to you sing, or I was the one singing. The distinction between you and me became blurred. Isn't that what you said *duende* meant?"

"*Duende* means different things to different people. Each listener experiences *duende* based on the emotion he or she brings to the experience. Whatever you bring–or whatever you seek–is magnified by *duende*, and the experience doesn't even have to be musical. That's just the context in which flamenco musicians speak. Like beauty, *duende* is in the eyes of the beholder."

"Then, in my eyes, you have *duende*."

"*Quizás*, Savannah. Perhaps you may be right." Again, he put forth a shy smile that reminded her of a dazzling light gleaming through the hairline crevices of a cracked wall.

༄

𝒯he sun began its descent towards the southwestern corner of the sky, as was its custom every fall. Alfonso put his guitar back into its case, sprang to his feet, and held his hand out to her. She took his hand, and he helped her to her feet, picking up the guitar case with his other hand. Savannah walked a few steps ahead of him as they made their way through the wooded area back towards the car. Alfonso watched her, loving everything about her, thanking God for creating such a fine specimen of womanhood for him to behold. Yet, even as he tried to fill his mind with ennobled visions of her, the savage part of him entertained a longing to possess her in the carnal sense.

Even as he joyfully looked forward to a few more hours alone in the car with her, he knew his masculine desire would prevail during the entire trip back, and he wasn't sure how he was going to subdue his feelings.

The first hour of the ride back to the city was quiet. The car radio was playing soft tunes, and Savannah hummed softly along with them. It seemed to Alfonso that something had happened between them that demanded silence and contemplation, and there was no need for conversation just then. Looking over at Savannah, it seemed that she, too, was at peace with her own thoughts. As he gazed at her, he wondered what distant thought put a smile upon her lips.

"You know what I was thinking?" she said, finally breaking the silence.

"Tell me, Savannah."

"You did something different a little while ago when you played your guitar and sang for me. You allowed the spirit to move in you. I just now realized the difference between the music you played for me today and the kind you play at the Club."

"What is that?"

"You were willing to express the emotions you rarely express. Isn't *duende* the willingness to turn yourself inside out for the world to see?"

"Why, yes, of course you're right," Alfonso replied,

He had always said that *duende* required extreme emotional demands from the singer. But until now, he hadn't been willing to express all but the most superficial emotions. As for those emotions that he did allow to surface, he did so with enough restraint as to render them meaningless. That's why his guitar-playing had always, in his view, fallen short of excellence.

It began to dawn on him that his love for Savannah enabled him to re-enter deep emotional realms where he was previously reluctant to go. With that realization came the sweetness of freedom, of being liberated from the shackles that had made his life a living prison. His heart pounded wildly, wondering about uncharted possibilities now that love had opened the door to that realm.

"And speaking of the willingness to turn one's self inside out for the world to see, isn't that the very definition of love as well?" Savannah ventured.

"I believe it is. It must be true what I've heard people from Andalucia say–that *duende* is love, one and the same."

"*Exactamente.*"

Alfonso smiled as the sun's amber rays turned to vermilion, signaling the approaching twilight. In the distance, he saw a train coming to the end of its journey. He imagined seeing a lone eagle emerge from it–its injured wings repaired–hurrying off to find its fragment of the sky, where it could learn to fly again.

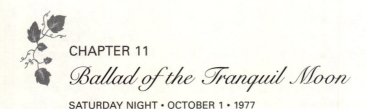

CHAPTER 11
Ballad of the Tranquil Moon
SATURDAY NIGHT • OCTOBER 1 • 1977

The glass panes of the city reflected the last glow of the Indian summer sun as the 1975 Buick wound its way past the Golden Gate Bridge toward Pacific Avenue.

Twilight is a fragile thing, Savannah mused, as she gazed at the fading light of the October day. *A priceless moment to be snatched from a daydream before the spell is broken.*

She couldn't remember when she'd felt the kind of bliss she experienced that day–was certain it was never. She longed for the moments with him to go on without end, clutching them to her heart, never wanting them to be over. She fantasized about running away with him, unencumbered, without a care in the world. She knew it was a dream, knew that reality would intrude upon her dream the moment he dropped her off at her apartment and drove home to his family.

She looked out the car window at the trees, whose shadows were longer than the trees themselves. These were the bewitching shadows of fall–the kind that photographers love to photograph and painters love to paint.

In the twinkling of a sigh, dusk rode off beyond the horizon. A waning moon appeared and the sky turned indigo as night fell. The air from nearby eucalyptus gardens infused the air with invigorating sweetness while the smell of burning leaves wafted up from somewhere in the distance.

As a gusty wind paid tribute to the falling leaves, the brown Buick approached 201 Pacific, and with it came the thought of the unspeakable loneliness of being without him. She wondered in desperation what time would be worthwhile if it were not spent with him.

He opened her car door and held his hand out to her as she slowly alighted. At the foot of the stairs, he stepped in close to her, hugging her, his fingertips feeling the skin of her bare back. Her arms went around him and her hand patted his back in a gesture of casual friendship.

Alfonso held her in his arms longer than social etiquette permitted. Even after Savannah's arms dropped to her side, he held her as though slow dancing to the ballad of the tranquil moon on a night that was vast and profoundly starlit.

Finally, she broke away from his embrace gently. "Thank you, Alfonso…thank you for…," she stammered as she sought the words to say, "…for an incredible day. I'll never forget it," she said, smiling at him.

He walked her up the steps to her door, holding her hand. She searched for the keys in her purse with her free hand, while holding on to his hand with the other, not wanting to let go for even a moment before she had to. The warmth of his hand made her skin ripple with small waves of tenderness. Still holding his hand, she slipped her key into the keyhole and turned the doorknob. Her head throbbed as she realized she must let him go now. It was the right thing to do.

She turned around to face him.

From out of the half darkness of the stair landing, he said, "Would you mind if I came in for a glass of water, Savannah?"

Her pulse quickened, sensing a prelude to danger. But perhaps it was temporary madness, perhaps it was falling in love with Alfonso Madrigál that made her lose her desire to live her life safely at that moment. For once, she dared to live dangerously.

"Of course," she said. "Please come in."

She turned around and walked to the kitchen, switching on the living room lamp along the way. She returned shortly with a glass of iced water. She brought no coaster. A coaster would seem an invitation for him to set down his glass and linger awhile. That was something she didn't quite know how to deal with.

Alfonso took the glass from her hand, trying not to look at her directly, not wanting her to see the longing in his eyes. He sipped quietly.

Warmth still ruled the October air, but the beads of perspiration that dotted his forehead and the rest of his body had little to do with the temperature in the air. As for Savannah, she could not look at his eyes, afraid of finding something lurking there that might overpower her. At that moment, if he had used any power at all over her, she could not have resisted, for she had no strength against him.

He sipped from the glass until it was almost empty–all the while looking at her, with intense, exploring eyes, as though emboldened by every long sip of water he took.

She stood in the lamplight, wanting him to kiss her, touch her, hold her, or say something to her. He said nothing. He stood by the open front door, sipping and watching her intently.

Suddenly, he leaned down and laid the glass on the side table. Then, he took her hand and kissed it, never taking his eyes away from her face. Something in her quivered, while another part of her stiffened, in a battle that tore her in opposite directions.

Alfonso felt her hand stiffen momentarily. Nonetheless, he drew her body close to his. His left arm circled her waist and the other gently cradled the back of her head. He started to stroke her hair softly while gazing at her, watching her eyes.

Savannah's eyes darted back and forth nervously even as her body slid into his. His hand slipped down her back, then moved to her chin, lifting it and kissing her lips first softy, then deeply. He cradled the back of her head with his other hand as he drew her mouth deeper into his.

Then, his hands moved slowly over the contours of her back, following the swell of her hips and slipping his arms around her waist. His lips explored the back of her neck and her bare shoulders. A soft, almost inaudible, gasp escaped her lips as her eyes were lulled shut by the throes of passion.

A cool breeze whistled idly through the front door, and a small wisp of drifting fog designed halos around the streetlamps. She leaned against him, feeling the warmth of his body spreading wherever it touched her body—her hands, her arms, her breasts, her belly and her pelvis.

"Savannah...," he moaned as her hands wandered across his chest and she felt her fingertips scorched by the heat of his flesh. He was breathing heavily and his forehead glistened with perspiration as she smelled the intoxicating headiness of his masculinity.

Suddenly, self-restraint made her pull away from him. A voice inside her head kept reminding her that there was a point beyond which she would not go, that she should never become intimately involved with Alfonso. With her eyes still half-closed with desire, her mind waged battles with propriety, morality and fidelity even while passion, desire, and longing ruled her body.

Savannah moved away from him, but he pulled her closer. An agony deep inside her begged to be indulged. Looking into his eyes and seeing the glaze of passion that burned in their ebony depths, she felt her limbs go weak again with desire. *God, how I want him*, she thought. But she fought back her desire, allowed composure to take over her senses, let her hands slip from around his back. She then reached behind her to take his hands into hers and clasped them tightly. Her eyes began to brim with shame over the impropriety of her desire. She had never before condoned women who had affairs with married men, and she scolded herself for entertaining the thought. She realized the horror of her mistake—the mistake of allowing herself to get into a compromising situation such as this. But walking away was still an option. She could do it....

"Alfonso, you should go," she whispered breathlessly. Her own words seemed the redemption as well as the death of her.

The night hummed and breathed an enormous sigh. She could hardly comprehend what was going on. She felt infinitely relieved even as her spirits sank. Her face was flushed, and her heart beat so fast she thought it would explode. She wanted him, needed him, loved him.

Alfonso brought both her hands to his lips. "Yes, I guess I should go," he finally replied.

As he turned to leave, she said, "Thanks again for everything, Alfonso. I'll never forget today."

"Neither will I. *Muchas gracias, Señorita* Savannah."

He kissed her lips again for a brief moment, and Savannah pulled away before the kiss had a chance to take hold of her again. Alfonso turned around and walked slowly down the stairs as she looked on.

A little voice inside Savannah cried in desperation, *Don't go! Don't leave, Alfonso. I need you. Stay with me!* Her mouth formed the words, but they remained unspoken as she watched him walk slowly down the stairs and out of her sight.

After several moments, she finally closed the door and turned off the lamp. She walked across the darkness of the living room, past the Japanese paper lantern that swayed as she walked by, past the framed pictures sitting on the antique chest, and into her bedroom.

The drapes were half-drawn and a street lamp lent sufficient light for her to remove her sandals, slip off her dress, find her silk kimono robe hanging on a hook in her closet, and put it on without having to turn the light on. Her face still burned from his kiss and his touch. She sank into her bed, stared at the ceiling and thought of him. She was in love for the first time in her life. Desperately in love with a man she could not have.

She began to ponder the events of that day. Her thoughts centered particularly around the afternoon on Heaven's Bluff when he sang to her. She summoned back the emotions that she felt while he sang, and she began to tremble again. Just as she thought of pulling out her journal and confessing her feelings to its waiting pages, she heard it.

A knock on the door. Soft and tentative at first, and then more certain. The palpitations of her heart became deafening. Reality merged with fantasy just then and she couldn't figure out which one she was in. As if in a trance, she slid out of her bed, and walked out of her bedroom and across the living room in her bare feet as she tied the sash of her robe securely around her waist. She reached the front door and looked into the peephole. *Alfonso.* The temperature in her body climbed higher than the mercury in the middle of an African jungle.

The doorknob seemed to turn on its own accord, as if directed by some mighty sorcerer, allowing the door to swing open.

∽

Alfonso stood there, looking at her framed in the doorway, his right hand propped high against the door jamb. Even in the darkness, she wielded an exquisitely controlled sensuality to which every fiber of his being responded. There in the dusky shadows of the entry way, like a beam of light from a lantern, shone the bewitching, inescapable eyes of Savannah. The rounded swell and the rising peaks of her breasts strained against the sheerness of her white silk robe, and her long mahogany hair was draped around her shoulders and back looking lustrous against the whiteness of the fabric. At that moment, he knew he had never seen any woman as desirable to him as she was.

In the silence that fell upon them, Savannah's mind hastened back to Alfonso's kisses just mere minutes ago. She felt the bones in her body dissolve into a powdery dust that floated in the weightlessness of her body. *God help me, I love this man.* Deep inside, she secretly hoped that her love for him would sanctify what she could no longer stop herself from allowing.

All day, Alfonso had silenced his untamed animal attraction to her. He knew he was losing the battle, but felt no remorse for the defeat to come. Forsaking all caution, he took her in his arms and kissed her with a passion born of a half-slumbering life discovering sweet wakefulness. Her arms slid up around his neck as if she couldn't bear to let him go. He pushed the door shut behind him with his heel while his arms held her close. His passion overwhelmed her and she melted into a small and helpless creature in his arms, and the resistance that possessed her only minutes ago was gone. Nothing could extinguish the flame that burned within her.

He pulled away from her for a moment and looked into her eyes. "Look at you…do you know how beautiful you are to me?" he whispered. Then, his mouth explored the contours of her neck, her shoulders and every crest and hollow of her body. She stood quivering in her bare feet on the plush carpet while his lips traveled forbidden roadways and his hands caressed silky slopes, down between the pillars, closer and closer to the bubbling spring of her desire, and awakening every river of her body with carnal fire. As if on cue, her sash came undone, flinging her robe open and revealing her body.

"Mi amor," he whispered, with a deep sigh. It was barely audible but it sent a quiver through her body, and she felt like a rose moistened by heavy dew. His eyes had a dreamy look in them while he kissed her neck, then her shoulders till he came to her breasts.

He kissed them gently, taking the nipples in his mouth in small caresses.

She shuddered, electrified by his hands and his lips upon her body. Rivulets sprang forth within her as she put her arms around him under his shirt and felt his smooth, firm, naked flesh. At first, she felt afraid–afraid of his overwhelming power over her, afraid of her desire for him. But as he fell to his knees on the velvet rug, caressing her abdomen with his face, planting kisses along the tops of her thighs, a viscous web of passion spun around her with a fervor so fierce that it melted every fiber inside of her.

She had no strength to protest, and no desire to disobey the desperation that dwelled in his eyes and her soul. He ran his fingers through her hair and smelled the aroma of the maritime nights of Málaga. It was the scent he smelled in her tonight. He was at the end of his journey and he found his home in her. All his searching now found its end in Savannah.

As he knelt on the velvet rug, he wrapped his arms tightly around her thighs with his head leaning against her lower belly. Her head towered above his, and all the while he kept thinking that this was the way Savannah deserved to be cherished and adored–above himself, and above all else.

"Oh, Alfonso," she murmured, unable to stop herself from quivering.

She couldn't remember how they made it to her bedroom, whether he carried her to the bed, or if they walked. She didn't remember where her robe had fallen and when she slipped into a nakedness that removed all barriers between her and Alfonso Madrigál. She only remembered being intoxicated by the sight of his blazing bronze skin upon her ivory skin, and being entranced by a power much greater than herself.

In the caverns of her trance, she felt herself as the midnight tide, growing restless under the wakefulness of a full moon, and in the distance, a noble stallion advancing first steadily toward her, then swiftly charging at full speed, and finally entering the warm waters of her ripeness with an indescribable rapture that emitted a muffled gasp like that of a desperate surf. Her mind reeled at the relentless entry inside her that felt fiercely overpowering like the thrust of a dagger, yet strangely tender. Dark waves, silent beforehand, rose in a frenzy, rolling, undulating and stimulating the perfumed waters of the sea as the stallion moved by leaps and amorous gallops, penetrating deep into her private ecstasy. Somewhere inside her, the waves parted and she yielded to him with the wild abandon of Andalusian gypsies, flung her discernment to the wind, while the undertow pulled the awesome prime of him deeper still into her, tenderly plunging into the depths of her with a silent primordial force and domination, touching the abyss that had been untouched before. Soft moaning sounds escaped her as she felt the exhilaration of his sweet invasion, and she heaved to meet him in a rapturous rhythm. Under the watchful eye of the waning moon, they rode a tempest of surging, quivering, aching, and throbbing in unutterable ecstasy. The water engulfed the stallion in an increasingly relentless grip, and the ocean heaved and swelled into a great crest that suddenly, without warning, crashed thunderously upon the rocks in a soaking, shattering convulsion, bringing to full circle the delirium of lunacy.

Afterwards, she shuddered with spent passion as the Kahili ginger flowers permeated the warm air with their inebriating fragrance. She held him close, feeling like she held everything in her arms. More than anything, she remembered feeling like a woman–drenched and pulsating with life for the very first time.

Alfonso felt an indescribable bliss as he rested his cheek upon her breasts, thinking he could live the rest of his days like this. He remembered everything, relished everything, especially when all the aching subsided and his body entered a place of ecstasy completely unfamiliar to him until that moment. Making love to the woman he loved had a new dimension of pleasure, transcending all human experiences he had ever known. He suddenly understood the secret language of the planets, the bolt of lightning in the desert, the songs of the rainforest, and the mysteries of the universe.

She gently laid his head upon a pillow and placed her face upon his chest, smelling the Mediterranean Sea and the citrus fruits of Málaga on him, letting the scent engulf her.

No one could buy the happiness she felt at that moment–happiness born of an intense love for one man. Happiness born of a certainty that there was no one else with whom she would rather be, now or ever. And sorry no one could see how happy they were.

∽

It was almost midnight when Alfonso finally left. Almost as soon as he was gone, the phone rang. It was Russell. Savannah let the answering machine pick up.

"Hi, sweet pea," Russell's voice said. "Where are you? I've been trying to reach you all day. Pick up the phone if you're there." There were a few seconds of silence. "Well, I just wanted to tell you that it looks like I'm going to be here a few more days. I won't be flying back from Chicago tomorrow after all, but I'll definitely be back on Thursday night. I'll call later and give you the flight details. Love you."

She felt a little guilty being happy that Russell wasn't going to be back so soon. She smiled, relishing the thought that she had five more days to spend exclusively with Alfonso. Slowly, she unclasped the silver chain from around her neck and stored it, along with the globe-shaped silver charm dangling on it, in an oak chest where she kept mementoes from her past.

CHAPTER 12
To Be Alone with Love

SUNDAY MORNING • OCTOBER 2 • 1977

The smile on Alfonso's face when he arrived at 201 Pacific at ten o'clock didn't reflect the discord he had experienced at home that morning.

Isabel had quarreled with him–complained about his being gone all day Saturday, and not coming home until late. She demanded to know where he was off to again today, reminding him it was her day off. He didn't like lying to Isabel, but he made up some excuse that he hoped she'd believe. On his way out the door, Cristina tugged at his shirt sleeve, reminding him that he had promised to take her to the Palace of Fine Arts to see the swans.

He knelt on the floor in front of her, put his hands gently on her shoulders and said, "Cristina, I can't take you to see the swans today because I have things I need to do. I'll take you on Thursday instead, okay?"

Cristina rubbed her eyes with the back of her hands and stared at him, surveying his entire face, as though looking for some kind of clue as to what sort of things he needed to do on a Sunday morning. Just then, she momentarily turned her eyes towards Savannah's painting that was hanging on the wall, and then searched his face.

"So Thursday it is, Cristina?" he asked again, feeling uneasy under the weight of her stare.

"Okay," she finally replied. Her face was expressionless. If she was disappointed, she didn't show it just then.

Alfonso walked out the front door and walked down the steps to his car. As he began to pull away, he caught a glimpse of Cristina standing behind the screen door clutching the door's aluminum brace. Her eyes strangled his heart with grief. They were the same eyes he had seen in the orphaned children at *Orfanato Pedregalejo* when Abuelita and he went to the orphanage to donate goods and funds. A sharp dagger stabbed him deep in the chest. For a brief moment, he considered turning off the engine, going back to Cristina and telling her that the things he needed to do could wait, and that he'd take her to see the swans after all. But instead, he bit his lower lip and looked away.

Then, just as he stepped on the clutch and shifted to first gear, he noticed Isabel at their bedroom window watching him drive away.

It would have been easier for Alfonso to tell Savannah he would see her on Monday. But the night before, as they lay in bed, Savannah had casually mentioned how she wanted to go to the *Infiorata Festival* on Sunday. He had offered to take her there. He would have found any reason—and overcome greater obstacles—for the chance to see her again.

Alfonso was consumed by the need to show Savannah that her needs were important to him. That she wasn't his second priority, but his first. He felt a need to make her feel fully loved—and convince her that he cared enough about her to rearrange his life to be with her. It was a need born of the guilt he felt for being married, instead of an unencumbered single man with all the time in the world to devote to her.

Nothing from Alfonso's earlier battles was evident when he arrived at Savannah's doorstep at ten o'clock that Sunday morning. When he took her in his arms and held her close, he quickly put behind him all thoughts of Isabel and Cristina. Nothing else seemed to matter to him when Savannah was in his arms.

Even as he held her, masculine longings arose in him that made him want to carry her into the bedroom and make passionate love to her again. But instead of obeying his carnal desires, he chose to defer the satisfaction of his own needs in favor of hers. Savannah was already dressed and ready to leave for the *Infiorata Festival*. He would just have to silence the urgency of his need until later.

                                                             ~

They arrived at Sharon Meadow just minutes after the *Infiorata Festival* officially opened. It was a festival celebrating flower artists from Italy who created beautiful murals on the pavement using flower petals. The practice of making flower-petal art originated in Italy decades ago when artists created the art on sidewalks and streets. The most renowned of the festivals was the *Infiorata di Noto* in Sicily, which was held annually at the end of May.

Savannah's eyes lit up and an audible gasp escaped her lips when they walked by the nearest set of displays. There were intricate flower mural "carpets" depicting frescos of the Sistine Chapel.

"These are splendid," she gushed.

"Yes, they are," he replied, amused by the childlike side of Savannah that he hadn't seen before—glad he had offered to come with her to the festival. Savannah seemed transformed into a little girl discovering toyland.

His thoughts turned to Cristina and how she, too, would enjoy seeing these flower murals. He was certain she would probably pay less attention to the works of art than she would the quivering of the flower petals every time even the slightest breeze swept by. He slipped his hand into Savannah's, feeling overjoyed just walking beside her. He tried to remember which poet wrote the words, *Time not spent with you is lost.* Indeed, time not spent with Savannah was lost.

The main pavilion at the festival featured artists from Sicily who demonstrated how the flower petal murals were created. Savannah stood among the first row of onlookers, and Alfonso stood behind her, his arms circling her from the back, as they watched. He kissed the top of her head, exhilarated by the sweet smell of hyacinth in her hair.

The flower artists demonstrated how they built an earthen berm out of organic soil. "Creating flower art is similar to making a stained glass window," one of the Sicilian artists said, "except that glass stays in place while flower petals obey the wind." They then used spoons and hands to fashion a cross-section of the berm, getting it ready to adhere the petals inside. The soil was kept moist by spraying it constantly with water.

⁓

Like a well-watered garden beside a running stream whose waters never fail. That was how Savannah felt at that moment. *Parched land blessed by eternal rain.* It occurred to her she must be dreaming. Here she was, standing in the arms of a man she had just met six days ago, yet feeling cared for by him much more than she ever felt cared for by Russell.

In the context of her life, Savannah had never dared dream of finding a man like Alfonso. A man who called his guitar *Guernica*, who spoke in metaphors, wrote poetry, sang with a voice like a country stream, and fantasized about eagles on trains. A man who moved and made love like a noble stallion. Men like Alfonso were reserved for beauty queens, prom queens, debutantes, and girls with silver spoons in their mouths—girls whose daddies loved them.

She had convinced herself that her life was a parched terrain in which poetry and handsome Spanish balladeers had no place, and she had long forgotten how to fantasize about knights in shining armor. Yet for the first time in years, a voice within her admitted that she longed for a taste of that kind of life. Wanted a man to cherish her, write poems for her, sing to her, and tell her she was a sunbeam in a field of clover.

"What makes you happy?" Alfonso asked her out of the blue.

"I'm sorry, what?"

"I want to know the things that make you happy, Savannah. The things that put a smile on your face, make you laugh. The things that make you feel special." He kissed her on the cheek affectionately, letting his arms close in around her waist from the back.

Everything inside her wanted to answer, *"You, Alfonso. You, you and you."* But instead, she smiled and said, "Trees of green, red roses too, the ones that bloom for me and you...."

"And you say to yourself, what a wonderful world," he paraphrased the remaining lyrics of the song into her ear, filling every sinew of her body with rapture.

Across the way, an elderly couple had turned their attention away from the flower artists' demonstration, and started watching them instead, smiling and remembering the days when they, too, were that much in love.

Savannah turned her face toward Alfonso, lifted her chin, and kissed him on the lips while he held her close from behind. She felt the eyes of the elderly couple upon them. *Yes, take a look at us,* Savannah shouted in her mind, wanting the whole world to hear. *Look at me! Have you ever seen anyone as deliriously happy?*

The flower artists carefully began to affix the petals between the beams, creating a three-dimensional effect that made the flower art appear to be a hand-loomed carpet to the onlooker.

It was a process that would take a few hours.

―――

In the car, on the way back to Savannah's apartment, Alfonso held her hand while he drove. With her free hand, Savannah caressed his forearm gently, not realizing what fires she was igniting in him as she did.

As soon as she turned the key to the front door and opened it, Alfonso gave up the pretense of propriety and pulled her into him, fervidly kissing her neck, her shoulders and her breasts with lips that smoldered. He lifted her off her feet and carried her to the bedroom just as he had wanted to do the moment he saw her that morning. In a flash, the clothes came off and he reveled in the sight of her nakedness.

Savannah closed her eyes in breathless anticipation, aching to be invaded by his noble sword once again. But instead of going into her, Alfonso positioned his body just above hers, like a wild panther waiting to pounce on its prey—with his body barely touching hers. He began to move his body over her breasts, her belly, and her thighs causing her skin to ignite wherever his body touched hers. Over and over again, his body swept over hers, the scepter of his manhood brushing first lightly, then urgently, against her flesh in a frenzied rhythm that wielded a fire of desperate longing. She wrapped her legs around his hips as he continued the hallucinated dance without going inside her–faster and faster still until muffled screams escaped her lips and she climaxed, throbbing helplessly through cerulean waves of ecstasy. He whispered Spanish words of love into her ear and kissed her body between phrases.

When her throbbing subsided, he proceeded to conquer every crevice and every fleshy mound of her, awakening the flower that bloomed between her columns. He made love to her again and again with the kind of fervor that made every nerve of her body weep with pleasure, taking her deep within the labyrinth of love's private heaven. He was to her like a tropical typhoon that began as a warm, gentle rain, followed by high and sultry monsoon winds that turned into a raging tempest, leaving her body quivering in its wake. And afterwards, they lay in each other's arms, still and enraptured, with no other purpose than that of loving each other in silence. It was with a sense of awe and astonishment that Alfonso realized he was utterly and completely defined by his love for Savannah.

As they lay in bed, holding each other close, he asked her, "What do you dream of?"

"Huh?" she said, still dreamy-eyed from their passionate love-making.

"What are your hopes, your dreams, your ambitions?"

"You really wanna know?" Savannah asked, dumbfounded that he would even be interested.

"Yes, I do," he answered.

She couldn't quite understand why his question made her eyes brim with tears. She turned her face away from him briefly and blinked her eyes repeatedly to disperse the tears. She didn't want him to see her cry again. For the first time in her life, she felt that she mattered, and whatever feelings she voiced would be acknowledged. She felt as though Alfonso had handed her a blank canvas that represented the realm of all possibilities, one wherein she could design a life that fully expressed her values and her dreams.

"I want to start a school where I can teach emotionally traumatized children how to paint," she said tentatively. She half expected the perfunctory, "Oh, that's nice, sweet pea" reaction that Russell often gave her whenever she broached a subject that neither interested nor concerned him.

Instead, Alfonso folded his pillow in half, propped his head a little higher, and looked at her intently. "That sounds like an excellent idea. Tell me more about this school."

"I want a school where I can not only teach children concepts such as contrasting colors, curves, angles, and awareness of texture, but for them to receive the therapeutic effects of art expression. Children have an organic way of expressing through play–so I want a school where drawing and painting can help them convey complex feelings as a way of helping them cope with whatever trauma they've experienced."

Savannah pursed her lips, her eyes glazed over as if trying to recall a distant memory. Then she continued, "I would have child psychologists on staff, of course, and together, we would gently ask the children questions about their art, and get them to express feelings they have been unable or reluctant to put into words. For instance, if a child has been traumatized by having been abandoned by her father, I'd like to see art become a means of expressing and dealing with that trauma."

Savannah became conscious of the fact that she had been rambling on and on, so she suddenly stopped talking. *Perhaps I've said too much,* she thought. She searched his face to check if he was still interested in what she was saying, or if he had tuned out and dismissed her silly ideas...like all the other men she ever knew.

Alfonso had tucked his left arm under his head on the pillow. He clung to her every word, realizing that this was the closest that Savannah had come to talking about her father and her trauma over losing him.

Noticing that she had become quiet, he nudged at her to continue. "Please go on, Savannah. I really want to know how you envision this school. I want to know what it looks like in your mind's eye, down to the color of the walls."

"Okay," she said, relieved that she wasn't boring him. "You see, grief in children has a natural progression, and they need to be supported every step of the way or they're liable to form unhealthy attitudes that will scar them for life. And sometimes, therapy is not sufficient. Art can be used as a means of expression, wherein the children do not have to rely on verbal skills."

Savannah continued talking. Alfonso listened. He didn't offer solutions, suggestions, or refinements. He just listened, and that was more than enough for her. She felt that she was in a safe environment where she could voice her innermost thoughts. She sensed herself becoming bolder, more ambitious about her ideas, as he prodded her to go on. For the first time, she didn't have to tailor her dream to support another person's dreams. Her dreams didn't have to take a back seat to anyone else's.

"I've learned that what children say is not necessarily what they're feeling. When they draw or paint, however, their feelings are often expressed on paper, and their work offers important clues to their fears, concerns and worries."

Savannah hesitated again for a moment, and Alfonso said, "Go ahead, I'm still listening."

"Alfonso, I could talk about this all night, but it's 8:35, and I think you'd better start getting ready. Your first set starts in twenty-five minutes."

Alfonso was unwilling to go back to work just yet, after having spent two glorious days with her, but he knew he needed to. "Would it be alright if I came back after my last set?"

"Of course it's alright. I'll wait up for you," she said, savoring the thought of spending more time with him. "There are fresh towels in the rattan cabinet in the bathroom, if you want to wash up."

Alfonso took a quick shower, and emerged from the bathroom minutes later wearing nothing but a bath towel slung around his neck. She watched his bronzed, hard body move across the floor with the stride of a prize-winning racehorse. His belly was flat as a board, and the musculature of his body reminded her of ancient Greek sculptures. His chest, arm and leg muscles were defined and elongated, not stuffed with over-bulging muscles of men who spent the better part of their lives at the gym.

As he turned his back towards her and bent over to pick up his change of clothes on the side chair, Savannah couldn't help but stare admiringly at his broad shoulders, his strong, wide back and narrow waist that gave him the sculpted, V-shaped torso she'd seen in swimmers' physiques. His gluteus muscles protruded prominently from the back of his pelvis, and the curvature gave his buttocks a sculpted shape she had seldom seen in a man.

"Savannah, if you don't mind, I'd like to continue talking about this school of yours when I come back later," he said while pulling a high-collared white shirt over his head and fastening the buttons. "That is, if you're not too sleepy by then."

"Sure," she answered, getting up from the bed and slipping on her white kimono. She wondered how she could possibly be sleepy around a man like him when he had reawakened dreams that had slumbered for too long.

She walked over to him, helping him fasten the buttons on the cuffs of his sleeves, straightening his collar, feeling his gaze upon her. Then, she picked up his straight-legged, slender-fitted pants and his belt from the chair and handed them to him. As he pulled them on and put the leather strap of his belt through the loops, she walked behind him and hugged him from the back, smelling his muskiness beneath the lemony scent of bath soap. *God, how I love this man, she thought,* leaning her head against his back.

Finally, Alfonso put on a black bolero jacket, and having finished dressing, he turned around, put his arms around her, and held her close, running his hands through her hair. His heart began its unrehearsed dance again, running wild and carefree through the

113

golden meadows of Savannah. He longed to find a metaphor or a poem to tell her that loving her was the ultimate fulfillment of himself, the supreme purpose of his life. That to love her eradicated all the rage and the sorrow of all his years. But words seemed inadequate to convey how profoundly he loved her. He then laid his fervent lips upon hers, and decided that silence said it much better.

From her bedroom window, Savannah watched him walk to his car, looking like a Spanish matador in his bolero jacket with the dramatic epaulets, feeling grateful that he would be back in her arms again in a few hours. She sank onto her bed, lying on the spot where he lay, burying her face in the pillow on which his head had been just minutes ago, feeling every pore of her body imbibe his essence. With him, she felt like the *prima ballerina* of Swan Lake, not the supporting dancer she had always been. Like the swan, not the ugly duckling. She soaked herself in her reverie, basked in it, drenched herself in the love of Alfonso Madrigál.

Savannah Curtis, forsaken daughter of Lyndon and Elaine Curtis, felt herself enter a blissful fantasy from which she would never quite return.

CHAPTER 13
Amber Days and Nights of Indigo
MONDAY–WEDNESDAY • OCTOBER 3-5 • 1977

Alfonso planned his days around Savannah over the following week. Every morning, after dropping off Cristina at day care, he would spend all day with her. And except for the necessary task of shipping the rest of her art to the Shaughnessy Gallery in Los Angeles, Savannah planned her days around him.

The Indian summer had lingered past its prime, but now it had taken its final bow, giving way to the damp, nippy autumn that San Franciscans knew so well. The infamous fog had returned from its brief vacation, and the cold weather announced that it was there to stay.

Savannah was wearing a red oversized sweatshirt and a pair of blue jeans when Alfonso arrived at her apartment on Monday morning.

"I just got off the phone with François," she told him.

"François?"

"François Sauvigny. He's that friend of mine I told you about that I sent your painting to for further evaluation. He gave me some news about the painting. I'll tell you as soon as I get dressed. I lost track of time talking to him, so I didn't get a chance to change. It'll take me only a few minutes, okay?"

"What's wrong with what you have on?" he asked.

"You're joking, right?" she asked, incredulous. Her incredulity stemmed from years of getting used to the protocol of dressing that Russell demanded. To Russell, a sweatshirt and jeans did not constitute attire suitable enough to be seen in public, unless you were going to engage in sports. It was suitable for common people, perhaps, but not for Savannah. At all times, Savannah needed to be dressed in a manner that would make Russell proud to introduce her to his friends, acquaintances, or business associates–in case they bumped into them somewhere. Although he disliked overly done make-up, he always preferred to have her wear a sufficient amount of powder and blush, a hint of eye shadow, a dab of mascara and a tasteful application of pale–not bright–lipstick, so she would look presentable to others.

"You want me to go out in this?" she asked Alfonso again just to make sure she heard him right.

"*Mi corazón*, you would look beautiful to me if you wore a

burlap sack. You look perfectly fine in that, but if you prefer to change into something else, that's up to you. But don't change for my sake."

Savannah thought that she ought to at least change into the navy blue LaCoste turtleneck that Russell had bought for her. *For casual outings*, he had said. Everything about Russell Parker was beginning to seem annoying to her now.

"Okay, then," she said finally. "I'll keep what I have on."

"*Muy bien,*" he said with a smile.

"So ... do you wanna know what François said?"

"Oh, yes. Tell me, what did he say?"

"He confirmed what I initially thought…that the painting is the work of Picasso. And also verified through further analysis that it was indeed created in 1897. That makes it one of the rarest finds to come around in a long time."

"That's good news," he said with lukewarm interest.

"What's wrong, Alfonso? I thought you'd be overjoyed."

"I am overjoyed, *mi amor*. But not more than I'm overjoyed by you," he said, taking her into his arms.

Savannah blushed.

"Don't you even want to know the price François thinks the painting would fetch on the auction block?"

"If you told me how much the painting is worth, would it make me feel richer than I feel right now knowing that you're in my life?" he asked, looking tenderly into her eyes. "If not, then you need not tell me."

༄

*A*utumn seemed the best time to visit the wine country, with its grape vines a medley of vivid colors and the harvest in full regalia. On Monday, Alfonso and Savannah drove to the idyllic countryside of Napa Valley. On their drive into the valley, Savannah was enchanted by a charming, tile-roofed Tuscan villa sitting on top of a hill surrounded by olive trees and grape vines. When it turned out to be one of the wineries, the Borrelli Vineyard, Alfonso took her there for lunch. He held her hands across the table, gazing at her in a way that left little doubt about how he felt about her.

On Tuesday, Alfonso wanted to visit the town where Savannah had spent most of her growing-up years. So they drove to the Ferry Building at the foot of Market and Embarcadero and took the ferry to Tiburon. The ferry took them to the Tiburon dock on the corner of Tiburon Boulevard and Main Street, a street which still retained much of its Victorian charm. At the tail end of Main Street was a wooden deck dotted with benches and picnic tables. Savannah had packed a picnic basket filled with lunch fare she had prepared the previous evening–a small Cornish hen roasted with lemon and rosemary, mini Gruyere cheese sandwiches on freshly baked rosemary bread, bow-tie pasta with a creamy pesto sauce, baby spinach salad with sweet grape tomatoes and feta cheese–and a bottle of red Burgundy wine. They decided to enjoy their lunch on one of the tables while watching sailboats and ferries on the bay.

After lunch, as they browsed the shops on Main Street, Alfonso asked her what it was like growing up in Tiburon. Savannah said she didn't grow up in Tiburon, insisting that it was just the place where she lived with Sabine after her mother died. It occurred to her that although she had spent nine of her growing years in Tiburon, she felt emotionally detached from the place and instead, considered the apartment on Kings Road in San Francisco–where she had lived with her parents–home.

Suddenly, Alfonso asked her the dreaded question again. "Whatever happened to your father?"

There was a painful silence as Savannah's eyes searched the skies of Tiburon for an answer. After a few moments, she said in an overly animated voice, "Oh, there's the high school I went to!" She pointed to a newly renovated building perched on top of a hill, with the words *Tiburon Catholic High School* inscribed in white relief letters on a short brick wall. "It's co-ed now," she continued, "but back when I used to go there, it was an all-girl's school."

For the second time in the space of a few days, Savannah berated herself for keeping Alfonso at arm's length. Scolded herself for treating him like someone who couldn't be trusted with her deepest confidence. How could she not let him in, when he himself had opened up about his own private hell just a few days before? Just then, she felt Alfonso's arms slip around her shoulders, and he held her close to him right there in the midst of Main Street's bustle. A tender wave of comfort engulfed her, and it was then that she realized that her self-admonition had lost its voice.

On Wednesday, they talked about going to Muir Woods after having an early lunch, which Alfonso insisted on preparing. Savannah rode with him in his Buick to an international food market on Bay Street, where he proceeded to buy a whole lobster, large prawns, squid, shrimp, clams, mussels, assorted white fish, Spanish brandy, a dry white wine and a dozen other ingredients. It became clear to her that this was not an ordinary lunch Alfonso was getting ready to prepare. "*Sarsuela* is a wonderful fish stew that is served in many coastal towns in Spain," he said to her, upon seeing her amazement over the assortment of ingredients. "I'm making you a special version of *sarsuela* from a recipe passed down by my great grandparents, who were both originally from Cataluña." It was an exceptional treat for Savannah, who had never had the pleasure of having a man cook a gourmet meal for her before.

After lunch, they drove to Muir Woods, the only remaining stand of old-growth redwoods in the San Francisco area, and walked through the ancient forest of centuries-old giant redwoods.

On all three days, they would return to Savannah's apartment in the mid-afternoon. The mellow days made them look forward with breathless anticipation to their intimate moments together. Alfonso would again make love to her, and she would throb at his fingertips, yield to his exquisitely controlled sexuality, and quiver, shudder and climax again and again, being drenched in the nectarous masculinity of him. After the lovemaking, they would lie in each other's arms for an hour–sometimes talking, sometimes relishing the silence that spoke volumes between them–until he had to leave to pick up Cristina at the day care center and take her home.

During those days, Savannah knew that the time Alfonso was spending with her was more–much more–than she could dare ask of him. She wondered how long it could last, how long he could continue making excuses to see her. She was also painfully aware that they were both avoiding the conversation they knew had to occur. The conversation that would have to start with, "Where do we go from here?"

Savannah worried that she was embarking on a perilous affair with Alfonso, and agonized about the repercussions their affair would have on Isabel and Cristina. She worried about what to say to Russell when he returned from Chicago, and wondered if she would ever allow him to touch her again–after Alfonso.

On his end, Alfonso struggled with responsibilities to his family and his love for Savannah. Deep down, he knew that if forced to make a choice, there was no question which decision his heart would make.

He felt a great sorrow for Isabel. Now that he had come to know what it was like to love a woman, he knew he could never love her the way a woman wants to be loved by a man. *'Does a man have to stay married to his wife because of marital obligation–even if he knew deep in his heart that he loved another?'* he wondered. *'That wouldn't seem fair to him or his wife, would it? If I left Isabel, wouldn't I be doing her a favor by freeing her to find a man who truly loves her?'* Alfonso wasn't certain he knew all the answers, but he was certain he cared about Isabel enough not to want to hurt her. He felt an even greater sorrow for Cristina. It grieved him how easily he could decide to give her up, if necessary, to be with Savannah—when just three weeks ago, there was nothing and no one that could ever make him forsake her. He secretly wished that there would never come a time when he would have to choose between Cristina and Savannah. His gaze fixed upon Savannah, who was lying beside him with her eyes half-closed, and remembered how she had never really recovered from the heartbreak of her father's abandonment. It was something he would never want Cristina to suffer. He was comforted by the fact that if ever the time came that he had to leave Isabel to be with Savannah, he would not need to abandon Cristina. He could still continue to see her while living with Savannah. *It happens all the time with children of divorced parents,* he argued. He smiled tentatively, feeling grateful there could somehow be a happy medium. *But what if Isabel were to move back to Spain and take Cristina with him?*

The digital clock on Savannah's bedside table—which read 4:40—didn't allow him the luxury to ponder the question. He needed to get ready to pick up Cristina at five.

Just as he was getting up from bed, Savannah suddenly said, "Stay with me, Alfonso. Please don't go!"

"What's the matter, *mi amor*?" he said, taking her into his arms again. "I'm not leaving you for good. I won't see you tomorrow because I promised Cristina I'd take her to see the swans. But I can be back here with you on Friday, if you'll have me." Even as he said the words, he began to feel the pain of not being with her—even for just a day. It was the same ache and inexplicable loneliness that he felt the night he watched her walk away from him at *Club La Cibeles* the week before.

"Don't worry about me, Alfonso. I don't know what came over me. Of course, I'll see you again." Savannah began to calm down, perplexed by the way she just behaved. "By the way, Russell's flying back from Chicago tomorrow evening."

At that moment, Alfonso felt an insane jealousy that another man was going to be with Savannah tomorrow night. What would any normal red-blooded man want to do with his fiancée after having been away for more than two weeks? His stomach tightened and his insides clenched at the thought of Savannah in the arms of Russell.

Before he finally walked out the door of 201 Pacific, he held her in his arms for a long time. Once again, he was engulfed with the need to find the words to tell her how much she meant to him, how much he loved her, and how much the last five glorious days and nights with her had made him a better man. But again, he chose to kiss her instead, hoping that silence would say it much better.

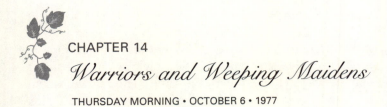

CHAPTER 14
Warriors and Weeping Maidens
THURSDAY MORNING • OCTOBER 6 • 1977

Isabel stood next to the dining room table flipping through a stack of pictures Cristina and Alfonso had taken. She put each picture down on the table, one by one, as she finished looking at them.

"These pictures are very good, Cristina. Did you take all of them?" she asked.

"Yes, Mama," Cristina replied. Pointing to a picture of sea lions lazing the afternoon away on wooden platforms along the pier while seagulls clustered on another platform, she said, "I took a picture of these seagulls and sea lions at Fisherman's Wharf. They're smart like the geese. Look…the sea lions know to stay right here in this area and they don't bother the seagulls in that area. And the seagulls do the same thing. They know their place. Papa said it's like they can read invisible signs that say 'Reserved for Sea Lions' or 'Reserved for Seagulls' or something like that."

"Hmmm…" A twinge of jealousy stabbed at Isabel's heart. It was an irrational but familiar jealousy she always felt when she realized how close Alfonso and Cristina were. She wasn't sure whether she was jealous of Cristina's fondness of Alfonso, or Alfonso's fondness of Cristina, or whether she just simply felt excluded.

"I took this picture of the boats at Pier 39," Cristina continued, pointing to the picture of sail boats on the bay. "This picture of the pigeons, I took at *Geerdelly* Square."

"Ghirardelli Square," Isabel corrected her.

"That's what I said. *Geerdelly* Square."

"I'll start a photo album for you, Cristina–and you can put all the pictures you took in it, okay?"

"Good idea, Mama. My own photo album–wow!"

Isabel was down to the last few pictures in the stack. She smiled when she saw the picture of Cristina in the park, with a Victorian apartment in the background. Cristina had a curious expression on her face, as though she wasn't quite ready to have the picture taken.

"Oh, this is a picture that Papa took of me."

"Where was it taken, Cristina?" Isabel asked, holding the photograph in her hand, wondering why Alfonso had shot the picture with Cristina off-center.

"At the park. Summerhill Park. It was the first time we went there."

The last picture in the stack was yet another off-centered picture of Cristina taken in the same spot as the previous one. Cristina's image was all the way to the left, with the same Victorian apartment to the right. The Victorian was painted a bright yellow and white, and had an address marker bordered in iron scrollwork. The number within the address marker was quite small, but it was still legible. *201 Pacific.* Then, she noticed the figure of a woman looking out through the parted curtains on the upper floor of the Victorian. The image was too small to discern her features. Suddenly, Isabel's heart felt like lead as she realized why Cristina's image was off-center on the photograph.

Just then, Alfonso came in the front door. He had been outside, warming up the car. "*Vamos!* It's time to go see the swans, Cristina."

Isabel quietly slipped the pictures back into the photo sleeve. "Wait for me while I get dressed. I'm coming with you," she said.

⁓

Savannah wasn't certain what compelled her to drive to the Palace of Fine Arts that day. What sort of perverted pleasure would she get out of watching Alfonso spend time with his daughter? The parking lot was half filled when she drove up in her black Toyota Celica. She parked her car in a dark corner of the lot, where she was sure Alfonso wouldn't spot it.

She sauntered down the walkway through the neo-classical portico toward the main grounds, watching in awe as the ochre-tinted Corinthian colonnades and the grand Romanesque rotunda with the massive dome loomed into view. She was always dazzled by the beautiful structures that comprised the reconstructed Palace. Beneath the dome of the rotunda, Greek statues and ornamentation projected from eight curved panels in low relief, depicting centaurs, warriors and weeping maidens of Greek mythology.

Savannah walked past the colonnades and the rotunda, her eyes skimming the lagoon in front of the Palace, searching among the tourists for Alfonso and his daughter. Just then, she heard the sound of his voice.

"You'll hear it better if you go to the middle, Cristina."

She turned around and spotted Alfonso standing under one of the towering arches of the rotunda, holding the hand of a chubby-cheeked little girl with long, jet-black corkscrew curls spilling out from a knitted beret.

Savannah moved behind one of the columns so that she would remain out of sight. From where she stood, she saw Cristina let go of Alfonso's hand, run to the center of the rotunda, clap her hands together, then listen to the eerie reverberation her clapping made.

Standing near them was a dark-haired woman wearing a teal-colored dress. Her back was towards her, and Savannah couldn't see her face, but she heard her tell Alfonso that she would walk down to the garden fountain and meet up with them there. *It's Isabel,* Savannah thought, her heart pounding nervously.

"Esta bien," she heard Alfonso say.

Isabel turned around and started walking towards the colonnade where Savannah hid behind a column. As Isabel passed her by, she saw her face up close, and was startled to see how physically attractive she was. She hadn't expected Alfonso's wife to look so stunning. She looked just like the porcelain Spanish dolls that Kimberley displayed on top of her living room *étagère* in glass cases. Isabel had large, doe-shaped eyes fringed with long upturned lashes, and neatly upswept ebony-black hair adorned with ornamental combs. She wore a slim-fitting dress that accentuated her voluptuous figure, with a ruffled hemline that flashed her shapely legs when she walked.

For a split second, Savannah saw Isabel turn her eyes towards her. She imagined seeing a flicker of recognition, but dismissed it as soon as Isabel looked quickly away. As Isabel continued walking down the serpentine pathway towards the fountain, Savannah noticed that she had attracted the attention of two men in their thirties, who stopped to stare admiringly at Isabel, uttering compliments loud enough for her to hear. Isabel pretended she didn't see or hear them, and continued to walk on.

A sickening feeling gripped Savannah, as though icy water were injected into her veins. That old, familiar inadequacy she felt whenever she beheld other women who were born with attributes she desired to have–beauty, brains, or talent–and who didn't have to work as hard as she did to get them. She somehow always felt diminished, less special, even inferior in comparison to them–like the poor relative of some pedigreed gentry.

An irrational barrage of thoughts began to overrun her mind. She thought, *How could Alfonso possibly love me when he has such a beautiful wife who's much more worthy of him than me?* She began to wonder if perhaps she was just a notch in Alfonso's long string of romances, and that maybe Alfonso was just the stereotypical Latin lover after all–one who knew how to charm women into thinking he loved them.

Get a hold of yourself, Savannah, she scolded herself as she quickly dismissed the disquieting thoughts that plagued her. She tried to recall instead how thoughtful, attentive and loving Alfonso had been to her over the last several days, and concluded that her nagging doubts were unfounded.

Yet even as she persuaded herself that Alfonso loved her, despite the fact that she wasn't as genetically endowed as Isabel, she felt the stab of guilt for her secret delight in winning Alfonso's affection away from her, to whom Alfonso rightfully belonged. She tried to mitigate her guilt by recalling the emotional detachment she sensed in the brief interaction she witnessed between Alfonso and Isabel–as though the absence of warmth between them gave her pardon for her wrongdoing.

Her gaze turned back to Alfonso and Cristina, who had started walking away from the rotunda. She heard Cristina squealing as she ran towards the lagoon, where white swans were gliding regally through the water, and ducks, geese and pigeons loitered at the water's edge. Savannah followed a short distance behind them, hiding behind trees to make sure they wouldn't see her.

Cristina sat herself down on one of the park benches scattered on the periphery of the lagoon. She sat with her legs crossed at the knees as she viewed the graceful swans gliding by. As Alfonso sat himself next to her, Savannah noticed that Cristina closed her eyes, raised her right hand in front of her with her palm perpendicular to her chest, fingers outstretched, and bowed her head ever so slowly.

When she reopened her eyes, Alfonso asked, "What were you doing just now?"

"I was saying hello to the swans–telling them how beautiful they are," she said. "Look, here they come now. They heard me."

Two white swans floated from the center of the pond, the water lapping gently as they paddled toward the edge of the lagoon where Cristina and Alfonso sat. When they were several feet away, Cristina closed her eyes again and made the gesture with her right hand, as if bestowing reverence upon the swans. One of the swans let out a brass-like honk, and Cristina giggled.

"The swans know me," she said, beaming. She pulled a small plastic bag out of her purse, half-filled with chunks of bread, and tossed a few in the water. The swans quickly ate the bread, and moved in closer.

"Can I get the swans to eat out of my hand, Papa?"

"You're not allowed to go past that point," he said, pointing to the chain-link fence surrounding the edge of the lagoon. "Why don't you just throw the bread into the water like you just did?"

"Okay," she said, as she doled out a few more chunks of bread into the water, watching as the swans dipped their elegant necks up and down as they ate. "Sssshhh…we have to be very quiet. The swans spook easily."

"How do you know that?"

"I saw it on TV. They're also very skittish."

"And what do you think skittish means?" Alfonso asked, visibly amused that Cristina knew such big words.

"It means they're excitable because they can't move their big bodies very well. On TV, they showed how the papa swans help the mama swans guard the nest and take care of the young swans–the *signuts*."

"Cygnets," Alfonso corrected.

"How do the papa swans learn how to guard the nest and take care of the cygnets?"

"They don't learn it. Sometimes animals just naturally know how to do certain things without being taught. Birds know how to build a nest so that they can lay eggs in it. Spiders know how to spin a web. Skunks know when they are in danger and they start giving off a stinky smell to keep their enemies away." Alfonso pinched his nose and frowned in exaggerated disgust, and Cristina chuckled.

"It comes naturally," Alfonso continued. "It's called instinct."

Just then, the swans bobbed their heads exuberantly and raised their wings, and paddled back to the middle of the pond.

Cristina waved at them, saying, "Bye, I'll see you again soon."

She watched the swans swim away. All of a sudden, she sneezed.

"God bless you!" Alfonso said.

"Thank you," she replied. Then, she turned to look at the heavens, as if in deep thought. After a long moment of silence, he asked, "What are you thinking of?"

"I was wondering what I would say to God if he sneezed," she said with a twinkle in her eyes.

Alfonso laughed.

"You know what else I was thinking, Papa?"

"No, what?"

She answered, with a faraway look in her eyes. "I was thinking …this is the only childhood I'm going to have. I wanna hold on to it."

Savannah heard every word Cristina said. Coming from a child who wasn't even halfway done with her own childhood, her comment seemed comical to her. Yet it made her wonder how Cristina could possibly know that childhood was a precious time worth hanging on to. Even as she wondered, she found himself longing for her own forgotten childhood.

A trio of musicians had set up chairs in one of the acoustically favorable nooks on the north side of the colonnade, and a crowd of tourists had begun to gather around them. As the flautist began to play, the chirp-like sound of his flute pierced the air in and around the colonnade, the rotunda and the lagoon, as though electrically amplified. Before long, the flute was joined by the strains of the cello and the silvery notes of the clarinet in a classical melody that gave Savannah visions of 18th century Viennese ladies taking a stroll in the Austrian countryside in their frilly frocks and parasols.

When she turned to look back at Alfonso and Cristina, she noticed Cristina turning her head towards the direction of the music. All of a sudden, Savannah felt Cristina's eyes upon her. She quickly ducked out of sight behind a tree, relieved that it wasn't Alfonso who spotted her.

"Look, Cristina, do you see Mama over there behind the fountain? Let's walk over there so we can all go to the Exploratorium together," he said, lifting Cristina off the park bench with both hands, and straightening the folds of her dress.

Out of the blue, Cristina asked, "Papa, why don't you love Mama?"

"Of course, I love her." Alfonso meant it. "Why do you ask this question?"

"Oh, I know you love her…only because she's my mother and your wife. But I feel it in my bones that you're not in love with her."

"How can you say that?"

"*Instink*, I guess."

Alfonso turned quiet, and Savannah waited with bated breath, wondering what he would say to Cristina.

"Instinct, huh? Well, let's see how good your instinct is. How do you tell when a boy is in love with a girl?"

"Oh, he gets goosepimples on his skin…he dreams about her all the time even when it's not night time. He writes poems for her, he plays the guitar and sings songs to her, and his head is in the clouds, mostly. Oh, and he likes to kiss her a lot. On the lips…not on the cheeks or on the forehead like you kiss Mama. And he crashes his bicycle into the trash can and he goes *loco*." She crossed her eyes and twirled her forefinger next to her temple.

The freshness and simplicity of her insight startled Savannah. Her observations were unfettered by analysis and held a good helping of truth. For what is love, indeed, but a flurry of irrational and inexplicable behavior that is closely akin to madness?

"Wait a minute, are you saying that when I play my guitar and sing *Paloma Blanca* to you, then I'm in love with you?" he teased.

"No, silly," she said, rolling her eyes in mock exasperation. "You can't be in love with me. I'm just a little girl. A big boy like you falls in love with a big girl. And I don't mean a big girl like…*gorda*." She lifted her arms out to her side and puffed up her cheeks. "I mean a tall girl, but not as tall as you. And I don't mean a song like *Paloma*

Blanca. I mean a romantic song," she said, putting on a serious face, "like the one you were singing last Saturday night on your guitar when you came home from work."

"So you heard me singing that song? I thought you were asleep."

"I was, but I woke up when I heard you singing."

"Do you think I'm in love with a woman, then?"

"Yes, Papa. And she makes you very happy. I never saw you smile so much."

Alfonso turned quiet again. What could he say?

"Papa, remember that woman who made the painting–the one whose daddy left her? Her daddy left because he was in love with a woman–not his wife, but another woman." She began to cry as she continued, "You wouldn't do that, would you, Papa? You wouldn't leave Mama and me to be with another woman, would you?" Her mouth was downturned, and her voice was pleading now. "Would you?"

Savannah saw the raw neediness in her plea, the same neediness that still lurked in the deep recesses of her own heart. Tears began to run down her face. She heard the long pause before Alfonso was able to answer.

He took Cristina in his arms. "Sshhh, *mi amor. No llore*...don't cry. No matter what happens, I will always love you. I will never just disappear from your life."

"Papa, please...if you ever go away, promise me you'll take me with you. Who's going to turn off the dark? Where would I find another papa like you?" She began to cry inconsolably.

"I promise I will always be with you, Cristina," he said in a choking voice.

Just then, Savannah saw Isabel walking towards Alfonso and Cristina. Isabel asked Cristina why she was crying, and Cristina shrugged her shoulders and said nothing. As Isabel bent down to embrace Cristina's trembling body, her arms encircled Alfonso as well.

Gazing at the three of them, huddled together as a family on the banks of the lagoon, Savannah felt a sharp dagger tear at her heart. All of a sudden, she felt like an outsider who had no right to intrude on the sanctity of Alfonso's family. How easy it had been for her to push away all thoughts of Alfonso's wife and daughter, pretending they didn't exist, whenever she was alone with him. How easy it had been to rationalize that Alfonso needed to be rescued from a stormy marriage, and to convince herself that she deserved a much-needed respite from her own loveless existence.

But now, there they were in the flesh. The wife and daughter that until now had only been imaginary beings in the fantasy life she had created around Alfonso. Isabel and Cristina were living, breathing human beings whose lives could be irreparably destroyed if she continued her relationship with Alfonso.

She saw how close Alfonso was to Cristina, and what a good father he was to her. She remembered her own father, and how he, too, had been a good father to her, even if all she could recall now was the last hurtful thing he did. She remembered how her mother loved her father deeply, and how her father rarely reciprocated her love.

All she had ever known about Isabel before was how unhappy she was for having married Alfonso. Now, looking at her, she understood the cause of her unhappiness. It wasn't because she didn't love Alfonso. It was because she was hurting inside, and she struck verbal blows at him for not loving her the way she wanted him to love her. Savannah wept for Isabel now, imagining the pain of loving Alfonso and not have him love her back. She cried for her own mother whose unrequited love for her father followed her to her grave. At that moment, there prevailed upon her heart the unbearable agony of unloved wives everywhere, who turned their faces to the wall, their passions lying unrequited in their breasts.

Her mind began to play back every minute of a Saturday in autumn, three days before she turned eight. Lyndon Curtis awoke early that morning, but he didn't wake his little girl. Savannah didn't know why, and would spend her life wondering why....

∽

She woke up when the sun was well past the grasp of the horizon, looked up at the pink cuckoo clock on the wall, which told her it was ten after eight. She jumped out of bed, walked down the hall to Mommy and Daddy's bedroom, rubbing her eyes sleepily.

The door was closed, and she knocked on it.

"Daddy, are you up? You forgot to wake me up."

There was no answer from within. She turned the knob and pushed the door open. Mommy was sitting at the edge of the bed, staring at the wall. When Savannah moved towards her, Mommy took her into her arms. She wouldn't stop crying. Savannah had never seen Mommy cry before.

"What's wrong, Mommy? Where's Daddy?"

"He's gone, Savannah. He's just...gone."

"Where has he gone?"

"I don't know, sweetie. I wish I knew." And then she started to cry again.

At first, Savannah thought her mother was lying. Daddy would not just get up and leave without a word. There had to be an explanation.

It occurred to her that Daddy was playing a prank on them. He had always been a prankster. Her eighth birthday was three days away. Of course! Daddy would come back then and surprise her with presents and say, "Wasn't that a good surprise, Princess?"

Her birthday came. She put on the new dress that Daddy had bought for her a week before. Aunt Sabine came over with a cake and balloons. Mommy told her they'd take her to the shopping mall, and she could pick any birthday gift she wanted. She said, 'Okay, Mom, but let's wait for Daddy so he can come with us.'

She sat in the living room all day—as close to the front door as she could sit. She wouldn't even turn the TV set on because she wanted to be able to hear Daddy's footsteps when he came to the door. Every time she heard a car door open or slam shut, she'd look out the window, waiting to hear him say, "Happy Birthday, Princess! Miss me?"

But he didn't come. When she saw the mailman walking down the street carrying a package, she raced out the door to ask him if the package was for her, and he said it was for the house next door.

When Aunt Sabine suggested it was time for cake, Savannah refused to blow out her candles or cut the cake until Daddy came home. She didn't eat all day, although Mommy kept coaxing her to eat. Then, she finally fell asleep on the living room sofa, and woke up at a quarter past nine that night. Aunt Sabine had carried her to bed, took off her new dress and put pajamas on her. Through the open door, Savannah caught a glimpse of her mother sitting at the kitchen table, crying.

Savannah didn't ask if her Daddy had come while she was sleeping. She knew then that he wasn't coming back.

◦

*N*ow Savannah's thoughts turned to Cristina. What a precious child she was, and what an amazing person she would grow up to be if Alfonso could always be there to care for her. What kind of person might she herself have become had her own father been with her instead of forsaking her?

Tears blinded her eyes, and she wiped them with the back of her fingers as she turned around and started walking toward a throng of tourists, hoping to blend in with the crowd. The tears continued to gush furiously as the familiar image of the faceless specter wearing a black hood flashed into her memory again. This time, the specter was standing beside a tombstone, and the image struck terror into her heart and made her blood run cold.

All of a sudden, she realized that the herd of gremlins she had consigned to the attic of her mind had returned with a vengeance, and they blurred her vision as she quickened her pace towards the parking lot. A voice deep inside implored her to run as far away as she could from Alfonso Madrigál–and she found no strength to disobey.

Just as she stepped into her car, she heard the trio of musicians in the colonnade begin to play Albinoni's *Adagio in G Minor*. Savannah buried her face in her hands and sobbed quietly, feeling more alone than she had ever been.

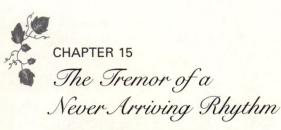

CHAPTER 15
The Tremor of a Never Arriving Rhythm

THURSDAY NIGHT • OCTOBER 6 • 1977

Savannah parked her car across from the front entrance of *Club La Cibeles*, crossed her arms over the steering wheel, and stared out the windshield. Then, she fixed her gaze on the peach-colored linen envelope that lay on the passenger seat right next to her purse. She slowly picked up the envelope and turned it over. *Alfonso Madrigál.* His name, inked in black against the pastel paper, jumped out at her.

She looked out the window at the still darkened entryway of the Club. She glanced at the time on the car radio clock. *5:49.* The Club's parking valets had not yet arrived at their posts, but she was sure the club manager, the kitchen and wait staff would already be inside. The entrance to the Club was only thirty feet away from her, and yet the distance seemed like an ocean to cross. Her hand was on the door handle, but she knew she could still change her mind. She could turn on the ignition and drive away. Forget she ever wrote the letter.

She sat frozen by the image of Alfonso, Isabel and Cristina huddled together as a family by the lagoon at the Palace of Fine Arts. She remembered how Cristina had somehow perceived her secret pain through her painting, and begged Alfonso not to let the same fate befall her.

With a heart that felt like lead, she alighted from her car and made her way across the street, through the curvy entryway of *Club La Cibeles*, with its Spanish murals and metal sculptures on the wall. Far ahead, she could hear the clatter of kitchen activity and the sound of friendly chatter.

The dining area was still half-dark, so she didn't notice a man appear in front of her out of the shadows.

"Hola, Señorita."

"Oh...," Savannah gasped, taking a step back.

"I'm sorry. I didn't mean to startle you, Miss. How can I help you?"

"Are you the manager?"

"Yes, I'm Gonzalo Arguelles *a su ordenes*," he said, tilting his head slightly in a half bow.

"Mr. Arguelles, if I leave this letter with you, would you make sure Alfonso Madrigál gets it when he comes in this evening?"

"Why, of course. He should be in any minute now. You're welcome to wait for him, if you wish."

"Doesn't he play at nine?"

"On regular days. But tonight, we have a flamenco troupe from Seville coming in, and Alfonso will be performing with them. That's why he's coming in at six to coordinate their numbers."

"Oh, I see...." Savannah thought her heart was going to burst out of her chest. "I'm in a bit of a rush, so I don't think I can wait for him."

"Okay, then. I'll make sure he gets this as soon as he walks in."

"Thank you, Mr. Arguelles," she said, whereupon she turned around and walked out of the Club. She quickened her pace as she neared the entrance, and nearly bumped into a parking valet, who had just arrived and was busy setting up a sign.

She ran across Portofino Boulevard to her car, turned on the ignition, and pulled away. As she did, she looked in her rear view mirror just in time to see Alfonso's Buick pulling up fifty yards behind her.

She was relieved that he didn't see her. She checked the time on her car radio clock. *5:57.* As if in a daze, she drove towards the freeway entrance to 101 South. Russell's flight would be arriving at 6:20. She prayed there wouldn't be a lot of rush hour traffic so that she could get to the airport on time. She hated how annoyed Russell could get whenever she was late even by just a few minutes.

Traffic was backed up for a couple of miles on the 101. At this rate, she was going to be late. Somewhere inside her, a rebellious voice screamed, *Why should I care?* The only thing she cared about right then was how Alfonso would react upon reading her letter.

Earlier that day, after sealing her letter to Alfonso, she had put down all her thoughts in her journal, writing feverishly for almost three hours without stopping—lest the thoughts slip away from her. After she was done writing, she put the journal back in the hidden drawer of the built-in china cabinet where she had kept it away from prying eyes for the last thirteen days. It would be the last time she would write on her journal.

∽

"You just missed her. She left a few minutes ago," Gonzalo said.

"*¿Quien?* Who are you talking about?" Alfonso asked.

"The woman who's been making you smile lately," Gonzalo replied, winking mischievously. "I always knew there was a woman. A beautiful one at that."

"A woman came to see me, Gonzalo?"

"*Si, Señor.* Here...she left this for you," Gonzalo said.

He handed the letter to Alfonso and disappeared into the kitchen. Alfonso looked at the peach-colored envelope. He caught a whiff of Savannah's perfume on it, and smiled.

He sat himself on a bar stool, and there, in the half-darkness of the empty room, he opened Savannah's letter. The letter was on monogrammed stationery, elegant linen stationery that had the initials of Savannah Karenina Curtis—SCK—in raised lettering.

October 6, 1977

Dear Alfonso,

Where should I begin? Maybe an appropriate beginning would be to let you know how remarkable you have been in my experience.

Since that Friday you first spoke to me at Sutton Hall, you have been the most extraordinary man I've known. You possess a combination of qualities I've rarely seen in a human being. I have been moved by your music, stirred by your passion, fascinated by your profound insights and humbled by your deep devotion for those whom you love.

When not in your presence, I have found myself caring for nothing else but to know where you are and what you are doing. I've found myself wondering what thoughts would be worthwhile without you in them.

You have been to me a comet piercing the murky skies of my life, the fulfillment of every dream my heart has ever imagined. You have opened my eyes to a beautiful world that was unknown to me. Most of all, you have made me feel more cherished and cared for than I've been in a long time.

Over the last few days, I've wondered how you could have known I was in desperate need of your kind of affection when I had become so adept at hiding my need. It was as though you looked deeper into my heart than anyone else had cared to look, found what I was starving for, and took it upon yourself to give it to me. It makes me feel that God put you in my life, even for just this brief interlude, to remind me that such devotion still exists, although I've seldom known it.

You are warmhearted, affectionate, and capable of giving so much, Alfonso, and I have no doubt you will accomplish great things in your life, especially in your music. For this very reason, please understand why I must say goodbye. If we allow our relationship to blossom any further, it would complicate both our lives and would not serve those who love us and depend on us.

A few days ago, I wrote the beginnings of a poem:

> Sparrows fly on their way to you
> And if I knew the way, I'd hurry, too
> Midwinter turns to spring
> And I remember things I never said to you.

I've known the desperation of losing someone I loved without having had the chance to say goodbye or tell them how much they meant to me, so I refuse to let this opportunity pass me by now.

Know that I love you, Alfonso, and I will love you for as long as I have breath, for as long as my heart beats in my chest, and even when distance and time finally separate us. Know that I've never loved anyone the way I love you, nor do I think I will ever love this way again. But I'd rather let you soar upon my love and be ennobled by it, rather than let it compromise the things you hold dear, especially your precious daughter, Cristina. I'd rather lose you than turn you into less of a man than the one I've come to know and love.

My only wish is for you to remember me the way I'll remember you.

Yours forever,
Savannah

P.S. I'll be in Los Angeles for my gallery opening next week, but please call my answering service with your address so that I can send your Picasso painting back to you.

Alfonso folded the pages of Savannah's letter and slowly slipped them back into the envelope. From somewhere deep within his chest, he heard an animal cry, like the plaintive wail of a mourning, heart-stricken wolf, a lonely sound piercing the air with anguish. His hands balled into fists of their own accord, and he saw the knuckles turn white from his grip.

Later that night, as he shared the stage with the *Danza Española* Flamenco Troupe's acoustical guitarist, Sebastian Robledo, he looked out at the audience, strummed the first few chords of the song he had agreed to perform with Sebastian. Then, he stopped suddenly and found himself playing a tune he had not previously rehearsed–a *Lorqueña*, a poem of Lorca transformed into song. One he used to sing a long time ago in the back streets of Málaga. It was a *Lorqueña* taught to him by his friend, Ruben, one for which he had felt no affinity–until now.

Sebastian looked puzzled, wondering why Alfonso had decided to switch to another song without letting him know. Upon listening to the piece Alfonso began to play, he recognized the *Lorqueña* and, being familiar with the chords to the song, played right along with Alfonso

Alfonso thought he had forgotten the words of the song, but the words flowed out of his lips easily, as his guitar played on its own accord, as though detached from his fingers and his hands.

He sang with a voice that he hardly recognized as his own.

The people in the audience were startled, particularly the regulars who had heard him play but never sing. Even Gonzalo, who was poring over the reservation list, trying to figure out how to accommodate the late arrivals, looked up at Alfonso to see what he was up to.

"*Entre mariposas negras, va una muchacha morena junto a una blanca serpiente de niebla,*" he sang. *Among black butterflies goes a dark-haired girl next to a white serpent of mist.*

Federico García Lorca's words had never before expressed a tragic drama such as the one raging in his chest.

The crowd grew quiet as Alfonso sang with an escalating emotional tension. His verses were punctuated by sudden cries of anguish. During the long silences in between lines, even the softest sighs in the back of the room could be heard as people waited in anticipation for what he would do next.

He was feeling bolder with every note that he sang, and his fingers ran unencumbered across the frets of *Guernica*. His tones became more confident and free. The audience was mesmerized. Even the clinking of glasses at the bar eerily seemed to be in perfect sync with the guitar's rhythm.

"*Va encadenada a tremblor de un ritmo qué nunca llega,*" he continued singing, letting the music take a life of its own, and just riding the waves of the music. *She is chained to the tremor of a never arriving rhythm.*

Alfonso was so engulfed in the emotion of his song that he hardly heard the first "*Olé!*" that came from somewhere in the crowd. Neither did he hear the second one, or the third. Then he heard a thundering sound come to his ears, the sound of rapid rhythmic clapping, and heels stomping, interspersed with "*Olé!*" after "*Olé!*" after "*Olé!*" as the crowd became delirious. He dared not open his eyes for fear the magic would disappear and the fantasy would end. He stomped the heel of his boot down into the stage in time with the guitar.

He strained his voice into tortured, emotional notes, cries of pain transformed into music. His passion overwhelmed the audience, and his adrenalin reached fever pitch as the crowd cheered him. He sang the final words, *"Tierra de luz, cielo de tierra,"* with vocal nuances that twisted his passion into more intense knots of cathartic emotion. Then he ended with his trademark flourish by thumping the sound board of his guitar.

The crowd broke out into the most ecstatic applause he had ever heard. He felt spent, having turned his soul inside out for the world to see. The line between the artist and the audience had all but vanished. The audience and the artist had become one. He opened his eyes and it was really happening–he had not just dreamed it.

The crowd was bewildered. Many of them didn't have a word to describe what just happened. The flamenco aficionados insisted, "That's *duende.*"

It may have been *duende*, but to Alfonso, it was his pain made flesh. Of that, he was certain.

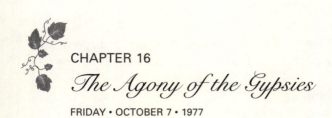

CHAPTER 16
The Agony of the Gypsies
FRIDAY • OCTOBER 7 • 1977

Alfonso dropped Cristina off at the Penguin Educational Day Care Center on Friday morning. There was a phone booth just around the corner from the center. Alfonso walked over to it and dialed Savannah's home number. No answer. He began speaking on her answering machine:

Savannah, I received your letter. I need to talk to you. Please call me at the Club tonight–555-3891. I'll be there from eight until twelve.

At the Club that night, after he finished playing his first set, he asked Gonzalo if anyone had called him.

"No, the lady didn't call," Gonzalo said, genuinely sorry to see that Alfonso, who had finally learned how to smile, was again slipping back to his former sullen self.

Over the next two days, he called Savannah again a few times. Still no answer. Again, he left a message for her to call him back at the Club. The return call didn't come.

On Sunday afternoon, he thought he'd call again before Savannah left for Los Angeles the next day. This time, he left a different message:

Savannah, it's Alfonso. About the painting. You don't have to send it back to me. I'd like you to have it.

Then, on second thought, knowing that she would never accept such a valuable gift, he continued:

Or if you don't wish to accept it as my gift, at least keep it in your custody for me until I see you again. Whichever way you decide is fine by me.

That night, when Alfonso arrived at the Club, a jubilant Gonzalo announced, "The lady called, *amigo*."

"Did she leave a message?"

"*Si, si!* She said…here, let me read what I wrote down. She said she'd be glad to take custody of it for you."

"That's it?"

"That's everything. *No mas, no menos*. What's this thing she agreed to take custody of?"

"Just something I lent her," Alfonso shrugged. "What time did she call?"

"Oh, about seven-thirty or so. Half an hour ago."

"*Gracias*, Gonzalo."

"Oh, I almost forgot. This guy just called to make a reservation for tomorrow night. His name is Miguel Castillo. Have you heard of him?"

"No, I don't think so."

"He's the Artists & Repertoire VP of Polygram Records. It turns out he just happened to be in town and he heard about your performance on Thursday night. So he's coming to check you out. You might want to play that *Lorqueña* again tomorrow."

"*Ciertamente*, Gonzalo. If that's what you want."

On any other night, news such as this might have come as a big thrill to Alfonso. To attract the interest of a record company executive, especially a label that was already negotiating to take Paco de Lucía to global stardom, was a big deal. But tonight, the message Savannah left was all he could think of.

She'd be glad to take custody of it for you, Gonzalo had said.

He detected a note of detachment and finality in her brief message. Clearly, she was reluctant to talk to him or she would have called at eight or later to talk to him directly.

It was almost midnight after he played his last set. Just as he did every night since he received her letter, he drove his Buick down Portofino Boulevard and turned left on Pacific Avenue. Hoping to catch a glimpse of her, but dreading the possibility of seeing Russell with her.

Tonight, as on previous nights, 201 Pacific was totally dark and all the curtains were drawn shut. Again, an agonizing jealousy gnawed at him at the thought of Savannah spending the night at Russell's.

His thoughts went back to Wednesday afternoon, the last time he was with Savannah. She had been reluctant to see him go. *"Stay with me, Alfonso. Please don't go,"* she had said with a note of urgency in her voice. It was as though if he walked out the door, they would never see each other again.

It was ironic that less than twenty-four hours later, she herself would say goodbye in a letter. *What happened in that short span of time,* he wondered woefully, *that caused her change of heart?*

❦

*K*nowing that Savannah would be in Los Angeles for a couple of weeks, Alfonso didn't try calling her again until the second week of November. He dialed Savannah's home number again.

The recording at the other end of the line said, "The number you have dialed has been disconnected and is no longer in service. Please check the number or try your call again."

His pulse quickened as his finger clicked on the receiver button and dialed again, slowly and carefully. He felt himself bristle as the same recording came on.

With hands trembling, he searched his wallet for the business card Savannah had handed him at Café Marcel. He found it, and dialed the number to her answering service.

A woman answered, "Devereaux Agency."

"Pardon me. Isn't this the number of Savannah Curtis?"

"Please hold on."

After a few moments, the operator returned to the phone line. "This used to be the number for Savannah Curtis, but now it's the Devereaux Agency's."

"Do you have a forwarding number for Miss Curtis?"

"No, I'm afraid not. There's a note in our file that says she's relocated out of town and she didn't leave a forwarding number."

"Thanks for your help," he mumbled.

Putting the phone back on its cradle, he glanced at the clock on the wall. Ten past four. Before he knew it, he was in his Buick driving towards Pacific Heights.

He parked his car across the street from 201 Pacific, in the same spot where he had parked frequently in days past. From where he sat, he looked up at her apartment and noticed that the drapes on all the windows were flung wide open. As he crossed the street and climbed the steps towards her front door, his blood turned cold as he realized that the drapes weren't flung wide open at all. They were gone. The windows were curtainless.

Halfway up the steps, he peered into the bay window and saw what his heart already suspected. Savannah's apartment was empty.

He felt himself floating in a strange dimension–a dimension where Savannah never existed, where Savannah was just a dream. He just stood there, transfixed by her vacant apartment, wondering whether the events of early October ever happened at all. Wasn't that the bay window from where she waved at him every morning when he came to spend the day with her? Wasn't it just a month ago that he climbed these very steps to her front door? Things he remembered and the stark reality of what he saw in front of his very eyes split apart in painful and confusing disparity.

With limbs that felt like lead, he climbed the last few steps. He stared at her front door for a few moments, gasping for breath, fearing the inevitable. Finally, he rang the doorbell. When the door opened, he half expected to catch a whiff of the Kahili ginger flowers that had grown familiar to his nostrils. But there was no scent.

A heavy-set, gray-haired woman in her sixties appeared at the doorway. "May I help you?" she asked.

Alfonso hardly heard her words as he stared beyond her and his eyes combed the stark emptiness of what used to be Savannah's place. Gone was the moon-shaped black lacquer screen with inlaid mother-of-pearl pagodas, gone was the bamboo tree in a reed basket, the coffee table entwined with braided hemp, the white orchid plant in the porcelain planter. Gone was the canister-shaped Japanese lantern. In their place was wall-to-wall nothingness. Further beyond, the door to Savannah's bedroom was ajar, and he saw that it, too, was empty. Alfonso felt something inside him come unhinged.

"May I help you?" the lady asked again.

"I'm looking for Savannah Curtis," he finally mumbled, noticing the fracture in his own voice when he said her name.

"Oh, I'm sorry. She just moved out a few days ago. I'm Maxine Bennett, her landlady," she said, a half-moon smile appearing on her face. "At least, I was her landlady until a few days ago."

"Do you know where she moved to, Mrs. Bennett?"

"I'm afraid not. She said something about moving out of state… or maybe out of the country, I can't remember. All I know is that she had to leave in a hurry. She gave me her notice last week, and then before I knew it, she had moved everything out of here. She didn't have to move out so quickly, though. She's paid up through the end of the month." Then, turning her gaze towards the interior of the apartment, she said, "I've gotta hand it to her, though. No matter how much of a hurry she was in, she sure left this place as clean as the day she moved in."

Mrs. Bennett was still talking, but Alfonso didn't hear her words. Blindly, quickly, he nearly stumbled down the stairs, ran across the street, got into his car and drove off without looking back.

◆

Cristina had been sitting in the waiting room of the Penguin Educational Day Care Center for fifteen minutes when Alfonso pulled up to the curb. She jumped to her feet when she saw him coming.

"Cristina, wait for your Dad to come in and get you," Miss Luisa called out to her. "You know the rules. You mustn't go running out the door…"

"… for my own safety," she said, finishing Miss Luisa's sentence absently while watching Alfonso alighting from the car and walking towards the glass doors leading to the waiting room.

Upon entering, Alfonso tipped his head slightly towards Cristina's teacher, then without a word, took Cristina by the hand and led her out the door.

"What's wrong, Papa?"

"*Nada, amor,*" he answered. "Nothing at all."

Alfonso drove home in silence. Cristina didn't dare speak to him. She kept perfectly still and barely breathed. She looked out the window, watching the cars, the houses and the scenery flying by while a furrow began to creep upon her brow. Then, she closed her eyes and pretended to fall asleep.

༄

After parking the car in the garage, Alfonso carried Cristina up the front steps, through the front door, past the grandfather clock that was getting ready to strike six, past the mantel laden with framed pictures, past *The Fern in the Clearing*, and past Bubbles who was pondering her fishbowl life. He pushed her bedroom door open with his knee and nestled Cristina beneath a cotton sheet on her bed and kissed her closed eyelids before shutting the door behind him.

Alfonso sat himself down on the sofa, staring absently at the play of shadows on the window shades as the day melted into twilight, his chest feeling like the rubble that was left behind by the earthquake of 1906. The heat of a blast furnace seemed to scorch his veins, and his temples throbbed with no mercy. His face was livid and his eyes brandished daggers as he mulled over the events of the day. He could not contain his outrage over how easily Savannah could cut him out of her life completely. How effortlessly she could go about her life, leaving him to wander lost without her. Angry that she could say she loved him, and yet behave as if she didn't give a damn about him and wanted nothing more to do with him.

He reckoned that Savannah was going ahead with her plans to marry Russell. Wondered how she could marry him after what had happened between them in the last twelve days. Even as he pondered, he berated himself for his arrogance—his idiocy in assuming that the twelve days they had together would eclipse the four years Savannah has had with Russell.

He remembered Savannah saying that Russell and she were to relocate to Connecticut after the wedding—or sooner, if need be—at Russell's suggestion. *Maybe her departure for Connecticut was hastened by her need to distance herself from me*, he thought bitterly.

Night began to fall, and Alfonso looked out the window, searching the sky, quadrant by quadrant, for solace from his tortured spirit. Even the waning moon mocked him. The world closed in on him, and he felt his insides being wound up more tightly than he could bear. He punched a fist into his palm and realized that the caged beast in his soul that had once been tamed by Savannah had returned with a vengeance. The floorboards trembled as he paced the floor with wrathful steps, his fingers clawing the wounding edges of the peach-colored envelope that bore his name. He read her words again, one by one, and his anger turned into an anguish like an elemental strife at sea. He suddenly understood the agony of the gypsies who fled from India and sought refuge in Andalucia, singing their songs of mournful woe. Felt the disembodied pain of the beheaded, Dionysian scream of Silverio's *siguiriya*. He grasped the horror of Guernica's townsfolk as their homes were pillaged, and felt the ominous tragedy that left women weeping and animals screaming in terror.

Alfonso could not decide which fate was worse, having Savannah ripped from his life, or death itself. He never knew there would come a time he'd long for his vicious days in Málaga, preferring its cruel punishment to a day without her. His kind of pain could send others rushing for solace in the universe of a liquor glass. He grappled with the thought of drowning his sorrow in a glass of spirits. A hand-cut crystal decanter filled with Spanish brandy, flanked by an assortment of unopened bottles of whisky, vodka, and wine, beckoned to him from atop the wet bar. Ignoring the lure of liquor, he reached for his guitar and started to play.

 ～

Cristina stood behind her bedroom door, her ear pressed against the crevice, listening to the sounds of madness coming from the living room, fearful of stepping outside. There was a hideous presence out there, and it didn't seem to be her father. It sounded like a fierce, wild animal foaming at the mouth, and it made her body tremble with terror.

Suddenly, she heard Alfonso's guitar playing a distraught melody, accented by maniacal rhythms and a deranged progression of chords. It seemed as though a disembodied entity was playing the demented tune. An excruciating pain ran through her body as the strains of the guitar reached her ears. She was certain that every time she heard the sound, she lost a few of her days on earth.

Frantically, she cupped her hands over her ears to drown out the sound, ran to her bed and pulled her pillow over her head. Big tears began to run down her cheeks. Soundless tears that sprang from the unbearable grief told by her father's guitar.

"Papa, I'm sorry," she whispered under her breath, between sobs. "I'm sorry for what I've done."

Isabel walked in the front door at seven thirty-five. Cristina was relieved to hear her footsteps and her voice. When she heard Alfonso tell her he was leaving for the Club, she finally began breathing full breaths again. She didn't know how much more of his guitar-playing she could bear.

While he played his crazed rhapsodies, she was certain her blood was being squeezed out of her body drop by drop from her fingertips. So sure was she that every few minutes, she would raise her head to see if a pool of blood had formed on the floor where her hands hung beyond the edge of her bed. There was no pool of blood, but she found herself exhausted and unable to move.

～

Just as Alfonso pulled away in the Buick, Isabel called Cristina to dinner. "I bought you your favorite, *chiquitica. Vamos a comer.*"

When Cristina didn't answer, she walked into her room and found the bed cover, sheets and pillows strewn all over the floor and Cristina's little body face down on the bed, her limbs splayed in all directions.

"Cristina!" Isabel screamed with a voice fraught with panic.

She raced to Cristina's side, lifted her from the bed, and held her closely. "My God, you're as cold as ice!" she cried, looking upon Cristina's face, which had the pallid color of death. Picking up a woolen blanket off the floor, she bundled Cristina in it and whispered, "*Mi hija,* I'm going to call for an ambulance. You stay right here and I'll be right back."

She jumped to her feet and headed towards the door when Cristina cried out to her, "I'm okay, Mama. You don't have to take me to the hospital."

Isabel turned around and saw her little girl sitting up in bed, tugging at the woolen cocoon in which Isabel had wrapped her tightly. The color quickly returned to her cheeks. When Isabel took her in her arms, her skin was no longer cold.

"*Mi hija,* you almost gave me a heart attack," she said, hugging her. "What happened to you?"

Ignoring her mother's question, she said, "Did I hear you say you bought my favorite? Fish and chips?"

"Yes, yes, I did, *amorcito,*" she answered, smiling. *"Tienes hambre?"*

"Starving," Cristina said, jumping off the bed and scurrying out the door.

～

Cristina was fast asleep when Alfonso came home at half past midnight, but when he picked up his guitar and started playing, her eyes flew open, and fear began to paralyze her. A chill crept into her bones again like an early frost on the grapevines of autumn. She wanted to run, but her body seemed glued to her bed. Every time he played his guitar, she felt an electric shock shoot through her little body. So excruciating was it that she thought she would swallow her own tongue and choke to death. Then came that sickening feeling that her blood was draining out of her body through her fingertips. During the moments when the guitar was silent, Cristina gasped for breath as if those breaths would be her last. Then, the guitar would play again, and volts of electricity would course through her body until she went into convulsions or, once in a while, lapsed into unconsciousness. She prayed for the relief of unconsciousness, but those episodes never lasted for more than a few minutes. And whenever she came to, she would feel numb and paralyzed.

Cristina wondered if she could bear an entire night of her father's pain. Several times during the night, she was tempted to walk out to the living room and beg him to stop playing. But each time, she stopped herself. *It's my fault that he's in pain*, she thought. *This is my punishment.*

Cristina heard Isabel's footsteps coming down the hall headed towards the living room. "*Por Dios*, Alfonso. Why do you play this hideous music? And at this ungodly hour, no less!"

There was a pause, then Alfonso resumed playing the furious, enslaving tunes of his torment.

Isabel stormed off, muttering terms of exasperation as she went back to their bedroom and slammed the door.

Cristina jumped off her bed, opened the drawer of the nightstand, took the yellow plastic locket out of it and walked out into the living room.

"Papa," she called out.

༄

Alfonso stopped playing his guitar. He looked up and saw Cristina looking disheveled, her pajama top hanging off her shoulders. His face softened slightly as he looked at her.

"Did I wake you up, *mi hija*?"

"No, Papa. I've been awake all night."

Alfonso grimaced as he got on his feet. "Then, I'm going to have to sing you to sleep."

"No!" she cried adamantly.

He was taken aback by her response.

"I mean ... thanks, Papa, but you don't have to sing me a song tonight. I just came to give you this," she said, holding out the yellow plastic heart-shaped locket to him.

"I can't take that from you, *mi amor*." The locket was one of Cristina's most prized possessions.

"But I want you to have it. It has eighty-two jewels and fifty-three kisses. I counted them. And I put them in there for you...so you won't forget someone loves you."

And just then, Alfonso Madrigal, who had not cried since Doña Carmen Madrigál's funeral, who would rather bite his lips until they bled instead of exhibit tears, took his daughter into his arms and wept tears that stung like cayenne.

"*Gracias. Muchas gracias,*" he said when he finally let her go.

Cristina turned around and started walking back to her bedroom. Then she turned her head back towards him and said, "Some flowers don't bloom all the time."

"What do you mean, Cristina?"

"Miss Luisa said some flowers have seasons. Some bloom every year. Some bloom in the summer. Some in autumn. So even if you don't see them for awhile, they'll come back next season."

"*Absolutamente.* Miss Luisa is right."

∽

The guitar was silent the rest of that night, and Cristina was finally able to sleep. It wasn't the last time the guitar would play songs of woe, but from that night forward, the music would begin to seek the dawn.

∽

MARCH 25 • 1978

Fighting bulls quarreled in the marshes of the Guadalquivir River, wails echoed in the cathedrals of Mallorca, and squalls were tamed by the lassoes of a guitar as Alfonso Madrigál emerged from the somber shadows of winter to the dappled light of spring. It wasn't quite daybreak but he arose, knowing that this was the day that he'd once again look upon the light.

Four months and ten days since he found Savannah's Victorian apartment at 201 Pacific empty, he opened his eyes without hearing the plaintive cry of a wounded animal in his chest, without hearing the sound of his heart breaking. His body stopped floating between a tortured slumber and a waking hell, and he could finally think of Savannah being gone without wanting to die.

In the past one hundred twenty-nine days, he had staggered on the brink of madness, attended only by the music that bloomed in the midst of heartbreak. It was as if his rage, his anguish and his pain had found a sanctuary in the hidden, aching melodies which became his salvation. Every day, the music that sprung forth from his guitar went from demented cacophony worthy of a strait jacket, to musical chaos, to melancholy ranting, and finally to somber melodies that wept. Wept for all the distance that separated him from Savannah.

Somewhere in the caverns of his solitude, Alfonso had heard a voice speaking through the trees in the forest, saying, *"When you learn to be still, you will know me."* And his soul finally entered that stillness where silence ruled, peace prevailed, recrimination had no voice, and knowingness emerged. The knowingness that reassured him that loving another human being was God's way of affording him glimpses of his unfathomable love. In his spiritual awakening, he came to terms with the magnitude of his love for Savannah, and it was then that he realized he could continue loving her even when she wasn't with him.

Alfonso felt as though he had fallen from a steep precipice, passing from the carnal through the ephemeral and into the eternal on the wings of music–and inexplicably falling right back into the clearing that was Savannah.

As the sun began to rise, a cloud passed across it, fracturing the light of dawn. Alfonso stared at his reflection in the mirror hanging above the mantel and saw a man forever changed by his love for Savannah Curtis. For the first time in months, Alfonso was smiling.

When the grandfather clock struck ten that morning, Alfonso picked up the phone and dialed Zendrik's number.

"Hello," came Zendrik's voice on the other end of the line.

"Hombre!"

"Hey, *amigo*. What happened to you? Where've you been?"

"I've been doing penance for my transgressions."

"Seriously, man, you got me worried there for a while. I called you several times but I didn't hear back from you."

"Sorry about that, *amigo*. I've been goin' through hell for a while."

"Well, you know what I always say about going through hell."

"Yeah, I know. Don't stop there. Just keep on going. That's what I did, *hombre*, and I came out in one piece."

"It must've been rough, huh? How long were you out of circulation? Three months?"

"More like four months. One hundred twenty-nine days, to be exact."

"And how're you doin' now? You doin' okay?"

"More than okay. I'm a changed man, *amigo*."

"I suppose you had some kind of an epiphany, huh? I wanna hear all about it, man." Then, a moment later, he asked, "This doesn't have anything to do with Savannah Curtis, does it?"

"You remember her name?"

"You, my friend, are a man of few words, so when I saw that poem you wrote for her–man, I could tell she'd turn your world upside down."

"That, she did."

"So when are you going to tell me all about *Señorita* Savannah?"

"How much time do you have?"

"All the time in the world, *amigo*. I'm just here hangin'. I don't have to leave for the Grease Monkey until eight. Wanna come over?"

"I'll be there in half an hour."

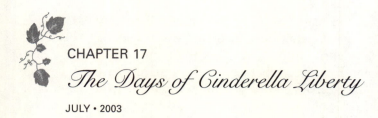

CHAPTER 17
The Days of Cinderella Liberty
JULY • 2003

"A story once begun knows not where to end..."

The noontide clamored for completion, a waning moon galloped towards oblivion, and an invisible hand rewrote the fates of strangers. Cassidy Hamilton awoke at daybreak on a Sunday morning in July.

The remnants of the night's shadows dispersed outside in the flares of dawn. As she had done many times before, Cassidy stared at the ceiling and wondered whether the Victorian apartment was too large for her needs. A three-bedroom dwelling for a single girl with a modest income seemed more than a little excessive by most standards of prudence. That it was also a coveted Victorian located in an upscale, high-rent neighborhood rendered it that much more out of her league. To Cassidy, spending more than half of her paycheck on rent was an extravagance that would infuriate her mother's sensibilities. A defiant smile crept onto her lips as she secretly savored any opportunity to go against her mother's wishes.

But oh, the space. The space! she gushed to herself, surveying the high ceilings and the airiness of 201 Pacific. Years of living in the suburban community of Merit Grove, with its clusters of identical stucco-walled track homes, her shoebox bedroom, and her mother's smothering presence made her crave space with an obsession that bordered on neurosis. The cramped dorms and studios of Berkeley offered little to ease the claustrophobia of a world closing in on her. Once again, the magistrates of her mind ruled in favor of 201 Pacific. For all its superfluous space, this Victorian apartment was exactly what she needed to blur the mind-numbing, suffocating sameness and mediocrity that had characterized her life thus far. Here, she could rattle in wild abandon to her heart's content, and she was more than willing to pay the price for the delicious indulgence.

When she first started apartment-hunting last September, Cassidy had immediately been enamored with the genteel Victorian apartment and its vintage personality that seemed frozen in time. Walking through room after room of 201 Pacific, accompanied by Kerrigan Bennett, the apartment owner's son, she had been consumed by thoughts of a bygone era. She had fantasized about the people who may have once lived there. *What fascinating lives they must have led.* She imagined that this might have been the home of a celebrity from the turn of the century, or maybe a diva from the San Francisco Opera, a family of privilege from Victorian times—maybe even a miner-turned-nouveaux-riche from the days of the Gold Rush.

If these walls could talk, she had said to herself, *what secrets they would tell.*

Throwing caution to the wind, she signed the lease on 201 Pacific in late September 2002, knowing fully well she could barely afford the rent. Less than a month later, Cassidy Hamilton, seeker of remembrances from a bygone era, came upon a hidden drawer, tucked behind the baseboard of a built-in china cabinet, holding the journal of Savannah Curtis.

෴

On this Sunday morning in July, Cassidy lingered in bed longer than usual. Her eyes glazed over a cluster of framed pictures sitting on her night table, and became transfixed on a photograph of herself wearing a toga at her high school graduation, with her dad standing beside her.

Her thoughts traveled back to her days at Logan High School eight years ago. Logan had more than its share of highly intelligent students who were also, curiously enough, social misfits. Cassidy had often wondered whether it was because most of the kids at Logan came from broken families. She had read somewhere that seventy-three percent of high school kids come from broken families, even higher in communities with the lowest quintile of earnings. While Logan High consisted of students from households with median incomes, it certainly had more kids from broken families than the national average. Indeed, practically everyone Cassidy knew in school had either divorced, separated or unwed parents. That realization dawned on her the day a classmate of hers, Danica Rollins, recited her composition in class at the prompting of her English teacher, Miss Daniels.

The topic of Danica's composition was her parents' fifteenth wedding anniversary. Halfway through her recitation, Bruce Cavanaugh, one of the kids sitting in the back of the room, yelled in a voice loud enough for everyone to hear, "What kind of a freak has parents who ain't divorced?" While Bruce's words were met with glares and snide remarks, it didn't escape Cassidy's notice that from that day on, Danica was regarded as some kind of oddity. It seemed that the kids began to eye her with suspicion, as though she didn't belong—that she wasn't one of them. Cassidy had wondered if it was just human nature at work—distrusting strangers who weren't like themselves. Or maybe the kids secretly envied Danica for actually having some kind of unfair advantage that the rest of them didn't have. Through it all, Cassidy couldn't help but think what a screwed up world it was, where you're considered normal if you come from a broken family, and a freak if you don't.

Her own parents, Jack and Diane Hamilton, were no better at staying married than everybody else. Cassidy never really knew the cause of their breakup when she was barely three. Whenever she asked her dad why they got a divorce, he would make light of things by putting on a comical face and singing his own words to John Mellencamp's song.

> *Here's a little song about Jack and Diane*
> *Just two young kids doin' the best they can*

But he never really answered her question.

In the context of Cassidy's life, there was no such thing as living happily ever after. While some people had long-married grandparents that they could look to for hope, her own grandparents on her father's side had both perished in a car accident long before she was born, and her grandparents on her mother's side had divorced when her mom was just in her teens. Cassidy often thought that her mom's dysfunctional family caused her mom to have a jaded, devil-may-care attitude and a "Murphy's Law" mentality that if anything can go wrong, it will. Although Cassidy refused to admit it, she was influenced in no small way by her mom's mantra in life: "Love never lasts. Never count on love because it will betray you sooner or later."

Cassidy wished she could find a reason to be fond of her mother. After all, it was only normal for a daughter to detest certain characteristics of her mom, and yet find redeeming qualities that she could love her for. Cassidy found it hard to love a self-absorbed, uncaring, overly critical, and domineering person whose voice echoed over and over in her ears. "Don't tell people I'm your mother, Cassidy. Just tell them I'm your big sister. And stop calling me Mom. Call me Diane." She called her Diane from the time she was old enough to follow orders.

Cassidy lived at Amalfi Circle in the suburban town of Merit Grove until she went off to Berkeley, yet she always called the two-bedroom dwelling *Diane's townhouse*. She had never called it home. In truth, she couldn't think of the townhouse or Diane without getting a taste of bile in her mouth. She couldn't remember the number of times Diane had told her she never wanted children. And Diane never tired of dropping thinly disguised hints as to what her life might have become if Cassidy hadn't come along.

Diane had a phenomenal singing voice that could put a rock spin to traditional country music. For someone born and raised in California, she could make her guitar tell stories of broken hearts, cheating lovers and lonely lives better than any country star "wannabe" in Nashville could. "I would have taken my show on the road," she often told Cassidy with a disgruntled sigh, "but then I got pregnant with you. And that was the end of that."

Diane once invited a guy named Hank to the townhouse for dinner. When Hank commented how beautiful she looked in the pictures she displayed on the living room mantle for his benefit, she said, "Oh, yeah, I was quite a knock-out in my younger days. Until I had Cassidy, that is."

One summer, a friend of Diane's came back from a trip abroad, and Diane had said, "Oh, you're so lucky, Maureen, that you're free to travel whenever you want. I'd travel the world, too, if I didn't have Cassidy to worry about."

The innuendos made Cassidy feel as welcome as a nest of termites at Diane's townhouse. She often wondered whether Diane looked upon her and saw nothing but the demise of her youth, her freedom and her dreams. *If I died,* Cassidy would often say to herself ruefully, *Diane would probably be happy that I'm out of her hair.*

In the summer of 1993, Diane asked Cassidy to drive her to San Jose. Having just gotten her driver's license two weeks earlier, Cassidy was eager to exercise her new driving privileges, and didn't bother asking Diane the purpose of their excursion. As she steered Diane's blue Corvette up to the curb in front of a rambling bungalow in a seedy neighborhood of San Jose, she began to wonder what business Diane had in this underbelly of the woods. Still, she asked no questions.

The bungalow, which was in an advanced state of disrepair, turned out to be the home of a Mexican woman named Socorro, who hardly spoke any English. Cassidy was instructed to sit in the dank living room that smelled of cat's urine while Socorro led Diane to an adjoining room and shut the door. It was then that it began to dawn on Cassidy what Diane had come here to do.

Every sinew in Cassidy's body rebelled against the slaughter to come. *What kind of monster decides to get an abortion and asks her own daughter to drive her there?* Her mind was tormented by a nightmarish vision of Diane cackling wickedly, "You escaped the blade, my pretty. But this one here ain't gonna be as lucky," pointing to her belly. Then out of Diane's mouth spewed the diabolical laughter of villains, scoundrels, murderers and evildoers. Cassidy was still pondering dark thoughts when Diane emerged from the adjoining room. There was no trace of remorse on her face, no emptiness or sense of loss. Instead, she wore the triumphant look of a woman who had just escaped an 18-year prison sentence. Walking right behind Diane was Socorro, wearing a dingy white butcher's apron. The sight of her in slaughterhouse garb made Cassidy bolt out the door.

"I'll wait in the car, Diane," she hollered, as she walked down the front steps. Once outside, she gasped for air and clutched at her belly to keep from throwing up. Acids were still raging in her abdomen as she sat herself behind the wheel of Diane's blue corvette. Through the open front door of the bungalow, she saw Diane give Socorro a wad of cash, and Socorro, in turn, handed Diane a small brown paper bag.

Not a word was exchanged between them on the ride home. *Maybe I don't deserve the courtesy of an explanation,* Cassidy muttered to herself bitterly. *After all, who am I anyway but the other unwanted child? The lucky one who escaped the blade?*

Upon returning to the townhouse, Diane retired to her room to take a nap. Cassidy thought to anesthetize her mind with television, and sat herself on the recliner in the living room. As she reached for the TV remote, she saw it. The small brown paper bag Socorro had handed to Diane earlier that day. Diane had left it on the coffee table. Whether it was on purpose or by accident, Cassidy was uncertain. She slowly opened the bag and saw inside a glass container the size of a pickle jar. She lifted the jar out of the bag, and there, suspended in water, was Diane's souvenir from her evil-doing. A bloody mass floating in limbo.

Cassidy's mouth hung open, and she swallowed hard. She was certain the faceless being inside the jar was the sister she had always wished for–severed from its mother like a worthless body part. She would have named her Skye. Skye would have been a lovely child with a beautiful spirit, and a light that shone from within. Skye would have had a sweet disposition, unlike the embittered, hell-bent, jaded temperament Cassidy had acquired in her life with Diane.

Tears stung Cassidy's eyes as she realized that Skye's life had been extinguished with no regard to the wonderful human being she could have been. Simply because Diane viewed her as yet another threat to her freedom. *I would have taken care of Skye, Diane, if you didn't want to,* Cassidy cried to herself. *I would have been willing to quit school to look after her, to love her the way she deserved to be loved. I'd have taken her to live with me when I turned eighteen, and raised her as my own, if you wanted nothing to do with her. Why'd you have to kill her?*

Cassidy walked to the back of the townhouse carrying the bottled remains of Skye. She opened the glass sliding door that led to Diane's small backyard garden. Diane had built a picket fence around the garden to keep the neighborhood pets from trampling over and nibbling on her prized blossoms. Diane nurtured her flowers the way a mama bear nurtured its young. Protected them with a vigilance reserved for botanicals instead of humans.

Cassidy laid the jar on the ground. With a spade, she began to uproot one of the *passionata* plants that Diane prized more than all the others. The plant had a single blossom that held two long cup-shaped petals facing each other, resembling hands in prayer. The petals were the color of blood, and that seemed a fair exchange to Cassidy. Blood for blood. After removing the *passionata* plant from the ground, with its roots still intact, she continued digging until she had a hole large enough to hold Skye's remains. She slowly unscrewed the lid off the jar, poured Skye into her eternal resting place, and scooped a mound of dirt over her unmarked grave.

Into the brown paper bag, she put the uprooted *passionata* plant. When Diane saw the plant with its blood-red blossom spilling out beyond the rim of the paper bag later that evening, she appeared unruffled as she proceeded to cut off the plant's roots with her garden shears, and put the leafy stems, along with its single blossom, into a crystal vase. She said nothing to Cassidy. Neither did she say anything when she saw the gaping space in her garden where the *passionata* plant had been, and saw the mound of dirt in its place.

A thought occurred to Cassidy that chilled her bones. *Diane would have killed me, too, if she could have.* She had no doubt that Diane would have gotten rid of her as easily as she did Skye, had her dad not been around to stop her. Diane had never wanted children, and Jack had wanted as many as God could give. The more she thought about it, the more certain Cassidy became that her dad had persuaded Diane to keep the unplanned baby, and Diane reluctantly did so. Later, when she felt robbed of her life, her youth and her dreams after the birth of Cassidy, she blamed her misery on Jack, and that's what caused her to eventually file for divorce.

That weekend, Cassidy had asked her dad if her suspicions were true. Again, he had put on his comical face and proceeded to sing his version of John Mellencamp's song.

> *Here's a little song about Jack and Diane*
> *Just two young kids doin' the best they can*

With the same intensity that she disliked Diane, Cassidy had adored her dad. Jack Hamilton was warm, affectionate and nurturing. Cassidy sometimes wondered whether God had made a mistake by handing her dad all the maternal instincts that should have been given to Diane.

To Jack Hamilton, life was a song. There was always an abundance of singing and merriment around him, and there was a song for every occasion, every circumstance, every insight. He wasn't the polished singer that Diane was–in truth, he sang off-key and invented his own lyrics most of the time–but he more than made up for it with the spirit and conviction with which he sang. He would jump out of bed on Sunday morning and sing his own version of Lionel Ritchie's song, with all the fervor he could muster:

> *That's why I'm breezy*
> *I'm breezy like a Sunday morning, yeah*
> *That's why I'm breezy*
> *I'm breezy like a Sunday mooooooooorning*

He would do exaggerated gestures with his body, as though doing an interpretative dance, and it would make Cassidy laugh until her belly hurt. She would often join him in his singing, and make him laugh in turn whenever she made up nonsensical words in place of song lyrics she didn't know.

Cassidy remembered how Jack would sing his caricature version of the Four Tops song, "I Can't Help Myself," while performing his own exaggerated version of the suave dance moves of The Temptations.

> *Sugar Pie, pumpkin doll*
> *You know that you're mine, all mine*
> *I can't help myself*
> *I wanna kiss you a thousand times*

Over the years, Jack had used the song to cajole her, cheer her up when she was feeling down, and coax her out of a bad mood. It was Cassidy's "feel good" song, and years later when she entered adulthood, it was still the song that would put a smile on her face. She liked it so much that Jack began calling her "Sugar Pie."

"You're looking more like your mom everyday, Sugar Pie," he had told her when she was seven. "You even sing just like her." Cassidy remembered feeling a little annoyed to be compared to Diane, although Diane's looks and her singing voice were probably her most admirable attributes.

"I may look like her and sing like her, but I'm more like you in everything else, Daddy," she insisted.

Cassidy spent weekends and half of every summer vacation with her Dad, and they were the best times of her life. She could still remember looking out the large picture window of Diane's townhouse, her elbows on the window sill and her face cradled in her cupped palms, waiting for the sight of Dad's Honda Civic coming down the road. Her heart would jump with glee whenever she saw the gleaming red hatchback wheeling around the bend, and heard the familiar rumble coming from its broken muffler. And as she scampered out the door to meet him, he'd step out from behind the wheel, close the car door behind him, drop to his knees at the end of the breezeway, and stretch out his arms, waiting for Cassidy to fill them. "There's Daddy's little girl," he would say, hugging her tightly and rocking her gently to and fro. And then, he'd flash his smile at her. Daddy's smile. The one that told her that nothing else in the world mattered to him but her.

She called those times her "Cinderella Liberty" days. For a glorious day-and-a-half every weekend—and six weeks every summer—she was the belle of the ball. She could frolic and sing and be as merry as she wanted to be before going back to the cinders of her life with Diane.

Her Dad's one-bedroom apartment in Burlingame was modest, but to Cassidy, it was a palace where she was convinced laughter lived. It always smelled of burning incense, something which fit the character of the Birkenstock-wearing, peace-loving, transcendental-meditating remnant of the flower-child generation that Jack Hamilton was. As far as she could see, her father had a modest income from his occupation as a violinist who taught classical music appreciation and conducted a college orchestra, but he would often say to her, "One day, Sugar Pie, when I earn more money, I'll get myself a bigger apartment in the city with a second bedroom just for you. Maybe I'll even get one of those fancy Victorian apartments that you love so much."

"If you like, Daddy," she would answer. "Right here's fine, too."

Cassidy often worried how her dad would find time to date if he had her over all day Saturday through Sunday afternoon.

"Don't worry yourself about such things, Sugar Pie."

"But it's not fair that Diane gets to date men all the time, and have boyfriends and such, and you're stuck with me on weekends."

"Let Diane do what she wants to do. And I'll do what I like doing best, and that's spending time with my favorite girl." Then he grinned at her, and she knew he meant every word.

Early one Sunday morning when she was eight, Cassidy crept out of her dad's bed and tiptoed to the kitchen to make him a surprise breakfast for Father's Day. Half an hour later, carrying a serving tray with a plate of pancakes and a glass of orange juice, she ceremoniously walked back into her Dad's bedroom and nudged him awake. Jack opened his eyes and looked at the plate of misshapen pancakes slathered with butter and syrup.

"I tried my best to make them heart-shaped, Daddy, but they look funny, don't they?"

Jack took the tray from her hands, laid it down on the bed next to him, and took Cassidy in his arms.

"Daddy, why are you crying? They're not that bad, are they?"

"Nothing wrong with them, Sugar Pie. They're perfect. I was just wondering what I've ever done to deserve you."

For as long as she lived, Cassidy would never forget her dad's words. The words that gave her life, made her feel what it was like to be loved, even without the words "I love you" being spoken. Jack Hamilton loved being a dad. Not just anybody's dad, but her dad. She couldn't remember a long walk they took together when he didn't stop to pluck a small white flower and put it in her hair, nestled above her left ear. Then, he'd lapse into his own rendition of the Cowsills song, from the sixties.

Flowers in your hair, flowers everywhere
I love you, flower girl
You crept into my heart
Oh, I don't know just how

Jack Hamilton was not necessarily what women would call a good catch, but to Cassidy, he had qualities that far outweighed material possessions and other worldly accomplishments that women consider desirable. Little did she know that Jack would become the barometer by which she would appraise the value of every man she would encounter.

It was not until Cassidy went off to UC Berkeley on a scholarship, and started living in a dorm on campus, that Jack began dating a woman named Sharon Davis. It was then that she saw a glimpse of the wonderful husband he could have been to Diane, had Diane given him the opportunity. It was not hard to see that he had begun caring deeply about Sharon, a divorced mother with two sons. To Sharon, Jack Hamilton was the prince she had been waiting for all her life, and they had made plans to be married the following summer.

For all the attention he paid Sharon, Cassidy never felt she took a back seat in her father's affections. There was enough love in Jack Hamilton's heart for both of them, not to mention Sharon's sons, and no one ever felt shortchanged in the process. Sharon once told Cassidy that when she and Jack first started dating, she had asked him what he looked for in a woman.

"The most important thing is for the woman to know that she

can't compete with my daughter for my affection…because she will lose."

"And how did that make you feel?" Cassidy asked Sharon.

"I thought it was perfect," she said. "That's exactly how I feel about my sons. No one comes before them. Not even myself."

Cassidy was nineteen, and in her second year at Berkeley, when the phone rang at her dorm. It was Sharon, crying hysterically. Jack had died in his sleep just before dawn. He had long suffered from sleep apnea, which caused his throat to close repeatedly during sleep and his breathing to stop for several seconds at a time. That morning, his breathing had stopped for several minutes, leading to death from lack of oxygen.

Cassidy felt her life lose its only luster the day her father died. But even as she mourned his death, she grieved for Sharon and wondered if Sharon felt any less pain than she herself did for losing the man she loved. During Jack's funeral, Diane Hamilton lost no opportunity to spread her gospel of doom. "If they don't leave you, they die on you," she had told Sharon, honestly thinking her words would somehow provide some comfort.

It took Cassidy five years to recover from her father's death and to fill the moments that used to be filled by him. It was only after five years that she was able to remember the times she shared with her dad without cursing God for taking him away from her. During one of her visits to his grave, Sharon's words became a source of solace. "You had nineteen years with your dad, Cassidy. Some people aren't as lucky."

∽

As Cassidy rolled onto her back and stretched out on the bed, luxuriating in the sense that she had all the time in the world to laze about, her thoughts turned to Savannah. Savannah wasn't as lucky. She had less than eight years with her own dad. Cassidy wondered how her life would have turned out if she lost her dad before she turned eight. Wondered how it would have felt if it hadn't been God who had taken him away, but if her dad had just left of his own volition without saying goodbye.

Tears began to pour out of her eyes for Savannah now. It was neither the first nor the last tears she shed for her since the day she found her journal.

Looking back, she realized it was probably one of the reasons she was obsessed by Savannah and Alfonso's love affair for the last nine months of her life. She wanted desperately for Alfonso to mend the hole in Savannah's heart for good. His love was pure and deep, with none of the artifice that often accompanies love. Deep in her heart, Cassidy, too, wanted a man to love her and make all her pain go away. At that moment, she wondered how many women in the world sought the love of a man as a substitute for their father's love—and how many have suffered the sting of disenchantment as a result.

Cassidy finally rolled out of bed, slipped on her robe and slippers, walked to the kitchen to put the coffee on, opened the front door and stooped to pick up the Sunday paper at her doorstep. Then, she sat on her overstuffed sofa and began to spread the various sections of the *San Francisco Journal* over her coffee table. She reached for the *Calendar* section, and her eyes gravitated towards an article concerning a special display at the San Francisco Museum of Modern Art. It read:

> SAN FRANCISCO, CA – A painting Pablo Picasso completed when he was only 17, and heretofore unseen in public, is on display at the San Francisco Museum of Modern Art. This rare work of art surfaced in late 1977, four years after Picasso's death on April 8, 1973. Its authenticity has been verified by three international art authenticators.
>
> The painting is creating a stir in the international art scene because it is one of the few known works done by Picasso during his adolescent years, prior to completing his formal art training at the Barcelona School of Fine Arts. It is also one of the rare works of art whose *pentimento* (underlying image depicting the artist's original intent) has come to the surface in complete detail. The untitled painting, created in 1897, is expected to fetch the highest price paid for an artwork, if put on auction.
>
> It is on loan to the Museum by an unnamed private individual who is holding the art work in custody for its undisclosed owner.

A large picture of the painting was prominently featured with the article. It was a hauntingly beautiful portrait of a woman with black tresses and a red dress sitting on the grass. Behind her was a dark-haired man with a slight build kissing the woman on the left cheek.

The picture had so completely riveted her attention that she had not even noticed that the feature article was titled *Pentimento de Picasso*. At first, Cassidy failed to make the connection. Then, she saw the signature on the bottom right corner of the painting. *Ruiz 1897*.

The feature article included an interview with the woman who loaned the painting to the Museum. A woman who wished to remain anonymous.

The woman claimed that custody of the painting was given to her by the grandson of the lady who was the subject of the picture.

She explained that Picasso had painted the image of a man into the original picture, locked in an amorous kiss with the lady, then changed his mind. He then painted a seascape over his image. The seascape was barely visible now because the brushstrokes, color and impasto of the pentimento were far bolder than those of the seascape. The pentimento had started to appear sometime in 1957. Now, 106 years after the painting's creation, the *pentimento* had emerged more completely than any other known *pentimento*.

The interview went on to say that the painting has been in the custody of the unnamed woman since 1977. At that time, the *pentimento* was about 15% apparent, but infra-red and x-ray equipment were able to discern the image that was yet to surface. The piece has caused art experts to speculate that the image of the man in the pentimento was that of Picasso himself because it resembled a self-portrait that he created in 1896. Picasso biographers even speculate that Picasso had painted himself out in order to conceal his youthful courtship of a 16-year-old Málaga girl identified only as Carmen. Reports had it that although Picasso and Carmen never married, he presented her with a gift, the likes of which he had never given to anyone before: a tambourine on which he painted the most elaborate bouquet of flowers.

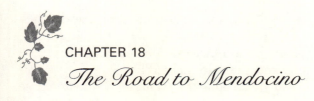

CHAPTER 18
The Road to Mendocino

On Monday morning, Cassidy phoned the San Francisco Museum of Modern Art. She spoke to the curator, Frederick Carlisle, who was naturally reluctant to divulge any information about the woman who had loaned the Picasso to the museum.

"Please, Mr. Carlisle," she pleaded. "I'm acquainted with the woman who loaned you the painting. Her name is Savannah Curtis, isn't it?"

Mr. Carlisle hesitated, and then said, "I'm not at liberty to reveal her name or her whereabouts to anyone for any reason, Miss."

"Perhaps she goes under her married name?" Cassidy ventured. "Parker? Savannah Parker, perhaps? She's a friend of mine whom I've spent years looking for. Please, would you tell me how to get in touch with her?" Then, on second thought, she said," Or would it be possible for me to leave my phone number with you, and you can ask her to call me, would that be alright?"

"I'm sorry, but we've received so many calls requesting the same, and I'm afraid we simply have neither the personnel nor the resources to handle such requests. We also have an obligation to safeguard her privacy."

Undaunted, Cassidy contacted the art delivery service company that the museum used to transport art into and out of the museum. Although she was unable to get a specific address, she managed to obtain the county from which the painting originated. Mendocino.

On the following Saturday, Cassidy drove to Mendocino without a clear course of action as to how she would find Savannah. After poring over the Mendocino county records, the name of Savannah Curtis could not be found. But there were three residents with the first name Savannah. She quickly scribbled their addresses on a piece of note paper.

With a *Thomas Guide* in hand, she located all three addresses and set out to knock on their doors. The first one, Savannah Redfield, turned out to be a blond woman in her early thirties. Savannah Robinson turned out to be an elderly Norwegian woman who'd lived in Mendocino since the 1960s. The third address, 335 Castlebrook Lane, belonged to a Savannah Fairchild.

Cassidy parked her car curbside across from the yellow cottage nestled in a quiet cul-de-sac. There was an exquisite flower garden in the front yard, framed by a candlestick fence. She walked up the cobblestone pathway leading to the front door, rang the doorbell and waited a minute. There was no answer.

As she started walking back to her car, someone finally came to the door. "You rang?" came the voice behind her.

She turned around to see a young man standing at the door. He appeared to be in his mid-twenties, stood about six feet tall, dark brown hair, dark eyebrows, a five-o'clock-shadow, and a goatee on his chin that accentuated his chiseled facial features. In his slate-colored sweatshirt and faded blue jeans, he looked ruggedly handsome.

"Oh ... yes, I did ring. I was beginning to think no one was home," Cassidy said, retracing her steps back towards the cottage. "I'm looking for Savannah Fairchild."

"I'm afraid she isn't here right now, but she'll be home in about fifteen minutes."

She couldn't quite place his accent. It sounded part American, part Spanish, and part British.

"May I wait for her?" she asked.

"Yes, of course," he said, opening the door to let her in. "Would you mind telling me the purpose of your visit?"

"Well, first of all, I just wanted to make sure I've come to the right place. Was Savannah ever referred to as Savannah Curtis in the past? Her maiden name, perhaps?"

"Fairchild is her married name, but yes, Curtis was her maiden name."

"Well, in that case, I'm here to return something that belongs to her. A journal. I think it's fairly important to her."

He closed the door behind him. "Please have a seat. May I offer you a cup of coffee or tea?"

"No, but a glass of water would be nice, thanks."

When he disappeared into the kitchen, Cassidy was able to take a closer look inside the cottage. There was an enormous stone fireplace against the north wall. An overstuffed sofa and loveseat upholstered in antique-rose chenille, surrounding a coffee table of mottled rosewood. Hardwood floors stained with three different shades–mahogany, maple and redwood. On the walls hung what she presumed were Savannah's paintings. She noticed that she signed them *Karenina*.

The glass of water arrived in a few moments.

"I hope you don't mind my asking, but how are you related to Savannah?"

"I'm her son. I'm sorry I didn't introduce myself. I'm Brandon Fairchild. And you're ...?"

"Cassidy Hamilton."

Brandon said he was visiting his mother for the weekend. He said his mother had just moved back to the States a few months earlier from Switzerland, where she had spent the last twenty-six years.

"I was born in Switzerland myself," Brandon volunteered. "Raised there, for the most part. But I've also lived in London, Paris and Madrid. Now, I call San Francisco home."

"So I suppose you're able to speak French and Spanish fluently then?"

"Fluently, I'm not sure. I guess you could say I know enough French and Spanish to be dangerous." He chuckled and threw back his head in merriment. He had carefree hair and a carefree attitude. There was a wildness in his eyes that startled her every time he flashed them at her.

"I suppose your dad lives here with your mom?" I ventured.

"My mother lives alone. My dad died before I was born, and she never remarried. I worry about her living all by herself. That's why I often come up here on weekends to keep her company."

"Why did she decide to live here? Wouldn't it have been better if she lived in San Francisco so she can live close to you?"

"There's no reasoning with my mother the moment her mind's made up. Well, actually, she said she'd always dreamed of retiring here one day. She's still far from retirement age, but she's an artist by profession." He gestured in the direction of the art on the wall. "These are all her paintings, by the way."

"I was looking at them earlier. They're quite beautiful."

"Mendocino is home to a growing community of artists," he continued. "So she feels quite comfortable here. Her work is carried by art galleries in the village."

There was a brief lull in the conversation. Suddenly, he asked, "Do you live here in Mendocino?"

"No, I actually live in San Francisco. I work as a paralegal in a downtown law firm."

"And you drove all the way out here to return something that belongs to my mother? What did you say it was?"

"Her journal. I found it in a Victorian apartment I just moved into last October. Apparently, your mother lived in the same apartment back in 1977."

"That long ago, huh? That was just before I was born."

"When were you born?" she asked, her heart beginning to pound loudly.

"June of '78," he replied.

It didn't take much mental calculation for Cassidy to know that Brandon was born exactly nine months after Alfonso's affair with

Savannah. *Could he be Alfonso's son?* she wondered. She couldn't be certain. He could very well be Russell Parker's son.

"Do you know when your mother moved to Switzerland?"

"Before the end of 1977, if I remember correctly. She said it was the year before I was born."

"Was your father's name Russell, by any chance?"

For the first time since she arrived at 335 Castlebrook Lane, Brandon looked askance at her as though to ask, *Why all these questions?* She suddenly felt embarrassed by her own behavior, by her endless barrage of questions. She must have seemed like a stalker, interrogating him and prying into his mother's affairs. The blood rushed to her face in shame.

Nonetheless, he answered politely, "No. His name was Warren. Warren Fairchild. He died in October of '77 right after I was conceived. That's why my mother moved to Switzerland soon thereafter and lived with Nana Sabine, my adoptive grandmother."

All of a sudden, Cassidy felt she didn't have the right to be there, violating Savannah's privacy. It dawned on her that Savannah would find her visit intrusive. *What right have I to pry into her private life, discover her secrets, and interrogate her son?* Her head was spinning, and she was tempted to bolt out the door without saying a word.

Instead, she tried to compose herself as much as she could, and said, "There's something I need to do right now, Brandon. Maybe I should just come back later."

"Are you sure? She should be here any minute now."

"I'll be back in half an hour. Would that be okay?"

"Okay. Sure."

She walked hurriedly to her car for fear she would run into Savannah as she was returning home. When she got into the car, she drove. And she kept on driving without looking back.

On the long drive back to San Francisco, she scolded herself for trying to meddle in an affair she had no business getting involved in. She wondered whether it was her way of lending color and excitement to her otherwise dismal life. Then, it occurred to her that Alfonso might still be married to Isabel, or Savannah may already be involved with another man. Suddenly, she felt like a silly, love-struck girl desperately trying to revive the love between a man and a woman that lasted a mere two weeks, twenty-six years ago. A love that was probably a long-forgotten chapter of Alfonso's and Savannah's lives by now.

No matter how hard she tried to convince herself otherwise, something inside her still believed that Alfonso and Savannah were destined to be with each other. But she made herself a promise that she'd do one last thing, after which she'd stop being a meddlesome busybody and start minding her own business.

Upon returning home, she did a search for Alfonso Madrigál on the Internet. If he was still playing flamenco music somewhere, maybe his name would show up in the search results. It did.

She wondered why she hadn't thought to do this before. The Internet turned up quite a few search results for Alfonso Madrigál. Apparently, he was a flamenco recording artist who has produced three albums since 1977. There was an e-mail address for his record company.

Cassidy placed the clipping from the San Francisco Journal into her scanner, and uploaded the scanned image to her computer. Then she typed the following e-mail:

SUBJECT: About Savannah Curtis...
Alfonso,
    The attached article was in the San Francisco Journal a few days ago. I believe it's the painting of your grandmother.
    I also found Savannah. She now lives at 335 Castlebrook Lane in Mendocino. She goes by the name, Savannah Fairchild.
    Good wishes,
    A Secret Friend

CHAPTER 19
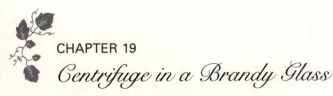
Centrifuge in a Brandy Glass
MONDAY NIGHT • JULY 21 • 2003

Cristina Madrigál-Vargas gently laid her sleeping child on his bed. She tiptoed quietly out of the room and closed the door behind her. She then walked down the hallway past the two guest rooms, the family room and the kitchen.

Alfonso was in the living room, standing next to the floor-to-ceiling glass window, sipping a cognac, looking out into the park across the street and the lights of Madrid in the distance. He still wore his hair fairly long, just past his nape. Except for a few strands of gray, his hair made him look younger than his fifty-one years.

Cristina poured herself an amaretto and sat herself down on the leather-upholstered easy chair. "Papa, it's about time."

Alfonso turned around and began to walk toward her. "Time for what?"

"Time to find the Kahili ginger flower."

He froze in mid-step for a moment, then continued walking towards the settee, sat himself down, and faced her.

Cristina set her glass down on the coffee table. The next moment, she buried her face in her hands and began to weep. "It's all my fault," she said tearfully.

"What on earth are you talking about, Cristina?"

"It's all my fault that you're not with her. I robbed you of your happiness." Hot tears began to fall heavy from Cristina's eyes.

"You did no such thing. You've brought me nothing but pride and happiness, *mi hija*."

"No, I haven't. I made you choose between Savannah and me, and now she's gone."

"You had nothing to do with that. It was her decision to leave me."

"Because I made her do it, Papa. I made her do it. Don't you see? She was there that day. At the Palace of Fine Arts. The day we went to see the swans."

"She was?"

"Yes. You didn't see her, but I did. I knew she was watching us, listening to us. I spoke loudly enough so she'd hear me beg you not to leave Mama and me."

"You were a child, Cristina. Barely four years old. You can't blame yourself for the actions of others."

167

"No, Papa. It was my fault. I played to her emotions. I knew she wouldn't be able to bear it if she saw me being needy of you. How hurt and broken I'd be if you ran away with her. I knew she'd remember how hurt and broken she was after her daddy left her."

Alfonso was silent as he pondered that day, twenty-six years ago. Most of all, he remembered the day after when he received the letter from Savannah.

"And Papa, don't think I don't know the great sacrifice you've made so as not to hurt me that way. You could have gone after her, searched the world for her, but you didn't. You stayed with me even when you knew I wasn't your daughter."

Alfonso stared at his hands, not knowing what to say.

"I've known for a long time, Papa, even before that day at the Palace of Fine Arts. One night, I overheard Mama and you quarreling, and she threatened to take me away from you since she said you weren't my father."

Alfonso heaved a deep sigh, knowing that the moment he dreaded had come. "*Mi hija,* I've known even before you were born, that you weren't my biological child…but that hasn't stopped me from loving you as though you're my own flesh and blood."

"I know, Papa, I know. You've never made me feel like anything else than your own daughter. But I fell apart when I heard Mama say I was the child of another man. I cried for days thinking that it wouldn't be long till you left Mama and me. And when Savannah came into your life, I started getting nightmares that I would wake up one day, like Savannah did when she was little, and find you gone. So when I saw her at the Palace of Fine Arts hiding behind the trees, I staged an emotional outburst for her to see. And it worked like a charm, Papa. But when she disappeared from your life, I immediately regretted what I had done when I saw what it did to you. I'm sorry, Papa. I'm so sorry I put you through all the pain." Her tears dripped into the amber pool of Amaretto. Her grip on the liqueur glass tightened until she nearly broke its stem.

Alfonso sat silently, swirling his cognac until it created a centrifuge in the brandy snifter. Cristina's revelation stunned him, and he was at a loss for words. He grieved the torment Cristina must have endured as a child, the kind of torment he would have done everything to shield her from experiencing. He recalled the dark days following Savannah's letter, how he took leave of his senses, how he had filled the apartment on Potrero Hill with the blinding pain of his heart that bled out of his guitar, how preoccupied he had been bemoaning his own misery that he couldn't see what was happening to Cristina. During the four months that Alfonso had given full expression to his pain and nursed his wounds, Cristina had turned from an outgoing, cheerful, spiritually grounded child into a reclusive, rebellious and temperamental creature. When he finally emerged from the dark days, he saw what his turmoil had done to Cristina, and set about trying to restore her to her former self. Cristina's spirits eventually came around, but Alfonso knew that something in her had died. Perhaps it was her innocence. He remembered the words she said to him at the Palace of Fine Arts. *I was thinking…this is the only childhood I'm going to have. I wanna hold on to it.* Alfonso felt he had stolen his daughter's childhood, for she was never quite the same after that.

Cristina's words continued echoing in Alfonso's ears. She had spoken of the "great sacrifice" he had made by not going after Savannah and leaving Isabel and her behind. He knew he didn't deserve the credit for such noble acts, but he said nothing. Left to his own devices, he'd have thrown caution to the wind and gone after the only woman he had ever loved, without considering his wife and daughter.

It was, in fact, Savannah who had encouraged him to remain faithful to his filial obligation. Savannah had made him see that he held the power to nurture or destroy his little girl's life. She had written, *I'd rather let you soar upon my love and be ennobled by it, rather than let it compromise the things you hold dear, especially your precious daughter, Cristina. I'd rather lose you than turn you into less of a man than the one I've come to know and love.*

Alfonso's thoughts were interrupted by the sound of Cristina's voice. "But now I see you could have loved me, too, while loving her."

"And that's what I've done, Cristina. That's what I've done. Love is something you can do whether the object of your love is in or out of your sight. Even as I loved you, there has never been a day that I haven't loved her."

Alfonso had a faraway look in his eyes as he continued to speak. "When I was growing up in Málaga, there were many mornings when I sat on my grandmother's terrazza facing west. Even when I didn't see the sun rising directly in front of my eyes, I knew it was there because its brilliance shimmered off the white-washed walls of the village houses. Its light was ablaze on a thousand window panes. That's the way it is with Savannah. Whether she's in or out of my direction, I know she's there."

"Papa, I know you've managed to survive without her, but you need not be without her any more. In case you haven't noticed, I'm grown up now and have a family of my own. Now, it's time for you to be happy."

"Cristina, loving her from a distance all these years has given me a deep happiness I can't explain. She made me realize the extent to which I can love a woman...that's a reward in itself. Because of her, I know the secrets of my own heart. Some people go through their whole lives never knowing this.

"All you see with your eyes, *mi hija*, is me without her. But she's with me all the time. There isn't a thought, word or deed of mine that isn't colored by her in some way. When I play my guitar, she's the one cheering me on. When I sing, she's the one I sing about. When I go to sleep at night, she's in my arms and in my dreams. Every man should be so lucky to love a woman as much as I have, and for as long as I have."

"Papa, you were so good to Mama while she was alive. You tried to love her as much as you could for my sake. I know she appreciated that—even if you couldn't love her the way you loved Savannah. But Mama's been gone for over a year now. Isn't it about time you looked for Savannah?"

"If I knew how to get to her, *mi hija*, I would. I started looking for her a few months after Mama died, but I have yet to find her. But I'm not worried. Remember what I always used to tell you when you were a child?"

"Don't go looking for love, for if love finds you worthy, it will find you."

"*Exactamente.*"

⁓

Alfonso said goodnight to Cristina and her husband, Antonio, at half past eleven that night. He drove three miles to his villa on the corner of Valladolid and Coscoluella. He hummed a Spanish bolero softly as he turned the key and entered the back door of the villa.

On his way towards the staircase, he passed by the study. The desktop computer screen had a blinking icon that signaled that he had mail. He decided to read his e-mail before turning in.

There were dozens of messages in his e-mail box. He scanned the subject column to see if there was any e-mail important enough to open. His heart leaped when he got to the line that read:

SUBJECT: About Savannah Curtis ...

CHAPTER 20
Ablaze on a Thousand Window Panes

WEDNESDAY AFTERNOON • JULY 23 • 2003

Cassidy had just poured herself a mid-afternoon cup of coffee at the staff lounge when she was paged overhead. "Cassidy, you have a phone call on line 3."

She picked up the phone on the back wall of the staff lounge.

"This is Cassidy."

"Hi, this is Brandon Fairchild. Remember me?"

Blood rushed to her face. She heard a throbbing in her ears and instantly regretted picking up the phone in the staff lounge instead of her office.

"Hello, Brandon," she said, trying to act nonchalant. "What a surprise to hear from you. How on earth did you find me?"

"Well, you mentioned you worked for a law office downtown. I looked in the yellow pages and the third number I dialed, I got you. I hope you don't mind my calling, but you left so abruptly the other day that I actually thought I had offended you."

"Oh, no...you didn't offend me at all. To tell you the truth, I just changed my mind. I no longer thought it was a good idea for me to be there."

"I respect whatever you've chosen to do, but when I told my mother you had stopped by about her journal, but left without waiting for her, she was quite disappointed. She wishes you could've waited for her to return. Oh, and she said she definitely would like to have the journal back."

"Sure. How about if I mail it back tomorrow? Should I send it to the Castlebrook Lane address?"

"Actually, I have a better idea. If you wouldn't mind another trip to Mendocino, I'd like to invite you to drive up with me on Saturday. Then, you can give it to her in person."

Cassidy had promised herself that she would no longer meddle in anything concerning Alfonso and Savannah. *I guess this is different because now, I'm being invited,* she thought.

"Are you sure it's okay with Savannah...I mean, your mom?"

"I told her I'd invite you back and she was delighted. She even told me you can plan to spend the entire weekend, if you want. Her cottage has two guest bedrooms and she's a wonderful cook."

"I did have a few things lined up for the weekend, Brandon, but I think I can clear my schedule so I can drive up with you."

"*Fantástico!*" Brandon exclaimed, and Cassidy could almost see him tossing his carefree hair back, grinning.

∽

Cassidy heard a knock on her door at 7:48 Saturday morning. *He's early,* she thought as she zipped her overnighter, thankful she had finished packing. She opened the front door and was taken aback. The man standing at the door hardly looked like the Brandon she remembered from the week before.

He looked striking in a pair of black jeans topped with a black V-necked cotton shirt, with its long sleeves folded to just below his elbows. A pewter crucifix on a black leather cord hung from his neck and rested on the part of his upper chest that peered above his shirt's neckline. He had a calculatedly disheveled ruggedness with a two-day stubble, hair tousled about without looking unruly. Standing in the doorway with his hands resting on his hips, he had an edgy, untamed countenance that reminded her of James Dean or a young Brando.

"Hey, Cassidy. Am I too early?" he asked, cocking his head to one side and flashing his wild eyes at her.

"Well, you are…but I don't mind, Brandon. Please come in. I'll be ready in a minute."

He stepped in and closed the door behind him. Cassidy watched from the corner of her eye as he walked over to the sofa in a natural swagger that she hadn't noticed the last time. He sat himself down on the sofa, stretched his legs in front of him, crossed them at the ankles, and spread both of his arms on the seatback. His eyes wandered around the apartment, and his eyes squinted slightly as he did.

"So this is where my parents lived before I was born," he said, finally.

"Why, yes, you're right," I replied, not wanting to contradict what Savannah might have told him.

"You like Kahili ginger flowers, too, I see?" he asked.

"Yes, don't they smell wonderful?" I said, not admitting I had never heard of them until I read about them in Savannah's journal.

Excusing herself, she walked over to the coat closet, pulled a small canvas satchel out, and carefully put Savannah's journal and Zendrik's CD into it. Then, she went into her bedroom, carried her overnighter out to the living room, and said, "Okay, all set to go."

Brandon took the overnighter from her hand, and said, "By the way, did I tell you that you look absolutely beautiful?"

Cassidy had made it a habit to gloss over men's perfunctory compliments. Therefore, she was surprised to find herself feeling flushed by his comment.

"Thanks," she murmured, thinking it must be the dress.

As if reading her thoughts, he said, "I didn't mean just today, Cassidy. Or just in that dress. What I mean is, well…you look beautiful to me." Brandon didn't speak in poetic metaphors. But his words made Cassidy feel like a sunbeam in a field of clover.

༄

The sky throbbed, wisps of fog quarreled and the ocean's foam hummed as Brandon drove the cobalt-blue BMW sedan down Geary Boulevard, down through Fort Mason, past the Marina Green and the Palace of Fine Arts. Then, across the Golden Gate Bridge, descending into Marin County. All traces of fog that dotted the summer sky were nowhere to be found when they reached the Mill Valley area.

Brandon pressed a pre-set button on the car radio to listen to a classical music station. "Do you like classical music?"

"I grew up listening to classical music. My father was a violinist who taught classical music appreciation and conducted a college orchestra."

"Did I hear you say he 'was' a violinist?"

"Yes, my father passed away almost six years ago. I still miss him terribly. He was the best dad in the world."

Brandon smiled. "I love hearing people talk fondly about their dads. It makes me imagine how things would have been between my dad and me…had he lived."

"Oh, I'm sorry, Brandon. I didn't mean to make you feel like you had less of a childhood…"

"No need to feel sorry, Cassidy. I honestly like hearing people talk about their dads. Growing up, my mother told me wonderful stories about her dad. As for me, yeah, sometimes I wish I grew up with a father…but my mom's the best mom in the world, so that more than makes up for it."

It was Cassidy's turn to smile. Somehow, she couldn't picture Savannah being anything less than an excellent mother. She wished she could say the same about Diane.

"Speaking of classical music, are you familiar with Albinoni's *Adagio in G Minor?*" Cassidy asked.

"Funny you asked. I listened to that piece my entire childhood," he said with a carefree laugh. "My mother used to put me to sleep listening to it."

The drive through the rest of Marin County was filled with small talk accompanied by the classical tunes of KDFC.

"What kind of work do you do, Brandon?"

"What kind of work do you think I do?"

"Hmmm...looking at you, I'd guess you're a musician."

"Close enough. I'm a stockbroker." His laughter was infectious, and Cassidy couldn't help but laugh with him.

"I would never have guessed. Maybe because of your hair ...?"

"Oh, I wear my hair slicked back and I'm clean shaven when I'm wearing my pin-striped broker attire. What you see today is my Bohemian, weekend warrior garb. Oh, and by the way, you weren't too far off when you guessed that I'm a musician. I moonlight as a flamenco guitarist. Wednesdays and Friday nights at the *Casbah* with a couple of my musician friends."

"Stockbroker by day...flamenco guitarist by night. What an interesting dichotomy."

Brandon chuckled.

"How did you learn to play flamenco guitar?"

"I actually took formal lessons with a guitar teacher named Jose Montoya when I lived in Madrid."

Brandon became very animated talking about his adventures in Spain and his forays into the flamenco culture. He spoke of the train ride he took from Madrid to Cádiz, the last train stop in the south of Spain. How he took the bus from Cádiz to various towns in Andalucia. He talked about the fiery flamenco shows that he saw in Sevilla, Granada, Jerez de la Frontera, and as far as Alicante, the easternmost tip of Andalucia.

He spoke of a *tablao* that he visited in Ronda, where a fat, middle-aged waitress unceremoniously walked up to the stage and sang a *cante jondo* that set his blood ablaze. At every turn, the locals warned him about the gypsies that ran wild along the highways and byways of Andalucia, gypsies that were notorious for robbing tourists of their money and belongings. Brandon had heeded their advice and kept his money tucked in his socks, and his passport tucked in a plastic pouch clipped inside his boxer shorts–and thus avoided untoward incidents. From Cádiz, he took a four-hour bus ride that climbed through winding roads and dangerous terrains to the picturesque port of Algeciras, where he boarded a ferry boat that crossed the Strait of Gibraltar and docked in exotic Morocco. In Morocco, he experienced flamenco fusion, a unique incarnation of flamenco guitar collaborating beautifully with the Arabic Orchestra of Tangier.

Suddenly, Brandon stopped short, and said, "I'm sorry I've just been rambling on and on. I never even asked you if this is at all interesting to you. Do you like flamenco music?"

"Yes, I do. I can't say I've listened to a lot of it, but I know some artists like Paco de Lucía, Armik, Strunz and Farah, and the Gypsy Kings."

"I like all of those you mentioned. But this guy here's my absolute favorite." He switched from the radio to the CD player, selected one of the albums, and played the first track.

Brandon turned up the volume and the two of them sat quietly for a minute, listening to the skillful guitar-playing set to a rumba beat.

"Wow, it sounds great," Cassidy said, after listening to half of the first track. "Who's the artist?"

"Alfonso Madrigál."

"No way!" Her knee-jerk reaction came across as a loud squeal.

Brandon was startled by her response. "Have you heard of him?"

"Yes...I mean, no. Okay, let me say this right. Yes, I've heard of him, but no, I haven't heard him play. Didn't he used to play in the Bay Area some time back?"

"Before you and I were born. Now, he's based in Madrid. This is his third album. I also have the first two. Do you know what people call him?"

"No. What?"

"They call him the 'untutored genius, the Michelangelo of flamenco music.' He's had very limited training, and yet he's one of the best I've seen."

"Have you met him?"

"Actually, I saw him in concert when I lived in Madrid. He's quite well known in Spain."

"Has your mother heard this album?"

Brandon looked at her as though she had asked a strange question, which indeed her question was.

"No, I don't think so. She likes flamenco music. She's the one who got me interested in flamenco when I was a kid, but she hasn't kept herself up to date on the artists."

Just then, they spotted a train in the distance going south on its way to Mill Valley.

"Do you know what's in that train, Cassidy?" he asked.

"Let me guess," she said. "I'd have to say it's a flock of wild eagles with injured wings, waiting to be taken to a place where they can find their fragment of the sky–and learn to fly again."

Brandon cast a puzzled glance at her. Then, he threw back his head in his carefree way and chuckled.

"How is it that you know what I'm about to say next? Are you with the CIA or something?"

"Try 'mind reader'–or 'stalker,'" she said, giggling.

"No, seriously. Could it just be a series of coincidences that you live in the same apartment where my mother used to live, that you like Kahili ginger flowers, flamenco music, *Adagio in G. Minor*...

and now, you even know word-for-word the story my mother tells me about what's in those trains? If I didn't know any better, I'd think you're a blond clone of Savannah Fairchild!"

Childlike laughter escaped Cassidy's lips, the kind of laughter that she thought resided only within the walls of Jack Hamilton's one-bedroom apartment in Burlingame that smelled of incense.

Even as she laughed, she wondered whether she should play it cool when it came to letting on how much she knew about his mother. She decided against it, thinking that he'd eventually figure out she knew what she knew from reading Savannah's journal.

⁓

Cassidy couldn't recall how the conversation turned to the subject of absurd movie plots.

"My vote has to go to *Titanic*," she declared. "While I appreciate the parts of the plot that have to do with historical fact, the story of the fictional characters is absurd."

"How so?"

"I think it's ridiculous to idealize the relationship between a 17-year-old woman traveling in first-class and a 20-year-old boy who won his third-class passage through a lucky hand in poker, since their relationship was founded on such a lame premise."

"And what premise was that?"

"Well, you know the story. Rose, a 17-year-old woman, depressed over the prospect of having to marry a man she didn't love, and live a life of endless protocol, tries to commit suicide by jumping off the ship. Jack, the 20-year-old starving artist, persuades Rose not to jump. Then, later, their relationship is further cemented when Rose coaxes Jack to sketch a portrait of her in the nude, which to me, is as idiotic a foundation for a relationship as I've ever seen. This, then, begs the question, 'Can a 17-year-old woman, who's accustomed to wealth, find happiness with a poor boy after the novelty of their differences wears off?' More importantly, suppose they both survived the Titanic and made it to dry land, would they have any chance of living happily ever after?"

"If they choose to," came Brandon's quick reply.

"What are you saying? This relationship is as doomed as they come, Brandon!"

"According to whom?"

Slightly exasperated that Brandon wasn't seeing things her way, she ventured, "So you're saying you like the plot of *Titanic*?"

"I didn't say that. I'm just surprised at how easily you dismiss the prospects of a relationship just because it appears doomed to you. You don't know the characters intimately, and neither do you know the intensity of their love for each other, or their level of commitment. Yet you're willing to doom their relationship."

"So let me get this straight. Are you saying that if Rose and Jack were alive today, having both survived the Titanic, you believe they'd have a successful relationship?"

"If both of them choose to," he replied, without blinking an eye.

"But don't you think love has a shelf life, and that at some point, it loses its luster and dies a natural death?"

"No, I believe true love endures."

"You sound like someone whose heart has never been broken."

"On the contrary, I've had my heart broken enough times that I've come to recognize what love really is…and isn't."

"Well, then, tell me. How can you tell when something isn't love?"

"When it's based purely on feelings, for one."

Cassidy sat in deep thought. Nothing in her experience or knowledge could comprehend what he was saying. What is love if not a feeling? Even *Webster's* dictionary defines love as a deep, tender feeling of affection toward a person arising from any number of events or elements.

As if reading her thoughts, Brandon continued, "Love is not just a feeling. It is a choice, a commitment, a way of behaving toward another. Feelings and emotions are fickle, and the circumstances that give rise to them, even more so. Therefore, if love were based on feelings, it would be as fleeting as a passing fever. And a passing fever, love is not."

Cassidy pondered Brandon's words, knowing that they made more sense than all the drivel that has been administered to her by her mother and her failed relationships in small, lethal doses for so many years. "Am I therefore mistaken in thinking that love is transient, and that it abandons you when you need it most?"

Brandon threw his head back in his carefree way, and laughed. "Now, you're beginning to sound like someone whose heart has been broken a few times!"

"And then some," she added, laughing with him.

After a few moments of silence, Brandon said, "In my humble opinion, love is not simply an event that happens to you. Rather, love is something you choose to do. The state of being in love is simply a prelude to love. But most people make the mistake of thinking they're one and the same thing. I believe that you're given circumstances by which you can exercise the choice to love. I call it the thunderbolt that God supplies. It's that instant attraction to another person, those warm, fuzzy feelings, that fever akin to drunkenness or madness that causes you to know that you're in love. But it's what you choose to do after that thunderbolt has passed that matters. You choose whether you're going to continue loving the other person after the drunkenness has dissipated, after the frills of romance have fallen away. You choose whether you're going to continue to seek the best interests of the other person, and care about him or her through any and all circumstances–and for how long. Love is a conscious choice."

Brandon had certainly presented a better paradigm of love than Cassidy had ever considered before. It was one that provided comfort, hope. Cassidy had always feared the volatility of love as she knew it. *One day you could feel you love someone, other days you may not. Some days you could feel loved, and other days you don't.* She figured that even if she found Mr. Right one day, there was never any certainty that she would still love him five, ten, fifteen years down the road–or if he would her. She would always have to wake up every morning, asking herself, "Is this the day that love will fly the coop?" She'd hated the feeling of helplessness that some deity can simply decide whether to keep love in our midst or not.

In contrast to that was Brandon's assertion that love–at least the love that one gives to someone–could endure for as long as one chooses. It was the first of many conversations Brandon and Cassidy would have on the subject of love.

One of the things Brandon said echoed in her ears. He had said, "A man must love a woman not because of the way the moon hangs in the sky, or the way a woman's face catches the glow of starlight. True love is the ability to choose one person above all, and the ability to celebrate that choice for as long as you live."

Cassidy sat in silence for a minute or two, savoring the words Brandon said. Wishing they were not just words uttered for the applause of women, but an ideal to which all men could aspire. For if all men regarded women with such reverence, she was certain there would be no unhappy women in the world.

It occurred to her that Brandon's view of a man's love for a woman was coincidentally aligned with that of Alfonso–"an unchanging heart that chooses every moment to be amazed by her on any day, in any light, in any season, and any night."

A chip off the old block, Cassidy said to herself, smiling.

∽

After the last track on the CD ended, Brandon pressed on one of the pre-set buttons on the radio. An oldies station began playing "I Can't Help Myself" by the Four Tops.

As if possessed, Cassidy began to sing along animatedly, mimicking her father's exaggerated dance movements as she did.

"You've got a great voice," Brandon said, watching her from the corner of his eye. She was so engrossed in her singing that she didn't seem to hear his comment. He marveled at how quickly Cassidy's mood had turned from pensive to jubilant upon hearing the song. He had not seen this side of her before, and he rather liked it.

When the song ended, she said, "Oh, I do love that song. My daddy used to sing it to me all the time. And he used to call me 'Sugar Pie.'"

"Ahh … so there's the missing piece of the puzzle." He winked at her, then threw back his head and laughed his carefree laugh.

It was eleven by the time Brandon pulled up into the driveway of Savannah's cottage. He turned off the engine, and as he opened the car door and began to step out from behind the wheel, Cassidy asked, "Would you mind if we brought Alfonso's CD into the house so we can listen to the album again?"

"Sure. You really like it, don't you?" He grinned.

"More than you know," she replied.

They entered the cottage through the kitchen door. Cassidy had not seen the inside of the kitchen the first time she visited. It was bright and airy, with spacious counter tops of multi-colored tile.

"Mama, we're here," Brandon called out.

They heard Savannah's footsteps as she walked hurriedly down the hall from one of the bedrooms in the back. She ran to Brandon, embracing him warmly. Brandon, in turn, lifted her up off the ground with his hands on her waist. When he put her back down, he kissed her on the cheek while hugging her affectionately.

She was beaming. Both of them looked at each other as though they hadn't seen each other in years.

Brandon finally turned to Cassidy and said, "You'll have to excuse us. We're not used to living in the same country, let alone the same state. So we're both thrilled when we see each other even after just one week."

"I think that's sweet," Cassidy said, smiling.

"Mama, this is Cassidy Hamilton. Cassidy, this is my mother, Savannah Fairchild."

Savannah gave her a warm hug. "Wonderful to meet you, Mrs. Fairchild."

"I'm so glad you could come. Brandon can't seem to stop talking about you. Oh, and do call me Savannah."

Cassidy figured she must be in her early fifties, yet she looked as though she was only in her late thirties. She wore a pink floral dress and white sandals. She had a slim figure and had the posture of a ballerina. Her face lit up every time she spoke. She had a genuinely warm personality that made Cassidy feel immediately at home.

"I have iced tea and lemonade in the refrigerator. Which would you prefer?" she asked her.

"I'll have iced tea, please."

"I'll get it, Mama. What can I get for you?"

"I'll have a lemonade, thanks."

When Brandon left for the kitchen, Savannah turned to Cassidy and said, "So how do you like living at 201 Pacific?"

"Oh, I love it. I just moved in last October. I'll probably stay forever…for as long as I can afford it, that is," she said.

"That's what I said when I first moved there. When I relocated to Switzerland, I left in a hurry and I forgot to take the journal out of that hidden drawer. So many times, I've thought of going there and getting it back. So many times, I wondered if someone would find it. I'm glad you did, and I thank you for going out of your way to return it to me."

Cassidy wanted to tell her what her journal has meant to her, and how it has affected her life in so many ways, but decided there would be time to tell her that later.

"Cassidy, I meant to ask you. How did you find me?"

"I saw the article about the Picasso painting in the *San Francisco Journal* and tracked you down here."

She smiled.

Brandon appeared in a few minutes with the refreshments. He took a quick sip of his iced tea, and without skipping a beat, took the CD out of his pocket and walked to the entertainment center.

Alfonso's music filled the room. Savannah continued making conversation with Cassidy. After having heard two or three of the tracks on the album, she said, "I love this music, Brandon. Who's the artist?"

"Alfonso Madrigál."

Savannah froze when she heard Alfonso's name. Then, she turned her eyes towards Cassidy. Cassidy smiled, knowingly, and Savannah managed a tentative smile.

"Let me take a look at the CD case, sweetie."

Brandon handed it to her. She looked at the CD cover and gazed at the picture of Alfonso playing the guitar with his eyes closed. Cassidy watched her, while trying not to look too obvious that she watched her.

She thought she saw Savannah's eyes welling up. Then Savannah flipped the CD case to look at the other side. She glanced at the track titles and all the other back cover copy, but her eyes were glazed over.

"You'll have to excuse me for a minute. I'll be right back," she murmured, not looking directly at Brandon or Cassidy.

Brandon's eyes followed her as she bolted to her bedroom, Alfonso's CD in hand. He had a bewildered look on his face.

After about five minutes, Savannah called out from her bedroom. "Brandon, would you ask Cassidy to come in here, please?"

He looked at Cassidy, looking as confused as ever.

Cassidy walked into Savannah's bedroom and shut the door behind her.

Savannah was sitting on the edge of the bed, crying. Cassidy sat herself down next to her and put her hand on Savannah's shoulder. Sitting next to her, she watched Savannah staring intently at Alfonso's picture on the CD, tears streaming down her cheeks, while her other hand fidgeted with the folds of her dress with her manicured fingers.

"You must think I'm strange," Savannah finally said, regaining her composure.

"Why would I think that, Savannah?"

"You're here no more than ten minutes and I'm bolting out the door like a bat out of hell. Please forgive my dreadful behavior. My manners are appalling–"

"There's nothing to forgive, and I would hardly call what you did dreadful," Cassidy interrupted her in mid-sentence. "And under the circumstances, I can't really blame you for reacting the way you did. I guess you never knew Alfonso was a recording artist?"

"I've spent the last twenty-six years trying to know as little as I could about his whereabouts. I was afraid if I knew where he was, I might leave everything and run to him. I wasn't prepared for the consequences that would bring. I've never even seen a single picture of him until Brandon handed me this CD." Tears began to fall heavy from her eyes, dripping down her chin and onto the straps and bodice of her dress, soaking through its cotton fabric.

Cassidy moved in a little closer, putting her arm around Savannah's back and grasping her forearm.

Savannah turned her gaze away from Alfonso's picture and stared out the window, beseeching the air above Mendocino. "How much of my journal did you read, Cassidy?" she asked.

"Every word. I hope you're not upset that I've read it. When I found it, I had no idea to whom it belonged ..."

"Upset? Why should I be upset? I'm actually relieved I can finally talk to someone who understands what I'm going through, or I think I'll go crazy. Thanks for being here."

"I met one of Alfonso's friends. His name is Zendrik. Have you heard of him?"

Savannah nodded. "Alfonso once told me about him. What did he tell you?"

"He told me what Alfonso went through after you sent him your letter."

Savannah began to weep again. "I'm afraid. I'm afraid," she cried, her eyes glazing over as though in a hypnotic trance.

"What are you afraid of, Savannah? I want to understand."

Savannah laid Alfonso's CD on her bedside table and began to wring her hands as she struggled for the words to say. "Five months ago, when I was still living in Lucerne, I woke up at midnight in a pool of sweat. I had a dream about Alfonso. In my dream, he said to me, 'I want to see my grandmother's painting, Savannah. Where have you hidden it?' That's all he said, and then he disappeared. In my dream, I went to the storage warehouse, where I had kept the painting. When I looked at the painting, my blood froze. The *pentimento* had completely surfaced, and it bore the grisly image of an ogre painted in ghastly colors the likes of which I've never seen, with a face so hideous that it turned my body into stone. When I tried to run or scream for help, I couldn't move. I could feel my heart beating loudly in my chest. The beating became louder and louder until it was deafening, and then, suddenly, my heart exploded and shattered me into a thousand pieces. That's when I woke up in a pool of sweat." Savannah stopped talking momentarily and closed her eyes, breathing heavily.

"Please go on."

"It was midnight when I awoke. I didn't sleep one more wink that night. I waited for daylight, for the time the storage warehouse would open. I hadn't seen the painting since the day I put it there when I first arrived in Lucerne. My hands were trembling just before I opened the storage unit to look at the painting, afraid of what I'd find there. What I found is that the *pentimento* had not turned into the image of an ogre, but the image of a man, such as you saw in the picture in the newspaper."

Cassidy was silent, waiting for Savannah to continue speaking.

"That's when I realized that I needed to return the painting to Alfonso. The very thought of it terrified me more than I could bear. That would mean that I would have to take myself out of hiding, and put myself in a place where he could find me. It was an agonizing thought, but that very day, I called the San Francisco Museum of Modern Art and told them I'd loan them the painting. I also started making immediate arrangements to move myself and all my belongings out of Switzerland and back to the States– Mendocino, in particular. Everything I did that day, that week…in fact, these last five months, have been excruciating to me in a way I can't explain. And yet I did it as though some unseen force was prompting my hands and feet to hurry, as though time was running out. But through it all, Cassidy, I've felt my body dying a slow, painful death."

As Savannah spoke, Cassidy stared at the floor while watching Savannah from the corner of her eye. Watching her face contort every time she winced, watching her body tremble almost to the point of convulsion, watching her hands clench and unclench erratically, and watching her tears continue to pour out as she spoke of her dream and its aftermath. She could almost see the complex cascade of associations in Savannah's mind, and the memories that erupted to torment her. They were as explosive as land mines of unknown locations.

"I would have thought you'd be happy to see Alfonso again… instead of being fearful like this…"

"One would think I would," Savannah replied. "But somehow, I can't get myself to feel joy. I can only feel trepidation. You may think I sound insane, but I have this feeling I can't explain that if and when I see Alfonso again, I will surely die."

It was the second time Savannah had spoken of death and dying. Cassidy tried to remember her conversation with Zendrik a few months back. He had recounted an incident that Alfonso had told him about his daughter, Cristina, and how, upon viewing Savannah's painting, *The Fern in the Clearing*, she had said, "The lady who made the painting…her daddy's gone away and her Mama died of a broken heart." Cassidy wondered whether Savannah believed subconsciously that she, too, would die of a broken heart just like her mother.

Suddenly, words, phrases and sentences started streaming from Savannah's lips in rapid succession, half of them spoken aloud, and half mumbled. Mountains of words, an outburst of thoughts, concepts and images, some coherent, and some incomprehensible. Cassidy was convinced she had kept all these words bottled up inside of herself for a long time. She didn't catch all of the words, but from what she could make out, Savannah was saying, "What if Alfonso doesn't love me anymore? How could I possibly expect him to still love me after all these years have passed? How do I even know he really loved me in the first place, and that it wasn't just my neediness that made me want to believe that someone could actually love me? How can I be sure it wasn't just my imagination, particularly since he's never told me he loved me? How could any man love me when my own father didn't love me?"

Cassidy found herself weeping now. She wondered how empty and meaningless her own life would be if she didn't have the comfort of knowing that her father loved her deeply and unconditionally. Savannah did not have that luxury.

After a long silence, Cassidy asked, "What is it that you fear most, Savannah?"

"I'm afraid that nothing is as I thought, or as I remembered. Do you know the real reason I wrote the letter to Alfonso ending our relationship? It's because I didn't want to stick around long enough to find out that he may not have really loved me. I preferred to say goodbye while I was still convinced he cared about me. So that I could continue to live in that fantasy. I couldn't bear it if his love for me wasn't real. I think I would die."

Cassidy stared at Savannah's face now, and wondered how a beautiful woman like her could ever be gripped by such self-loathing, and how she could feel so undeserving of love that she found it necessary to take leave of a relationship for fear it would turn out to be less than she wanted it to be. How miserable is a woman's existence if she feels she needs to invent a reality for herself wherein she could function–a world where she is cherished, loved and worthy.

All the while, Cassidy mourned how, in so doing, Savannah had deprived herself of experiencing the bliss of knowing that Alfonso Madrigál really did love her more than she could ever imagine a man could love a woman.

Cassidy's thoughts turned to Savannah's irrational visions of death. She had read somewhere that human beings are often unaware that myths wrought by emotionally charged events often masquerade as truths in their consciousness. Subconsciously, Savannah was probably unaware that her mind viewed her mother's death as having been caused by her broken heart. Savannah had allowed the myth to simmer over a long period of time until it had become as concrete and real as anything she could touch or taste.

"Savannah, I think I might have something that might be of some comfort to you. I'll be right back," Cassidy said, whereupon she walked down to the living room and picked up the canvas satchel she had set on the sofa. Her eyes spotted Brandon sitting out on the back porch.

She walked back to Savannah's bedroom and, without saying a word, pulled Zendrik's CD out of the satchel and handed it to her.

Savannah looked at the CD cover for a few moments. Her eyes widened when she realized the picture on the cover was Heaven's Bluff. Her mouth fell open when she read the title track, *Midwinter Turns to Spring*, recognizing the words she had written in her letter to Alfonso. Clearly bewildered, she turned her eyes towards Cassidy. "I don't understand. How did this happen?"

"After you ended your relationship with Alfonso, he poured his heart out to his friend, Zendrik. Told him everything about you and what you meant to him. Zendrik was so moved by what Alfonso told him that he was inspired to write the songs that are in this album. I know it must be hard to remember whether Alfonso's love for you was real, or if you just imagined the whole thing. Maybe these songs will help you remember."

Savannah looked dazed, barely able to comprehend what Cassidy said. Her eyes turned back to the CD in her hand, scanning the song titles on the back cover. A smile began to creep upon her lips when she opened the plastic jewel case, and there on the inside flap were the words of the poem Alfonso wrote for her.

> *Like the music of fresh fallen rain*
>   *and of swallow's wings*
>   *you are*
> *Like a young fern*
>   *uncoiling my fronds into a thousand tomorrows*
>   *am I*
> *Finding my way*
>   *to the clearing in the forest*
>   *and the serene, quiet shelter*
>   *of you*

And for the first time since Cassidy entered her room, Savannah looked tranquil.

CHAPTER 21
After the Thunderbolt Has Passed

SATURDAY MORNING • JULY 26 • 2003

Cassidy left Savannah alone in the living room to give her a chance to listen to Zendrik's CD on her own. She walked down the hall to the back porch, where she found Brandon on the porch swing, scribbling words onto a spiral notebook, his guitar lying on its side next to him. His mouth broke into a smile when he saw her coming, and she sat herself down on the Adirondack chair facing him.

She half expected him to ask what Savannah's emotional outburst was all about, and what they were talking about in her room for half an hour. But he didn't. In the days to come, Cassidy would discover that Brandon was the kind of person who seldom interfered in matters wherein he wasn't invited. Neither did he engage in idle gossip, nor try to pry anything out of anyone that they weren't ready to tell him. She liked that about him.

"Don't let me interrupt what you're doing," she said. "I just wanna sit here and relax a little bit," whereupon she laid her head back against the Adirondack chair, looked out upon the blue waters of the Pacific, and felt the ocean breezes on her face. She thought what a little slice of heaven this place was. Closing her eyes momentarily, she pondered how her life had changed virtually overnight, and how she had been transported to a place and time where music, love and poetry reigned supreme. One moment, she was just minding her own business, navigating the mundane issues of her life, when all of a sudden, she was thrust into the drama of a real-life paperback novel. Wasn't it just the other day that she found Savannah's journal–feeling like a star-struck fan of two screen idols, searching for a way to get backstage passes to watch them from the sidelines? All of a sudden, here she was–not backstage–but center stage in the unfolding drama of their lives.

Just then, Brandon's cell phone rang. Through half-closed eyes, Cassidy watched him pull the phone out of its case, which was hanging from a belt loop of his jeans. He glanced at the LCD screen to check the caller ID. With his other hand, he laid his pen down, closed the notebook, and got on his feet before answering the call.

"Hey," he said to the person on the other end of the line.

From where she sat, Cassidy could hear the voice of the caller coming in through the receiver. She could tell it was a woman.

"I'm in Mendocino visiting my mom," Brandon said. "I thought I told you."

She could hardly make out the caller's words, but whatever she said, she sounded quite annoyed. Her voice pitch went up by a few decibels, and her tirade went on for at least half a minute. Brandon's face remained calm, although he did walk down the porch steps and onto the lawn below.

"I won't be back till Sunday night," he said. After a long pause, "No, Allison, I didn't forget about Lindsey's party. I just didn't promise you I'd go." After another long silence, he said, "I'm sorry you feel that way. That was not my intention."

Before coming to Mendocino with Brandon, Cassidy had made a promise to herself that she would entertain no romantic fantasies about him. After nine years of dating, she felt burned out and had refrained from dating since she moved into 201 Pacific nine months before. Although she had never had a shortage of men asking her out, she chose to remain outside the dating scene for awhile. Even wondered whether she would ever want to date again. Her string of short-lived romances had left a bad taste in her mouth, and she didn't want to be disappointed yet again.

Cassidy Hamilton detested the man-pleasing culture that women's magazines had propagated among twenty-somethings. She was tired of competing with other women for men's attention. Tired of trying to be smarter, more beautiful, more successful or more sexually pleasing than the next woman. There would always be someone prettier, more intelligent, or better than herself in one thing or another, and it was as good a reason as any for a man to trade her in for a newer model. No, the next time, she would call the shots. The next man she dated would just have to love her for exactly who she was.

Cassidy wasn't surprised that she had swooned over Alfonso's far-flung ideal of love from his boyhood days. It had given her hope that it was possible for a woman to be loved unconditionally—and beyond all artifice. Brandon's voice interrupted her thoughts. "If that'll make you feel better, Allison, then do what you must do. But it sounds as though you're punishing me for something I didn't do."

Cassidy was amused. Brandon seemed to be navigating the treacherous waters of a woman's wrath. It was the first time she saw Brandon's carefree face turn somber. Nonetheless, he never lost his composure, even though he was obviously in a heated argument with this woman named Allison. Whatever she blasted at him, he countered with politeness and respect.

Brandon was on the phone for what seemed like twenty minutes. When he finally ended the call, he walked back up the porch steps.

Cassidy opened her eyes and he flashed a mischievous grin at her. The somber aspect that was on his face just a minute ago had disappeared completely.

He resumed his place on the porch swing and picked up his guitar.

"Play something for me," she said.

"I'll do better than that. I'll sing something for you."

"Will it be a flamenco song?"

"No, a *romancero*," he said.

"What's a *romancero*?"

"It's a Spanish ballad. Here goes ..."

He sang a melodic Spanish song in a voice that was fairly good. But it was the attitude with which he sang the song that struck Cassidy as remarkable. He didn't sing in the syrupy sweet singing style of balladeers, but instead gave the song an edge that made it more agreeable to her than the usual ballad. He seemed to tell a story with his face as well as his body. His shoulders were very expressive as they moved to the rhythm of the music, hunching forward dramatically in a half shrug while embracing the guitar in a semi-circle, not unlike the sensual flair with which a Latin dancer would handle his dance partner.

"Bravo," she said clapping her hands when he finished singing.

"Not bad, I guess," he said, as his fingers dove into a spirited Flamenco piece.

Cassidy listened as Brandon plucked complex melodies on his guitar, all the while hearing faint music coming from the living room where Savannah was listening to Zendrik's CD. Her thoughts turned to Alfonso and how enamored she had been with Alfonso's splendid view of love–and of women. In the universe of her experience, his perspectives were so supremely noble that she had come to revere him as a demi-god among mortal men.

Now, she gazed at Brandon as he played his guitar, wondering how much of Alfonso he had inherited. Brandon didn't tire of regaling Cassidy with one flamenco number after another, and she didn't tire of listening to him play.

"You're quite a performer," she said. He positively beamed over her compliment.

Cassidy suddenly realized what a wonderful time she was having. She felt a strange kinship with Brandon that she seldom felt with men she just met. But unlike the breathless tension that usually accompanied the start of her relationships with men, being with Brandon seemed agreeable and effortless to her. Best of all, it wasn't accompanied by the usual trepidation of wondering where the relationship would lead.

"Something smells good," Brandon exclaimed. Tantalizing aromas wafted out of the kitchen. "Shall we see what Mama's up to?"

"Sure," she said as she up and followed Brandon into the cottage. Zendrik's music was still playing in the living room, and Savannah was in the kitchen.

She was humming along with the music while stirring the contents of a sauce pan with a wooden spoon when Brandon and Cassidy walked in on her. She turned around and Cassidy noticed that her face was positively glowing. She looked blissful.

"I was just whipping us up something nice to eat. Lunch is almost ready," she said.

"I wish you would've told me you were starting lunch, Savannah. I would've liked to help out."

"Don't worry about it, Cassidy. I did most of the preparation for this meal last night. So all I had to do was just put it all together."

Looking at all the prepared food that was laid out on the kitchen counter, Cassidy exclaimed, "You call this a meal? It looks more like a gourmet feast to me! Let's see what you've got here… seared ahi tuna, garlic mashed potatoes, grilled Portobello mushrooms with caramelized onions…"

"And chocolate macadamia nut crème brulee for dessert—my favorite," Brandon chimed in. "My mother is always too modest about her cooking. In truth, she's probably the best cook in the world."

As Cassidy began setting the table, Brandon suddenly took notice of the music that was playing. After listening for a few moments, he asked, "Who's this you're listening to, Mama?"

"It's a singer named Zendrik. Cassidy just gave me the CD."

"It's pretty good. Sounds like something I've heard before."

"That could very well be, darling. This album has been around a long time. It was released the year you were born, actually. I'm surprised I've never heard the songs before."

"The album got a fair amount of airplay here in the States, from what I understand," Cassidy said. "You were living in Switzerland then. Maybe that's why?"

"You're probably right," Savannah replied, as she continued to hum along with the music.

෴

"*You* must have said something nice to her," Brandon said when Savannah was out of earshot. "I've never seen her this happy."

Cassidy smiled and said nothing, and he didn't press for an answer.

On Saturday afternoon, as wisps of fog gave way to clear blue skies, the threesome went down to the Village of Mendocino, where they poked around in Irish gift stores, bookstores and other quaint shops that lined historic Main Street. At the tail end of Main Street was a gallery with a yellow-and-white striped awning that bore the words "Fading Twilight" on the flap.

"You'll see some of my mother's best work here," Brandon whispered to Cassidy as he pushed the door open for her.

The gallery owner, a gray-haired, plump woman in her sixties, named Autumn Chenoweth, greeted Savannah warmly as they walked in the door; then she waddled over to Brandon and pinched his cheeks affectionately.

Autumn told Savannah that she had sold all but two of her art pieces, and asked when she might expect to bring in more of her art to sell.

"By next month, I hope," Savannah replied.

Brandon led Cassidy to Savannah's two remaining art pieces hanging on the east wall of the gallery. An audible gasp escaped Cassidy's lips when she saw Savannah's art. These were a far cry from the pieces hanging in the living room of Savannah's cottage.

One piece, titled *Abandonada*, had intricately detailed flower petals covering every square inch of the canvas. The flower petals were individually painted with gradations of monochromatic color that, when viewed as a whole, produced a ghostly image of a weeping woman among the petals.

"This is absolutely breathtaking!" Cassidy exclaimed, feeling goose bumps forming on her arms when she saw the subtle image appear, as if on cue.

Savannah was busy talking to Autumn and didn't hear Cassidy's remark.

"This is Mama's signature style," Brandon offered.

The second piece, titled *El Huérfano*, had every square inch of the canvas covered in leaves instead of petals. Leaves in every shade of gold, russet and burgundy, like the colors of leaves turning in the fall. They appeared to be irradiated, luminous, like the flower petals in *Abandonada*. Like the first piece, the leaves were individually tinted and shaded to reveal an underlying image, as though the leaves themselves were the canvas. Cassidy couldn't see the image at first, but when she took a step back, she perceived the image of a young boy squatting on the floor, his face buried in his lap.

"What makes her work amazing is that the underlying image is so vaporous and indistinct that you could miss it if you didn't look at it long enough. It makes it eerie, ethereal and melancholy at the same time," Cassidy said.

"Mama's art has always had a melancholy theme, for as long as I can remember."

"Does she always sign her name *Karenina*?"

"She used to sign her name *Savannah Curtis*. That was before I was born. Later, she decided to use her middle name, *Karenina*."

"I wonder why she did that."

"Mama has always kept a low profile…and has always stayed away from the public eye. I think she started using *Karenina* for anonymity."

After they left the gallery, they took a walk along the paths near the shops that overlooked the ocean. Savannah picked berries that grew wild along the grasses and trails. "These are edible berries, and they taste quite good," she said as she plucked a few of them and placed them in a handkerchief.

Among the berries grew a throng of white wild flowers. Brandon stooped to pluck one of the flowers, and took a step towards Cassidy. She was taken aback. "What are you doing?" she demanded.

"Don't worry. This is going to be painless," he replied, laughing at her curious reaction. Before Cassidy knew it, he had put the flower in her hair, nestled above her left ear. From that moment, she began to feel inexplicably warm feelings towards Brandon. The innocence of his gesture, and its lack of artifice, moved her. Instinctively, she started whistling the tune of the Cowsills song that Jack Hamilton sang, off-key and with made-up lyrics, to her years ago:

Flowers in your hair, flowers everywhere,
I love you, flower girl…

~

*O*n Saturday night, Savannah retired to her room early, and said she had some reading to catch up on. Clutched in her hand was her journal covered in handmade mulberry paper that Cassidy had given her earlier that day.

Brandon and Cassidy spent most of the night just talking. He talked about his childhood in Switzerland, his travels throughout Europe, his philosophies of God, life, love, art and music. And she talked about her dad, her work at the law office, and her own views of the world. In one of their conversations, Cassidy spoke of how she had been let down by love so often that she no longer believed in it. She found herself repeating Diane's mantra as if it were her own, "It just goes to show that love always fails. You can never count on it because it will betray you in the end."

Brandon threw her a sideways glance. "I hope you don't mind my saying, but you're quite a cynic for one so young," he said. "Do you make it a habit to compartmentalize things that way?"

"What do you mean?"

"With all due respect, you seem inclined to relegate things into neat little pigeon holes of your own design."

"And that's bad because…?"

"Because the narrower you set the borders on your beliefs, the more likely you are to be imprisoned by them. You run the risk of being unable to consider other ways of looking at things."

"Well, I'm not that way about all things. I'm just a little bit jaded about love."

"But that's exactly what I'm talking about. Love, of all things, is something that has far greater magnitude than any of us can fathom. How can you diminish it by labeling it as one thing, and ignoring all the other wonderful things it could be? Wouldn't you rather define love by its possibilities rather than its limitations?"

"I guess I could…provided I'd actually seen evidence of those possibilities with my own eyes."

"Have you ever considered that there might be possibilities out there that you may have never perceived with your own eyes, that you haven't yet begun to envision or comprehend, and yet you deprive yourself of knowing those possibilities because you choose to view love the only way you know?"

Cassidy felt embarrassed by her own narrow-mindedness. Brandon's question was a legitimate one, but no one had ever before challenged the comfortable beliefs that had become a part of her.

Brandon continued speaking, his eyes gazing up at the night sky. "The world is nothing if not a quantum soup of infinite possibilities, of which God is the Master Brewer." Then, turning his eyes towards Cassidy, he said, "All the possibilities are within your reach, and whichever ones you choose to focus on will determine the life you live. You alone create your own experience of the world by how you represent the world to your own mind. Think about it, Cassidy. Your life is just a printout of those thoughts with which you consistently fill your mind. *As a man thinketh, so is he.*"

Cassidy began to feel like a small-minded country bumpkin being led by the hand to ogle the skyscrapers of enlightenment. She looked back at all the naïve beliefs that she had allowed to govern her life, even paralyze her at times. She realized that all the years of men-bashing that she had engaged in with her female friends were nothing more than gripe sessions of women who have been hurt by men, but which had nothing to do with the true nature of love.

Cassidy found herself thinking about Brandon's qualities. He was handsome, intelligent, successful in his chosen profession, cultured, and had a wonderful sense of humor, uncommon wisdom and impeccable manners. She also sensed a deep spirituality in him, one which successfully combined Christian doctrines with quantum physics. She reminded herself that she mustn't entertain romantic notions about him. *Anyway, a man like him probably has a string of ladies hanging around him all the time,* Cassidy thought.

"I hope you don't think I'm prying, Brandon, but what's in the notebook?"

"The notebook?"

"Earlier today, I saw you scribbling on a spiral notebook."

"Oh, that," he said. "That's just a collection of my feeble attempts at poetry."

"Can you read me one of your poems?"

Brandon hesitated for a moment, saying, "My scribblings are just philosophical ramblings set into free verse, and they're far from polished. But if you insist…"

"I insist."

"Okay, I'll read you one poem then. But just one."

"Agreed."

Brandon left to fetch the spiral notebook and reappeared after a few minutes. He flipped through the pages of the notebook, looking for something suitable to read to her. "Okay, I've chosen one," he said finally.

"Let's hear it."

"I call this *The Dreamer or the Dream.* Here goes:

I am not I
  no more than you are you
For you and I are unsuspecting bursts of promise
  waiting to explode in a dance far more splendid than life
And I know not whether I am the rumba or the tango
  or the waltz
And you, in your twilight slumber, know not if you exist
  or if your life is the ethereal dream of the Supreme dreamer
And the dream which you thought was your own
  is it just a dream within a higher dream
    in an upward spiral that leads to the eternal?
Or is it the path that the Supreme dreamer dreamt for you
  to get to where you're going?
Are you the dreamer or the dream
  or are you one and the same?

"That's brilliant, Brandon."

"Thanks," he said, ceremoniously snapping the notebook shut with the same flourish that he thumped his guitar at the end of a song.

"How'd you learn to write poetry?"

"Like most people, I'm self-taught. As I said, my poetry is nothing more than my philosophical insights set into free verse. My mother told me that my father used to write poetry. Maybe some of that rubbed off on me, I don't know. She once read me a poem he wrote. I'll never forget it. 'Like the music of fresh fallen rain and of swallow's wings you are, like a young fern uncoiling leafy fronds into a thousand tomorrows am I, finding my way to the clearing in the forest…'"

"…and the serene, quiet shelter of you," Cassidy continued.

Brandon cocked his head to the side. "Why am I not surprised that you know this poem? I still think you're with the CIA."

"Yeah…the Culinary Institute of America, that is." They both laughed.

"The Culinary Institute, huh? Well, that remains to be proven, woman."

"Man, wait till I cook up a storm for you tomorrow!"

"Is that a threat?" he asked, recoiling his shoulders in mock defiance.

"No, it's a promise."

"Okay, Sugar Pie, you're on."

Her heart did a somersault when she heard him call her "Sugar Pie." Inside, she battled warm feelings towards Brandon even while she reprimanded herself for being charmed by a man who made her feel the way her dad did. Scolded herself for falling for what she suspected was a manipulative ploy to endear her to him.

⁂

The church, built of redwood and accented by stunning stained glass windows overlooking the Big River Beach, loomed up ahead as Brandon swerved into the parking lot. Savannah was saying that the Mendocino Presbyterian Church was the oldest church in continuous use in California. She had chosen to worship there ever since she moved to Mendocino a few months before.

The 8:30 service was small and intimate. As they walked through the entry doors, they received warm handshakes and hugs from the greeters, something to which Cassidy wasn't accustomed. It gave her a sense of belonging, of being a part of a family–an experience she had never had in a church setting before.

When Savannah had suggested on Saturday afternoon that the

three of them attend church service the next morning, Cassidy had been taken aback, not knowing how to react. She had agreed to go, but was still uncertain as to whether it was out of politeness that she went along with Savannah's request.

Cassidy's form of worship was so far removed from the practice of attending church services. Her mom, Diane, was not a church-goer, and if it had been up to Diane, Cassidy would never have attended church while she was growing up. Jack Hamilton, on the other hand, wanted to make sure Cassidy had the proper religious upbringing, and took her with him to attend Mass on Sunday mornings at the Holy Redeemer Catholic Church in Burlingame. As a child, she never really liked attending Mass. She wasn't particularly fond of its circumscribed rituals and the old-fashioned hymns that they sang, but she did enjoy just spending time with her dad–in church or out. When Jack Hamilton died almost six years earlier, she had stopped going to church altogether–even stopped praying–and thought that she had lost her faith for good.

Then one night, something happened that changed her faith and her relationship with God. Several months before, shortly after she moved in to her Victorian apartment at 201 Pacific, she had an epiphany of sorts. It was almost midnight and she was awakened from deep sleep by the howling sound of wind gusts entering a window she had left open. As she walked to the window to close it, the howling suddenly stopped and was replaced by complete and utter silence. The silence brought with it a deep, all-consuming peace that engulfed and permeated her body. Then, her skin began to tingle all over as though a pleasant electric current ran through it. Her ears heard no audible sound but her soul discerned soundless words that uttered, *"I am God. I'm still here, and I'm waiting for you."* Thereafter, an unseen presence swooped down upon her, filling her entire being with a light that was so radiant that it seemed almost palpable. Tears began streaming from her eyes on their own accord, and she fell to her knees without knowing why. When she told the story of the epiphany to her friend, Morgan, later that week, Cassidy had said, "From that moment on, I knew without a doubt that God exists…and that he loves me and takes care of me." Her supernatural encounter with God had restored her soul that had been spiritually bankrupt since the day Jack Hamilton died. Her orphaned heart had found a home in God.

Whereas she had previously regarded God as some divine entity somewhere out in the heavens, not really having a hand in her everyday life, after her epiphany God became a person with whom she had a relationship, with whom she had daily conversations. She realized then that this must be the real essence of faith. It was never about the religiosity espoused by organized religion, nor the pseudo-spirituality embraced by the spiritual junkies. Faith was simply a matter of having a personal relationship with the Almighty. Therefore, her worship of God consisted of her daily conversations with him, and she had not found it necessary to go to church to have those conversations.

Yet, here in the intimacy of the Mendocino Presbyterian Church, she suddenly no longer felt that attending church was just an outdated obligation, but rather another opportunity to experience God together with other people. *What a concept,* she said to herself. *Why, I just might end up liking church after all.*

Cassidy was flanked by Brandon on her left and Savannah on her right when the pastor called for everyone to join hands together around the communion table. From the corner of her eye, she noticed Brandon observing her with contemplative eyes. Her insides jumped, wondering what made him look at her that way. He had always maintained a cool, free-spirited attitude around her, and this seemed out of character for him. She decided to dismiss it as nothing more than the intimacy of the church getting the better of him.

After the service ended, they visited a local market for some provisions, then returned to Savannah's cottage.

"You get a break from cooking this morning, Mama. Cassidy has promised to show off her culinary skills today by making us brunch," Brandon said, winking at Cassidy.

"I'm fixin' to stir us up a mess o' somethin'. But no mattah what I cook, boy, it ain't evah gonna be as good as yo' Mama's cookin'," she said in the best Southern drawl she could manage.

"Well, darlin', we'all shall see about that," Brandon retorted, mimicking her Southern accent.

Savannah observed the banter between Brandon and Cassidy in amusement, and looked pleased that they were getting along so well.

"Okay, Cassidy. I hereby give you full command over my kitchen," Savannah declared with mock formality.

"Whoa! Consider yourself highly favored in the Fairchild home, Missy. My mother has never relinquished command of her kitchen to anyone before–not even Nana Sabine."

They all laughed.

Cassidy proceeded to prepare her grandmother's recipe for cornmeal pancakes. For a brief moment, she recalled the misshapen pancakes she had made for her dad on Father's Day, and remembered that it was the only time she ever saw him cry. When the cornmeal pancakes were done, she set them on the table with Canadian maple syrup. Then, she scrambled eggs with chives, *prosciutto* and *crème fraiche* and served them with toasted *focaccia* bread with melted cheese and smoked bacon. Lastly, she pulled out the tray of roasted red potatoes with rosemary that she had popped in the oven just before she started whipping up the pancake batter, slid them into a serving dish, and set the dish on the table.

"This is wonderful, Cassidy," Savannah gushed. "A perfect blend of old-fashioned and avant-garde cuisine. You were being modest when you said your cooking could never be as good as mine. This is delicious!"

"That's because she's with the CIA," Brandon teased, looking obviously pleased with her cooking himself.

"The CIA?" Savannah queried.

"The Culinary Institute of America," Brandon and Cassidy said in unison, laughing gleefully.

～

*B*randon lifted the last pieces of luggage into the trunk of his car, then walked back to where Savannah was standing on the cobblestone pathway. He kissed her goodbye on the forehead.

Cassidy thanked her for her hospitality, and gave her a warm hug.

"Thank you so much for coming, Cassidy," Savannah said. "You don't know how much your visit has meant to me. My home is open to you anytime, and I hope you find the chance to come back soon."

"Don't worry, Mama. She'll be back soon if I have to drag her out here myself," Brandon said as he opened the car door for her.

The trip back to the city couldn't have been more pleasant. Brandon kept Cassidy in stitches as he told of adventures and misadventures of his childhood and adolescent years.

Throughout the long drive, Cassidy noticed that Brandon would occasionally observe her with the same contemplative eyes she had seen earlier in church. Then, when he noticed that she was aware of his gaze, he would immediately revert back to his carefree persona.

They arrived back in San Francisco at six, and as Brandon walked her up the steps of her apartment, he said, "If you're not doing anything on Wednesday night, I'd like you to join me for dinner at the *Casbah*."

"Isn't that where you play flamenco guitar?"

"Yes. We start playing at ten so there'll be plenty of time for us to have a nice dinner before then."

"What would Allison have to say about your asking me to dinner?"

"Why would Allison have to know?"

"Isn't she your girlfriend?"

"I don't have a girlfriend. Allison's just a friend of mine. We were dating casually for a few months. If you're referring to that phone call I got from her last Saturday, that's just the way Allison is. She tends to get too territorial about me sometimes even though we're no longer dating."

Cassidy agreed to meet Brandon for dinner on Wednesday night. The next morning, when she walked into her office, there was a stunning floral arrangement of fragrant stargazer lilies and red roses accented with seeded eucalyptus in a tall crystal vase on her desk.

She was stunned by the note from Brandon that came with the flowers. It said: *I find a semblance of freedom every time I choose to love you.* Her eyes zeroed in on the word "love" and remained transfixed for what seemed a full minute or more. Her first impulse was to think Brandon was playing some kind of joke on her. *How could he use the word "love" in such a wanton manner?* She thought, *How gullible does he think I am to believe that he has fallen in love with me after having known me for nine days?*

An avalanche of memories came crashing down on her. Memories of a guy who bought tickets for a concert that was several months away with the objective of convincing her that he was planning on a long-term relationship with her, when all he really wanted was a roll in the hay that night. Memories of another man who said, "I love you" and, "I can't wait to spoil you" just to score a homerun as quickly as possible. Memories of yet another man who gave her a set of keys to his apartment, and another who drove her to Marin County and showed her a parcel of land he said he just bought, and on which he said he'd build her the house of her dreams. These men pretended they were in it for the long haul, but they were gone as soon as they got what they wanted, or as soon as they'd had their fill of her.

She had thought Brandon was different, but it now looked like he was just like the rest of them. He just had a more sophisticated modus operandi. He would charm women with his wit and his wisdom, and tug at their heartstrings a little, and when they were sufficiently primed, he'd spring the "love" word, send flowers and slide right into the same tricks men do to get women in the sack. Cassidy was convinced that even his timing was calculated. Flowers and words of love on Monday would translate to a night of passion on Wednesday. The artifice and the choreography of it all disgusted her, but she wasn't going to fall for it this time.

By the time mid-morning arrived, her disgust had turned into outright infuriation. Just then, the phone rang. It was Brandon. He couldn't have called at a worse time. She was seething mad, and determined to take it out on him.

"Oh, hi Brandon. How are you?" she asked in the most frigid voice she could muster.

"Whoa! What happened? Are you having a bad day?" he asked, sensing the foul mood she was in.

"Yes, the worst day."

"Well, didn't the flowers cheer you up even a little?" he asked in his usual charming way.

Cassidy was quiet for a moment, not even wanting to thank him for the flowers. Then, she hurriedly said to him, "Would you mind if I called you back later?"

"Sure, Cassidy. I'll wait for your call."

She attended a meeting in the conference room later that day, and when she returned to her office at a quarter past five, she noticed that Brandon had left her an e-mail message.

His message read:

Hi Cassidy,
I hope you're really just so busy that you haven't had a chance to return my call. But in case I'm wrong, and what's really bothering you is the note that came with the flowers, I'm truly sorry. But midwinter turns to spring and I don't ever wish to regret things I never said to you.
Brandon

Cassidy buried her face in her hands and chastised herself for the fool she'd been. She thought, *How could I allow my jaded self to turn the sincere sentiments of this wonderful man into an opportunity to vent my negative views about men? Have I come to distrust men so much that I couldn't recognize someone who had none but the purest intentions? How blind am I that I could not see Brandon falling in love with me because I was too busy pretending I was not falling in love with him?*

She wondered whether to send Brandon a reply e-mail or call him up on the phone, but before she had the chance to decide, another message in her e-mail box caught her eye. The subject line read:

SUBJECT: RE: About Savannah Curtis ...

It was a reply from Alfonso. She immediately opened the e-mail, and read Alfonso's message:

Dear Secret Friend,
Whoever you are, I want to thank you for e-mailing me the whereabouts of Savannah Fairchild. I've made plans to fly into San Francisco. I'll be arriving late at night on the 27th of July. I plan to spend the night at the St. Francis Hotel and drive to Mendocino the next day to see Savannah. Many thanks again for your kind e-mail.
Sincerely,
Alfonso

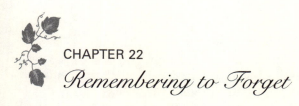

CHAPTER 22
Remembering to Forget

*I*t was on the twenty-seventh of July that Savannah met with her car accident on Highway 28 while driving towards San Francisco. The third of August was the day Alfonso walked into Room 739 of the Mendocino Coast Hospital with a brown linen portfolio clutched in his hand. It was then that he learned that Savannah sustained amnesia as a result of her accident.

The following day, after having spent nine days in the hospital, Savannah was discharged from the hospital. At ten in the morning, Brandon and Cassidy drove her back to the cottage.

Cassidy thereafter returned to San Francisco, while Brandon made plans to stay in Mendocino for as long as it took to make the necessary arrangements for Savannah's care.

※

*I*n the late afternoon on the fourth of August, Alfonso Madrigál parked his rented convertible in front of the yellow cottage at 335 Castlebrook Lane. He picked up the cellophane-wrapped Kahili ginger flowers that he had laid on the passenger seat, stepped out from behind the wheel of his car and walked up the cobblestone pathway to the front door. He rang the doorbell.

Brandon came to the door. He smiled when he saw Alfonso.

"*Señor* Madrigál, I'm Brandon Fairchild, Savannah's son. *Encantado en conocerlo.* Pleased to meet you," he said, holding out his hand.

Alfonso shook Brandon's hand. "*Mucho gusto.* I'm pleased to meet you, too, Brandon. *Habla Español?*"

"*Un poco.* Just enough to get by. Please come in," he said, stepping aside to let Alfonso through the door. "I see you've brought Kahili ginger flowers. My mother's favorite.

"Please have a seat while I go get her." Brandon went down the hall to Savannah's bedroom. He knocked softly on her door, and from where Alfonso sat, he heard him say, "Mama, there's someone here to see you." He barely heard her muffled response from within the room.

"She'll be out in a moment," Brandon said to Alfonso when he returned to the living room.

"*Muchas gracias.*"

"May I call you Alfonso?"

201

"Certainly."

"Alfonso, would you care for something to drink …?"

"No, thank you."

Brandon sat himself down on the settee that was situated perpendicular to the sofa, where Alfonso sat. "I have to say this is such a pleasant surprise. I've been a fan of yours for many years, and I had no idea my mother and you knew each other. When Cassidy told me you visited her at the hospital yesterday, it came as a shock to me."

"I'm glad you like my music, Brandon. And yes, I've known Savannah a long time, back when she used to live in San Francisco. But I've lost touch with her. I didn't know she had a son. I suppose your father is Russell Parker?"

Brandon found it odd that in the space of three weeks, two people had asked him if Russell Parker was his father. First, Cassidy, and now Alfonso. Whoever this Russell Parker was, his mother had never spoken of him.

"No. Russell Parker isn't my father. My father was someone I never knew. He died right before I was born."

"*Me siento.* I'm sorry to hear that."

"Oh, don't be," Brandon said. Then, changing the subject, "By the way, I saw you in concert in Madrid a few years ago. You probably don't remember, but I even went backstage with a friend of mine who knows you. His name is Hector Fernandez.…"

"Yes, now I know why you look so familiar. You're the young man who told me you were just learning to play *guitarra flamenca.*"

"Yes, that was me," Brandon said, grinning. "I'm surprised you remember."

"Well, you reminded me so much of myself when I was just getting started. So how's your guitar-playing now, Brandon?"

"I think my skills are adequate. My playing is fair, but I've still got far to go. I took formal lessons for two years in Madrid, and I've practiced until I thought my fingers would bleed, but I'm still not where I want to be in my playing."

"If you like, I can show you a different way of learning that will get you where you want faster. Since you already know the mechanics, I can teach you how to become your own best teacher."

"That'd be awesome! I'll hold you to that promise, man."

"*Ciertamente,*" Alfonso said. "Not many people know this, Brandon, but in many ways, it was Savannah who taught me how to play."

"My mother?" Brandon was taken aback.

"Sure, I learned the mechanics of playing back when I was a teenager in Málaga, but I was a mediocre, tourist-pleasing guitarist for years, hardly worthy of being called a Flamenco. It was Savannah who made me realize I could play from the spirit."

"Wow, I guess this is the week for surprises. Who'd have thought my mother had anything to do with your guitar skills?"

"Not only that. Before I met Savannah, I was strictly a guitarist. It wasn't until I met her that I became a singer as well."

"Did she make you do it?" Brandon asked, chuckling. "Mama has a way of making people step up to the plate and seize the opportunity."

"In a manner of speaking, I guess she made me do it. It's a long story that I'll tell you someday."

"I hope you don't mind my asking. How did you meet my mother?"

"I attended one of her lectures on Picasso, and she helped me authenticate a painting that once belonged to my grandmother."

"You don't mean the painting that Mama loaned to the San Francisco Museum of Modern Art, do you?"

"Yes, that's the one."

"So you own that painting? It's probably worth a fortune now, I'm sure you've heard...."

"If it's ever put to auction, I'm sure it would be worth much. But that's up to Savannah. I actually gave that painting to her a long time ago. It belongs to her now."

"She said a friend had left it in her custody, but that he'd be back someday to claim it."

"Well, her friend is back, but not to claim the painting. I gave it to her to keep."

Just then, Alfonso heard Savannah's footsteps as she walked across the hardwood floorboards of the hallway toward them. He looked up and there she stood, the Savannah of his memories–framed in the hall archway the way she'd been framed in the doorway of his mind for so many years. She looked to him every bit as graceful, elegant and beautiful as he remembered. And she was still the only woman who could arrest him in his tracks and lead him into loving contemplation.

"Mama," Brandon said out of habit. Seeing no response, he addressed her by her name instead. "Savannah ..."

She turned to look at Brandon, showing no signs of recognition. "I'm sorry, who are you?"

"I'm your son, Brandon," he answered. "And this," he said, directing his eyes across the room, "is your friend, Alfonso Madrigál."

Savannah's eyes fell upon Alfonso. Alfonso thought he saw a flicker of recognition but dismissed it as a figment of his hopes. He stepped up closer to her, took her right hand in his, and brought it to his lips, kissing it. Savannah's face flushed. After a few moments, her eyes widened. Her lips began to move, as though trying to say something to Alfonso, but no words came.

Just then, she wrinkled her nose, and her hands clutched her abdomen. "Something is making me nauseated. There's a very strong scent in here. Where is it coming from?" she asked as her eyes searched the room. "I think it's those," she said, pointing to the Kahili ginger flowers. "Would you take them away, please?"

Brandon darted a glance at Alfonso, and said, "Of course, Mama. Right away." He lifted the cellophane-wrapped flowers from the coffee table. Before taking them to the kitchen, he said to Alfonso, under his breath, "You'll have to excuse her. She has this new aversion to anything but the most subtle scents."

Savannah sat herself down on the sofa on the opposite end from where Alfonso was sitting, casting sideway glances at him as she did. "What was your name again?"

"Alfonso Madrigál."

"I have a problem remembering. Are we related in any way?"

"No, I'm a friend of yours … from a long time ago."

"How long ago?"

"Twenty-six years."

"How old am I–do you know?"

"You turned fifty-three on the ninth of February."

"I'm that old?" she asked, visibly dismayed.

"You're only as old as you feel," Alfonso said.

"Then, I must be twenty-three," she said, smiling.

Savannah's smile. There it was. It was the memory of that smile that had brightened his days, even when time and distance separated them.

Alfonso looked directly into her eyes, hoping that if their eyes met, she would see something–anything–that was familiar about him. He projected thoughts at her. *You know me, Savannah.*

Savannah was visibly uncomfortable, and she fidgeted with the folds of her dress to escape his stare.

"Where are you from, Alfonso Madrigál?"

It startled him when she spoke his name. "I'm from the city of Málaga in the south of Spain."

"Hmmm… Is that the place with the resort beaches, the sweet wine and the best fried fish in Spain?"

"*Sí, sí.* That's right!" Alfonso's face lit up, encouraged by her memory of what he had told her, word-for-word, at Café Marcel. "And it's also the birthplace of Picasso," he added, hoping to jog her memory a little more.

She was silent for a moment, deep in thought. Then she winced, as if in pain. "Picasso…Picasso. Does he play the guitar?"

It was apparent to Alfonso that Savannah's memory was not only checkered, but jumbled as well. However, he was encouraged that she did remember certain things. "No, Picasso was a famous artist. He did create a painting called *Guernica*. I'm the one who plays the guitar, and my guitar's name is *Guernica*. Do you remember, Savannah?"

She was frowning now. "I'm trying to remember, but when I think too hard, it gives me a headache. I'm sorry. I'm going to have to lay my head down. You'll have to excuse me." She stood up abruptly and walked down the hall. Instead of going to her bedroom at the end of the hall, she entered one of the guest bedrooms.

Brandon observed her walking into the wrong bedroom, and quickly walked in after her. "Maybe it would be better if you rest in your bedroom, Mama. You'll be much more comfortable there." Savannah followed him quietly.

When Brandon returned to the living room, he glanced at Alfonso apologetically. Then he sank himself onto the sofa and let out an enormous sigh.

"I can only imagine how hard this must be for you," Alfonso ventured.

"Put it this way. She's only been discharged from the hospital this morning, and I've only been taking care of her for barely six hours, and already I'm exhausted. But don't get me wrong. It's not the physical exhaustion but the emotional exhaustion that's draining to me. I have to grapple with my own feelings about her memory loss, and I guess the seriousness of the situation is just dawning on me now. It's not going to be easy."

"I'm sure it won't."

"I'm not sure if you already know this, Alfonso, but she has two kinds of amnesia. The first one is *retrograde* amnesia, wherein she remembers very little of what happened to her prior to her accident. That's the part that's okay for me to deal with. It's the other part that's tricky—the *anterograde* amnesia—which means she has difficulty forming new memories after the onset of the amnesia. She'll remember that George W. Bush is the President of the United States because that's an old memory her brain has retained, but it's the new memories she has trouble holding on to. You saw how she forgot who I was, even though I've told her my name every day for the past several days. She'll forget faces and conversations like the one you just had with her today. You try your best to make her remember, only to have her erase everything and start again the next day, or even the next minute. That's what's exhausting."

Alfonso turned pensive, clinging to every word Brandon was saying, not realizing until now how serious Savannah's condition really was.

"Then, of course, there's all those headaches. The doctors say we can look forward to a lot of those. They've prescribed some strong medicine, in case the headaches become severe. She'll also be increasingly irritable and intolerant of many things, even things she used to like...like Kahili ginger flowers."

"Who do you have in mind to take care of her, Brandon?"

"I've taken a whole week off from work, so I'll be taking care of her this week. Dr. Jackson says that the amnesia is severe enough that she requires a supervised living situation. So I'll be interviewing care providers starting tomorrow."

"You may not have to," Alfonso said quietly as he reached for his cell phone to make a call.

CHAPTER 23
One Profound Utterance of the Heart

MONDAY NIGHT • AUGUST 4 • 2003

It was early in the evening when the phone in the living room rang. Brandon walked over and answered it.

"It's the call from Madrid you've been waiting for," he said, handing the phone to Alfonso.

Alfonso took the phone from him. He wasted no time with pleasantries. "*Escúchame,* Gustavo." Then, he proceeded to give rapid instructions in Spanish.

Brandon couldn't help but overhear Alfonso's end of the conversation. The man on the other end of the line was Gustavo Martinez, who managed Alfonso's concert tours. Alfonso was telling him that he was going to have to cancel all his scheduled concerts. Gustavo must have protested because Alfonso appeared to say something accompanied with hand gestures to prompt Gustavo to calm down.

Alfonso proceeded to say that if it weren't for something of utmost importance, he wouldn't do something as drastic as this. He suggested to Gustavo that he tell everyone Alfonso had to take care of a family emergency.

From where he sat, Brandon could hear Gustavo through the receiver speaking in loud tones. "*Hasta cuándo,* Alfonso?" Until when?

Alfonso sighed and said he'd let Gustavo know. Then he said, yes, he realized there'd be hell to pay, but he was willing to pay the price.

Brandon was stunned. Not until just the day before did he even know that Alfonso Madrigál knew his mother. Today, he was beginning to realize that not only did he know her, but that he cared about her deeply enough to rearrange his life for her. *Who is this man,* he wondered, *and who was he to my mother?*

He was even more baffled when he called Nana Sabine in Switzerland to ask for her opinion about Alfonso's offer to be Savannah's care provider. Nana seemed surprisingly overjoyed. She told Brandon that Alfonso was one of Savannah's closest friends, and she could think of no one who could care for Savannah better. Brandon was astonished. He had never heard his mother speak of Alfonso before.

Alfonso finally finished his phone conversation with Gustavo.

He slowly put the receiver back on its cradle, as if in deep thought.

"You're sure this is what you want to do?" Brandon asked him again. "Being my mother's care provider is going to be a tough job–especially in her condition. It's a round-the-clock thing."

"I can handle it."

"And you do know that her amnesia may be permanent, right? It may take a long time before she regains her memory…if ever."

Despite Brandon's warnings, Alfonso remained unwavering in his intent. "If it were the other way around, I think Savannah would do the same for me."

Alfonso's statement left Brandon even more bewildered. He knew Savannah to be a caring mother, but he had never known her to care about any man at all. She never even spoke fondly of his father, Warren Fairchild. It was as though Warren Fairchild never even figured in her life at all. Savannah had always maintained an indifferent attitude towards men. Brandon pondered how little he really knew about her.

"Where do I sign?" Alfonso asked presently, as he picked up the Caregiver's Agreement where Brandon had left it on the side table.

Brandon watched as Alfonso filled out the Agreement in triplicate. He was not surprised when it came to the caregiver's remuneration that Alfonso put down a zero. Brandon couldn't help but wonder that a man would actually want to make this great sacrifice for a friend he hasn't seen in twenty-six years. Wondered if he himself would ever do it for any of his friends.

He had had reservations about leaving his mother in the care of someone he barely knew, particularly because Alfonso was a man. He would have preferred a female care provider. But Nana Sabine seemed to have no qualms about Alfonso, and had enthusiastically given her approval of Alfonso as Savannah's care provider.

⁓

Monday morning dawned upon Mendocino like a meadow lark descends upon a honeysuckle. Early light was beginning to crawl into view outside as Alfonso walked down the hall of the cottage in half-darkness towards the kitchen.

Brandon had driven back to San Francisco the night before, and Alfonso faced the first day of being Savannah's care provider. *Supervised living situation* was the term they used. He pondered the implications of his responsibility as he brewed a pot of coffee.

Caring for Savannah wouldn't be like caring for a child because she functioned like an adult in every sense. Neither was it like caring for an invalid because Savannah was not physically incapacitated in any way, nor was she senile. In fact, she seemed normal for the most part, except for the frequent headaches, the irritability, and the frequent lapses in her memory.

Alfonso was thankful that he had spent the previous week taking turns with Brandon to watch over Savannah. It gave him the opportunity to become emotionally grounded, and not grieve every time he saw Savannah look at him through a stranger's eyes. It also gave him the chance to get accustomed to Savannah's new personality.

She was unlike the Savannah he once knew. The Savannah he had known was timid, reserved, fragile, and plagued by fears he could not comprehend. The new Savannah was headstrong, outspoken, fearless and oblivious to the wounds of her past. Savannah's new persona was not altogether unattractive to him, just different. In some ways, even better.

Alfonso pondered these things as he sipped his morning coffee, perched on a kitchen stool.

Savannah appeared in the kitchen in her bare feet and a pink nightgown. Her hair was brushed neatly, her face scrubbed clean and fresh, her teeth a dazzling white. She looked ravishing to him even without a stitch of make-up on.

"*Buenos dias*, Savannah."

"*Buenos dias*…uh…" she muttered, and trailed off, trying to remember his name. "I'm sorry…I remember your face, but I can't remember your name."

Alfonso had gotten used to Savannah not remembering his name, even after he'd told her every day the previous week. It no longer bothered him. Today, he didn't feel the need to tell her again.

"Don't worry about remembering my name," he said, as he poured her a cup a coffee. Black, the way she wanted it. The Savannah of old always preferred her coffee with a little milk or cream.

Savannah's face flushed when he handed her the coffee cup cradled in a saucer.

"Are you going to live here from now on?" she asked.

Alfonso smiled. She had asked him that question every day since the day he arrived. "Yes, *amorcito*. I'm your care provider. I'm here to take care of you."

"But I don't need to be taken care of," she protested. "I can take care of myself."

"You've been in an accident, *corazón*," he said patiently. "You have amnesia, and I'm going to be here until you're better." He had had this same conversation with her many times before.

"Oh," she said, raising her eyebrows and looking surprised, as though she had heard it for the first time. "Amnesia…you mean loss of memory? Have I lost my memory?"

It always seemed like a rude awakening to her, no matter how many times she said it. Alfonso tried to make light of it. "Don't worry, *mi corazón*. You'll be okay soon."

"My name is Savannah Curtis, isn't it?"

"*Muy bien*. Yes, it is," Alfonso replied. It was a good start. At least she remembered her maiden name. Deep inside, though, he knew not to get his hopes up too high. It was more than likely she would forget her name just as soon as she remembered it.

"Do you remember your son's name?" Alfonso ventured.

"I don't have a son. I've never even been married."

"How about my name? Do you remember who I am?"

"I told you before. I remember your face, but I can't remember your name. I'm sorry...."

"Don't be sorry, *amorcito*," he said, kissing her hand. "Let's try something else. *Cierra tus ojos.* Close your eyes."

Savannah closed her eyes, and Alfonso took her hand and placed it on his chest. "Now, what do you hear?"

"Your heart beating?"

"Okay, listen closely. What do you think my heart is telling you? Just take your time and just feel what my heart is saying."

Savannah stood motionless, keeping her eyes closed, not saying a word. Alfonso allowed the undulant river of his unspoken feelings flow to her in silence.

A few moments later, Savannah's hand started to quiver slightly. The quivering turned to trembling. Then, she opened her eyes and smiled shyly at him.

"I feel like a...like a well-watered garden," she said, "beside a running stream whose waters never fail."

Her words fell upon his ears like dew on the grass. He remembered someone once saying that all the passionless speculations of the mind are not worth one profound utterance of the heart. It overjoyed him that Savannah had interpreted the pulsations of his heart as a nurturing spring.

He wondered if the heart had its own memory. Would Savannah's heart remember this moment, even while her brain found it difficult to form new memories?

"Speaking of gardens," she continued, "I think I'll do a little gardening today."

"*Esta bien.* Go ahead and spend time in the garden, and I'll prepare an early lunch for us before we go to Berkeley."

"We're going to Berkeley today?"

"Yes, you have an appointment with Gordon Marsh at 4:30 this afternoon."

"Who's Gordon Marsh?"

"He's a hypnotherapist recommended by Dr. Jackson. He may be able to help you with your amnesia. Then, afterwards, we're having dinner with Brandon."

"Who's Bran …?" Savannah trailed off. "Oh, never mind."

"What if I cooked us some *sarsuela* for lunch? Would you like that?" he asked, remembering how much she enjoyed it when he cooked it for her years ago.

"*Sarsuela?* What's that?" she asked.

"It's a delicious fish stew that's a popular dish in the town where I grew up. It has chunks of shrimp, mussels, squid, clams, and a variety of fish in a savory broth. If you like, we can go to the market and buy the ingredients.…"

"You know, that's really sweet of you, but I'm not very fond of seafood. I prefer vegetables," she said.

"Okay, then we'll just have lunch at that café in the village that you like." Alfonso felt himself getting adept at not being offended or disappointed by anything she said. He felt himself getting accustomed to the different person Savannah had become.

"Which café is that?"

～

It was 12:30 when Alfonso pulled the convertible out of the parking lot of the Dolphin Bay Café with Savannah, after having had a light lunch. It was a smooth drive to the Bay Area, and they arrived at Gordon Marsh's office in Berkeley at a quarter past four.

Alfonso sat next to Savannah in Gordon Marsh's waiting room, still wondering if hypnosis would be helpful at all for her condition. He recalled Dr. Jackson's words when he paid Savannah a house call a few days earlier: "There are no guarantees. Hypnotherapy is still regarded as experimental when it comes to amnesia. And if memory cells have been physically damaged, hypnosis cannot restore them. But it's worth a try. Gordon Marsh is one of the best in the field."

Savannah had been unusually upbeat and conversant during the drive into Berkeley. She spoke of God, of nature, and of love mostly. There was a childlike artlessness about her that Alfonso found appealing. She was unguarded and unafraid to speak her mind, and was not needy of anyone's approval. She knew exactly who she was, and fully accepted who she was. That seemed ironic to Alfonso because she could hardly remember the past that made her who she was. *Perhaps that's a good thing,* Alfonso surmised.

He thought back to the Savannah he used to know, who, in spite of her obvious assets, always seemed to feel inadequate, insecure, always trying to please, and always trying to be perfect.

"Why can't I ever remember your name?" Savannah had asked suddenly.

"Savannah, I told you not to worry about that. Do you at least remember what you felt when you listened to my heart this morning?"

"Yes, I do," she said. Her eyes took on a dreamy glaze.

"That's good enough for me." Alfonso smiled. "Okay, here's an idea. Do you know how the Sioux Indians name the people in their tribe?"

"No."

"They name their people after an event in their life, or a cultural concept or something in nature that makes an impact on them. Like 'Smoke Maker,' for example. Or 'Flies with Eagles.' Or 'Sitting Bull.'"

"Or 'Gallops with the Wind'?"

"*Exactamente*. So, do you think you can do that? Instead of trying to remember my name, just look at me and the first thing about me that makes an impact on you, that's what you should call me. And you can change my name any time you want."

"Yes, I can do that."

"So look at me and tell me what you think my name should be."

"Running Stream."

"*Fantástico*. I like my new name. I think I'll keep it."

༄

The one-hour session with Gordon Marsh restored a few of Savannah's memories, mostly from her early childhood. Memories that centered around her father–before her father abandoned her. Alfonso caught a rare glimpse of the kind of father Lyndon Curtis was to Savannah, and why she was devastated by his departure.

"When I was six, Daddy took me to see the Grand Canyon," Savannah had told Gordon Marsh. "It was so beautiful there that I said it was where God lived. Daddy said God lived wherever there was love. I pointed to his heart and said, 'So God lives in here?' and he said, 'You got that right, Princess'."

As she spoke of her Daddy, her face shone and she became starry-eyed.

All of a sudden, Savannah's memory switched to fast-forward and she remembered a part of her life well beyond her childhood. She recalled having a son.

"From the time I was pregnant with him, I knew he would be special. He was handsome from the day he was born, and always good-natured. I wished his father could've seen him. How happy he would've been."

"How is it that your husband never saw your son, Savannah?" asked Gordon Marsh.

Savannah ignored the question, and continued, "He got his father's eyes, hair, nose, hands and feet. From me, he got his skin coloring, his lips and his chin. He looked so much like him that it only made sense to name him after his father."

Just when Alfonso thought he had learned about enough kinds of amnesia, Gordon told him about yet another. *Posthypnotic amnesia.* It refers to a subject's difficulty in remembering, after hypnosis, the events and experiences that transpired while they were hypnotized. That was the case with Savannah. She recalled nothing of the memories she spoke of during hypnosis.

"Why did Savannah avoid answering some of the questions you asked?" Alfonso asked Gordon.

"There are events the unconscious deems better to remain out of conscious awareness," Gordon replied. "The unconscious continues to protect one throughout the process of hypnosis, and will only divulge information if it is certain that the subject can handle that information. In plain English, Savannah's unconscious is unwilling to reveal information about her son's father because the information is something she's not yet ready to face."

"Perhaps her husband's death is too painful a memory to remember. Maybe that's why she's never talked much about her husband, not even to her son."

"Perhaps you're right," Gordon replied.

༄

*B*randon was standing outside *Sol y Luna* when Alfonso pulled up to the parking valet on Portofino Boulevard at a few minutes past eight. He grinned as Alfonso and Savannah walked toward him.

"Sorry we're a little late," Alfonso said, glancing at his watch.

"A few minutes late. That's not what you Spaniards call late, is it?" Brandon said, winking.

"No, I guess not...but when in America..."

"Do as the Americans do," Brandon finished his sentence for him. Then, he slipped his arm around Savannah's shoulder and kissed her on the cheek. "Hello, Mama."

Savannah looked bewildered by the stranger's affectionate gesture, but she didn't pull away. She smiled at Brandon, pretending to know who he was.

Brandon knew better. "It's alright, Mama. It will all come back to you."

As they walked through the foyer of *Sol Y Luna* and into the dining room, Alfonso surveyed the place. The Spanish supper club was built in the same space where *Club La Cibeles* used to be. Except for the curvy entryway, it looked very little like its original incarnation. Alfonso looked over at Savannah to see if anything about the place jogged her memory at all. Nothing did.

When dinner was over, Savannah excused herself to go the powder room. Brandon ordered *tarte tartin*, a dessert he said Savannah used to love. Alfonso warned him not to be too disappointed if she didn't like it, telling him about the *sarsuela* he had suggested to make for her earlier.

"Don't worry. If she doesn't eat it, I will," Brandon said.

She didn't, and he did.

"Brandon, your mother spoke about you to the hypnotherapist," Alfonso said.

"Really?" Brandon was delighted. "What did she say?"

"Oh, she talked about what a great joy you've been to her ever since you were born, and how proud she is of you."

Brandon smiled and looked over at Savannah, who seemed unaware they were talking about her. Her visit to the hypnotherapist that afternoon was already foggy to her.

"She also said how much you look like your father. Do you have pictures of him?"

"He died before I was born, and I've never seen pictures of him."

"That probably explains why she didn't answer when Gordon Marsh asked her why your father never saw you. Oh, by the way, I didn't know you were a Junior."

"What do you mean, 'Junior?'"

"Wasn't your father's name Brandon Fairchild, too? That makes you Brandon Fairchild Junior, no?"

"No, actually my father's name was Warren Fairchild. Warren Timothy Fairchild."

Alfonso was puzzled. While under hypnosis, Savannah had told Gordon Marsh that she had named her son after his father.

Suddenly, Savannah asked Brandon, "Do you have a middle name?"

"Yes, I do. In fact, I think you'll get a kick out of this," he said, looking at Alfonso. "Mama must've liked your name a lot. My middle name is Alfonso."

CHAPTER 24
Sounding Brass and Clanging Cymbals
TUESDAY MORNING • AUGUST 12 • 2003

*B*randon sipped his coffee while leaning on the wooden railing of his Diamond Heights patio, watching the sun rise on the East Bay. Inside, Savannah packed the rest of her belongings, zipped her cosmetic bag and put it away in the side pocket of her black duffle bag. Alfonso stood in front of the hallway mirror, combing his hair with his fingers, and then giving the guest bedroom a once over, making sure they hadn't left anything behind.

Brandon turned to them and said, "Are you sure you won't have coffee at least?"

"We should really get going. Cassidy said she'd have breakfast waiting for us at her place. Thanks, anyway. And thank you for putting us up for the evening."

"Are you kidding? I wouldn't have it any other way. Besides, there was no sense for you to drive back to Mendocino last night since you plan to spend the day in the city today. So you've got your day all planned out?"

"Pretty much. We'll have breakfast at Cassidy's, then we'll spend most of the day at the museum, have an early dinner with Zendrik, and then head back to Mendocino."

"Well, if you find yourselves in the vicinity of Montgomery and Pine right around noon, call me at the office so I can meet you for lunch, okay?"

"Esta bien," Alfonso answered.

"If I don't see you later today, I'll be in Mendocino on Saturday."

"Wonderful! Don't forget to bring your guitar so I can give you the lessons I promised."

"I won't. We'll have a blast. Oh, and by the way, Nana Sabine is flying in from Lucerne on Friday night, so the two of us will drive up to Mendocino Saturday."

◠

*A*lfonso stood for a moment, gazing at the Victorian house at 201 Pacific. It was still exactly the way he remembered it, except that it was no longer yellow and white. It had been repainted periwinkle and gray. He knew every detail of this Victorian, every window sill, every curve of the millwork, and all its eaves. The snapshot he had taken of it from Summerhill Park twenty-six years ago was the only photograph he had of his time with Savannah. He had gazed at the photograph so often over the years that it had become a shrine of sorts to him.

Now, he watched as Savannah climbed the steps leading to Cassidy's front door. She took slow steps, stopping now and then to admire the details of the Victorian architecture. The gingerbread millwork, the turret-like corner tower, the bay windows. She seemed utterly fascinated, but she recognized none of it.

He walked up the steps right behind her. When she reached the landing, she turned around and said, "Let's just stand here for a minute and enjoy the view,"

"Of course. Why don't we?" It amused Alfonso to see her savoring the moment. Savannah held her hand out to him, bidding him to hold her hand, and he was thrilled. It was the first gesture of affection she had ever initiated.

∽

From the landing, Savannah fixed her gaze on the view. There was a lilac-and-pink "painted lady" across the street, and the rising sun cast leafy shadows upon its side wall. Then, there was shady Summerhill Park with dappled sunlight breaking through its lacework of foliage and overhanging trees, and a small glimpse of the bay in the distance. She inhaled deeply, taking it all in, enjoying just standing there. The smell of fresh brewed coffee and scrambled eggs wafted from inside.

Savannah was in high spirits. Something about the air, the view, the sounds of the city and standing close to this handsome man– close enough to smell his scent–took her breath away. She remembered last evening, and how he had slept in the same room with her. He had been such a gentleman, insisting on sleeping on the daybed so that she could have the queen-sized guest bed all to herself. She wouldn't have minded if he had slept with her on the bed, but didn't argue with him when he pulled out the daybed. It had been a warm night and he slept in cotton drawstring bottoms, naked from the waist up.

She remembered her heart pounding in her chest as she watched him from the corner of her eye while he spread the bedding and tossed the pillows on the sleeper. For the first time she admitted to herself how attracted she was to him. She had had a hard time falling asleep, just thinking about how near his body was to hers. She had finally fallen asleep around midnight, but awakened twice during the night, sat up and gazed at him, a feeling of tenderness sweeping over her. Everything about this man she called Running Stream seemed sensual to her these days.

Now, as she stood on the landing with his hand enfolding hers, she wondered what he was thinking of. She wondered once again if that thing she had felt from the palpitations of his heart was a true indication of how he felt about her.

Even as she did, she realized that she was remembering what had happened yesterday. *Is my memory coming back?* she wondered.

Just then, lace curtains inside the Victorian parted, and Cassidy's face peered out at them. She smiled when she saw them. "You're here!" she said, then disappeared from the window, and re-emerged at the front door.

"Hi," Savannah said cheerfully.

"Hello, Savannah! Hi, Alfonso! How long have you been standing out here?"

"Just for a minute, admiring your apartment and the view," Savannah said.

"Won't you come in? I've just finished preparing breakfast."

"I hope you didn't go through a lot of trouble," Savannah murmured politely as she walked through the front door.

"No, not at all."

"Thanks for inviting us over, Cassidy," Alfonso said, following right behind Savannah.

"Oh, I've really been looking forward to your visit. I'm hoping it will bring back a lot of memories."

"It certainly brings back a lot of memories for me," Alfonso said, then turned to look at Savannah. "What about you, Savannah? Does this place look familiar at all?"

"I'm not sure. It's certainly lovely, though. But I'm just not sure I've seen it before."

"Take your time. This is the apartment where you used to live twenty-six years ago. Take your time and maybe it'll come back to you."

"And what was your name again?"

"I'm Cassidy. I live here now. I found a journal you left behind when you used to live here. That's how you and I met. I returned the journal to you."

"I see...," Savannah said, surveying the apartment from the floor to the ceiling. "Can you show me where you found my journal?"

"Sure. I found it in that cabinet behind you...." Cassidy motioned with her eyes towards the built-in Victorian cabinet against the back wall of the living room.

Savannah turned around, walked over to the cabinet, and looked at it for a moment. Suddenly, she knelt down and pulled a section of the cabinet's baseboard to reveal the hidden drawer. "This is where you found it, right?"

Cassidy exchanged looks with Alfonso, who seemed delighted by Savannah's recollection. "Why, yes, of course, Savannah! That's where I found it. You remembered!"

Savannah smiled, but didn't take her eyes off the empty drawer. She stared at it long and hard, as though in doing so, it might awaken more memories. But nothing else came.

"Would you like to look around a little more, or shall we have breakfast first?"

Savannah shut the drawer, stood up, and said, "Let's have breakfast. I'm starving."

Cassidy had set the dining room table with a bouquet of summer flowers, a platter of strawberry pecan pancakes, and another platter of cheese omelette smothered with mushroom cream sauce, and grilled herb-cheese potato patties on the side. There was also a bowl of sliced fresh fruits, a pitcher of orange juice and a carton of milk.

Before they sat down to eat, Alfonso offered to say grace.

"Heavenly Father," Alfonso began. "We thank you for the wonderful blessing of food that Cassidy has prepared for us out of your bounty. And we thank you most of all that you have gathered us in this house that holds a special place in our hearts, and we trust that we'll find here what is in your will for us to find, knowing that your ways are past finding out and your timing is always perfect."

Savannah was convinced there was something more than just Running Stream's physical appearance that attracted her to him. Something deep inside told her that she shared a bond with him that transcended anything that was worldly. Hearing him say grace revealed a spiritual aspect of him that endeared her to him even more.

Breakfast was pleasant, and Cassidy was delighted that Savannah had eaten generous helpings of everything on the table with much gusto. "I'm glad to see your appetite has returned," Cassidy said.

"I think you've got me confused with someone else. I've always had a good appetite. I think it comes from my mother's side of the family. She's half German, half Italian. That says it all, doesn't it?"

Cassidy exchanged looks with Alfonso again, and smiled. "What's your mother's name, Savannah?"

"Elaine. And my daddy's name is Lyndon Curtis. He's a second-generation Welsh immigrant. His parents came from Swansea, Wales." The words seemed to slip out of Savannah's lips so easily that they startled her.

Her eyes widened as she looked first at Alfonso, then Cassidy. "Did I just remember all that? There's hope for me yet!" she said, giggling.

"You bet!" Cassidy said. "And have you ever been to Swansea?"

"Why, yes! I was six years old when my parents took me there. It's a small fishing village. The only thing I remember is my visit to a confectionery factory, where my daddy's brother, Uncle Dylan, worked as the manager. It was like a magical trip into Willy Wonka's chocolate factory. I'll never forget that," Savannah squealed with glee.

Over the next several minutes, Savannah spoke animatedly about her childhood memories. Even those that she failed to mention during her session with Gordon Marsh. She had an endless number of stories to tell. She seemed happiest when she talked about each one of her birthdays, all the way until her seventh birthday, when her daddy bought her a white birthday cake with the black tap shoes and red bows decorating the top, and the green lettering on the cake that read: *Happy 7th Birthday, Princess!* She remembered nothing beyond her seventh birthday.

One part of Alfonso wanted Savannah to snap out of her amnesia so that he could be with the Savannah he once knew and loved. Another part of him wanted her to stay just the way she was now—carefree, fearless, trusting, with a girlish innocence, and without the hurts, scars and demons that used to plague her.

Savannah excused herself presently, and asked Cassidy if she could use her bathroom.

"Sure. It's at the end of the hallway."

When Savannah walked away, she turned to Alfonso. "How do you do it?" she asked.

"How do I do what?"

"How do you continue to care about a woman who doesn't remember you? She obviously can't reciprocate your love, and she's a different person from the woman you once knew."

"You say that like it's a difficult thing to do."

"Well, isn't it? Here you are...a successful flamenco artist. I'm sure you have a swarm of young, admiring women at your feet, especially now that you're single again. You have fame, fortune, a mansion in Madrid, many friends, a daughter who adores you and a three-year old grandson. Why would you want to rekindle an old flame with a woman who hardly remembers you to begin with?"

Without skipping a beat, he said, "Because I choose to." His reply was so quick-on-the-draw that it startled her. He had needed no time to ponder the question. The answer came straight out of his conviction.

After a moment, Alfonso continued, "If I gave up on her, I wouldn't know what to do with the rest of my life. In the last twenty-six years, I could never forsake the hope of one day being with her again. Not without dying."

Alfonso was silent for a moment, looking afar off. Then, he stood up and started pacing the floor, his face punctuated by distant thoughts. "If I told you how many times I've performed on stage, and looked at every face in the audience hoping to find Savannah there, you probably wouldn't believe me." He paused for a moment. "If I told you the things I've done in the last twenty-six years in the hope of finding her, you'd find that hard to believe, too.

"There's a skeptic that lives in all of us, Cassidy. You're young and what you know of love is what you've seen in the media or what you've observed in the few experiences you've had thus far. I've no doubt you could speak all day long about the kind of love you've heard about through pop psychologists, magazines and second-hand sources, but have you experienced what it's like to truly love someone? Have you ever felt the heartbreak of being separated from the one you love…not for a day, or a week, but twenty-six years? Have you ever been given the choice to stop loving…and chose to love anyway despite the pain? Have you ever wanted to give your life just to know that the one you love is happy, wherever she is?

"When I met Savannah, I knew in my heart that of all the women God had given me the opportunity to love, I chose her and only her. That sounds like a romantic notion, but it's much more. Choosing Savannah was just the first step. To be deserving of love, one has to be willing to suffer long, endure all things, and give up everything one has, even one's own life, if that's what love requires.

"All of us yearn for a love that transcends height and depth, time and distance, life and even death. For some reason, we just don't believe it can happen to us. I didn't believe it could happen to me. When you sent me that e-mail, Cassidy, telling me where to find Savannah, you, too, embraced the hope that such a love exists. And it does."

After another long pause, Alfonso continued, "So now I find that Savannah has lost her memory. Yes, it grieves me, but that's no reason for me to stop loving her, is it? She's still Savannah to me."

Cassidy bowed her head and stared at the floor. She felt chastised and yet uplifted by Alfonso's sentiments. Yet, the skeptic persisted. "But what if she never regains her memory? What if she never returns to her old self? How long can you hold out without giving up on her?"

"I've asked myself those questions, Cassidy. Especially that day at the hospital when you first told me she had amnesia. I wondered if I could love a stranger who probably wouldn't love me back. I wondered how her handicap would inconvenience my life. I even wondered if I had the fortitude to stand by her whether she regains her memory or not. But during the last ten days, I realized that if I can't love what's left of the Savannah I know, perhaps I don't really love her. And there's nothing farther from the truth."

"So what if she stays just the way she is now and never returns to the way she used to be?"

"You may find this hard to believe but I already love her for what she is now, not just for some distant memory I have of her. If I met her for the first time while she's in this condition, I'd still choose her. If I do nothing else but look after her for the rest of my life, I'll have considered my life well spent."

Just then, Savannah emerged from the hallway. "Mind if I take a look around?" she asked Cassidy.

"Oh, not at all. Would you like me to give you the grand tour?"

"I think I can find my way around, Cassidy. Thanks." And with that, she proceeded to walk up the stairs. When she reached the fourth step, she skipped the fifth step and leaped directly to the sixth step.

"Why did you do that, Savannah?" Alfonso asked.

"Why did I do what?"

"Skip the fifth step."

"Because the fifth step creaks loudly," she replied.

Alfonso and Cassidy exchanged glances once again and smiled, as Savannah marched on up the stairs, not even noticing the small memory she had been able to recall.

When she was out of earshot, Cassidy turned to Alfonso. "Forgive me for asking you all these questions. I don't mean to play the devil's advocate or encourage you in any way to just get up and leave her. I guess I just wanted to know that you're not going to hurt her in the long run. God knows how much she's already been hurt."

"Yes, I think I have some idea."

"Alfonso, do you know why Savannah ended your relationship?"

"She couldn't bear to see me hurt Cristina the way her father hurt her."

"That was one of the reasons...."

"Was it because she found out she was pregnant with our child and didn't want me to know because it would cause me to leave my family?"

Cassidy was taken aback. "You know about Brandon?"

"I found out just yesterday. It came out during her hypnosis session. Brandon doesn't know yet."

"And how do you feel about that?"

"Knowing that Brandon's my son? I couldn't ask for a better gift. He's everything I've ever wanted in a son."

"Listen, Alfonso. There's something else about Savannah. Something not many people know, but she told me, and I think you ought to know it, too."

"What is it?"

"Savannah has long suffered from a psychological complex of not being good enough, not being worthy of love. She views the world through fractured lenses. It makes her do irrational things—makes her act out of a sense of poverty, unworthiness. One of the reasons she ended your relationship was because she didn't want to hang around long enough to find out that you really didn't love her. She's convinced herself that no one could truly love her. She blamed herself when her father abandoned her. She felt that if she only behaved better, if she were only prettier, if she were only smarter, then her father wouldn't have left her. So she's spent her life obsessively trying to be perfect because that's the only way she felt anyone would care to love her. But deep down, she's still convinced that if she let up for just a moment, if she's not at her best behavior, if she let her guard down long enough for people to see who she really is, they would not love her, but instead leave her just as her father left her. She always felt that even if a man did come to love her, he would end up leaving her when someone better came along. Believing that virtually every woman is better than she is, she never feels secure about her relationship with a man. She constantly battles feelings of inadequacy.

"So yes, it's true that she cared deeply about Cristina and didn't want her to suffer the way she had suffered. But the secret she's been keeping is that she ended your relationship while she still believed you loved her. She preferred to live in the fantasy that you loved her than know the truth that you just might be like all the others—that you could love only the version of herself that she manufactured. So she beat you to the door before you had the chance to walk out on her."

Alfonso wasn't certain how to process Cassidy's revelation about Savannah. Part of him wanted to weep for Savannah because she lived in a dark world of self-loathing and self-flagellation, and couldn't see how deserving she was of love. Part of him was saddened that he had failed to convince her that he loved her not for the surface embellishments that she allowed people to see, but because of who she was inside. Part of him was angry that her irresponsible father had distorted the way Savannah viewed herself for life. But somewhere, a small voice told him that he could have just as easily inflicted the same fate upon his own daughter, Cristina—had Savannah not intervened.

Just then, they noticed that Savannah had wandered into the den that used to be her studio. She seemed deeply engrossed, scrutinizing the Victorian moldings and architectural details of the room.

"Isn't it ironic?" Alfonso said, his gaze following Savannah. "Just look at her now. Her defenses are down, she's not trying to be anyone but herself, and she's far from perfect. And yet I love her nonetheless."

"Alfonso, I have a little confession to make. I find myself partly responsible for Savannah getting in that car accident in the first place. I was the one who told her that you were on your way to San Francisco. In your e-mail, you had said you'd be arriving on the 27th of July, and that you'd be staying at the St. Francis Hotel. I phoned Savannah and urged her to be at your hotel before you checked in. I thought it would be a romantic way for the two of you to get back together. It didn't take her long to decide. She immediately got in her car and drove off towards San Francisco. While on Highway 28, an SUV rammed into her car head on, and she fell into a coma."

Alfonso was silent. "Everything happens for a reason. Something good will come out of this, I'm sure. No sense in recriminations."

"You know what the ironic thing is?" he continued. "I didn't even bother checking into the St. Francis the day I landed in San Francisco. I just rented a car and drove straight to Mendocino. I couldn't wait to see her. I went to the address you gave me in your e-mail. There was no answer at the door, and I camped outside, thinking she'd be coming home sometime. I got a room at the Pines Hotel just to sleep and take a shower, but for several consecutive days, I parked outside the house and waited for her. It wasn't until the third of August that a neighbor told me that she had heard Savannah was in the hospital. That's why you saw me at the hospital that day."

CHAPTER 25
Lyndon and Elaine Don't Live Here Anymore

TUESDAY • AUGUST 12 • 2003

Alfonso felt jubilant that Savannah had rekindled a few memories during their visit to 201 Pacific. Even so, he accepted the fact that her memories were fragile, and that she could lose them just as fast as she recalled them.

After Cassidy left for work mid-morning, Savannah and Alfonso proceeded to the San Francisco Museum of Modern Art. The museum's exterior structure was imposing–comprised of textured brickwork, stepped-back concrete boxes and a truncated striped cylindrical tower. They walked past the gray-and-black granite zebra stripes of the entrance columns into the lobby. Halfway through the lobby, Alfonso heard a man's voice behind him saying, "Why, Mrs. Fairchild, what a surprise to see you!"

Savannah continued walking, not realizing that the man was talking to her. Alfonso tugged at her sleeve to make her take notice. She turned around and saw a tall, mustachioed gentleman in his early sixties standing in front of her, wearing a navy blue suit.

"Hello, Mrs. Fairchild," he said to her. "Martin Carlisle, remember?"

"Excuse me, Mr. Carlisle. I'm Alfonso Madrigál, Mrs. Fairchild's friend." Then in a hushed voice, he said, "I'm afraid Mrs. Fairchild won't recognize you. She's been in an accident, and has suffered some memory loss." Memory loss sounded less dreadful than that word–amnesia.

"I am so sorry to hear that," Mr. Carlisle said. "Now, I feel rather awkward. I just came over to thank her again for loaning us the Picasso. It's created quite a bit of excitement in the press, and has significantly increased the museum's visitors. We're so grateful."

"I'll make sure I extend your gratitude to her when the time comes, Mr. Carlisle."

"Thank you, Mr. Madrigál. Please tell her I wish her a speedy recovery."

"I certainly will," Alfonso said, nudging Savannah's elbow, suggesting that they should be on their way. Savannah caught the hint, smiled politely at Martin Carlisle, and started walking through the atrium toward one of the galleries.

225

"What was that all about? Did that man say I loaned them a Picasso? Is that true?"

"*Si, mi amor.* Back in 1977, I gave you a painting that my grandmother left me when she died. You had it authenticated. It turned out to be a Picasso. It's in this museum right now."

"How fascinating!" she said, with girlish glee. "Is that why you brought me here–to see it?"

"*Exactamente,*" he said, exceedingly amused by her childlike affectation.

It wasn't difficult to find the Picasso painting. It was centrally located in the West Gallery, and throngs of people milled around it. Among them was a group of about twenty-five Japanese tourists, with a tour group leader translating the painting's lengthy caption into Japanese.

It took almost five minutes before Alfonso and Savannah were able to inch their way through the crowd to take a close look at the painting. Upon seeing it up close, Alfonso felt a wave of nostalgia. He had forgotten how the image of the woman in the painting was such an accurate rendering of how Abuelita used to look–the creamy complexion, the widow's peak and the mole above the corner of her mouth. He remembered the mahogany-paneled drawing room at *Villa Madrigál*, where the painting once hung. He also felt something surreal about it because, although it was the same painting he knew and loved as a boy, it had also evolved into another painting altogether because of the appearance of the *pentimento*.

Viewing the painting in person brought forth a flood of emotions that he had not felt upon viewing its picture in the clipping Cassidy e-mailed to him.

"Tell me about this painting," Savannah said.

"This is a painting I inherited from my grandmother, which I gave to you twenty-six years ago. You loaned it to the museum a few weeks ago."

"Why did you give it to me? It must have been valuable to you."

"I gave it to you because I felt that one day it would bring you back to me."

Alfonso's emotional admission was lost on Savannah. It rang no bells for her. "So why is everyone so excited about the painting?"

"It's a work of Picasso that emerged after his death–and it was created in 1897 when Picasso was not even an adult. That's exciting enough to most people. But there's also a story behind it, which came out in the *San Francisco Journal*. All the other newspapers, magazines, TV and radio stations also ran the story, and so much drama and attention was focused on it."

"Tell me the story."

"People wanted to know who was this mystery woman that was the subject of Picasso's painting–this lady in red. Did Picasso have a love affair with her? Why did he paint himself into the picture, and then change his mind and take himself out in favor of a seascape? Then, of course, there's all the excitement about the image of the man in the painting."

"What about it? And why is it blurred compared to the rest of the painting?"

"That's because it's a *pentimento*," Alfonso explained.

"What's a *pentimento*?" she asked.

"In the early days, artists sometimes created an oil painting and then changed their mind and decided they didn't want to keep it, or they preferred to create another painting instead. When that happened, they frequently painted over the old painting beneath it. As the painting ages, the underlying image gradually comes to the surface." It felt odd to Alfonso that years ago, Savannah had been the one who explained to him the intricacies of a *pentimento*. And now, he was explaining to her the same things she had explained to him.

"So what you're saying is that Picasso painted over the image of the man?"

"Yes. When I gave you the painting, there was no man in the picture. It was a seascape. But now the seascape has vanished, and in its place is the original image of the man. Back in 1977, that man was just a small smudge on the painting. Now, the *pentimento* is completed. The art experts are speculating that Picasso originally painted himself onto the canvas kissing the woman but then, on second thought, he took himself out."

"The philosophical symbolism in that is pretty profound, don't you think?"

"What profound symbolism do you make of it?"

"It indicates the resurrection of an old love that was believed to be dead and gone, or that may have been taboo in the past. But now, it has become legitimized with the passage of time–paving the way for the reconciliation of separated lovers."

"I couldn't have said it better myself."

༺

It was late afternoon when they finished viewing the rest of the exhibitions in the South Gallery. As they left the gallery and headed back to the atrium, Savannah noticed a man and two women pointing at Alfonso and asking each other if he might possibly be Alfonso Madrigál.

She nudged Alfonso and said, "You've been spotted."

Alfonso turned around to see the threesome approaching him. The taller of the two women asked him pointedly, "Are you Alfonso Madrigál?"

"Yes, I am," Alfonso answered.

Savannah watched as they asked for Alfonso's autograph, and he was happy to accommodate. He was gracious and charming, quite accustomed to, and at ease, with his adoring public. She was proud of him. While he politely answered their questions and engaged in small talk with them, he cast occasional glances at her–and once, even winked at her, mischievously. Her heart pounded loudly when he did that, and she knew she was falling under the spell of this man she called Running Stream.

She looked at the clock in the atrium. *6:15*. She thought it would be a good idea to run to the powder room before they headed out the door to meet Alfonso's friend, Zendrik, for dinner.

As she walked down the hallway towards the powder room, she suddenly felt as though she was retreating into a dark salon, where the furniture was disappearing one by one. The powder room was brightly lit, but she suddenly felt disoriented. *"Where am I?"* she thought, not remembering why she was there or who she came with.

In a state of panic, she raced out the door, down the hallway, out the lobby and past the entrance columns of San Francisco Museum of Modern Art. Night was falling. There was a row of taxi cabs parked curbside, waiting for passengers. Hurriedly, she climbed aboard the first one and told the cab driver, "Take me to 950 Kings Road, please."

The cab arrived at the 900 block of Kings Road, with its identical rows of closely set two-story apartments with the steps to the front door situated on the left side, and the two-car garage underneath. The cab slowed to a crawl until it was directly in front of 950 Kings Road.

"Here we are, lady."

Savannah paid the cab driver and stepped out onto the curb, closing the cab door behind her. *How long has it been since I've seen them?* she thought to herself. *Won't they be surprised!*

She ran up the steps and rang the doorbell. A short, heavy-set, Hispanic man came to the door.

"Yes?" he said.

She was taken aback. Who was this stranger answering her parents' doorbell?

"Are my mom and dad home?" she asked, tiptoeing to see above and beyond him inside the living room. The TV set was on and two young girls were playing in front of it.

"Are you sure you've got the right address?"

"Is this not the home of Elaine and Lyndon Curtis?"

"No. The Lopez family lives here. For ten years now. Sorry." And with that, he shut the door.

Savannah felt lost. As lost and lonely as she could possibly be. She knew no one else she could turn to, nowhere else she could go. She was alone in the world. Slowly, she started walking down the stairs. Her knees began to buckle, so she sat herself down midway down the flight. The cement was cold and the night was dark, and she buried her face in her hands while the commercial jingles played on the TV set of the Lopez family.

After what seemed like an eternity to her, a pair of headlights appeared around the corner and started making its way down Kings Road. The car stopped and Alfonso came running out, leaving the car engine running and the door flung wide open.

Savannah looked up, her eyes stained with tears. Her pulse quickened when she saw him. "Running Stream, Running Stream! It's you!" He seemed like a bright comet piercing the murky skies of her life.

He ran up the steps, sat down beside her, and threw his arms around her. "Oh, Savannah, Savannah. What would I do if I lost you again?"

"And what would I do if you hadn't come for me? Mom and Dad are gone. Are they dead? Am I alone?"

"You'll never be alone, *dulce mio*. Remember this?" he said, placing her hand on his chest.

She closed her eyes and began to smile through her tears. "Yes, I remember this."

༄

Alfonso pulled up into the driveway of 335 Castlebrook after midnight. Savannah had slept in the car all the way from San Francisco. He was about to carry her into the house without waking her, but she opened her eyes as soon as she heard Alfonso open her door.

He walked Savannah to her bedroom door.

"Good night, Savannah," he whispered, kissing her on the cheek.

"Good night, Running Stream. Will you be here tomorrow?"

"I'll be here tomorrow, Savannah. I'll be here the day after tomorrow, too."

"And the day after that?"

229

"For as long as you need me, *mi corazón*. I'll just be in the next room."

She smiled warmly, trusting him at his word, and feeling safe and cared for.

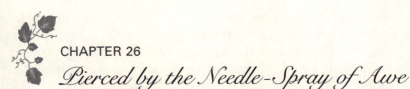

CHAPTER 26
Pierced by the Needle-Spray of Awe
SATURDAY • AUGUST 16 • 2003

The wind whipped the sand into a frenzy that Saturday morning in August, and a warm summer rain came down upon Mendocino in the early afternoon. The cypress leaves recorded every drop and the rain-kissed air sighed.

Savannah awoke from her afternoon nap, screaming. Alfonso ran to her side and took her trembling body into his arms.

"Running Stream, I don't know where Daddy is. I don't know if he's alive or dead. I had a dream…," she cried.

"Tell me all about your dream, *mi amor*."

"I woke up in the morning, and Daddy was nowhere to be found. Mommy was crying. She had been reading a letter Daddy left behind saying how sorry he was, that he had fallen in love with another woman, and that he was leaving," she said, breaking into sobs. "A few days later, it was my eighth birthday. He didn't come. He didn't call. He didn't write. He just forgot all about me." She buried her face in his chest, quivering like a kitten left out in the cold.

For the first time, Alfonso really felt the magnitude of Savannah's pain. It was as if by holding her in his arms, her pain had seeped into his pores and engulfed him. With a sense of despair, he realized that the demon which had haunted Savannah for decades, the same one that he had prayed would never surface in her memory-impaired state, was clawing its way to her again. He longed to gather her darkness in his hands and defeat it with the light of his love. He fought back the tears as he said, "I'm here, Savannah. I haven't forgotten about you."

Her sobbing subsided to a whimper, and she suddenly looked up into his eyes.

"Running Stream, I know who you are. I remember your face. Your eyes are familiar to me, and I've heard you sing. I even remember what you said…." Her voice trailed off, a frown creeping onto her brow as she struggled to remember.

"Tell me what I said to you, *mi amor*." Alfonso held his breath and waited for the sweet words of recognition from the lips of Savannah.

"'What do you dream of?' You wanted to know what I dream of, and I told you my dream."

"You said you want to start a school where you can teach emotionally traumatized children how to paint, yes?"

"Yes," she replied, looking afar off. "One of the rooms would have walls painted a deep blue, like the sky after sundown, because blue generates feelings of relaxation and well-being and would have a calming effect on the children. Another room would be painted a rosy pink because the wavelength of pink has been found to have a tranquilizing effect, and it suppresses hostile, aggressive, and anxious behavior. And another room would be painted green like a grassy meadow because green replenishes and restores the human spirit."

"Tell me more about this school, Savannah."

Savannah's eyes glazed over. "What? Did you say something about a school?"

Alfonso's heart sank. In the blink of an eye, just as swiftly as she came, Savannah Curtis was gone again like the migratory birds of winter.

"Running Stream, I'm afraid."

"What are you afraid of?"

"I'm afraid I'm going to die of a broken heart just like my mother did."

"No, you won't, *mi amor*. I'll make sure that never happens."

The next morning, Savannah awoke before the sun came up, put on a pair of cropped jeans, a short-sleeved cotton blouse the ends of which she tied in a knot just above her waist, and sneakers. She slung over her shoulder a canvas tote bag filled with gardening tools, and headed straight for the garden in the back lawn before anyone else was up. She smiled when she looked upon the horizon turning into light crimson with the first blush of day. She felt the stillness that permeated each blade of grass, each flower petal. The world was so tranquil at this time of the day that she could almost hear dawn breaking. The garden smelled sweet with the scent of flowers, and the air was soft and still as she knelt down to tend to her children.

Just after the sun came up, Alfonso awoke and walked to the kitchen to make the morning coffee. Brandon and Sabine had arrived at 335 Castlebrook just before midnight the previous evening after Savannah had gone to bed, and were still asleep in the cottage. While the coffee was percolating, Alfonso walked back towards his room and noticed the door to Savannah's bedroom wide open and the door to the back porch slightly ajar.

A momentary feeling of panic crept through him as he remembered how Savannah wandered off in a taxicab two nights before. His pace quickened as he approached the back porch. He was relieved to see Savannah in the garden.

He then disappeared back into the cottage, and emerged a few minutes later with a mug of fresh brewed coffee in his hand. He sat himself down on the Adirondack chair and sipped his coffee while watching her tending her garden.

Alfonso felt elated. It was turning out to be a warm summer day. White puffs of clouds appeared in rows, giving the clouds the rippling appearance that people called a "mackerel sky" because the clouds resemble the scales of a fish. Cypress trees framed the beautiful garden, where lavender, trumpet-shaped Oriental lilies, multi-colored gerber daisies, snapdragons and roses co-existed in harmony, without trying to upstage each other. The foliage and blossoms created an avalanche of colors that pierced him with the needle-spray of awe over God's craftsmanship. And there in the midst of it all was the woman he loved.

Savannah turned around and saw Alfonso watching her. "Good morning, Running Stream!" she exclaimed, waving at him.

A broad smile crept onto Alfonso's lips. This was the first time she had remembered his name for more than a day. At least the name she had given him.

"*Buenos dias*, Savannah."

Suddenly, Sabine's voice emerged from behind the screen door. "Savannah's taken up gardening?"

Alfonso turned around in his chair, not realizing Sabine had been standing there. "*Buenos dias*, Sabine. I didn't know you were up."

"Good morning to you, too, Alfonso," she said as she walked out into the porch. "And it is certainly a good morning, isn't it? Oh my God, this place is like a little paradise." She surveyed the garden and the view of the shimmering ocean beyond, and took in a deep breath.

"It's heaven to wake up to this every morning. Oh, and about Savannah's gardening. She seems to be very fond of it. Does that surprise you?"

Just then, Brandon emerged from the cottage, coffee mug in hand.

He interjected, "Mama never had a green thumb. Both the entry garden and this backyard garden were already planted and in full bloom when she bought this house. She hired a gardener to come in once a week because otherwise the garden would have died a natural death."

"Savannah never shared my passion for botanicals," Sabine said.

"And now, you can't tear her away from her garden," Alfonso said.

"Nana Sabine here has one of the most beautiful gardens in Lucerne. She's pretty active in horticulture circles and she's the Chairman of the Lucerne Garden Society, aren't you, Nana?"

Sabine smiled. "I have pictures of my garden, if you'd like to see them later, Alfonso. But Savannah's garden isn't too shabby either–especially the entry garden. Stunning!"

"I'd love to see your pictures, Sabine. Oh, by the way, would you like me to get you a cup of coffee?"

"No, thank you, dear. I'm not a coffee drinker. Looking out onto a garden is all the caffeine I need to get me going for the day," she said, sitting herself down on the porch swing. "I have a mind to do a little gardening with Savannah, but I'm just enjoying sitting here–watching her do something I've never seen her do."

Savannah, who was kneeling beside a lavender bush with a spade in her hand, looked up from her work and gazed at Brandon and Sabine. It looked to Alfonso like she might recognize Brandon, but clearly she did not recognize Sabine.

"Brandon showed me some of your books. You write beautiful poetry, Sabine," Alfonso said.

"And so do you, I've been told," said Sabine.

"You write poetry, Alfonso?" Brandon asked.

"Once upon a time, I did. But when I started writing songs, I fell out of the practice."

"I've started writing poetry myself. It's just not the kind of poetry you're probably accustomed to reading. It's pretty esoteric."

"You'll have to show me your poetry sometime, Brandon," Sabine said.

"If you promise you won't compare it to yours. I'm nowhere near as good as you."

"I promise," Sabine said, smiling.

Savannah was busy aerating the soil beneath her rose bushes. She seemed oblivious to the conversation that was in progress just steps away from her.

"Sabine, do you remember when Savannah moved to Switzerland?" Alfonso asked presently.

"I remember the exact date. November 28, 1977."

"That was just after my father died, wasn't it?"

Sabine fell silent for a moment. Her eyes darted furtively in the direction of Alfonso before replying. "I guess you can say that."

"Did you ever meet my father or see pictures of him?"

"No, I never did meet your father, nor have I seen pictures of him. But I've seen a painting of him."

"A painting?"

"Your mother painted a portrait of him…just for you. Hasn't she given it to you?"

"No, she hasn't. Where is that painting now?"

"I'm quite sure I saw her put it in her suitcase before she left Switzerland. It's probably around here somewhere."

"Do I really look a lot like my father? Like the painting of him, at least?"

Sabine looked directly at Alfonso, gazing at him for a few moments. Then, her eyes fixed squarely upon Brandon's face. "Yes, you do look a lot like him."

After a few moments, Sabine continued, "I may not have met your father, Brandon, but I certainly knew him well."

"How so?"

"Your mother wrote me letters throughout her relationship with your father. I remember the letter she wrote me on the day she met him. She wrote that she had a strange feeling he'd somehow figure in her life in some important way. She also spoke of him often during our phone conversations. Perhaps I knew your father well because of the person she became because of him."

"And what kind of person was that?"

"A person who was loved more than she thought it was possible to be loved," she replied, glancing once again at Alfonso.

"If he loved her that much, why is it that she's never spoken of him to me?"

"Perhaps it was because it was too painful to speak of him."

Then after a short pause, she continued, "There's one more thing, Brandon. Your mother suffered an emotional trauma when she was a child. Meeting your father was the closest thing she ever got to getting rid of the trauma."

"What kind of trauma, Nana?"

Just then, Savannah walked up the porch steps, wiping her brow.

"I'm starving," she announced. "Anyone for breakfast?"

CHAPTER 27
Artistry Blooms Best in Heartbreak
SUNDAY AFTERNOON • AUGUST 17 • 2003

The cottage was quiet that afternoon. Savannah was taking her afternoon nap, Sabine had gone out to do a little exploring of Mendocino on her own, and Alfonso and Brandon were sitting in the living room of 335 Castlebrook Lane.

"Did you remember to bring your guitar?" Alfonso asked.

"I knew I forgot something," Brandon said, slapping his forehead. Then, he grinned widely. "Just kidding. It's in the trunk of my car. I'll go get it."

He returned a few minutes later with his guitar case in hand. As he laid the case on the coffee table, he said, "Mama seems to be doing quite well."

"She's fine, for the most part. She still gets severe headaches once in a while, so I give her a headache pill and that seems to take care of it."

"Does she still sleep a lot?"

"Yes, more than the average person, but less than she did last week."

"Did she ever start taking the Amytal?"

"No, she doesn't want to take prescription pills at all. She seems to have a violent objection to drugs in general. Even after I explained that Amytal may help her regain her memory, she still wouldn't take it. She told me not to ask her again."

Brandon smiled. "That sounds like her, alright. She gave me the same rebuff when I tried to give her the Amytal the day she was discharged from the hospital." Then, lifting his guitar out of its case, he announced, *"Voila!"*

Alfonso looked it over and said, "That's a good-looking guitar. May I?" He held out his hand and Brandon handed him the guitar.

He examined the back and sides of the guitar made of Spanish cypress, strummed and plucked at the strings, fiddled with the push-pegs while keeping an eye on the LED tuning guide on the guitar tuner Brandon had placed on the coffee table. Then, he let his fingers tickle the strings with a slow rumba.

"Okay, it sounds the way it should," he said, handing the guitar back to Brandon.

"Before we get started, may I ask you a question?"

"Of course."

"Do you ever write music as a form of therapy?"

"I've often wondered how those who do not compose, paint, write or do something creative are able to escape the pain and the loneliness which often accompanies human life. When I first started writing music, the melodies emerged out of my wounded heart. It was as though my sorrow had struck an inexhaustible vein of creative inventiveness. That was how I eased my sorrow–so, yes, I've written music as a form of therapy. You know what they say. 'Artistry blooms best in heartbreak'."

After a brief pause, he continued, "But later, when I became more spiritually mature, I discovered that the ultimate therapy is to commune with one's Maker."

"Do you mean…"

"To be at one with the living God."

"I hear ya," Brandon said.

"So…are you ready to play?"

"Sure," Brandon said. "But I've warned you before. My guitar-playing is only fair."

"Compared to whom?"

"Well, I guess compared to you."

"Your first lesson: Compare yourself to no one but yourself. The only way to plow a straight furrow is to look straight ahead. At any given time, the thing you have to strive for is to be a better guitarist than you used to be. Compare yourself to no one but yourself. That way, you'll only keep getting better. Go ahead and start warming up while I get my guitar. Play anything you want."

Alfonso walked down the hall into his bedroom as Brandon began to play. He kept his ear on Brandon's playing and smiled, secretly pleased that his son took after him, and that Brandon wanted to master the same art for which he himself had the most passion. He sat down momentarily, listening to Brandon playing *bulerias*, one of the most complex rhythms in Flamenco. He was technically competent and had a flair all his own. He actually played better than he gave himself credit for. *The kid has his father's genes,* he mused.

He let Brandon finish playing before re-emerging with his guitar. "Bravo, Brandon. You're a much better flamenco guitarist than you pretended to be."

"Muchas gracias." Brandon grinned.

"Where did you learn how to play?"

"When I lived in Madrid, I took lessons from a flamenco guitarist who was known as *El Salvaje*. His name was Jose Montoya."

"So you learned from Pepito!"

"Pepito?"

"That's what his friends called Jose Montoya."

"You were friends with my guitar teacher?"

"For many years. He's one of the best teachers in Madrid for learning the mechanics of *guitarra flamenca*."

"He sure knew how to crack the whip. He growled and yelled at me until I got it right. I had weekly lessons for almost two years. Then, after I left Madrid, I just practiced on my own."

"*Muy bien*. Yes, a whip-cracker sounds like Pepito alright. He's not called *El Salvaje* for nothing. He's definitely the wild one."

"So is this the famous *Guernica*?" Brandon asked, eyeing Alfonso's guitar.

"I retired Guernica years ago. I dropped her accidentally while I was preparing for a concert in Granada, and she sustained a few cracks. She's never sounded the same since, but I didn't have the heart to let her go since she had been faithful to me for seventeen years. I keep her in a glass case in Madrid." He sat himself down on the easy chair, put his guitar on his lap, and rested his arms on its curves. "This lady's name is *Dora Maar*."

Brandon smiled, looking amused that Alfonso referred to his guitar as a lady. Alfonso sensed his amusement and said, "The longer you play *guitarra flamenca*, the more your guitar will become your lady. Cherish her and treat her well and she will sing for you like no bird has ever sung."

Brandon nodded.

"*Bueno…*," Alfonso said, putting on his teacher's hat. "I'm not going to teach you technique. Pepito has already taught you that. I'll teach you the spiritual side of Flamenco. Now listen well, Brandon. The mechanics of playing Flamenco you cannot completely divorce from the art. One must learn the mechanics first…like you have. But Flamenco is not simply about technique or the act of putting your fingers into various positions on the ebony board, or mastering the *compás*, or the rhythm. And it's not just about learning how to make your fingers fly across the strings. It's about telling a story that flows from here," he said pointing to his heart. "People will forget the way you played your guitar. But a story you tell from here will live on in their hearts forever."

"I've been going about it the wrong way, then. All I've been doing is practicing for hours so that I can develop the skill."

"Practicing for hours is a good thing, Brandon. But there comes a point when you've reached an adequate understanding of the mechanics and you have to ease up on them or you run the risk of getting lost in the structure, the motions and the modulations. Your music will be technically correct, but it will have no soul. Soul is what flamenco music is all about. Lorca once said we muddy songs simply because of education. I remember a story that your mother told me. It was about the time Pablo Picasso was just starting out as a student at the Barcelona School of Fine Arts in 1895. One of the first things he was taught to do was to write down the words, 'One must learn to paint, One must learn to paint, One must learn to paint' over and over again. But he was hardheaded, and wrote down instead, 'One must not learn to paint.' What that story taught me was that it's easy to lose the spontaneity of creation when we are overly instructed. That really took root in me. When I loosened my obsession on the mechanics, it freed me to be myself and express myself."

"How exactly do you do that?"

"That's another thing I credit your mother for having taught me. She taught me to allow the spirit in me to find its expression, how to play music from the inside. Every person needs something to make the spirit in him come alive. For me, it was these words: *'Be still and know that I am God'*."

"I know the words well."

"Insofar as you are creative, you partake of God's nature. Therefore, take every opportunity to escape from yourself into the thoughts of God. I find that, in stillness, I am transported to that remarkable place where I can know God and be aligned with his wisdom. Until I learned how to become still, I didn't realize that I spent much more time talking to God than I did listening to him. When I thought about the unlimited wisdom of God, what I had to say was nothing compared to what God had to say. Remember this always, Brandon. What God can create through you is much bigger than anything you can create on your own. So make it part of your process to sit quietly and let God do all the talking."

"You mean meditating, don't you?"

"Some people call it that. I call it 'entering the silence.' The object is not just to meditate, but to focus on tapping into God's abundance, for that's where all creativity flows from."

"I hear ya, man."

"Now for your second lesson. When you play, do not focus on pleasing the audience. Focus on the story you're telling with your song. Don't think about the audience or what they're thinking. Cicero once said, *'Nihil est incertius volgo.'* Nothing is more uncertain than the favor of the crowd. Your mother taught me that, too. When you focus on communicating the story well, you will automatically please the audience anyway. Now, let's play, shall we?"

Brandon grinned. "Okay, let's jam."

"Do you know the chords to *Los Sueños de los Malagueños*?"

"From your first album? I think I can wing them."

Brandon started playing the first few chords, tentatively at first, then with growing confidence.

Alfonso began to accompany Brandon, playing complex chords, yet harmonizing perfectly with his playing. His fingers moved like playful raindrops over the guitar strings, intuitively feeling their way around Brandon's playing without the benefit of a rhythm to play by, as if spiraling around an invisible pole with great ease.

Alfonso felt energized by the musical synergy they were enjoying, the affinity that enabled Brandon and him to perform in harmony, creating music of greater magnitude than the sum of their respective parts. In all the years he had been playing the guitar, he had rarely played with professional Flamencos with whom he achieved an organic "connectedness" the way he did with his son, Brandon. *Mi hijo. My son,* he said to himself, getting acquainted with the pleasure and pride the words brought him.

Suddenly, Alfonso became aware of what sounded like rhythmic clapping coming from somewhere. At first, he thought it was his imagination, for he was given to hearing hands clapping to the *compás*, the rhythm of every flamenco song that played in his head. Then it became clear the clapping was not imagined–the clapping came from somewhere behind him.

He glanced up quickly. Savannah emerged from the hallway, a faraway look in her eyes, and her arms raised at chest level as she clapped syncopated rhythms in unison with the guitars.

Brandon was so busy concentrating on the strings that it took him several seconds to notice that Savannah had entered the room and was herself caught in the web of the moment. He stared at her in amazement, all the while never missing a beat in his playing.

Savannah's rhythmic clapping grew louder as she stepped further into their midst. She seemed completely oblivious to the reactions she was getting from both Alfonso and Brandon, but instead appeared possessed by a disembodied entity that arose from the music, which was punctuated by the random tapping of fingernails on the *golpeadores*, the plastic plates attached to the guitars' soundboards. Suddenly, she stomped her foot hard on the redwood floor and swept her arms above her head, fingers tensed open, chin raised, her face a glowing expression of pain, and her mahogany hair falling over her white dress. Alfonso and Brandon continued playing while watching Savannah, and she began to dance in rhythm, her body moving with the music, her dress swaying from side to side. As the music approached its crescendo with a manic, restless rhythm, she danced as one possessed by the spirit of the music, like Lorca's "lunar epileptic" whose movements were keeping pace with explosive arm sweeps and the stacked heels of her sandals pounding on the floor. As the guitars finished *Los Sueños de los Malagueños*, Savannah dramatically dropped to the floor, hunched into a sorrowful heap.

Alfonso and Brandon looked at each other when they finished the piece. Then they stared at Savannah, crumpled into a ball on the floor.

"*Olé,*" Alfonso said. He put down his guitar and walked toward Savannah. He swept her off the floor in his arms and sat her down on the sofa, noticing that her face was stained with tears.

"How did you learn to do that?" Brandon asked Savannah.

"Learn to do what?" Savannah countered, looking disoriented.

"That…," he said, pointing to the floor where she had danced. "The dancing. Where'd you learn to dance like that?"

"I don't know what you mean. I don't dance. I've never been any good at it. Never will."

It became obvious to Alfonso and Brandon that Savannah had already forgotten what she had just done. They thought it best not to discuss it. Her memory lapses had always been erratic. Though there were some hopeful signs of memory retention, the lapses had become more frequent of late. Neither of them knew how to deal with it.

Savannah's eyes started to droop as she fought to stay awake. In a few seconds, her eyes closed.

"*Pobrecita,*" Alfonso said, barely audibly. Then, to Brandon, "The poor thing. She probably got exhausted from all the dancing. She seems to have fallen asleep."

With those words, he picked her up in his arms and carried her to her bedroom. He lay her down on her unmade bed and looked down upon her motionless body. The color seemed to have drained out of her face. Something about the way she looked lying there rang an alarm bell somewhere inside him.

He reached for her pulse. He felt none. He waved his palm in front of her nostrils. No breath. He searched for a pulse on the side her neck, just below her ear, his heart pounding wildly now. There was no pulse, no sign of life.

The room turned dark to Alfonso. Thoughts were racing through his head that he had no time to process. Savannah was all that mattered in his life. He swept her up in his arms again and carried her down the hallway to the living room, where Brandon still sat strumming his guitar.

"Get the car started, Brandon. The keys are on the mantel."

Brandon put his guitar down without delay. "What happened?" he asked as he sprang to his feet and lurched for the keys, a dose of apprehension in his voice.

"I don't know. She stopped breathing, and I can't feel her pulse. We've got to take her to the hospital." Alfonso's words were punctuated by shallow breaths. Beads of perspiration began to appear on his forehead. "Go ahead and start the car while I administer CPR on her."

Brandon raced to the front door, and in his haste, he flung the door so vigorously that it banged loudly against the wall. After Alfonso's efforts to revive Savannah failed, he carried her out the door while Brandon swung the rear car door open for them. As he walked with hurried steps around the car and got behind the wheel, Alfonso carefully laid Savannah on the back seat, gently propped her head on his lap after he sat himself next to her, and shut the car door.

Just before they arrived at the hospital, Alfonso saw Savannah's chest heaving slightly. He was relieved to see that she was breathing again, albeit shallowly, but her face still had the pallor of death.

CHAPTER 28

Vanquish the Darkness of the Human Soul

SUNDAY AFTERNOON • AUGUST 17 • 2003

The wheels of the hospital gurney that swept Savannah into the Emergency Room at the Mendocino County Hospital seemed to scream in Alfonso's ears. The gurney glided past the ER waiting room, past Triage, and straight through to the ER proper, and Alfonso followed a few steps behind as they wheeled Savannah into one of the rooms. He stood in the hallway outside the room while a nurse attached Savannah to a respirator, checked her vitals, and attended to her. In a few moments, one of the physicians on duty entered Savannah's room, accompanied by yet another nurse, and began examining her and doing a battery of tests.

An ER administrator walked up to Alfonso and asked him if he was related to the patient.

"I'm her friend and care provider," he answered.

"What is the patient's full name, please?"

"Savannah Curtis…I mean Fairchild. Savannah Fairchild." His head was throbbing and everything seemed foggy to him.

"Do you have her insurance information?"

"No. This emergency happened so fast that there was no time to find her insurance card. But if you'll check your hospital records, you'll find her insurance information, as well as all her personal information. She was just hospitalized here two weeks ago."

She disappeared momentarily, and Alfonso saw one of the nurses walking out of Savannah's room. He asked her, "Excuse me, how is she? How is Savannah?"

"Doctor Landon is attending to her. He should be with you as soon as he's done evaluating her."

The ER Administrator returned with documents for him to read and sign. Just then, he saw Brandon entering the ER after having parked the car. He motioned for Brandon to come over.

Brandon rushed to where Alfonso was standing, and asked, "Is she alright? What did the doctors say?"

"Nothing yet. They're trying to resuscitate her," Alfonso answered. "The doctor is in there with her right now, and will let us know her condition soon."

245

*F*ifteen minutes went by, and still no word from the attending physician. Brandon felt despondent. Seeing Alfonso looking forlorn didn't help him feel any better. Here was a man who normally exuded strength, was always self-assured and in control of things. Now, he looked helpless. If he ever had any doubts that Alfonso was in love with his mother, those thoughts were gone now. The devotion this man felt for Savannah was unlike any he had ever seen, and Alfonso's concern for her well-being surpassed even his own.

Brandon watched as Alfonso finally allowed himself to calm down enough to sit down on one of the guest chairs nearby. He watched as Alfonso leaned his elbows on his lap and rested his forehead on the palms of his hands, his eyes closed. He seemed to be praying. Brandon didn't want to disturb him with conversation, so he sat next to him, not saying a word. All the while, he worried about the condition of his mother, and remembered in horror how deathly pale she looked when Alfonso laid her on the back seat of his car.

The doctor finally emerged from Savannah's room.

"I'm Dr. Dermott Landon," he said, looking at both Alfonso and Brandon. "Are either of you related to Savannah Fairchild?"

"I'm her son," Brandon answered.

"Your mother is doing fine. We've resuscitated her and she's breathing on her own again."

Alfonso closed his eyes and let out an audible sigh of relief.

"That's great news, doctor. Thank you. What caused her to stop breathing?"

"She's had a mild seizure, which is not uncommon for those who have suffered brain injury such as the one she's had. It seems to me like it was an isolated unprovoked seizure that may or may not recur. Dr. Jackson is on his way here. He should be able to tell you the precise neurological implications of this episode since he's the specialist. In the meantime, she'll have to be admitted into the hospital. We'd like her to stay overnight for further observation."

"Of course, doctor. That would probably be best. Thank you."

*D*r. Jackson's opinion differed slightly from Dr. Landon's. He thought Savannah's seizure may have been provoked by an event.

"Seizures like these sometimes come from overexertion too soon after her brain injury. Did she engage in some vigorous activity that may have agitated her or caused her to be fatigued?" he asked.

"Alfonso and I were playing our guitars when suddenly she started dancing. Yes, I guess, you could say it was pretty vigorous."

"That may have been what triggered the seizure. You need to keep her from engaging in activities that may potentially be agitating or exhausting for at least six to eight more weeks."

Dr. Jackson didn't seem overly concerned about the seizure episode. He prescribed an antiepileptic medication to minimize a recurrence.

Alfonso realized that he should be even more vigilant in watching over Savannah. He was convinced, however, that any hardship he could ever experience looking after her would be nothing compared to losing her.

Alfonso and Brandon took Savannah home on Monday morning. Savannah's seizure had given Alfonso such a scare that he was changed forever by it. Later, after having laid Savannah on her bed to rest, he was sitting in the living room with Brandon, and he was able to put things into perspective.

"There's nothing like a brush with death–or even an imagined brush with death–that makes one realize what one values most," he told Brandon.

"You're right about that, man. I just went through that two weeks ago when Mama got into her car accident. And now this. I've learned that the value of anything–or anyone–is that part of your life you're willing to trade for it."

"Or give up for it," Alfonso added. After a short pause, he continued, "Speaking of giving up things, have you ever been in love with a woman, Brandon?"

"Yes, I have."

"When you first fall in love with a woman, you're willing to give this much," Alfonso said, placing his palms in front of his chest, facing each other, shoulder width apart. "Just a little bit, compared to all you can give. Then, you soon find out that love doesn't ask for a small part of yourself. It doesn't ask for a large part of yourself. It asks for everything you've got. And unless you're willing to give everything, you're never really in love."

"What would make a man want to love a woman enough to give everything he's got?"

"That's what separates those who love from those who seek only love's pleasure. Those who seek only love's pleasure do so with selfish motives, seeking only what they can get out of the love relationship. Why even bother calling it love at all? A man who truly loves is one who loves a woman because it's a privilege to love her, because loving her gives his life its meaning. A man, by his very nature, will always strive to keep his wits preserved, his heart intact. He will always want to be needed instead of being in need of someone–in control, rather than vulnerable. The capacity to love without regard to personal stakes is the greatest gift God has given us. For it is like a light that vanquishes the darkness of the human soul. But until you've loved a woman so much, Brandon, that you're willing to have your heart and soul turned inside out—unless your love causes you to halt what you're doing when she walks into view, and make you rejoice in your love for her—until you love so much that all you want is to see her blossom in your hands, you haven't really loved. Of this, I am sure. This is probably the only thing I can teach you that truly matters."

༄

Brandon swallowed hard, trying to digest the truth contained in Alfonso's words. Most of all, he was thankful that the woman Alfonso chose to bestow such a great love upon was his mother. He wondered if he would ever be capable of loving that way.

"I'm sure you're right, man, that this is one of the most important things I could ever learn from you. But you're not too shabby at teaching *guitarra flamenca* either." Brandon grinned.

"Speaking of *guitarra flamenca*...in case I forgot to tell you, Brandon, you're an outstanding guitar player. You're much more advanced than I was at your age."

"Coming from you, that's a great compliment, Alfonso. You're one of the greatest flamenco artists in the world. And if you don't mind the cliché, I'm your number one fan."

Alfonso's mood turned solemn. "A son is often his father's number one fan," he said, choosing his words carefully.

It took Brandon a few seconds to absorb Alfonso's words. His mouth hung open, unable to believe what he just heard. "What did you just say?"

"Brandon, what happened to your mother yesterday has got me thinking how fragile life is, and how fleeting. I know what it's like to have an opportunity to say something important to someone you care about, only to have fate snatch the opportunity away. Then you spend your life regretting what you didn't have a chance to say. I won't make that mistake with you."

"What are you saying, man?"

"There's something I failed to tell you last Monday. While your mother was under hypnosis, she mentioned something interesting. She said she named her son after his father. If that is so, it can only mean that Warren Fairchild wasn't your father."

"That can't be true...," Brandon said, trying to process the information.

"And you told me yourself that your middle name is ..."

"Alfonso," Sabine said, emerging out of nowhere, and finishing his sentence for him. "Your middle name is Alfonso, Brandon, because you were named after your father. It's about time you knew. You are Alfonso Madrigál's son."

Brandon was stunned, paralyzed where he sat, not knowing whether to be happy or angry. A thick vein pulsated on his neck. It wasn't the prospect of Alfonso being his father that bothered him. It was that his mother had deliberately kept this a secret from him. *Why did she tell me all those lies?* he asked himself. *Why didn't she let me know I had a father, and how could she deprive me of knowing him, growing up with him? And who was Warren Fairchild, if he wasn't my father?*

Sabine walked to the sofa and sat herself next to Brandon. "I've begged your mother to tell you the truth about your father since the time you turned eighteen, Brandon. But she said she wasn't quite ready. Now, I guess the responsibility rests on my shoulders to tell you everything."

A hush fell upon the room as Alfonso and Brandon waited for Sabine to speak again.

"Your mother met Alfonso in the fall of 1977 when she was already engaged to be married to another man...Russell Parker. Alfonso was the first and only man she'd ever fallen deeply in love with. But Alfonso was married when she met him, and he had a little girl named Cristina. Much as Alfonso loved Savannah and she him, she couldn't bear to have him leave his wife and his daughter. So she wrote Alfonso a letter ending their relationship. Before long, she found out she was pregnant with you, Brandon. So she broke off her engagement to Russell, left San Francisco to live with me in Lucerne so that she could give birth and raise her child away from prying eyes. She never told Alfonso about you because she didn't want to complicate his life.

"She changed her name legally from Curtis to Fairchild because if she named you Curtis, it would make people think you were illegitimate. Warren Timothy Fairchild never existed. She invented him so that if anyone asked, she could name Warren as your father who died before you were born."

Neither Sabine nor Brandon had noticed that Alfonso had slipped out for a minute. He returned later, holding a faded letter in his hand.

"Your mother is unable to speak for herself, so I hope this will help, son. This is the letter she wrote me twenty-six years ago," he said, handing the letter to Brandon.

Brandon took the letter from Alfonso, realizing that it was all beginning to make sense. This is why his mother had cried and bolted out of the room when he played Alfonso's CD. This is why he had never seen pictures of his father. This is why his mother had bought him a guitar when he was seven, saying that his father had also started playing the guitar at the age of seven.

He opened the letter, and read it silently to himself:

October 6, 1977

Dear Alfonso,
Where should I begin? Maybe an appropriate beginning would be to let you know how remarkable you have been in my experience.

Since that Friday you first spoke to me at Sutton Hall, you have been the most extraordinary man I've known. You possess a combination of qualities I've rarely seen in a human being. I have been moved by your music, stirred by your passion, fascinated by your profound insights and humbled by your deep devotion for those whom you love.

When not in your presence, I have found myself caring for nothing else but to know where you are and what you are doing. I've found myself wondering what thoughts would be worthwhile without you in them.

You have been to me a comet piercing the murky skies of my life, the fulfillment of every dream my heart has ever imagined. You have opened my eyes to a beautiful world that was unknown to me. Most of all, you have made me feel more cherished and cared for than I've been in a long time.

Over the last few days, I've wondered how you could have known I was in desperate need of your kind of affection when I had become so adept at hiding my need. It was as though you looked deeper into my heart than anyone else had cared to look, found what I was starving for, and took it upon yourself to give it to me. It makes me feel that God put you in my life, even for just this brief interlude, to remind me that such devotion still exists, although I've seldom known it.

You are warmhearted, affectionate, and capable of giving so much, Alfonso, and I have no doubt you will accomplish great things in your life, especially in your music. For this very reason, please understand why I must say goodbye. If we allow our relationship to blossom any further, it would complicate both our lives and would not serve those who love us and depend on us.

A few days ago, I wrote the beginnings of a poem:

> *Sparrows fly on their way to you*
> *And if I knew the way, I'd hurry, too*
> *Midwinter turns to spring*
> *And I remember things I never said to you.*

I've known the desperation of losing someone I loved without having had the chance to say goodbye or tell them how much they meant to me, so I refuse to let this opportunity pass me by now.

Know that I love you, Alfonso, and I will love you for as long as I have breath, for as long as my heart beats in my chest, and even when distance and time finally separate us. Know that I've never loved anyone the way I love you, nor do I think I will ever love this way again. But I'd rather let you soar upon my love and be ennobled by it, rather than let it compromise the things you hold dear, especially your precious daughter, Cristina. I'd rather lose you than turn you into less of a man than the one I've come to know and love.

My only wish is for you to remember me the way I'll remember you.

Yours forever,
Savannah

P.S. I'll be in Los Angeles for my gallery opening next week, but please call my answering service with your address so that I can send your Picasso painting back to you.

Brandon folded the letter slowly, having read every word. His eyes moistened as he pondered the circumstances that had led to his mother's actions. He felt ashamed now for even being angry with her for keeping this a secret from him. Knowing her, everything she did was for his own good, for his own protection. His heart ached for his mother, what she gave up, what she had to endure, the nights of loneliness she must have suffered without the man she loved.

His thoughts were interrupted by Sabine's voice. "Brandon, just before your mother drove off to see Alfonso at the St. Francis Hotel, just before her car accident, she called me. She told me she was on her way to see Alfonso, and that she would tell him about you. She also promised that she would finally tell you the truth about your father, and give you the painting she made of him. She said she kept it in the bottom drawer of her bureau. Would you like to go get it?"

Without a word, Brandon walked down the hall to Savannah's room, as if in a trance, still reeling from the startling news he'd just heard. Seeing Savannah asleep on her bed, he opened the bottom drawer of her bureau and found a brown-paper-wrapped package. A few moments later, he returned to the living room and handed the package to Sabine.

Sabine laid it on the coffee table and walked to the corner of the living room where Savannah had stored her easel. She carried the easel and set it next to the coffee table. Then, she began to carefully unwrap the package. When she was done, she tossed the brown paper on the floor, gazed at what appeared to be a framed painting and then placed it on the easel.

It was a painting of a young Alfonso, with dark piercing eyes, burnished bronze skin, a sovereign nose, and dark, shoulder-length hair with a lock spilling onto his forehead. Savannah's image was in the background. On the bottom right corner, it was signed:

To my son, Brandon
Love, Mama

"Savannah never had a picture of you, Alfonso. So she painted this from memory. She said she never wanted to forget how you looked to her." Then, turning to Brandon, "She created this while she was pregnant with you…right after she found out she was going to have a son. She said she'd give this to you when she was ready to tell you who your real father is."

Brandon glanced momentarily at Alfonso, then turned to Sabine. "What's written on the back, Nana? I saw something scribbled there as you were unwrapping the painting."

"Oh, it's something I wrote for her after she had ended her affair with Alfonso. She chose to put it here in the back of her painting," Sabine said. "Go ahead and read it, if you wish."

Brandon picked up the painting from the easel and turned it over. Glued to the back was a square-shaped piece of faded parchment paper with a feathery, deckled edge. In Sabine's ornate, calligraphy-like penmanship was scribbled a poem.

Brandon read it aloud:

"The anguish of a million stars
*   are concealed in restless trains that roam the countryside*
*   in secret cargoes*
*   to be delivered to the freedom of the sky*
Eagles fly not in the face of encumbrance
* but soar in the bosom of liberty*

They succumb only to the seduction
  of a muffled foghorn in misty waters
    and the lament of a Spanish guitar
The wayward foam of the Pacific
  surrenders itself to the arms of the Bay
    in the delirium of one Indian Summer
when he and she, though ice and fire
  were immortalized into a song
    that will live when both perish
      in one eternal sigh."

                              Sabine - April 1978

Sabine rose to her feet. "The way I see it is you've both lost precious time," she said, fixing her gaze upon Brandon, then Alfonso. "Don't lose any more."

Feeling awkward, Brandon turned to Alfonso, held out his hand, and said, "I'm glad to know you, Papa." The word Papa sounded foreign to him, but left a sweet taste in his mouth. "I couldn't ask for a better father than one who loves my mother the way you do."

Alfonso put his arms around him. "And I'm glad to know you're my son, Brandon. From the moment you visited me backstage in Madrid, I wished I had a son like you."

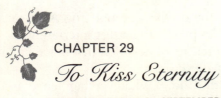

CHAPTER 29
To Kiss Eternity

SUNDAY MORNING • SEPTEMBER 14 • 2003

"*Hombre!*" Alfonso gave out a loud cry of surprise when he opened the door.

"*Hola, Alfonso!*" It was Zendrik. Standing behind him was a tall, lanky man with horn-rimmed glasses. "Oh, this is Monroe, a friend of mine," he said, motioning with his eyebrows to the man standing behind him. "Monroe, this is Alfonso Madrigál."

"I'm your humble fan, Señor Madrigál–for many years now," Monroe said, holding out his hand to Alfonso.

"*Mucho gusto.* Pleased to meet you," Alfonso said, shaking his hand. "Call me Alfonso, *por favor.*"

Then, turning to Zendrik, he said, "You're looking good for an old man."

"Hey, you don't look too bad yourself, buddy. Those streaks of grey in your hair make you look real distinguished."

"I apologize again for not meeting you for dinner last week. I told you what happened to Savannah, didn't I?"

"Yeah, you mentioned she took off from the museum and took a cab to the house where she lived as a child?"

"There was no sense in joining you for dinner after that episode. She fell apart. So did I, actually."

"Is Savannah here? I've been dying to meet her."

"She went to the village with Brandon, Cassidy, and Sabine. That's Savannah's adoptive mother, who's visiting from Switzerland. You'll meet her and the others when they get back."

They sat in the living room, with Zendrik chatting endlessly about old times, finding every opportunity to tease Alfonso about having an instant grown-up son. Alfonso, on the other hand, regaled them with his adventures in the flamenco world.

"What are you doing about the concerts you have scheduled?"

"I've canceled them until further notice."

"Man, I wish I had that kind of luxury to cancel concerts at a drop of a hat."

"It's not a luxury, amigo. It's a necessity. And it's not a drop of a hat. It's Savannah."

Zendrik understood what he meant. He knew what Savannah meant to his friend. He didn't bother asking why he shouldn't just hire a care provider for Savannah temporarily–at least on his concert dates. That would be out of the question for Alfonso. Alfonso Madrigál wasn't one to let practical matters interfere with matters of the heart. It was this intensity of devotion that made him different from anyone Zendrik had ever met.

Changing the subject, Zendrik said, "Whatever happened to your friend, Manolo? Didn't he used to live here in Mendocino?"

"He moved back to Spain after his wife died a few years ago. Poor man...he was never the same after she was gone. The last time I heard from him, he was living in *Chiclana*."

"Are you talking about Manolo Aragon?" Monroe asked.

"*Si, si.* Do you know him?"

"Not personally, but small world. I was in *Chiclana* for a couple of weeks last year, and I saw Manolo perform in a *tablao*."

"*No lo creo.* I can't believe it. What were you doing in Chiclana? It's not really a popular destination. The place is—*qué quiere decir*—what you call 'off the beaten track'."

"Oh, you won't believe it, but I went to every corner of Andalucia to get a taste of authentic flamenco music."

"You're a true flamenco aficionado, aren't you?"

"Monroe here is not only a flamenco aficionado. He's also a musicologist."

"A musicologist? What exactly is that?"

"He studies music as a field of research—quite distinct from composers and performers of music like you and me. You can say he's our geeky music sibling," Zendrik said, chuckling.

Monroe chuckled too at Zendrik's metaphor.

"On our way here, I told him about Savannah's amnesia, and he told me something really interesting. Tell him, Monroe."

"Well, the company I work for has been doing studies for twelve years on the effect of music. I've been working with them for five years, and we've developed what we call Harmonic Resonance Music. It's not music in the traditional sense, but rather harmonic music preparations used for medical purposes, not for entertainment."

"Very interesting. Please go on."

"We've developed various Harmonic Resonance Music programs for various indications, and have found that our music preparations have been successful in the alleviation of headaches, stress-related disorders, reduction of epileptic seizures, improvement of short-term memory, enhancement of learning abilities, all the way to easing gynecological problems in women."

"Get to the good part, dude," Zendrik said.

"Okay, okay. Well, we recently studied eighty-five patients with severe amnesia. In the experimental group, fifty-four of the patients received a treatment consisting of both conventional drugs, plus Harmonic Resonance Music designed especially for amnesiacs. In the control group, thirty-one patients received the conventional drugs only. Our finding showed that seventy-five percent of the patients that received a treatment with Harmonic Resonance Music showed a significant reduction in the degree of amnesia, and a marked improvement in memory restoration."

"That's impressive! Monroe, did you ever do a study of amnesia patients using only the music–that is, not in conjunction with the conventional drugs?"

"No, we haven't."

"It sounds like something Savannah ought to try. But she'll never go for the drugs. She won't even take the Amytal the doctor prescribed for her, as it is."

"Oh, yes, Amytal. I think that's one of the drugs used in the study, if I'm not mistaken."

"How can I get a hold of this music that's specially designed for amnesiacs?"

"That program is not yet available to the public, but I can probably make you a bootlegged copy of the recording on CD."

"As long as it won't get you in trouble."

"No, it won't if you don't tell anyone I gave it to you. There's no guarantee it will work without the drugs, but have Savannah listen to it anyway."

"Fantástico."

"I'll shoot the CD off to you in the mail next week."

"Muchas gracias, amigo. By the way, have you ever studied the therapeutic effects of commercial music recordings?"

"That's a good question. I've heard other companies attempting to do that, but our director won't even touch it because he's a stickler for music therapy that requires musicological or medical training. Personally, I think it's worth a shot. Anything from the strings of a mandolin to the sentiments of a pop song could potentially have a beneficial effect, although the effect may neither be measurable nor conclusive in the clinical sense."

"Now, you're beginning to sound just like a bona fide scientist."

"Actually, I consider myself more of a metaphysicist than a scientist. And the metaphysical side of me says that it's possible to listen to a song and viscerally feel the experience of the composer when he wrote the song. That's because sound can be felt in the physical and emotional body. Even before we become aware of the meaning of the song's lyrics, all the nuances of the music–its cadence, the arrangements of the notes, the flow of the melody–impinge upon the body and create a feeling, a mood or a sentiment.

"When it comes to amnesia, my theory is that a memory is more likely to take root when it's attached to an emotional event. And music is an emotional event. The emotional event bypasses the brain altogether and goes straight for the heart. It's the heart then–not the physical heart, mind you, but the emotional realm we call our heart– that restores the memory. That's just my theory."

"A theory definitely worth investigating."

"You've heard of the young boy who came out of a long coma when they played that funky theme song from *Seinfeld*, which happened to be his favorite show?"

"No, did that actually happen?"

"Yes. I think the key to healing is to find music to which Savannah can resonate–music that touches her heart."

~

*T*he cottage at 335 Castlebrook Lane had never seen a livelier crowd of people than the one that gathered around the dinner table that Sunday night in early September. There was Zendrik, Monroe, Alfonso, Savannah, Cassidy, Brandon and Sabine.

The ladies had cooked up a feast in the kitchen, exchanging stories that made them laugh or smile, while the men drank cold *cervezas* in the living room, played their guitars, listened to CDs, and indulged in all kinds of boisterous merriment as men often do.

At one point, Zendrik picked up his guitar and started playing the opening riff of "Midwinter Turns to Spring." Cassidy recognized the intro immediately, and found herself walking out of the kitchen and into the living room. Zendrik began to sing and Cassidy sang right along with him.

Before long, Savannah walked out of the kitchen, too, and stood beneath the archway leading to the living room. She appeared to be listening intently to the words that were being sung.

Alfonso looked up at her, watching her face for some kind of reaction. As Zendrik and Cassidy sang the words, "Sparrows fly on their way to you, and if I knew the way, I'd hurry, too…Midwinter turns to spring and I remember things I never said to you," Alfonso thought he saw Savannah's eyes brimming with tears. Just as he tried to catch a better look, Savannah turned around and walked back into the kitchen where Sabine was in the middle of pulling a perfectly done prime rib out of the oven.

The dinner table heaved under the weight of the culinary delights created by the ladies. There was salmon and scallop terrine and prime rib roast with merlot gravy prepared by Sabine; Chinese chicken salad and sun-dried tomato meatloaf made by Cassidy; grilled shiitake mushrooms and asparagus with Taleggio cheese, vegetable ribbons with saffron butter, and dessert, chocolate decadence made with sweet dark Ghirardelli chocolate and topped with a rich raspberry sauce–that Zendrik dubbed "orgasmic"– made by Savannah

Dinner was decidedly early–six o'clock–to give those who needed to return to San Francisco time to make the long trek home. During dinner, Zendrik posed a thought-provoking question that turned into a lively philosophical, and then spiritual, conversation. For the moment, no one remembered Savannah's amnesia, and they regarded her as just another normal human being at a dinner party contributing her share of views and philosophies.

At half past eight, the city folks decided it was time to head back to San Francisco. Alfonso insisted that there were enough sofa beds, day beds and sleeping bags to accommodate everyone for the night, but everyone had plans. Sabine was flying out of San Francisco back to Lucerne late the next morning. The rest of them had to go to work the next day.

∽

After the last guest had departed, Savannah told Alfonso what an enjoyable time she had. The day had tired her out, though, and she was ready to turn in.

Alfonso walked her to her bedroom. Just before she closed the door, she stood very close to Alfonso and looked up at him.

"Tell me your name again," she said.

"You know my name," he whispered.

"I know you as *Running Stream*. I want to know your real name. First and last."

"Alfonso Madrigál."

In the darkness of the hallway, with only pale beams from a sliver of moon streaming in through the back porch, she lifted her mouth to meet his. She melted into him as he returned her kiss with an ardor that almost startled her, enraptured her, made her want to be nowhere else but right there in his arms. *Oh, Alfonso Madrigál, I'm in love with you–whoever you are,* she thought. Her arms went around his neck and soft moans escaped her. She wished the moment would last forever, all the while fighting the urge to pull him into the desire that was growing inside of her.

He kissed her, again and again, with the fury of wild monsoon winds in the tropics. On her lips, he kissed eternity itself. There was no part of him that could remain indifferent from Savannah Curtis. There was something about her that no other woman possessed– something to which his whole being responded. It took all her strength to pull away from him. His hands were brushing over parts of her that made her insides ache, and she was determined not to lose control. Alfonso's eyes were still closed, his arms still reluctant to let her go, even as she gently pulled herself from him.

"Good night, Alfonso Madrigál," she whispered.

And he thought about how sweet his name sounded on her lips, while knowing that in the morning, her memory would erase his name once again. He could barely manage a weak, "Good night, Savannah *mia. Hasta mañana.*"

As she turned around and shut the door behind her, she remembered how by day, his gentlemanly ways and remarkable restraint had made her think he did not desire her–not as much as she did him. But by night, he smoldered like lava from an erupting volcano. As she shed all her clothes and slipped into the warm covers of her bed, she had no doubt her dreams would be of him that evening. She was not mistaken.

∽

Alfonso slowly made his way to his bedroom across the hall, feeling invigorated by her passion, her mouth, the heat from her body that he had felt when he held her in his arms. Beneath her feminine countenance, he sensed an aching sensuality that screamed to him like a siren in the night. As he lay in bed, he thought about how much he had wanted to take her in his arms and make passionate love to her since the moment he saw her framed in the hall archway–the day she was discharged from the hospital the first time. Every time she was near him, every time he held her hand, everything in him longed to dominate her, conquer her, possess her. It was all he could do to keep from imposing himself upon her–and throwing decorum, propriety and restraint to the wind. But he could never bring himself to take advantage of her, especially since she was in a vulnerable emotional state. Particularly after her seizure, he refused to put her health in peril by ignoring the doctor's orders–that Savannah should not be allowed to engage in activities that would agitate her or cause her undue exhaustion. It was three weeks and six more days until he would be free to be as close to her as he wanted to be. He felt no shame in counting the days. He had waited twenty-six years.

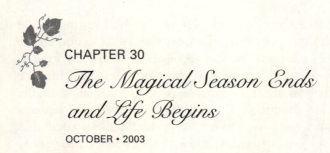

CHAPTER 30
The Magical Season Ends and Life Begins
OCTOBER • 2003

It had been three weeks since Alfonso received the Harmonic Resonance Music CD from Monroe. Day after day, he had played the CD for Savannah every morning after rising, in the evening before she fell asleep, and during the night, as Monroe had recommended.

So far, he had seen very little improvement in Savannah's memory restoration. So far, nothing he had tried had amounted to much by way of reducing Savannah's degree of amnesia.

Two subsequent hypnosis sessions with Gordon Marsh yielded marginal results. Savannah remembered very little about her life beyond early childhood while under hypnosis, and recalled nothing of the few things she did remember during hypnosis. Alfonso had also taken Savannah to see Preston Cummings, a Neuro-Linguistic Programming expert, who specialized in helping amnesiacs restore their memory. At first, the sessions showed promising improvements. Savannah was able to remember recalled memories for longer than a day, and even as long as a week. But the results were not long-lasting, as she would again lose the memories after the second week.

Bringing Savannah to all the places she was familiar with in hopes of jogging her memory also proved fruitless. She found nothing familiar about the Palace of Fine Arts, Café Marcel, Borrelli Vineyard, Tiburon, Muir Woods, Sutton Hall, or the Somerset Gallery. Finally, he took her to Heaven's Bluff, where he wanted her to smell the fragrance of the ocean that they loved together, and sit on the ground where they sat together, watching the water crest and fall. Still nothing.

Next, he put the journal that Cassidy found at 201 Pacific inside the drawer of her night table, hoping she would read it and recognize the story as her own. Before too long, Savannah found the journal, and he watched as she sat on the porch swing reading it intently for hours, watching for signs of recognition. When she came to the end, she closed the journal, walked back to her room and said nothing. Alfonso dismissed it as another dead end.

Unbeknownst to him, Savannah lay on her bed staring at the ceiling for a long time, pondering the story she had read and all the feelings it stirred up in her. She had recognized the handwriting in the journal as her own, and realized the story was hers, but she couldn't imagine that she was capable of loving a man with the magnitude she had described. Even as she wondered, she remembered how Alfonso—yes, that was his name—had made her feel that night when he took her in his arms and kissed her. She remembered how he made her feel whenever he was near, and whenever he slipped his hand in hers. She had no frame of reference for those intense feelings—until now. More than two decades ago, she had felt the same emotions that she was now feeling with Alfonso. It occurred to her that regardless of time, place and circumstance, she was destined to fall in love with Alfonso Madrigál. The realization seemed profound to her, yet she wondered how long it would take her to forget it.

And just as she expected, the memory was gone the very next day.

One night in October, Alfonso placed the brown linen portfolio he had brought with him from Spain on Savannah's bedside, allowing her to go through the items in it at her leisure. It contained her painting, *A Fern in the Clearing*, the letter she wrote to him, the faded picture of her walking past the parted curtains of her apartment at 201 Pacific, and the three CD albums of flamenco songs he had recorded over the last twenty-six years. She again acknowledged the handwriting on the letter and the signature on the painting as belonging to her, but the significance of the painting and the letter were lost on her.

The CDs piqued her curiosity, and she smiled because she saw Alfonso's picture on each of the album covers. "I've got to listen to this!" she had said excitedly.

Alfonso suddenly remembered Monroe's words: *A memory is more likely to take root when it's attached to an emotional event.*

This could be it, he thought. He could think of few things in his life that were as emotionally charged as the music he wrote on those CDs. Particularly his first album, titled *Triste*. He had written the songs when he was heartbroken over Savannah ending their relationship. *Perhaps that will get through to her,* he thought.

He was saddened when he realized that all Savannah could feel was an appreciation of his music. She could only comment on his awesome skill and the mechanics of his guitar-playing, but could not comprehend the heart of it, could not feel its emotional undercurrent. She failed to connect to his music the way he had hoped she would.

Alfonso thought of the things Savannah had no difficulty remembering. Like the name she had given him, *Running Stream*. She also had no trouble remembering his habit of kissing her hand. And she never could forget the night she took the taxi cab from the museum to the apartment where she used to live with her parents. She often talked about that night, and the emotions that accompanied the event.

"I remember that night when I was sitting on the cold front steps, crying my eyes out, thinking I was all alone. That there was no one in the world who cared about me, who even knew I existed," she would say to him as her chest slouched into a concave posture, her fists clenched tightly. Then, after a moment, she would straighten her back, unclench her fists, and smile. "And then you came for me."

Monroe was probably right in thinking that memory takes hold when it's attached to emotion. He had also said something else: "The key to healing is to find music to which Savannah can resonate–music that touches her heart." That statement had struck Alfonso like a bolt of lightning, and he had had a momentary flash–like a divine revelation or an epiphany of some sort. But the spark disappeared just as fast as it came, much like a nocturnal dream that's quickly forgotten the moment the dreamer awakens.

He tried to remember what long-lost memory Monroe's words had triggered in his own mind the moment Monroe said them. He was certain it would prove pivotal in helping bring back Savannah completely. Try as he did, he couldn't recall what it was.

Brandon had mentioned to Alfonso that at one time, before her accident, Savannah had been invited to exhibit her art at one of Mendocino Art Center's four gallery spaces. She hadn't gotten around to deciding which of her existing art works she should send, or whether she should create new ones.

Alfonso thought it might be a good idea for Savannah to visit the Art Center in hopes that it would reawaken her former passion for art and restore her art skills. Therefore, he drove her one morning to the top of the headlands, where the Art Center overlooked the Pacific Ocean. They took their time strolling through the beautifully landscaped grounds of the Center, which used to be the grounds where the historic Preston mansion was located.

As they walked through the Center's sculpture garden and the tiled courtyard, Savannah appeared to be mesmerized by the bustle of activity in the surrounding studios and classrooms for fine arts, jewelry, ceramics, sculpture, textiles and computer arts.

"One day, I would like to teach," Savannah declared, her eyes glazed with a faraway look. "If not in this place, then in a school of my own."

"What would you teach?" Alfonso inquired.

For a brief moment Alfonso imagined he saw a look of pain cross Savannah's face. He thought he saw her grimace and hold her breath, as though someone had plunged a sharp object into her chest. "I would teach emotionally traumatized children how to paint," she replied.

Alfonso's heart jumped. He remembered the night in 1977 when Savannah had told him about that project she often dreamed about and that afternoon a few weeks before when she woke up screaming.

"How exactly would you teach them to do that?" he queried, hoping to jog her memory a little more.

"I want to teach them how to draw and paint in a way that will help them cope with whatever trauma they've experienced."

"Would you teach them concepts such as colors, angles, texture …?"

"That would be part of it, of course, but there'll be so much more."

Alfonso noticed that Savannah's eyes flicked upwards as she spoke. He remembered what Preston Cummings, the Neuro-Linguistic Programming expert, told him about eye accessing cues: *When the eyes move upwards, the subject is imagining a past image or accessing a memory; as opposed to horizontal eye movements, which suggest that the subject is listening to remembered or invented sounds; or eye movements pointing downwards, which means that the subject is accessing his or her feelings.*

"Tell me all about it, Savannah."

"I would try to teach children to express through art the emotions they are unable or unwilling to put into words. If a little girl is suddenly orphaned, for instance, she needs to be supported every step of the way or her grief would produce unhealthy attitudes that will scar her emotionally for life."

The grimace appeared on Savannah's face again, and it soon turned into a visible wince, as though her hand was touching something excruciatingly hot, but she couldn't pull herself away from it. Alfonso couldn't bear to see her in pain. *God, spare her from that dreadful memory,* he prayed. He wanted Savannah's memory to be restored completely, but not if the terrible stigma from her childhood would continue to crucify her.

Savannah appeared to be limping along in pain as she continued speaking. "Allowing children to lose the opportunity to fly into the realm of their dreams because of emotional trauma is the worst crime of omission I can imagine," Savannah continued. "That's something I tried to teach Brandon when he was growing up."

Alfonso was startled. Savannah had never before remembered Brandon's name, nor remembered that he was her son, let alone recall what she taught him during his growing years.

"What did you just say?"

Savannah seemed to snap out of whatever trance she was in. Her face was serene once again. "Did I just say something? I don't remember."

∽

The weather in Mendocino was unpredictable. Although the morning had been sunny, some dappled clouds began to billow by mid-afternoon, and blustery winds began to blow. Savannah had not brought a sweater, so they decided to head back to the cottage.

On the drive back, Alfonso thought about the weeks he had spent with Savannah in Mendocino. The days were slow and largely uneventful, but he treasured them nonetheless. He knew that it sometimes took years for a man and a woman to get their togetherness in perspective, but he was feeling comfortable about the togetherness he shared with her. Having spent only twelve days with her in 1977, it was easy to imagine that the reality of living with her would have a sobering effect on him–that it would exhaust the initial euphoria of a romantic love affair and extinguish that astounding moment that lovers long to perpetuate.

That wasn't the case for Alfonso. For him, the evidence of love could be found not in the days when love is young, and emotions abound–but rather when its magical season ends and life begins. Life was beginning for Savannah and him, and he was savoring the joy of it more than he thought he would. The only thing missing was the physical intimacy, but he knew that would come in time.

As they stepped out of the cold into the warmth of the cottage, Savannah thought about how much she enjoyed being with him, and wondered about this man–no longer a stranger, but still a mystery to her–who never left her side.

"Would you look after me if you weren't paid for it?" Savannah asked out of the blue.

"What makes you think I get paid for looking after you?" Alfonso countered.

"Well, you said you're my care provider, didn't you? Don't care providers usually get paid for their services?"

"Not if they volunteered to do it without pay."

"You volunteered to take care of me? I must have meant a lot to you back then."

"You did. And you still do."

"Tell me what I was like before I lost my memory."

"You were an art expert and an accomplished artist. You painted the most beautiful landscapes that, to me, were deeply spiritual. They spoke to my soul." He motioned with his hand towards the paintings hanging on the living room wall. "You painted those."

"I did?"

She walked over to the paintings and scrutinized them.

"Why are they signed *Karenina*?"

"That is your middle name. You sometimes used it to sign your paintings, instead of your first and last name."

Savannah was curious to know what it was about the pre-amnesia Savannah that elicited such devotion from this man she called *Running Stream*. She had known him for many days—or perhaps weeks, she couldn't remember—and in all that time, she never gave this other Savannah a second thought. She had been comfortable in her own skin, and in the kind of person she was right now. But something about the way he talked about her made her want to acquaint herself with that other Savannah—even compete with her.

Gazing at the art work on the wall, she thought, *This is the work of the woman for whom his heart beats in that fashion,* recalling the cadenced palpitations of his heart. They spoke of tenderness and a profound devotion.

"Tell me more about the way I used to be."

"You loved Venetian classical music, and had an appreciation for Asian decor. You loved the work of the Welsh poet, Dylan Thomas, who lived in Swansea, where your father was born. You particularly liked Dylan's work, *Under Milk Wood*. You also loved Kahili ginger flowers and you loved seafood. You weren't much into disco music, but you loved the ballads of the Bee Gees."

"What about my personality?"

Alfonso smiled. "You had an incredible capacity for caring about other people, perhaps more so than yourself. As though other people were more important than you. You were sweet and affectionate. When it came to your profession, you were confident and self-assured. But when it came to your personal self, you were very reserved, almost to the point of timidity. *Fragile* is the word I used to describe you—like someone that I needed to protect. You had a fear of people hurting you, but you seldom spoke of it."

Her eyes still immersed in the paintings, she pondered this

Savannah of whom he lovingly spoke. This feminine, meek and vulnerable creature–this damsel in distress. The kind of woman that men wanted to rescue–wanted to fall in love with. And she thought of herself in comparison to her–independent and sufficient unto herself, never needy of attention, fearless, stubborn, outspoken, always insisting on her own way–even mule-headed at times. Quite the opposite of the Savannah Alfonso cared about. She was happy being the way she was, and didn't care to be like the other Savannah at all. Even so, her heart was a little jealous, although she didn't want to admit it.

She wondered if Alfonso would even take an interest in her if she didn't happen to have the physical appearance of the Savannah he once knew. She wondered if he'd even be remotely attracted to her personality. Deep down, she hoped he would be. For the first time since she met him, she worried. *If I never return to the person he once knew, would he still want to be with me? Would he still want to look after me and never leave my side?*

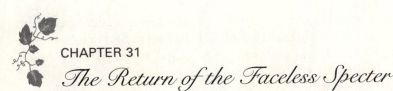

CHAPTER 31

The Return of the Faceless Specter

SUNDAY • OCTOBER 26 • 2003

While Savannah was taking an afternoon nap, the fleeting memory that had surfaced in Alfonso's mind upon hearing Monroe's words came back to him.

He had almost forgotten it altogether because it happened a long time ago. He had mistakenly thought that the music from his three CD albums would cause an emotional reaction in Savannah. But he suddenly realized that Savannah had no recollection for that music. On Heaven's Bluff, twenty-six years ago, he had sung a song to her—the first song he had ever written. Upon hearing it, she had cried and her body had trembled. And one of the things she said was, "Your music touched my heart."

There it was. By her own words, his song had touched her heart. Now, he wondered whether it was the key to restoring her memory.

Alfonso hurriedly fetched his guitar, *Dora Maar*, from his bedroom and quietly entered Savannah's room across the hall. She was fast asleep. At first, he groped for the chords, strummed them softly so as not to awaken her prematurely while he familiarized himself with the song he had not sung in over two decades. Then, when he was confident he remembered all the chords, his fingers started dancing over the strings as he plucked at them in melodic succession.

"La ultima vez," he sang. "Te fuiste de prisa sin adios ..."

༄

Savannah felt herself in a kind of twilight sleep, not yet fully awake. A song was tugging on her heartstrings. What was it that made tears run from her eyes down her temples? What memory was awakening?

She opened her eyes a crack to peek at the man who was strumming a guitar and singing, eyes closed. He appeared engrossed in his song, oblivious to what it was doing to her insides. She began to feel the way she did long ago, at a place called Heaven's Bluff, in 1977.

She was fully awake now, but couldn't dare open her eyes until he sang through to the end. Just as he finished his song, the doorbell rang. It was an urgent, insistent kind of ring, and Alfonso got up quickly, as if compelled to answer it.

269

He leaned his guitar next to Savannah's bedroom door before he hurried out. He didn't take a look behind him to find that Savannah had opened her eyes and was looking right at him, knowing him, remembering everything.

Savannah lay still, thinking she must be dreaming. Could that really have been Alfonso singing to her just now? The last thing she remembered was getting into her car and driving off toward San Francisco to see him at the St. Francis Hotel, where Cassidy had told her he was staying.

Yet, between that time and now, she also remembered bits and pieces of things that happened, things that involved doctors, a hospital, Alfonso, Brandon, Sabine and others. She was just a bit too groggy to understand how it all fit together. The only thing now that gripped her attention was that Alfonso was here with her again. She felt an immense joy, but also sensed within her a dark fear of impending doom. She pushed that aside.

She got up off the bed, thinking she couldn't wait a moment longer to be with him. She looked down upon the dress she had on. A beautiful magenta-colored summer dress. She vaguely remembered buying it–at a small boutique on Main Street, perhaps?

She could hear Alfonso talking to the postman, who had rung the doorbell with a package to deliver. She heard a soft thud as Alfonso put the package down on the hardwood floor. Her heart was pounding hard at the prospect of having him near her again. She decided to wait a few moments to give him time to walk back into her room.

When he didn't come, she moved across the room, around the periphery of her bed, past her dressing table, past the chest of drawers, past his guitar that was leaning next to her door. All was quiet as she walked down the hallway.

Just as the postman was walking away, a young woman who was driving by the cottage brought her car to a sudden stop and called out to Alfonso from the street.

"Excuse me, sir," she hollered. Alfonso figured it was someone in need of directions.

Not wanting to awaken Savannah by hollering back, he closed the front door behind him and walked toward the young woman. She, in turn, had quickly parked her car and stepped out from behind the wheel. Despite the blustery weather, she was clad in a tight, yellow tank top and a short, pleated denim mini-skirt.

"May I help you?" he asked.

"I'm sorry to bother you. I hope I haven't made a mistake, but I couldn't help but notice you while I was driving. By any chance, are you Alfonso Madrigál?"

"Why, yes, I am," he answered.

～

At that moment, Savannah had walked into the living room, and not finding Alfonso anywhere, she looked out the front window and saw him talking to a very attractive blonde, blue-eyed woman who had more curves than the final stretch of coastal highway leading into Mendocino.

"I knew it!" Savannah heard the woman scream in a shrill voice. "Oh, I'm such a big fan of your music, Alfonso. I have all your albums, and I even saw you in concert in Granada when I visited there last year. Is it okay if I gave you a hug? I'm just so excited to meet you in person!"

From where she stood, Savannah could hear every word the nubile, twenty-something bombshell said to Alfonso.

The woman had already struck a pose—arms outstretched. He opened his arms and she hugged him—longer, tighter, and more intimately than Savannah cared to see. Then, in a moment of total abandon, she kissed Alfonso on the lips. Savannah looked away as her blood drained to her feet, not wanting to see if he would reciprocate her kiss. A sudden chill crawled down her spine. Something was coming back to her with a certain male-volence—something that made her heart beat with a tumultuous rhythm.

This is the kind of pain I had hoped to avoid all these years, she said to herself. *Is this my worst nightmare coming true?* Feelings welled up inside of her that she knew only too well.

Outside, Alfonso had drawn back from the young woman's ardent kiss. The young woman, who introduced herself as Rachel, seemed to want to talk to him forever. She wanted his autograph on his three CDs, all of which she had in her car because she listened to him all the time.

As she listened to the woman chatter on, Savannah looked at her reflection in the mirror above the fireplace. She was still quite attractive, but the signs of middle age were beginning to creep on her. Even when she was a young woman, like this Rachel girl, she couldn't bear competing with another woman, especially for the affection of a man. How could she compete now, when she was not half as attractive as these nubile, young nymphets that, given his fame, must constantly surround him?

Then, the thought occurred to her. The thought that she knew was coming. What if Alfonso and she got together again, and he later decided to leave her—for this Rachel woman, for any woman, for any reason? Could she live with herself then? The answer came quickly. *I've done quite well without him for twenty-six years,* she thought. *I can do it again. I can't bear to be hurt that way.*

Deep within Savannah Curtis, the faceless specter wearing a black hood began to spin a viscous web around her that obscured all reason. She found it difficult to breathe, and she froze in terror when she heard the same voice from long ago imploring her to run before Alfonso outran her out the door. She felt the irrational need to preserve herself from the certainty of death.

∽

After about ten minutes of Rachel talking up a storm, Alfonso excused himself by telling her he had someone waiting for him in the house. Rachel drove away, waving her hand at him as she did.

Alfonso walked back to the house and found the front door locked. He didn't remember locking it. Thinking Savannah was still fast asleep, he didn't want to ring the doorbell or knock on the door. Instead, he walked around to the side of the house, and let himself into the back lawn through the candlestick gate. He tried the door to the kitchen, and it, too, was locked.

He peered into Savannah's bedroom window and found that her bed was empty. He started calling out her name. "Savannah." No answer. He called out louder. Again, there was no answer, nor was there any stirring inside the house.

Finally, he went back to the front door, knocked loudly and rang the doorbell. Savannah approached the door without opening it. "Who is it?" she asked.

"It's me, Savannah. *Running Stream.* I've locked myself out. Open the door, please."

"I'm sorry. I don't know who you are. I can't let you in. There's no one here by the name of Savannah."

Alfonso's stomach tightened in a slight panic. Could this be another memory lapse, or had she regressed further back in time? He walked to the back of the house and tried the door to the back porch. It swung open. He walked down the hallway, looking for her in every bedroom that he passed. He found her sitting on the sofa in the living room with the drapes drawn, her hands folded on her lap, her eyes closed.

"Savannah, there you are."

"I will thank you for not calling me Savannah, sir. It isn't my name," she said.

He sat beside her on the sofa and put his arms around her, kissing her hand the way he always did whenever he saw her.

"*Abre tus ojos.* Open your eyes, Savannah. Look at me. You know who I am."

She opened her eyes. Everything inside her ached to hold him and kiss him and tell him how much she loved him and missed him, but she said, "I don't know who you are, sir. I already told you my name is not Savannah. You better leave now."

Alfonso took her hand and held it to his chest. "If you don't remember me, you'll remember this," he said. His heart was pounding loudly now, unable to comprehend what was going on, feeling that Savannah was slipping beyond his reach.

"What do you expect me to remember by feeling your heart beat?"

She pushed him away and rose to her feet. "Sir, don't make this any harder than it is. I think you'd better go," she said, walking to the front door and opening it.

Alfonso looked at her, feeling as forlorn as he did at the hospital when he first found out she had amnesia. But something inside him was sure he could reach her and bring her back. He had thought he was making progress, and now this. He was a total stranger to her again. Farther from her than he'd ever been before.

Now, she didn't even know her own name.

He walked over to where she was standing, put his arm around her waist, gently pulled her close, and kissed her. For a moment he could swear that she was melting into him like she had many years ago. But the next second she pulled away and slapped him hard on the cheek.

"How dare you? What kind of gall gave you the permission to do that? Leave my house now, or I'll be forced to call the police."

Alfonso felt the sting of a thousand invisible needles on his cheek where Savannah had slapped him. The image of his mother suddenly flashed in his memory, and the smell of his mother's excruciatingly sweet French perfume with spicy undertones invaded his nostrils.

Tears began to well up in his eyes. To keep them from falling, he bit hard on his lower lip until drops of blood trickled out.

Finally, he said, "I can't just leave you without calling Brandon. He'll have to drive out here before I go. Someone has to take care of you," Alfonso said, walking towards the phone on the kitchen wall. He dialed Brandon's number, hoping he'd be home.

"I don't need anyone to take care of me, sir. Not you, not my son, not anyone."

"Hello," Brandon answered, slightly breathless. He had just walked in the door and had run to the phone when he heard it ringing.

"Hello, son. I'm glad I caught you home. Is there any way you can drive out here today?"

"Why? What happened?"

"It's Savannah. She's turned into someone else again. She doesn't recognize me and has repeatedly asked me to leave. She plans to call the police if I don't. I can't just go without someone here with her."

"I'll be there as soon as I can," Brandon said, "but if she doesn't recognize you, how do we know she'll recognize me?"

~

"*I* know it's here somewhere," Alfonso said, riffling through the chest of drawers. "Here it is," he muttered under his breath as he pulled the Caregiver Agreement out of the bottom drawer.

He walked back into the living room and handed the Agreement to Savannah. "Your name is Savannah Fairchild. You've had an accident and you've lost your memory. You have amnesia, do you understand? I've been appointed by your son...our son, Brandon, to be your caregiver. I want to respect your wishes, and I'll start packing my bags right away, but do you see why I can't leave until Brandon gets here? You're my responsibility."

Savannah eyed the document that Alfonso had handed to her, pretending to read it, but looking right through it. Alfonso's words hit her like a ton of bricks. "You're my responsibility," he had said. *Yes, that's all I am to him. His responsibility.* If she remembered correctly, that was the very reason she had kept Brandon a secret from him in the first place. Because his sense of responsibility toward his son would forever tie him to her, and she wouldn't be able to make a clean break. But now, something else Alfonso had said bothered her. "Our son, Brandon," he had said. *How did he know that Brandon is our son? No, he can't know. It would complicate everything. And does Brandon know, too? It would complicate everything.*

"This Agreement means nothing, Mr. Madrigál. It doesn't matter that you are the caregiver of this Savannah Curtis mentioned in this document. I am not Savannah Curtis."

"Then what is your name?" Alfonso asked.

"I don't know. I don't remember," she answered, shrugging her shoulders. She wondered how long she could keep up the act of pretending that she was yet another incarnation emerging from her amnesia. "All I know is that I would prefer it if you leave my house now. Please."

Alfonso was out of options. Was this God's way of telling him to just give up on this part of his life? Was it time to take a bow, say he's given it his best shot, and call it a day? The door was wide open. All he had to do was walk out. It would be hard, but not unbearable. Not when the woman he loved has struck a blow to his face that made his blood curdle with stinging venom. Not when she couldn't bear to be under the same roof with him.

While it was true that Savannah couldn't bear to be under the same roof with him, it wasn't because she couldn't stand to be with him. God knows how long she had waited to finally be with him. It was because if he stayed any longer, she might want him to stay. And she feared what would happen if he did.

Even as she feared, she took a perverse comfort in her familiarity with the fear. The sinister, foreboding fear that dominated her life. The fear that had become her friend. The fear that knew her like no one else did. It was her faithful companion, and it never failed her. If there was anything she could rely on, it was that dislocating fear of being left behind. It paralyzed her from doing things that could potentially hurt her. She was thankful for having the fear. It was her protector.

*

*B*randon arrived at a quarter past seven. The sun had just disappeared beyond the horizon and darkness was falling. Crickets whined about the coming cold as the clover swayed in the winds of Mendocino.

"Brandon, I'm so glad you're here," Savannah said when he walked in the door. She embraced him warmly.

"You know me, Mama?"

"Of course, I know you, son. What did you expect?"

Brandon was bewildered, but thrilled that his mother finally remembered who he was.

"Where's Papa?" he asked.

"Son, you know your father died before you were born."

"That's what you told me, Mama, but he didn't die. My father is standing right here. Yes, Mama, that's right. Alfonso is my father, isn't he?"

"What are you talking about, son? Who is Alfonso?"

Brandon turned around, expecting to see Alfonso standing there, but he had gone into his bedroom.

"No worries, Brandon. We've always been alright—just you and me."

"Of course, Mama. Of course, you're right."

"But son, you'll have to ask that man to leave. He doesn't belong here. Promise me you'll ask him to leave."

Alfonso emerged from the hallway, carrying his suitcase in one hand, his guitar case in the other, setting them down by the front door.

"He doesn't have to ask me to leave, Savannah. I'm going." He turned around to face them.

"Where will you be going? Where can I reach you?" Brandon asked.

"I'll probably be staying at the Fairmont tonight. I may stay a day or two before flying back to Madrid."

Savannah took a step toward Alfonso, and held out her hand. "Goodbye, sir. I hope you have a safe trip."

Alfonso took her hand and brought it to his lips to kiss it. "Goodbye, Savannah," he said, searching Savannah's eyes one last time. *Give me a sign, a clue, a reason, any reason why I should stay, Savannah,* he said to himself. But her eyes were glazed over, as though he wasn't even there.

Alfonso turned to Brandon, gave him a hug, and said, "I love you, son. Take good care of your mother for me." And with those words, he turned around to open the door, picked up his suitcase and guitar case, and walked down the cobblestone path to his car, which was parked in the driveway behind hers.

Through the open door, Savannah watched as the man she loved walked out of her life, never to return. It's just as well, she thought. Better now than later. Everything leads to goodbye anyway. Remembering her father, she thought, *Sometimes there are even no goodbyes. This is better than the last time, isn't it, Alfonso? This time at least we had a chance to say goodbye to each other.*

Alfonso stopped by his car door to look at her one last time. Then, he was behind the wheel, shutting the door after him. And as he drove away, she watched with shipwrecked eyes as his car disappeared around the bend, until the sound of his engine faded away. And in the Mendocino dusk, all was so tranquil that Savannah was sure Brandon could hear her heart breaking.

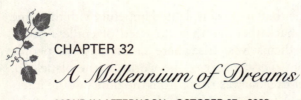

CHAPTER 32
A Millennium of Dreams
MONDAY AFTERNOON • OCTOBER 27 • 2003

In the light of day, some things are left behind by the savage frontiers of the night that keep us remembering those of whom we dream, those in whose company we flourish, those for whom we endure enormous agony, and those without whom we perish like children in the wilderness.

That afternoon in October, the late-blooming jasmines lingered past their prime, unsure what season it was. The clock tower at the *Embarcadero* rang in a new hour and bid farewell to the hour gone by with rhythmic regularity. The leaves of the oak trees were turning. And a hundred miles away, trains headed for Mendocino slowed down at journey's end. The world revolved in that manner for Alfonso Madrigál as he made his way to the San Francisco International Airport.

The town car weaved itself in and out of afternoon rush hour traffic on its way to the international terminal. Sitting in the back seat, Alfonso hardly saw the endless sea of people spinning an intricate web of comings and goings, people saying hello, saying goodbye, and wondering when they'd see each other again.

The driver of the town car pulled up to the curb. Alfonso looked out the window from the back seat and read the sign: *Iberian Airlines*. He took his wallet from the inside pocket of his coat, pulled out a fifty dollar bill and handed it to the driver, who murmured his thanks. Alfonso picked up his suitcase and his guitar case and was inside the terminal within a few moments. He had no time to lose. He looked at his watch. *5:47*. Just forty-five minutes until his flight to Madrid was scheduled to depart. He had his ticket, passport and boarding pass. After ascending two flights of escalators and going through security check, he hastened his pace as he approached Gate 7. There were about eighty people sitting in the lounge outside Gate 7. The airline had not yet started boarding.

There was something about this airport that made him sentimental. This was the first U.S. soil he stepped onto when he first arrived from Spain on the twenty-third of September 1976. He remembered the day quite well. His heart was full of a profound mixture of liberation, hope, and a conviction that here in this country anything was possible. Just a floor beneath him was the Arrival area where right now an Iberian Airlines plane would be disembarking another batch of transplanted hopefuls with the same starry eyes he had back then, as they dreamed of endless possibilities to reinvent themselves. Elsewhere in the airport, people were coming in from every corner of the world by the planeload, and a millennium of dreams was rising from the floors of the international terminal. Alfonso pondered their restlessness as he remembered how he had felt in Spain years ago—as birds must feel before their first migration—a gut instinct that they should fly away to another place in order to survive. Like eagles with injured wings searching for a fragment of the sky in which to fly.

Little did he know on that day in 1976 that he was flying straight to Savannah Curtis.

He thought of the two months, three weeks and one day he had spent with Savannah in Mendocino. Other men would have considered that a waste of time. But for Alfonso, there was no wasted time. For as long as he was with her, he was alive.

Alfonso sat himself down on a chair in the waiting area, next to a woman in her late twenties and her young son. He glanced at the boy, who was seated next to him, reading a book. He appeared to be about five years old. He wondered how Brandon must have looked at that age. He wondered what things he'd have done and places he'd have gone with him in his growing years. How would his presence in his son's childhood have changed Brandon? Would he have turned out better or worse than he is now? What difference could he have made as his father? Was it fair for Savannah to rob him of the pleasure of knowing his son and being there for him? He decided that Savannah probably did the right thing in not telling him. He already had a daughter to raise, and he would have been torn between Brandon and Cristina. How could he fault Savannah when she did such a fine job raising Brandon? If he were to list all the things he'd have wanted in a son, he couldn't ask for more than Brandon.

Alfonso tried to push away all thoughts of Savannah, but something kept bothering him. There was something that didn't seem right.

He tried to remember the details of the previous day. They seemed a blur to him because they happened so fast. When Savannah was looking at the Caregiver Agreement he had handed her, she had said, "This Agreement means nothing, Mr. Madrigál. It doesn't matter that you are the caregiver of this Savannah Curtis. I am not Savannah Curtis."

Nowhere on the Agreement did the surname, "Curtis," appear. The name given as care receiver was Savannah Fairchild. Yet, she had said *Savannah Curtis*. How could she have known the surname she had before she legally changed her name to Fairchild...unless she was Savannah Curtis herself?

A crazy notion entered his head. What if Savannah had regained her memory sometime between the time he sang to her on his guitar and the time he returned to the front door after having spoken to the young woman named Rachel? And what if she was pretending she still had amnesia so that she could use it as an excuse for not knowing who he was, not remembering her own name, but conveniently remember Brandon?

But why would she do that? he asked himself. *Why would she want to push me away?*

He tried to retrace his steps to see if there was anything he might have done to trigger her irrational behavior. The doorbell rang. The postman delivered a package. A young woman called to him from the street asking if he was Alfonso Madrigál, the flamenco artist. He walked a few steps from the house to speak to her so as not to awaken Savannah.

Could that be it? he wondered. Could Savannah have heard him talking to the young woman, seen her hugging and kissing him, and decided she couldn't cope with female fans flirting with him and showering him with attention?

He remembered what Cassidy had told him about Savannah. *Savannah always felt that even if a man did come to love her, he would end up leaving her when someone better came along. Believing that virtually every woman is better than she is, she never feels secure about her relationship with a man. She constantly battles feelings of inadequacy.*

He also remembered what Savannah herself had said during one of the episodes when her memory was temporarily restored: *"I'm afraid I'm going to die of a broken heart just like my mother did."*

Alfonso decided that Savannah's irrational behavior was consistent with her psychological complex. Could it be that Savannah had pushed him away because she wanted to beat him to the door before he had the chance to walk out on her?

"Ladies and gentlemen, Iberian Airlines Flight 387 bound for Madrid is now boarding. We will begin boarding handicapped passengers, as well as passengers with little children first, and then we will proceed with general boarding."

Alfonso rose to his feet, lifted his carry-on satchel off the floor and walked hurriedly out of Gate 7, into the airport's main concourse, and toward the car rental counter.

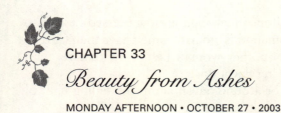

CHAPTER 33
Beauty from Ashes
MONDAY AFTERNOON • OCTOBER 27 • 2003

It was late afternoon when Alfonso parked his rental car behind Savannah's Ford in the driveway of 335 Castlebrook Lane. He thought of ringing the doorbell, but decided against it. Instead, he walked down the darkening cobblestone path to the candlestick fence, undid the latch on the gate and let himself into the back lawn as he had done many times over the past several weeks.

Savannah was sitting alone on the porch swing, her arms folded across her chest, waiting for the sunset, for redemption. The wind carried her sighs out onto the blue Pacific as the sky turned orange, and dusk reached full bloom. *The world is so tranquil that I can almost hear night falling,* she mused.

Upon approaching the south side of the porch, he called out to her. "Savannah."

Startled by the voice coming from behind her, she turned around, and said, "Yes?"

Upon seeing Alfonso, she froze, and hastily looked away.

"Savannah Curtis. It is you, isn't it? The Savannah I once knew …my Savannah?"

She remained quiet, looking out upon the horizon, wondering how he knew. Somehow, he had seen through her act and realized she had awakened from her amnesia.

He continued walking around the periphery of the porch, and walked up the steps toward where she was, and sat on the Adirondack chair facing the swing.

Neither of them spoke, but there was no uneasiness in the silence. They had both known solitude, and had found peace with it.

Savannah sat quietly, slowly unfolding her arms and bringing them to rest on her lap. She felt the impulse to push him out of her life again, but seeing him sitting there brought to mind only the good memories. She remembered everything about that dreamlike Indian summer, twenty-six years ago. Every detail from the way he looked, the way he smelled, the way he was when he was with her. The way she was when she was with him. The time they spent together. And how she felt pity for all the women who could not have Alfonso Madrigál standing, sitting or lying beside them. And singing to them the way he sang to her.

In his own silence, Alfonso marveled at how blessed he was to be able to behold one woman—this woman named Savannah Curtis—as he had never beheld another woman before. With awe, with reverence, and with undying devotion.

Nothing moved near or around Savannah in the fading light of autumn. If it did, he wouldn't have noticed.

Savannah watched Alfonso from the corner of her eye, this man who had traveled a great distance to see her, realizing that none of the love she had for him had faded with the passage of time. To her, he was still the only man who could make time stand still the way it did now.

He arose from his chair, sat next to her on the porch swing, took her hand, and brought it to his lips to kiss it. "I love you, Savannah," he said softly, looking upon her tenderly.

The unsaid words that had haunted him for twenty-six years, that he regretted never having said to her, now came freely from his lips. The words that needed no embellishment for they said exactly what was in his heart.

And Savannah, who had waited a long time to see him again, who had wondered what she wanted him to say to her when they saw each other again, could think of no better words.

She longed to tell him she loved him, too, but she feared its consequences. *Savannah,* she told herself, *you mustn't say or do anything that will give him a reason to stay. You know fully well what that would mean.*

The ancient fear that still burned within her chest swept over her yet again. Long were the days she had spent within its walls, and painful were the nights when she was alone with it. How could she withdraw from fear's company without losing a part of herself? She had known fear longer and more intimately than Alfonso Madrigál. To give up the safety of fear would be madness.

"Don't pin your hopes on me, Alfonso. I would be impossible to live with. You will tire of my insecurities, and you'll soon realize I'm not worth the trouble. I'm setting you free so you can soar as high as you can without being encumbered by me."

There's the Savannah of old, Alfonso thought to himself. *Always self-effacing. Always fearful of taking risks. Always underestimating the depth of my love for her.*

"I didn't come back to change your mind. You have your reasons for not wanting me in your life, and I will respect your decision. I've come back because, while sitting at the airport waiting to board a plane, I realized that somewhere in Mendocino is the Savannah who knows me, the one who used to love me. And I didn't want to leave without telling her the things I've wanted to tell her. I don't intend to stay. I still have my one-way ticket back to Madrid, and I'll be flying out tomorrow."

Savannah began to relax, unclenching the grip that her right hand had over her left wrist. Even as she felt relieved, the thought of him being gone forever also pierced her with an unspeakable sorrow. She thought about the words he had said, "...out in Mendocino is the Savannah who knows me, the one who used to love me." *Used to love him.* There had never been a moment in the past twenty-six years that she didn't love him with all her heart. *If he only knew,* she thought.

"There are many things for which I want to thank you, Savannah. One of them is my music."

"What did I have to do with that?"

"I became a recording artist because of you. You and I were at Heaven's Bluff when you told me that I needed to let the spirit move in me. I started to do just that and I found that songs started to flow right out of me...the same way words come at me when I look upon a thing of beauty...when I look at you, Savannah."

Savannah reveled in his words, allowing herself to feel the pleasure of being beautiful to the man who meant the world to her. Nonetheless, her face remained nonchalant.

"I started ignoring the rules, and stopped worrying whether I was doing it right or wrong. Instead, I focused on letting the spirit move in me. When I did that, the melodies I created no longer resembled anyone else's."

"Your music is amazing, Alfonso. You've done very well. I'm so proud of you."

"In case I didn't make myself clear, I owe my music career to you, Savannah. Because you saw something in me that I didn't see in myself."

Deep down, Savannah was not willing to take any credit for his success. "You've always been so talented, Alfonso. But it isn't I whom you need to thank but God, who gave you the gift. I'm so glad you've made a wonderful life for yourself. I, too, have made a good life for myself. It would be best to leave well enough alone."

"I'll leave you be," he said, finally resigning himself to the fact that she wasn't going to change her mind. Then, he reached into his pocket and pulled out an envelope folded in half. "But not until I give you this."

"What is it?"

"Before I left Madrid, Cristina gave me this letter and asked me to give it to you."

She took the envelope he handed her, wondering what on earth Cristina would want to write to her about.

She opened the sealed envelope, carefully unfolded the letter, and began to read.

Dear Savannah,

If you're reading this letter, it can only mean that my father has found you. He's waited so patiently for this day to come.

You may not know much about me, but through my father, I've known you more intimately than you know. More importantly, I know how our lives—my father's, my mother's, and mine—have been forever changed because you happened to us.

I've never seen my father as happy as during the time he spent with you in 1977. Although I was only 4 then, God had blessed me with a depth of understanding uncommon for a child my age. I remember that time in 1977 made an impression on me because the change in my father was quite evident. It was as though he had become another person, able to overcome the rage, the bitterness, and the grief that had marred his younger days. Before he met you, I rarely saw him smile. And yet, from the moment he brought home your painting, A Fern in the Clearing, he could neither hide nor contain his joy.

I was therefore saddened when I saw how destroyed he was when you disappeared from his life. Broken-hearted could not even begin to describe the depression he sank into during the weeks and months after you left. I felt his pain, every bit of it. As a child, I didn't understand much about affairs of the heart, but I realized that something happened between the two of you that I hoped to understand one day.

Once, I asked him about you, and I saw him turn his face away from me and pinch the inner corners of both eyelids with his thumb and forefinger. I never brought your name up again after that. We moved back to Spain in 1979 when Papa got his first recording contract.

When Mama died last year from an illness that was both painful and lingering, my father never left her side. I'll never forget what she said to him before she passed away. She said, "Alfonso, you've been as good a husband to me as any man could be. But I also know that I'm not the woman you've loved in your private moments." When he started to protest to give her comfort in her final hours, she said, "Hush, Alfonso, a woman knows these things. You no longer need to hide it from me because I know this as sure as I know my days are numbered. I saw her, you know, at the Palace of Fine Arts when Cristina, you and I spent the morning there in the fall of 1977, remember? I had noticed her watching Cristina and you as you watched the swans, and she was trying to keep you from seeing her. Then, I watched as she walked quickly away, wiping her eyes as she went."

Then, Mama said, "I went to the Victorian apartment at 201 Pacific the next morning—the one you had taken a picture of—across from Summerhill Park. I knocked and the same woman I saw at the Palace of Fine Arts came to the door. I pretended I had the wrong apartment, but I could tell she recognized who I was. I knew then that she was the one who inspired the beautiful love song you wrote that one night when the heat kept us all awake. You had stayed up until close to dawn playing your guitar and singing the most beautiful song I had every heard." Then she said, "I can't ask for more of you than the part of your life you've already given me, Alfonso. I can't give you back the time you could've spent with her, but I can die in peace knowing that you have yet a chance to be with her, and that you'll do whatever you need to do to grab that chance. Be happy, mi amor, and tell her to take good care of you for me."

Savannah, I'm grateful for the great sacrifice you made, that of breaking off your relationship with my father back in 1977 so as not to destroy his family, and so as not to hurt me in the process. You could have chosen to be selfish by asking my father to leave my mother and me so he could be with you. I know he would have done that, if you asked him to, because I knew how much he loved you.

As an adult, and having been in love myself, I still don't condone, but I fully understand why a man would leave his family for the woman he loves. There's no standing in the way of a man and a woman in love. Even if I know that now, I didn't know it when I was a little girl. If my father had run away with you and left me at the age of 4, I know I would have been scarred for life.

Although a man is seldom justified for leaving his wife for another woman, knowing how much my father loved you, I would have found it in my heart to forgive him if he had left my mother to be with you. A man's love for a woman sometimes causes men to do things that are rational only to them. That love often eclipses their love for their child. I hope that knowing this, you can find peace with what your own father has done.

Thank you for sacrificing your own happiness, and

enabling me to grow up as a whole, functional human being, which would not have been possible without my father's presence. I thank you, too, on behalf of my mother. Although my father could never love her as much as he loved you, you encouraged him to honor his commitment to her, and that enabled him to love her and care for her as much as he could until the day she died.

When I was old enough to understand, my father shared with me his idea of how a man should love a woman. This is what he said: "If I must love a woman, let it be for love's own sake. Let it not be for the mere loveliness of her face, the way she speaks, the silhouette of her body, or for a quality that falls in well with mine, that makes a day or a season magical. For these things might not linger, or we might momentarily change for one another, and love thus made may be unmade as swiftly. Let me not love for superlative things that she is or isn't, has or hasn't–for how easy would it be to find another who embodies such things and more, and lose my love thereby. But rather, let love carve in me an unchanging heart that chooses every moment to be amazed by her on any day, in any light, in any season, and any night. Let me love with spellbound fascination over her soul touching mine, that forever I may stand in the radiance that is her."

I wept because of the beauty of his sentiment. I wept, too, because I knew then that the woman he chose to bestow that kind of love upon was you. And finally, I wept because I longed to have a man love me the same way, and I wasn't certain whether I would ever find it.

That's when my father first told me, "Don't go looking for love, for if love finds you worthy, it will find you." Love did not find me for many years. I've had to endure a string of painful relationships that masqueraded as love, but were just a poor facsimile of it. But five years ago, I was blessed to have met, fallen in love with, and been cherished by my husband, Antonio, who loves me deeply–not in the way my father loves you–but in his own special way, which suits me perfectly. We've been married for 4 years now, and have a 3-year old son, Lorenzo.

Savannah, for a long time now, I've wanted to meet you. I've wanted to tell you how you've changed Alfonso Madrigál's life, and that his memory of you and the wisdom you brought him have brightened his days in infinite ways, and brought him music that healed him. For that, I sincerely thank you.

> *My father has spent the last 26 years of his life regretting that he never told you he loved you. He believes that had he been able to convince you that he could love you more than you could ever think it's possible for a man to love a woman, and that he could fill the hollow parts of your heart that your father left behind, that you might never have disappeared from his life the way you did. Even as I say this, I apologize for any trouble I might be causing for I don't know whether you're presently married or involved with a man, nor do I know if my letter dredges up a past you'd rather not revisit. But I write it anyway because if, for any reason, this is not the opportune time for him to say it to you because of attachments that you may already have, I need to say it for him. Not because he wanted me to tell you, but because a love of this magnitude should never be left unspoken. Savannah, he has loved you from the first day he met you with a love even he can't comprehend–and he loves you still and always will. There's a part of Alfonso Madrigál that yearns to live, for he has known what it's like to live, even if only for twelve days in 1977.*
>
> *I wish upon you the wholeness that only true love can give. I thank you for loving my father, and for making him the wonderful man that he is today.*
>
> *With love and gratitude,*
Cristina Madrigál-Vargas

Savannah thought she had wept all her tears, but upon reading Cristina's letter, she struck a hidden vein. Her hands shook, and sobs came from the deepest part of her.

She had always known that Alfonso loved her, even if he had not said the words. But this love of which Cristina spoke–she had no frame of reference by which to comprehend it. Didn't know a man could love a woman that way–least of all, her. Every fiber in her being denied that this could even remotely be true.

"Savannah…" Alfonso's voice interrupted her thoughts. "Last month, Brandon and I took you to the hospital because you had stopped breathing and you had no pulse. Do you remember that?"

She nodded. The memories from her post-injury persona were a little cloudy, but she remembered almost everything.

"When I saw you lying on your bed, lifeless, thinking that you might already be dead, I wanted to die myself. I just didn't care to live in a world without you in it. Wherever life takes you, Savannah, even if it is continents away from me, I want you to know that you don't have to be anyone but yourself because I love you. I love the entire universe of you. I love who you are, who you were, and who you will ever be. I love all the good and not-so-good about you—including any dysfunctions, imperfections, insecurities, and limitations you might have, whether real or imagined."

Savannah pondered his words but said nothing.

"And now before I go, I want to thank you for giving me the best gift a man could ask for."

"And what is that?"

"You've given me a son."

"You know about Brandon?"

"*Si, mi amor.* Brandon is a wonderful surprise I never expected to receive at this stage in life."

Savannah's eyes started welling up with tears again.

"And he has been your wonderful gift to me for the last twenty-six years. You had your music to occupy your days, and I had Brandon. The very first time I was able to think of you without wanting to weep was when he was born. Sometimes I'd look at him—this living, breathing flesh-and-blood human being who's part you and part me—and I would have more joy than I could bear. I even began to feel that it was unfair to you that I had the pleasure of having him in my life, and you didn't. Will you ever forgive me for depriving you of seeing your son grow up?"

"I still have many years to give Brandon. I don't blame you for keeping him from me. I understand why you've had to do it. I'm not angry. Instead, I'm overjoyed. You've raised our son beautifully and I couldn't ask for more."

"In truth, I had very little to do with how well he turned out, Alfonso. I think God raised him in the way he should go…to become what he's become." Savannah's eyes were sparkling as she spoke of Brandon. "He's the beauty that arose out of the ashes of my life."

Alfonso was quiet. He watched as a smile crept onto Savannah's lips.

She continued speaking, "I've always felt that I ought to be punished because I wanted you though you belonged to another woman. But instead, I was given a reward that I don't deserve—and that's our son, Brandon." Savannah's eyes were far away.

"Beauty from ashes," Alfonso repeated Savannah's words slowly. "You probably remember the story of a king who desired another man's wife. So he sent the woman's husband away into battle to be killed so that he could have her for himself. Even so, he was forgiven by God. And though he ought to have been punished, he and the woman were given a son, who would become the greatest king of Israel."

"The story of David. There's undeserved redemption for sinners like him. Like us."

"God's ways are past finding out," Alfonso said. "I like to think Cristina and Brandon are our undeserved rewards for the sacrifices we've made."

~

Alfonso sat silently for a few moments, realizing that he had said everything that needed to be spoken. And all his devotion for Savannah had been conveyed over the days and weeks that he had cared for her while she suffered from amnesia. He felt he could finally be at peace and never have to look back on things unsaid and undone.

"I'll be on my way now, Savannah. *Adios, mi corazón.*"

He put his arm around her waist, gently pulled her close, and kissed her with the hunger of a hundred famines and the thirst of a thousand droughts. Savannah smelled the Mediterranean Sea and the citrus fruits of Málaga on him as she had many years ago. She was spinning in the spiral universe of his kiss, and something in her wanted to stay there forever.

Then, he slowly pulled himself away from her, kissed her hand once again, and stood up to leave.

"Thank you, Alfonso," she said as he made his way toward the porch steps.

Looking back over his shoulder, he said, "For what?"

"Thank you for taking care of me these last two months."

"Two months, three weeks and a day," he said wistfully. "It's far more than the twelve days I had with you in 1977. Maybe this will tide me over till the end of my days."

For the first time in her life, Savannah realized that the certainty of Alfonso's love is what had healed, deepened and renewed her. And finally set her free to be whoever she was. For the first time in her life, she felt so loved, so accepted, so awesome, so beautiful, and so cherished that she needed no further guarantees. Gone was the stigma that made her hide her real self, for fear of being abandoned again. Gone was the ugly and unworthy person she had convinced herself she was. Gone was the need to run before he outran her to the door. All the nightmares, doubts and fears of her life saw their demise that very moment.

All because of the indescribable love of this man she once called Running Stream. This man named Alfonso Madrigál.

Unaware of her thoughts, Alfonso walked down the porch steps and headed for the wooden gate leading out to the driveway. He walked hurriedly so that she wouldn't see that tears had begun to pour from his eyes, wondering if he could ever get used to spending a day, an hour, or even a moment without her.

"Alfonso," she cried softly after him, as she leaned against the railing of the porch.

He didn't hear her calling him as he unlatched the gate, walked through, and closed it behind him. He could feel the cobblestone pathway through the soles of his shoes as he wiped his eyes with the back of his hands.

"Alfonso, wait," Savannah pleaded, as she ran across the lawn after him.

Alfonso heard her unlatch the gate, but kept on walking.

"*Running Stream*," she called to him, and he turned around to look at her. She caught up with him halfway down the pathway and grabbed his arm. "Do you believe that people can die of a broken heart?

"If that were true, I'd have died of a broken heart a long time ago. Love doesn't kill you, Savannah. It lets you know you're alive."

She said nothing, but inside she already knew that her love for him and the son she had with him were the only things that had kept her alive.

"Do you ever fear that all your love will amount to nothing? That the person you love may one day disappear from your life?"

"There is no fear in love. I've learned that perfect love drives out fear. One who fears has not been made perfect in love. Whenever it's love you give, it will never amount to nothing."

Suddenly, an unfamiliar peace swathed Savannah's heart and she finally understood things she didn't know before. She slowly stepped in closer to him, feeling his arms encircle her body, cradling her in a safe haven where fear could never enter. She knew then that in his arms was the only place where she cared to be, now and always.

Alfonso held her for several moments without saying a word. Then he pulled back from her slowly, still holding her body close to his. He gazed at her tear-stained face, knowing in his heart that Savannah Curtis was entirely worthy of all the love he could give.

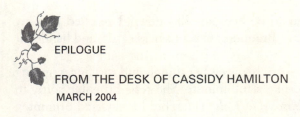

EPILOGUE

FROM THE DESK OF CASSIDY HAMILTON
MARCH 2004

"A rose makes no reference to former roses or to better ones. They exist for what they are and there is no time to them. There is simply the rose, perfect in every moment of its existence."

—Ralph Waldo Emerson

Savannah and I sat at one of the tables fronting the stage at the *Casbah*. It seemed as though all the flamenco music aficionados of San Francisco had flocked to the club that night and had snatched up all the available seats, not to mention the aisles, the hallways and the corridors. I half expected the fire marshal to come barging in to slap the owner with a citation for filling the club well over capacity. The atmosphere inside the *Casbah* was electric, and the breathless anticipation for the event of the evening was palpable.

Savannah was sipping on a *sangría*, and I, a *margarita*, and we had to raise our voices in order to hear each other above the escalating noise level of the club. She was telling me how excited she was that Cristina, Antonio and Lorenzo were flying in from Madrid the following Wednesday. They were coming to attend the wedding.

Alfonso and Savannah were to be married in Mendocino on the twentieth of March, the first Saturday of spring when the village wears its loveliest hue and the gray whales begin their 10,000-mile migration from Alaska to the warm lagoons of Baja California, grazing the shore of Mendocino on their way. The wedding was to be held at Heaven's Bluff.

After poring over the details of the wedding, our conversation turned to Brandon. I told her that just last week, Brandon received a notice from the County that his application for a name change had been approved.

"Really? He never told me he was going to do that."

"He filed for the name change the week after Alfonso and Sabine told him that Alfonso was his father. You still had amnesia at that time, Savannah. It took a couple of months to get his name changed, but that's not the end of it. He's now in the process of having the U.S. Department of State issue him a new birth certificate with his new name. Since he's a U.S. citizen born outside the United States, he had to send for the original SRS letter from the doctor who delivered him in Switzerland. It should be here any day now." I reached into my purse, pulled out one of Brandon's new business cards, and handed it to Savannah.

Savannah held the card between her thumb and forefinger, gazing at it for what seemed like a full minute. She read his name softly to herself. *Brandon Alfonso Madrigál.* Then, her eyes started brimming with tears. "It's the name I've always wanted him to have," she said as she finally put away the card and tucked it into her purse.

We talked about the Picasso painting, and how speculators expected it to sell for at least three million dollars at auction–maybe more, depending on the vagaries of the auction block.

Savannah said, "I think it's expected to fetch such an unthinkable price not only because Picasso paintings created before the turn of the century are scarce, but also because there has rarely been a *pentimento* that has rendered itself visible in its entirety through its overlay."

"It's as if the painter had purposely wanted it to reappear after a period of time," I said. "Sort of like a time-released *pentimento*."

We both laughed.

"Do you think Alfonso will ever put it on the auction block?" I asked.

"Never," Savannah replied.

"He seemed willing to part with it before. He gave it to you, didn't he?"

"In his mind, he gave it to me, but I've had to remind him that twenty-six years ago, I refused to accept it as a gift. All I agreed to was to take custody of it. The authentication documents have him down as the owner, not me."

"How long are you going to keep it on loan at the San Francisco Museum of Modern Art?"

"Only until the end of March. In April, Alfonso and I will fly to Málaga and loan it to the *Museo Picasso* that just opened there last October."

I was stunned. "Alfonso is actually going back to Malaga? I thought he swore never to set foot there again."

"He was much younger then, and full of rage. Time has refined him." Then wistfully, she sighed, "I'm more in love with Alfonso now than I've ever been.

"Just last week, out of the blue, he called his father, who still lives in Malaga. They talked for more than an hour, and Alfonso promised we'd visit him when we go there next month."

"Will he ever cease to amaze us?" I asked.

"Perhaps not," she replied, her eyes sparkling. "Oh, and going back to your question as to whether Alfonso will ever sell the painting ...for the time being, at least starting next month, it will be on loan at the *Museo Picasso*. Thereafter, it will be up to Brandon because Alfonso will be giving it to him. Not too long ago, he gave the tambourine to Cristina."

"You mean the one on which Picasso painted a bouquet of flowers? Has that been authenticated, too?"

"Yes, it has, and it's worth a small fortune because it's not just a painting, it's also a rare artifact."

Savannah looked at her watch. It was five minutes before ten.

"I wanted to ask you about that song," I said.

"What song?"

"The song Alfonso sang to you on Heaven's Bluff. The one that awakened you out of amnesia."

"Oh, you mean the one written by a Malagueño singer?" she grinned.

"And the Malagueño singer's name turned out to be Alfonso Madrigal?" I grinned back at her. "Why is it that it was never recorded and put in one of Alfonso's albums?"

"He said when he wrote it, he meant it to be heard by my ears only. I told him it's about time he shared it with the world. So he's agreed to include it as a bonus track on his upcoming CD."

Carlos Reynoso, the owner of *Casbah*, tapped on the microphone that he had carried onstage. The mike test gave off a piercing feedback. After making the necessary adjustments to get it to the proper volume and balance, he finally pulled the mike off its stand and said, "Ladies and gentlemen. Those of you who've been to the *Casbah* before are already familiar with our tradition of bringing you the best local Flamenco artists. But tonight, you're in for a treat such as you've never experienced in your life. A gentleman from Spain has just dropped in on us …"

The audience started cheering.

"If you're a flamenco aficionado, there's no doubt you know and love the music of this Spanish gentleman."

The crowd roared even louder.

"The *Casbah* never advertised this special event, but from the looks of the throngs of people outside clamoring to get into our already overflowing club, it seems to me that the word has spread like wildfire that this unbelievably talented *gitano* from the south of Spain would be here tonight. So without further ado, I bring you the untutored genius of flamenco music…Alfonso Madrigál."

The crowd went wild.

Alfonso appeared from backstage carrying his guitar in one hand. He walked to the center of the stage, moving with the gait of a proud stallion. He finally sat on one of the two stools on stage and brought his mouth up to the mike.

"Carlos promised you a treat tonight such as you've never experienced in your life. What he forgot to tell you is that the real treat is not that I will be playing for you tonight, but that my son will be playing for you, and I have the privilege of accompanying him. I'm so proud to introduce him to you. Brandon Alfonso Madrigál."

Brandon stepped out from backstage and swaggered onstage with his guitar in hand, amidst the thunderous applause. From the corner of my eye, I watched as Savannah pulled a handkerchief out of her purse and started dabbing her eyes.

༄

*T*he twentieth of March was a glorious day for a wedding at Heaven's Bluff. The surrounding meadows and fields were ablaze with golden poppies, scarlet prairie wildflowers and purple irises, yellow mustard and multicolored wild radish on carpets of emerald green grass–looking no less than God's own palette. In the midst of the splendor, I spotted a rare Calypso orchid standing solitary like a bride waiting for her groom.

The sun spread its topaz glow in the air above Mendocino as whales escorted their young southward, fairly close to shore, as though eager to witness the wedding that had waited twenty-six years to take place.

Zendrik had written a song to honor Alfonso and Savannah's marriage. And there, in the pinnacle of the world, where the horizon blurs the lines between heaven and earth, he sang:

> *Let me come eagerly to her*
> *Let me surrender to her arms with no doubt*
> *Let me know there'll be no one else but her*
> *And that she's everything that my life's all about*
>
> *Let me be strong for her*
> *Steadfast in my love for her*
> *Let me remember she has dreams, as well as I*
> *Let me be faithful when*
> *Temptation rears its head*
> *Let me look forward to be with her all my life.*
>
> *If our lives encounter pain*
> *We will stay together and*
> *Most of all our love will see us through*

So let me come eagerly to her
Let me remember when it's dark that she's there
Let me know as I do now that she's mine
And that no synergy could be as right as ours…

෴

ℐ had never attended a wedding wherein no one, not even the bride, knew where the reception was going to be held. Savannah had said that Alfonso had insisted on taking care of all the arrangements himself. The invitation had simply read:

Reception to follow at an undisclosed location.

After the wedding, at Alfonso's prompting, Brandon handed out directions to the reception venue, which was three miles from Heaven's Bluff.

The reception site turned out to be a stunning, single story building fashioned out of light gray travertine stone, with a spacious and beautifully landscaped lawn abounding with lush cascades of bougainvillea, where round white tables had been set up for the wedding reception. The catering staff had made certain everything was impeccable, from the food, to the service and the décor.

Everyone, including myself, thought that Alfonso had rented the building for the occasion, but we were soon to find out differently.

It wasn't until after everyone had dined that Alfonso stood to his feet.

"Friends and loved ones," he began. "Twenty-six years ago, my bride told me she dreamed of one day starting a school where she could teach emotionally traumatized children how to paint. For the last twenty-six years, I've wanted to make her dream come true…the way she has made mine come true. Therefore, today, in the sight of all those who love and care about her, I want to give her the place where her dream can take flight."

Having said those words, he led a tearful Savannah by the hand down a walkway flanked by colonnades and flowering vines, into the building.

The large classroom facing north was painted a deep blue, the color of the sky after sundown. There were two smaller classrooms, facing east and south, one painted a rosy pink, and the other green like a grassy meadow. In the grand foyer, painted a pristine white, a banner hung from the ceiling that read:

Savannah's Fragment of the Sky

If you enjoyed this book...

Here are **3 things** you can do now:

✓ Order **autographed** copies of
to give away as gifts (see quantity discounts below).

✓ E-mail your friends a sample chapter of
delivered in an enjoyable, full-color **Digital Web Book** with <u>actual turning pages</u> – for FREE. This will take you just a few seconds to do. Just go to:
http://www.MidwinterTurnsToSpring.com/DigitalWebBook.htm

✓ Share your comments in the "Reader's Corner" at the
website located at:
http://www.MidwinterTurnsToSpring.com

(**Autographed** Book and Companion Music CD)

PRICE LIST

1-2 copies	@ $27.00	(S & H only $5.00 for up to 2 copies)
3-6 copies	@ $24.00	(S & H only $8.00 for up to 6 copies)
7-11 copies	@ $20.00	(S & H only $12.00 for up to 11 copies)
12 or more copies	@ $15.00	(S & H $15.00 for every 12 copies)

Go to the secure online order form at:
http://www.MidwinterTurnsToSpring.com/quantityorder.htm

or send a check or money order to:

Think-Outside-the-Book Publishing, Inc.
311 N. Robertson Boulevard
Suite 323
Beverly Hills, California 90211

Note: All prices above are in U.S. Dollars. Shipping and handling prices are within United States only. To obtain S & H prices for delivery to non-U.S. destinations, send e-mail to: foreignorders@MidwinterTurnsToSpring.com